A DISPLACED PERSON

A DISPLACED PERSON

LATER LIFE AND EXTRAORDINARY
ADVENTURES
OF
PRIVATE IVAN CHONKIN

Vladimir Voinovich

TRANSLATED FROM THE RUSSIAN BY ANDREW BROMFIELD

NORTHWESTERN UNIVERSITY PRESS
EVANSTON, ILLINOIS

Northwestern University Press
www.nupress.northwestern.edu

 transcript

This book was published under the auspices of the Mikhail Prokhorov Foundation
TRANSCRIPT Programme to Support Translations of Russian Literature.

Printed in the United States of America

10   9   8   7   6   5   4   3   2   1

Library of Congress Cataloging-in-Publication Data

Voinovich, Vladimir, 1932–
    [Peremeshchennoe litso. English]
    A displaced person : the later life and extraordinary adventures of Private Ivan
Chonkin / Vladimir Voinovich ; translated from the Russian by Andrew Bromfield.
        p. cm.
    "Originally published in Russian as Peremeshchennoe litso by EKSMO, 2007."
    ISBN 978-0-8101-2662-6 (pbk. : alk. paper)
    1. Soldiers—Soviet Union—Fiction. 2. Adventure stories. I. Bromfield, Andrew.
II. Title.
PG3489.4.I53P413 2012
891.7344—dc23
                                                                        2012020231

Contents

Preface

I think I deserve a place in the record books. Writing this novel in three volumes has taken me just one year short of half a century. The story of Chonkin was conceived in 1958 and completed in 2007—conceived from the very start as an epic composition extending over a long period of time. Hence the initial title, *The Life and Extraordinary Adventures*. It has always surprised me that not a single person reading the book in the form in which it has existed thus far has asked, "There are adventures all right, but where's the life?" The only life in the first two volumes is the summer and early autumn of 1941.

At the very beginning, when I conceived this work, I mostly composed it in my own mind, thinking about various twists of the plot and comic situations and telling them to my friends, and I was satisfied with that. I was in no hurry to write anything down, assuming that I had plenty of time ahead of me. In fact, I was granted more than enough time, but not all of it proved to be suitable for calm writing. It seems to me that to write something on an epic scale, you need to be in an epic state of mind, and that was not my condition from the late 1960s until at least the mid-1980s. A nuclear superpower declared war on me and tried to "halt my pen," as they put it. When they were trying to talk some sense into me at the Union of Writers, the author Georgii Berezko appealed to me neurotically: "Voinovich, stop writing that terrible Chonkin of yours." In the KGB they repeated the same request insistently, adducing more cogent arguments in the form of poisoned cigarettes.

They didn't put me in prison, but they created conditions less conducive to the composition of an epic canvas than the open letters, either irate or sarcastic, that I employed from time to time to repel attacks by the superior forces of the enemy. I did not abandon attempts to continue with my main work but, exasperated by the constant stings and bites of my adversaries, I constantly veered into a journalistic style, into attempts to caricature Brezhnev or Andropov, although these individuals were of no interest at all as characters or prototypes for potential literary images. They deserved precisely caricature and nothing more, but I had not conceived the novel as a grotesque.

As a matter of fact, I had described the genre of the work as a joke-novel, from which certain critics drew various different conclusions, but this designation was simply a ruse, a hint that this was a light-hearted piece of work, and there was no point in nitpicking over it.

Having left the U.S.S.R. and then returned to it, free now of the constant pressure to which I had been subjected for so many years, I made numerous attempts to resume my interrupted work, covered several reams of paper with writing and threw out almost everything I had written. I wasn't getting anywhere. The plot turned out labored and the phrases were stunted, which pained and surprised me terribly. I wondered how this was possible—after all, not so long ago I had had something in me that attracted the attention of the reading public. Nonetheless, I continued my efforts, pushing my rock up the mountain with dogged perseverance. Some of my readers assured me that *Chonkin* was fine as it was and did not require any continuation, but having written the first two books, I felt I had no right to die without finishing the third. My condition could have been compared to that of a woman who has borne three children to term but only given birth to two, with the third remaining inside her for an indefinite period.

There came a moment when I suddenly felt absolutely sick of "the art of setting word after word" (Bella Akhmadullina), and gave up writing altogether, swapping the pen (or, rather, the computer) for the brush. For forty years in succession I had written at least something, either well or badly, practically every day. I had never experienced any lack of subjects or characters. Now the life flowing past in front of my eyes had ceased to provoke the need to reflect it in some way. My hand did not reach for the pen, or the pen for the paper, and the computer gathered dust. Later I made only a partial return to literature, writing journalistic essays and memoirs. Incidentally, they also cost me a serious effort. And in attempting to compose even a short story, I experienced the total helplessness of a beginner. As if I had never written anything.

Eventually I decided that this was probably the end, the well had run dry and clattering the bucket against the empty bottom was a waste of time. It was time to say good-bye to the idea of a conclusion for *Chonkin*.

But the powers on high proved indulgent and allowed me to live until the moment when I realized with joy that the sentence I had pronounced on myself was premature.

At this point I shall allow myself the liberty of a lyrical diversion and initiate the reader into certain details of my personal life. Although I am an advocate of lifelong marriage, nonetheless until recently I had already been married twice. I separated from my first wife after eight years and lived with my second wife for forty, until she drew her final breath. It happened that the first book of *Chonkin* was written while I was with one wife, and the second while I was with the other. One way or another, their presence in my life influenced this work, and the form in which it was realized sometimes caused serious complications in my life and the lives of my wives, who shared with me all the consequences of my plans and actions. I have therefore decided that it would be right to dedicate, albeit retrospectively, the first book to the memory of Valentina, and the second to the memory of Irina.

Irina's death was protracted and painful. When it was all over, I felt totally desolated and apathetic, and simply started pining away. That is, I lived after a fashion, did something after a fashion, wrote something feeble, but I took no pleasure in any of this, or in my own existence. I was returned to life by Svetlana, who had also lost the person closest to her some time before. Being a selfless creature, she had always been used to caring for someone and, having been deprived of the main object of her attention, she was in a condition similar to my own. It seems to me that we found each other at just the right time.

Svetlana surrounded me with such great physical and emotional comfort that I had no choice but to rise from the ashes. I realized that I wanted once again to live, to write, and strangely enough, I could actually do it. It turned out that something had accumulated in the well after all. I wiped the dust off the computer and started hammering away furiously at the keyboard, feeling an extraordinary, long-forgotten inspiration. In my seventy-fifth year of life, I worked as I had done in my youth. I confused day with night, hurrying to keep up with my characters, who created themselves, as they had done earlier. I can say quite confidently that without Svetlana, this would not have happened. And so it is entirely appropriate that I dedicate the third book to her, with love.

A DISPLACED PERSON

PART ONE

The Colonel's Widow

1

WHEN IVAN KUZMICH DRYNOV was awarded the rank of general yet again, along with the title of Hero of the Soviet Union, it naturally attracted the attention of Soviet journalists. Especially since it happened at the beginning of the war, when the Red Army was retreating on all fronts, and generals were more often shot than decorated. But here was a general regarded benevolently by the authorities, and rumors even circulated that Comrade Stalin in person had virtually drunk to *bruderschaft* with him. Of course, journalists made a dash for the general from all sides but, as usual, the quickest off the mark was the *Pravda* correspondent, Alexander Krinitsky, who had already written about Drynov's heroic exploits. Since he was personally acquainted with the general and represented the major Party newspaper, he was granted a repeat audience with Drynov ahead of all the others. The audience took place in a sanatorium not far from Moscow, where the general had been sent to take a brief rest and restore his strength.

Krinitsky found the general strolling along the carpet runners on the ground floor in striped pajamas with his Gold Star pinned on. They settled down in the foyer under a ficus tree. Krinitsky took a notepad out of his dispatch case and Drynov took a pack of Palmyra of the North *papyrosas** out of his pocket. In response to the journalist's questions, the general declared that he had indeed succeeded in carrying through a brilliant military operation, but it should not be forgotten that generals only enjoyed such good fortune when the men they led fought courageously. He recalled Chonkin as a case in point and told Krinitsky in detail about this dauntless warrior's heroism—how he had defended a plane that made a forced landing, valiantly doing battle with an entire

---

* A *papyrosa* is a Russian kind of cigarette with a cardboard tube through which the tobacco smoke is inhaled.

regiment, but at this late stage the general didn't specify exactly which regiment it was.

Since both participants in the conversation were extremely drunk, Krinitsky's recall of the general's story was somewhat inexact, and he also happened to lose his notepad on the way to his newspaper's offices. As he tried to reconstitute the general's tale, what he recalled was that Chonkin had defended a plane on which he himself had apparently arrived. So Krinitsky decided that Chonkin must be an airman. After that he drew on his own imagination, which had never let him down, to compensate for his lack of information. It was he, I believe, who created the mythical feat of the twenty-eight heroes from General Ivan Panfilov's division that has been recorded in the history textbooks as an indisputable deed of great valor, at which Krinitsky himself was virtually present in person. He it was who invented these heroes, who supposedly fought and perished in an uneven battle against German tanks at the Dubosekovo railway siding, and he it was who attributed to the mythical commissar Kliuchkov the mythical phrase which, naturally, he also invented, and on which he prided himself until the day he died: "There is nowhere to retreat, Moscow is behind us!" Not only did he pride himself on it—if anyone ever doubted the absolute or, at least, partial veracity of the legend, he subjected them to such scathing criticism in the press that the doubters suffered grave tribulations as a result.

So, on the subject of the heroic feat of Chonkin the airman, Krinitsky penned a feature article that the editors chose as the best material of the week, and then of the month, and it was hung up on a special board. Krinitsky walked about for an entire month feeling extremely pleased with himself, proudly thrusting out his chest and stomach. In fact, it wasn't just for that month: he always walked about proudly thrusting out anything that he could, and in addition, a month later, to the envy of his journalist colleagues, it turned out that he had again written the best article, about something else that he had not seen. The issue of the paper with the feature on Chonkin was distributed right across the country, and it could have reached the Dolgov district immediately, but it didn't, because the district was still occupied by the Germans, who mostly read the *Völkischer Beobachter,* and not *Pravda.*

ONE OF THESE ASSIDUOUS READERS of the *Völkischer Beobachter* was the military commandant of the town of Dolgov, SS Obersturmführer Herr Horst Schlegel. Right now he was sitting in his office, the former office of the former local secretary of the All-Russian Communist Party (Bolsheviks), Andrei Revkin, who had died a hero's death. This change of power had brought no significant changes to the office: there was the same twin-column desk covered with green baize for the incumbent with the same long table set against the desk to form a letter T, formerly for sessions of the bureau of the District Committee, and now apparently not for anything in particular. Only the portraits had been affected by the change. Previously portraits of Lenin and Stalin had hung behind the Party secretary, while now there was a portrait of Hitler hanging behind the commandant. But Lenin and Stalin had left two dark, unfaded patches on the wall.

At the precise moment under description, the commandant was engaged in assembling a parcel for his wife, Sabina, who was in the city of Ingolstat, while whistling the well-known German song "Ich weiss nicht, was soll es bedeuten," with lyrics by the Jewish poet Heine. This was the way in which he had decided, at long last, to reply to her numerous absurd requests to send her silk stockings, lace panties, and French perfume because she supposedly had nothing to wear to church or the theater. On the first occasion he had written in reply that lace underwear was not really essential for going to church, or even the theater, and he hoped very much that no one was peeping under her skirt either in the theater or at confession, and if somebody was peeping, then not only did he not wish to facilitate them, he could not, because the things she was asking for simply did not exist here. Sabina had turned a deaf ear to the remark concerning potential under-the-skirt peepers, but expressed bewilderment: surely there were women there in the place where he was stationed, and if so, then what did they wear to visit the churches and theaters? She referred Horst to the example of their former neighbor, the soap maker Johan Zeller, who regularly sent his Berbel both underwear and overwear and even cosmetics. "*Mein Schatz* (my treasure)," Schlegel replied to her acidly, "as far as I am aware, my friend Johan is stationed in Paris, while I am presently in a small Russian town that cannot even be found on the map. Believe me, the difference between this town and

Paris is very great indeed, and the range of goods on offer here does not entirely correspond to what can be found in French boutiques."

Since she ignored his explanations and repeated the same requests in every letter, he had decided to teach her a lesson and, on the advice of his assistant, Frau Katalina von Heiss, he had put together a package in which he included what the local women wore—knitted-fabric pantaloons with elastic below the knees, woolly socks, cotton-wadded trousers, and a cotton-wadded jacket—accompanied by a written explanation that this was a typical outfit for the local ladies, and for good measure he added a bottle of Soviet triple eau-de-cologne. He was arranging his gifts in a cardboard parcel box when the aforementioned Katalina von Heiss looked in at the door. Anyone who had ever happened to meet Captain Milyaga and remain alive would have recognized this heavily made-up blonde as Kapitolina Goryacheva, the former secretary of the head of the NKVD. The former Kapitolina was now living under her real name, or perhaps another invented one—some spies change their names so often that they themselves can't always remember exactly what name they were originally given by Mom and Dad. Whether under her own name or a false one, this woman (or perhaps she wasn't even a woman) now worked for the benefit of the Great Reich (or someone else) in the same office, which was now the property of the German "Right Place," performing approximately the same duties (only for appearances' sake, of course—spies only pretend to do what everyone can see, their real goals are quite different). From time to time she also performed extra-budgetary duties of the same kind as she had in Captain Milyaga's time. This allows us to assume that she was, after all, a woman, because if she was not, Milyaga or Schlegel, or at least one of the two, would have got to the bottom of things. In short, Katalina von Heiss (that is what we shall call her) glanced into the office of the man we shall assume to be her boss and informed him that a certain local plant breeder was seeking a meeting with him.

"Who?" queried Schlegel.

"A local madman," said Katalina. "A very amusing individual."

"Well, all right. Send him in."

Schlegel took the box off the desk, sat down in his chair, and pretended to be writing something exceptionally important.

The door opened and a strange man bowed in the doorway before walking into the office, accompanied by Katalina. He was wearing a groundsheet cloak over a padded jacket and striped canvas trousers tucked into the tops of cowhide boots with handmade galoshes glued together out of pieces of automobile tire rubber. He had a battered map case hanging over his shoulder and was holding a wide-brimmed straw hat in his left hand.

The visitor approached the commandant's table, smiled, and said: "Good health to you, *guten Tag*, Mr. Commandant, allow me to introduce myself: Kuzma Matveevich Gladishev, self-made genius of plant-breeding."

Katalina's Russian was excellent (no worse than Captain Milyaga's), and German was her native language, but she couldn't find an appropriate German term for the Russian word meaning "self-made," and she translated it as *selbstgeborene*—"self-born."

"What do you mean, self-born?" the Obersturmführer asked in amazement. "Even Jesus Christ was born of woman. Did he hatch from an egg or something of the sort?"

Katalina laughed and translated the question for the visitor, who replied with dignity that he hadn't hatched himself out of anything but, despite lacking adequate education, he had succeeded, thanks to his own personal efforts and talent, in acquiring extensive knowledge and in some respects had surpassed even the most highly educated academicians and bred a vegetable hybrid with which he wished to feed the German army.

Naturally, the commandant inquired as to what kind of hybrid this was. Gladishev put his hat down on the chair beside him, hastily opened his map case, took out several newspaper cuttings with articles, both long and short, devoted to himself, with photographs, and laid them out on the desk in front of the commandant.

Katalina offered to translate the texts, but the commandant said "Don't bother" and fixed his eyes on one of the photographs, in which Gladishev was shown with a bundle of the hybrid. Then he looked up at the live Gladishev and exchanged glances with his assistant.

"The Soviet newspapers have written so much about you. Are you a Bolshevik?"

"Absolutely not!" said Gladishev, throwing his hands up to his chest in fright. "On the contrary. I am categorically opposed to the Soviet order, for which I have been subjected to repeated persecution . . ."

Schlegel folded his arms and leaned back in his chair. "Interesting! Tell him that all the Russians I meet here claim to have been persecuted by the Communists. And how did they persecute him? Did they arrest him? Put him in prison? Torture him? Stick needles under his finger-nails?"

Frau von Heiss translated.

Gladishev admitted that he had, thank God, managed to avoid un-pleasantness of that sort. But the Soviet authorities had refused to rec-ognize his scientific achievements and denied him the opportunity to cultivate the hybrid he had created, which he had called ROTNAS, i.e., the Road to National Socialism.

"If the German authorities would give me enough land for my hybrid, I could supply the entire German army," said Gladishev, clutching his hat between his knees and flinging his arms out wide, as if trying to embrace all those whom he was prepared to feed. "Can you imagine it, Mr. Officer, a huge area of land from which we could gather a double harvest of potatoes and tomatoes at the same time!"

"Very well," the Obersturmführer said through his interpreter, "we may perhaps consider your proposal at a later time, when we finish this war. Do you have anything else to say?"

"Anything else?" Gladishev hesitated, uncertain of how to set forth a hypothesis that some people might find incredible. Of course, he hadn't been able to share ideas of this kind with any Soviet bureaucrat. But now he was facing the representative of a new and more advanced civiliza-tion, who ought to take a broader view of things.

"You see . . . how can I put it . . . you'll say it sounds crazy . . . and I would agree with you . . . but I have personally witnessed the transfor-mation of a horse into a man."

"A horse into a man?" Katalina asked.

"I can understand why you might not believe me," Gladishev admit-ted, "but I even have written evidence. Here . . ." He rummaged in the map case, took out a scrap of paper and smoothed it out as he laid it on the desk. There was a single phrase traced out on it in round, almost childish writing.

"What's this?" the commandant asked, grimacing at the paper in dis-gust.

"It says: 'If I die, please consider me a Communist,'" Frau von Heiss translated.

"What does that mean?" the commandant asked, bewildered. "Con-sider whom? You?"

"Oh no!" Gladishev said with a smile when he heard the translation.

"Not me, of course not. I never made any applications to join the Party. It's Osya . . ."

"Osya?" Schlegel asked, demonstrating that he too spoke Russian quite well. "I believe Osya is a Jewish name. Isn't that so, Frau von Heiss?"

"Jewish?" Gladishev exclaimed, startled. And he smiled: "No, he wasn't a Jew. Osya, Osoaviakhim, he wasn't Jewish, he was a gelding, that is, a horse, but he'd been, you know, castrated."

"A Jew, Mr. Scientist," Schlegel said with a frown, "is a racial concept. And a Jew, whether he's castrated, circumcised, or baptized, is still a Jew as far as we're concerned and must be handed over to the German authorities."

"And especially," added the former Kapitolina, "if he wants to be a Communist."

"He doesn't wasn't to," Gladishev babbled rapidly, getting flustered. "He wanted to. But they shot him. He was a gelding, but they shot him just at the point when, as a result of unremitting toil, he turned into . . ."

"Into a Jew?" the Obersturmführer prompted.

"Absolutely not," Gladishev protested vehemently. "He turned into . . . simply a man."

"What does 'simply a man' mean?" the SS officer countered. "And what's so simple about it, if even before he changed, he was already asking to be considered a Communist?"

"Well, he did that out of sheer stupidity," Kuzma Matveevich tried to explain. "Out of stupidity and ignorance, especially since he grew up on a Soviet collective farm and, you understand, he had outmoded views of the world. But if the German High Command is interested in principle . . ."

"No," the Obersturmführer said decisively. "The German High Command has no interest in this. In fact," he said, raising one finger, "we would be more interested in the reverse process of transforming a man into a horse. But in the meantime, My Dear Sir Who Gave Birth to Himself, I would advise you to go back home and, if you genuinely wish to forward the ideals of National Socialism, start by exposing the Jews and Communists hiding among you."

"Yes, sir!" Gladishev replied obediently and set off toward the exit, but then he stopped in the doorway. "Pardon me, Mr. Officer, but what about my hybrid?"

"We'll talk about it some other time," the Obersturmführer promised.

"And now I have a question for you. Excuse me, but what is that you have on your feet? Not the boots, I mean, but those things on top of them."

"Those?" Gladishev looked down at his feet and shrugged, unable to understand how his footwear could be of interest to such an important representative of Great Germany. "Why, those are rubber goods."

"Something like galoshes?" the SS officer asked, seeking a more specific answer.

"You could say that."

"They're Soviet galoshes," the former Kapitolina laughed. "If I recall correctly, the Russians call them slush-stompers, condoms, shit crushers, and CTPs. CTP," she explained to Schlegel, "is the Chelyabinsk Tractor Plant."

"Very interesting," said Schlegel. "And do they really not let through moisture?"

"Never," Gladishev assured him. "They're very high-quality goods."

"Really?" Schlegel got up from behind his desk, walked around Gladishev, and prodded the slush-stompers with his foot. "Listen, Mr. Scientist, would you be willing to sell me these things of yours . . ."

"These things of mine?" Gladishev asked, bewildered. "Do you need them?" he asked with a start. "Oh, if you need them, then of course." And he started pulling off the slush-stompers, stepping on the heel of one foot with the toe of the other. "I'd be happy to make you a present of them. As a token of my great respect."

"Not as a present," said Schlegel, dampening his enthusiasm. "You should know that a German officer does not take bribes. I'll pay you for your tractor plants—twent . . . that is, fifteen occupation marks."

After Gladishev left, Schlegel added the goods he had bought to what was already packed in the parcel box, and added a note to his wife with the explanation that the local ladies wore this footwear when they went to the theater, the cabaret, and other places of entertainment.

IN KUZMA MATVEEVICH GLADISHEV'S DEFENSE, it should be said he was by no means a principled opponent of Soviet power; neither was he a convinced adherent of National Socialism. But, like many scientists, he would have liked to stand aside from politics, he regarded the completion of his scientific research as the most important task of his life, and it was all the same to him who assisted him to achieve his goal.

Nonetheless, he was pleased with his visit to Dolgov. He thought he had managed to get on the right side of the German commandant. Of course, he must have done, since the commandant had entered into a commercial arrangement with him and given him a counter-assignment, which Gladishev set about carrying out immediately upon his return to the village. He tore two pages out of a standard exercise book: on one of them he wrote "List of Jews in the village of Krasnoye," and on the other, "List of Communists in the village of Krasnoye." In the list of Communists he entered only one name—that of the former Party organizer, Kilin, who, as it happened, was no longer in the village at that time—and in the other list, which was empty, Kuzma Matveevich wrote: "Unfortunately, there are no Jews living in the village of Krasnoye at present."

ALTHOUGH THE GERMANS HAD NOT OFFERED to support his hybrid either, his zeal had been noted, and soon Kuzma Matveevich was summoned to Obersturmführer Schlegel and asked if he wished to become the elder of the village of Krasnoye. He accepted the proposal because ever since his young days he had dreamed of occupying a position of leadership, but under the Soviet regime he had never been offered anything of the kind.

He didn't have enough time to cause much damage to his fellow villagers in his position as elder, but there was one particular matter in which he made his mark. When an order arrived from the Germans stipulating that ten head of cattle must be requisitioned from the most prosperous peasants in the village, the first animal he entered in the list of those to be expropriated was Nyura's Beauty, whom he hated so furiously following a certain incident that he wanted her to die as an arch-enemy of mankind. He had started to hate Chonkin at the same time, and Nyura, but more than anyone else in the world, more than Chonkin and Nyura, more than Stalin and Hitler, he hated Beauty. He often recalled, and sometimes even dreamed about, the way she had destroyed his vegetable plot, how insolently she had devoured the final plant of ROTS (the Road to Socialism—there had not been any "National" in the name then), and he had hoped, in fact he had dreamed passionately, of seeing the fatal hour when they would take hold of that horned so-and-so's tether and lead her off, resisting desperately, to the slaughterhouse. And now he had indeed lived to see that happy moment.

Early in the morning six bandy-legged soldiers from the German *Sonderkommando* led Beauty out of Nyura's cowshed and, as Gladishev had foreseen, the cow resisted obstinately, bracing her front legs against the ground, lowering her head and shaking it about, as Nyura tried helplessly to take her back. Gladishev watched through the window and exulted.

The soldiers kept pushing Nyura away harder and harder, but when she fell down, she just got up again and dashed back to the cow. Gladishev saw her trying to explain something to an elderly *Feldwebel* with a bandaged throat. She folded her hands together imploringly into a boat shape, fell to her knees, and grabbed hold of the *Feldwebel*'s legs. Perhaps he was from a peasant family himself and understood the Russian woman's despair; he didn't want to do her any harm, and so he didn't hit her straightaway. First he freed himself and tried to frighten her off by swinging his rifle butt, but when she dashed to the cow again, grabbed hold of the tether, and pulled the animal toward her, he lost his temper and thumped her in the stomach so hard that she fell down, doubled up, and lay there by the road for a long time, twitching in agony, until Ninka Kurzova lifted her up and led her home.

The expropriated cows were quickly assembled on the edge of the village and led off in tight formation in the direction of Dolgov, down the half-frozen road along which someone or other had always been driven—kulaks to Siberia or men into the army, all along the same road and in the same direction—toward the hillock behind which there was a kind of black hole. Many had set off in that direction, but very rarely had anyone come back.

Gladishev went out onto the porch to look at the cattle being driven away. He saw Nyura trying to save her cow, saw the German first push her aside and then finally hit her. The plant-breeder had not yet completely lost the ability to feel human sympathy, but his hatred for Beauty and his thirst for vengeance overrode his other feelings and, once he was sure that the devastator of his scientific research would receive the punishment she deserved, he went back into his house and downed a whole tumbler of his own moonshine in his delight.

"Eh-ha-ha!" he cackled, rubbing his hands together fervently.

"What are you so delighted about?" asked his Aphrodite, who had only just woken up.

"I'm delighting in life!" he replied joyfully. "Delighting in the fact that we're still alive while some others are already ooh-hoo-hoo!"

But the self-made scientist's joy did not last long. In a snowy, frosty December the Red Army, after sacrificing the lives of millions of its soldiers, won its first victory in the war against the invaders at Moscow. The Dolgov district was liberated by partisans under the command of Aglaya Stepanovna Revkina. On her orders, German collaborators were rounded up and then strung up in the Square of Fallen Warriors, without any time-wasting investigations. But then someone pointed out that this made the hanged criminals fallen warriors as well. This embarrassing argument obliged the authorities to reconsider their actions, and reprisals against the German lackeys were temporarily discontinued.

Gladishev was lucky. He was handed over for trial. Since he had not apparently done anything particularly bad and his case was not dealt with in the heat of the moment, his sentence was relatively mild: five years of exile to the distant regions of Siberia.

STRANGELY ENOUGH, AFTER THE GERMANS ARRIVED, the post office in Dolgov carried on working in almost exactly the same way as before. The volume of incoming correspondence was reduced, certainly, but it did not dry up completely. And the same Lyubov Mikhailovna Dulova remained in charge of the post office, despite the fact that she was a Communist. The Germans at first intended to do something nasty to her, but she presented them with proof that she was the daughter of a repressed kulak, that one of her grandfathers had been a merchant and the other a priest and that she had joined the Party out of fear of losing her job, but had not paid her Party dues for the last three months.

Obersturmführer Schlegel decided that these explanations were acceptable, since he regarded himself as a liberal (by SS standards) and understood very well that someone could join any party, including the Communists or National Socialists, out of ordinary mercantile considerations rather than ideological conviction. Schlegel also took into account the petitions made on Lyubov Mikhailovna's behalf by Oberfeldwebel

Schultz, who had entered into a relationship with her. And so Lyubov Mikhailovna remained in her job, but her happiness was short-lived.

When the Germans retreated, she attempted to retreat with them and Oberfeldwebel Schultz, and she had already packed two suitcases when she was seized by Aglaya Revkina's partisans while in the process of packing the third. The partisans wanted to hang her immediately, but in view of her sex they took pity on her and came up with a less severe punishment. They shaved half her head, led her around the Square of Fallen Warriors, and tied her to a whipping post, barefoot and wearing nothing but a shirt, with a sign around her neck that said: "I SLEPT WITH A FASCIST." It was not entirely just of the partisans to write that, because Oberfeldwebel Schultz was not a fascist at all and not a member of the Nazi Party; he was a cook by trade and had gone to war against his own will. However, it was not Schultz but his erstwhile mistress who was the issue.

While she was standing there tied to the post, barefoot and barely even dressed, people came up, called her a bitch, and spat in her face. Nyura, who happened to be walking across the square, saw her in this situation. Nyura probably ought to have been delighted, recalling how Lyubov Mikhailovna had given her the sack, and she ought to have taken revenge by spitting in her face and asking which one of them had slept with a German, but Nyura was not a vengeful woman, she was soft-hearted. Looking at her former boss, the only thing she felt was sympathy. She even started appealing to the people there: "What is all this? Just what do you think you're doing? What kind of animals are you? She's got no shoes and no clothes, she'll turn into an icicle soon, and you're spitting at her."

But the people there, mostly of the female sex, were in a truly vicious mood by then. Actually, people can always be vicious, in easy times and hard times, but at that time they could be especially nasty. Nyura started defending her former boss, the people didn't like it, and one woman wearing a man's city coat asked: "Just who is this pushy bitch and why's she standing up for the other one?" And another suggested: "Probably she's the same kind, that's why she's interfering." A third woman said they ought to tie her to the other side of the same post to balance things up. And the crowd started thickening around Nyura. But then there was a shout: "What are you women yelling about and what are you crowding round here for? That's Nyura Belyashova, her husband's an airman, fighting at the front."

The women standing around were confused, and while they were wondering if they should consider Nyura's airman a circumstance that mitigated her guilt, Katya the telegraph operator (she was the one who had shouted) led Nyura out of the crowd by the hand and started abusing her for being too kind-hearted by half and forgetting how Lyubov Mikhailovna had treated her. And then she asked, "Will you come back to the post office?"

"I'll come back," Nyura replied, "but who'll take me?"

"I'll take you," said Katya. "I'm going to be in charge at the post office now. And I'll take you. Especially since your Ivan's turned up."

"Wo-ot?" Nyura exclaimed, unable to believe her ears.

"Never mind wo-ot, he's turned up. Come on, I'll show you wo-ot."

THEY RAN QUICKLY TO THE POST OFFICE and there on the right, just on the way in, on the board with the specimens of postcards and telegrams hanging on it, where they hung up all sorts of announcements and the order announcing Nyura's dismissal had once hung, there was an article from the newspaper *Pravda* pinned up with thumbtacks. Nyura immediately saw the headline printed in big letters:

IVAN CHONKIN'S HEROIC FEAT

Still unable to believe her eyes, she fell on the text and read it right through, moving her lips, from the beginning to the end. The author of the article described events as follows:

A flyer of the N command [during that great war, for reasons
of secrecy, all military units mentioned in the Soviet press were
referred to as N], Ivan Chonkin, who had been shot down in an
unequal battle against fascist vultures, had been obliged to land
his fighter plane in territory occupied by the enemy in the area
of the town of N. Naturally, the Germans had decided to take
him prisoner and capture the plane. The detachment of crack SS
cutthroats sent to accomplish this not only failed in their mission but were taken prisoner by the valiant warrior. And then
an entire regiment joined in. Chonkin put up valiant resistance
and, even though he suffered a concussion, maintained his

defense singlehanded for several hours until general Drynov's
N division arrived to relieve him.

Everyone who was in the post office at the time was happy for Nyura
and congratulated her. Verka from New Kliukvino was the only one who
angered Nyura by doubting.

"But is it your Chonkin?"

"Whose could it be, if not mine?" Nyura answered back. "Mine's an airman, and this one's an airman. Mine's Ivan Chonkin, and this one's Ivan
Chonkin. How many Ivan Chonkins do you think there are in the world?"

"Quite a lot, I reckon," said Verka, with a shake of her head. "It's not
such an unusual name."

There are some people like that, especially women, who just can't hold
back—not even out of spite, but out of sheer stupidity—they just have to
say something to spoil your mood and ruin your appetite.

But no matter what Verka said, she couldn't shake Nyura's certainty
that the Ivan Chonkin who had turned up was her own Ivan Chonkin,
hers and not any other. And she also had another reason that she didn't
tell anyone but kept in her own head: there was probably no one apart
from her Ivan who was capable of such a heroic feat, but he was capable
of it, and had already done things exactly like that in front of her very
eyes with the modest help she had been able to give him.

NYURA CAME RUNNING BACK to Krasnoye with the newspaper, went
around to all the houses, and showed the article about Ivan to everyone:
to Taika Gorshkova and Zinaida Volkova, not even leaving out granny
Dunya. Some were genuinely glad, others pretended to be, and yet others
were openly envious. Ninka Kurzova, like Verka from New Kliukvino,
tried to dampen Nyura's enthusiasm with the argument that, even sup-
posing it was the same Ivan Chonkin, what good was that, even if he was
alive, when he hadn't ever written a single little letter?

"My blockhead writes nigh on every day. I can't even imagine how he
does any fighting and where he gets so much paper from."

And indeed, Nikolai did surprise and delight his wife with his mis-
sives almost every single day, and not just ordinary letters either, but

letters written in verse. Ninka had never suspected that Nikolai had any poetic ability before, but now that he was at war, for some unknown reason Kurzov had suddenly developed a talent as a versifier, and he wrote one long, long letter after another in rhymed text on subjects like this:

> Yesterday to battle led,
> We beat the fascist roundly
> And then our young commander said:
> You fought that fight right soundly . . .

> Dear aged mother, shed no tear,
> Or wife of sweetest charms,
> My eager feet will speed me there
> To fold you in my arms . . .

"It's all lies, all lies," Ninka grumbled angrily. "He writes any old thing, whether it's true or not, all he cares about is if it sounds good. He's even put his aged mother in, and his aged mother's been dead for three years already. Why bother to write trash like that?"

"Whatever he writes, if he writes, it means he's alive," said Nyura. "And that's the most important thing."

"That's right, of course," Ninka agreed with a sigh, and tossed the letter into the corner of the counter, where the other letters were already lying in a big heap.

NYURA HAD HAD THE PILE OF SCHOOL EXERCISE BOOKS with crooked ruled lines since before the war. She found some ink, too. And the thick office pen with the number 86 nib hadn't gone rusty on the shelf yet. That evening Nyura took one of the exercise books, tore a double page out of the middle, and blithely composed:

> Happy times and good day, tell me what you have to say, dear
> Vanya! I'm getting on well, and I wish you the same with all my
> lonely woman's heart. And also sound health and a good mood.
> I'm working as a postwoman at the post office as I did in former

times, and I read about you in the newspaper, about how you fought an uneven battle with fascist vultures in your frighter plane. Vanya, battle the enemy valiantly, with all possible caution and come back victorious, alive and well to your Nyura, who's waiting for you with impatient love. And if you come back without an arm or a leg or some other part of your body like that, then I'll be regretfully glad of it and I'll take care of you like a little child until the end of your life or mine, anything as long as you're content. With that I end my short letter and await a speedy reply as the nightingale waits for summer.

With greetings,

Your Anna Belyashova from Krasnoye village, if you haven't forgotten.

Before she put in the final period, she paused doubtfully, because she hadn't written the most important thing, and perhaps she ought to. She hadn't mentioned a word about her pregnancy. Then she decided: "Well, all right, when he answers, I'll write about it."

She folded the letter into a triangle with the text on the inside, and then all that was left was to write the address on the clean side. That wasn't a difficult task. From Krinitsky's article, Nyura knew that Chonkin was serving in the N command. And the N command, as she remembered, was the very finest command in the Red Army, because it was mentioned in all the newspapers. Nyura didn't have a very clear idea about army structures. That was why it didn't seem strange to her that the N command included airmen, tank troops, artillerymen, infantrymen, and others. Nor was she surprised that the N command was fighting simultaneously on all fronts: defending the N elevation, taking the town of N, and advancing along route N.

In short, Nyura knew the address. She dashed it off on the clean side of the triangle:

"U.S.S.R. N command, Airman Ivan Chonkin in person."

And she was very sure that he would reply straightaway. She told all the women that she'd written a letter and was expecting a quick reply. And she really was. As soon as the usual sacks of post arrived from the train, she was the first to dash to sort them out. But all to no avail.

IT SEEMED LIKE SOMEONE WAS WRITING SOMETHING to everyone except Nyura. Even Old Man Shapkin, first when he was alive and
then after he was dead, was regularly sent letters from the front by his
great-nephew Timosha, who had only turned up recently. In 1930, when
he was still a teenager, Timosha had been exiled to some unknown des-
tination, together with his father, mother, two sisters, grandfather, and
grandmother, and not so much as a whisper had been heard about them
right up until the war. Now he wrote long, detailed letters, about how
they had been transported in some unknown direction in frozen freight
cars for many winter days and nights, being fed on small, frozen potatoes that weren't either cleaned or boiled, as if they were pigs. His grandmother slept right beside the door and she died there in the night, after
wetting herself and freezing to the floor.

They took them all the way to Kazakhstan, put them into big wagons,
drove them further and further into the steppe, and dumped them. They
gave everyone eighteen pounds of flour and said: "Live here any way you
like; if you die, then that's your lot, and if you survive, good for you." And
they left behind a few spades, rakes, pitchforks, and one axe.

Fortunately, when they got there the freezing weather was over and
the snow was melting, but rain set in and for many days the heavens
poured down on them without a break, soaking them to the bone, and
on all sides as far as the eye could see there was tall feather-grass and
sagebrush, and it was impossible to imagine any way they could live
there.

It wasn't only the women—the grown men cried like children. But
Timosha's father, Timofei Shapkin, said there was no point in crying,
tears wouldn't fix anything, and he ordered everyone to pick up the tools.
He stuck his spade into the ground first and started excavating a dugout.
Those who weren't involved in the main job were sent off into the steppe
to search for wild millet, sage, and other herbs, to pull up the feather
grass and sagebrush by hand for fuel and, if they could manage it, catch
gophers or even mice—to lay in supplies. They wouldn't have lasted long
on those provisions, but one day Timosha's father went off to somewhere
far away and came back on a horse. They killed the horse and then ate its
meat all winter. Luckily for them, the snow fell again, a hard frost set in,
and the meat didn't spoil. By that time they had already excavated two

dugouts and cobbled together a little stove, and that was how they lived, but not everyone survived. The first to depart for the next world was Timosha's grandfather, and in early spring both of his sisters came down with some short, deadly sickness and soon passed away, too.

In spring Timosha's father took him and they made a run for it. They didn't mind being caught and put in prison or killed—anything would be better than dying there.

They walked through the steppe as far as the Esil Junction and climbed into a freight car full of sheep's milk cheese. Timosha's father gorged himself on the cheese and died right there in the car from a twisted bowel. And Timosha was caught by the railroad guards while he was traveling, after which he was beaten and sent to an orphanage, where he attended an ordinary school at first, then an industrial training school. And before he was drafted into the army, he worked as a plasterer.

Timosha wrote so punctiliously that the dirty-yellow triangles of his letters arrived almost every day. He depicted his own past and present life in the minutest detail and talked about his army comrades who were killed or wounded, but he never asked Old Man Shapkin about his life, as if he assumed that nothing ever happened to the old man and nothing ever could happen. The old man had died a long time ago, but Timosha kept on and on writing, without noticing that no answers ever reached him from Krasnoye.

10

"WELL, WHAT THEN?" NINKA ASKED IMPATIENTLY. "Anything from N command?"

"Nothing," Nyura admitted. "And I've written another letter already. Not a word or a whisper."

But Ninka was one of those people who put on an air of friendly sympathy because they just have to go and say something really nasty to a dear friend that will upset her and make her feel sick at heart.

"Well, he'll write for sure, won't he!" she said, shaking her head. "Just grab a pencil and write this very minute, he will. I'll tell you straight, Nyura, you're wasting your time, eating your heart out. I don't like saying this to you, honest to God, I don't, but I say it as one friend to another: don't wait, don't hope, you can't trust anyone but yourself."

"What on earth are you saying!" Nyura said resentfully. "Why shouldn't I hope? Our love was that strong. You don't know the way he held me tight and the things he whispered in my ear."

"Oi, Nyur, don't make me laugh! Whispered in your ear, did he, oi-yoi-yoi! He really had it easy with you, from the moment he landed here. Down a glass of vodka, have a bit of fun with a woman, scratch his itchy head a bit—why wouldn't he do some whispering! And now what? He's an airman, get it? Here today and somewhere else tomorrow. And everywhere out there, Nyura, the ground's swarming with women just like you and me."

"Don't they chase your Kolka, then?"

"Don't get angry, Nyur, but Kolka and me are married, and even then I don't trust him, but you and that Vanka of yours . . ."

Ninka waved her hand despairingly and gave up.

The other women didn't say anything like that, but Nyura noticed them giving each other looks that meant they didn't believe Chonkin would ever answer her letters.

11

DURING THE LAST WEEK OF JANUARY and the first week of February there were strong winds. The blizzard swirled snow around the houses and it settled layer upon layer, got packed down, and then trampled into firm drifts. The drifts grew and grew until they rose higher than the roofs, and all life came to a standstill in Krasnoye. The people waited out the fury of the elements, huddling inside their houses. And what would anyone go out for, when they couldn't see a man or a tree or a bush two steps in front of them? At night they had no light; they didn't have any matches, or kerosene for a lamp with a glass chimney or a floating wick, and they weren't used to living by the light of a wooden spill any longer. They carried burning coals to each other's houses to light the stoves and the only light they had was the fire in a stove with its flap open. They used the flour they still had, mixed with oilcake, bran, and dried goosefoot, to bake sticky, crumbly flapjacks.

During the coldest period, Olympiada Petrovna, the refugee, and her grandson Vadik moved in with Nyura again to save on firewood. Nyura willingly agreed to this invasion of her living space: although she'd got used to living alone, she still felt the need to have another living soul nearby. And especially in winter, when it gets so lonesome on your own that you could howl like a wolf. But now she had something like a temporary family. With her character, Nyura was always getting involved with someone else's problems: taking care of someone, doing someone's laundry, cooking someone's food, and feeling delighted if she managed to please someone. Nyura gave her lodgers her own bed and moved up onto the stove. She volunteered to wash Vadik's little trousers, shirts, and underpants. Olympiada Petrovna threw her own things in for good measure, and Nyura didn't object. And so she turned into a servant in her own house, working for her guests. And Olympiada Petrovna treated her like a servant, but she always addressed her formally, as Anna Alexeevna. Olympiada Petrovna was a pampered city woman, she didn't want to go to the river to wash out her underwear in a hole in the ice, she didn't know how to chop firewood, and was quite incapable of pulling an iron pot out of the stove with the oven fork, but she liked to give orders and lecture people, and she was capricious. Either the hut was too hot for her or there was a draft blowing through the cracks, or she complained that the bedbugs bothered her all the time.

"I simply can't imagine it, Anna Alexeevna, have you really lived with bedbugs all your life?"

Nyura shrugged in embarrassment. "How can you get away from them? Where there's people, there's bedbugs."

Olympiada Petrovna read Vadik poems, which he memorized easily, then declaimed in a loud voice:

> Wonnay inna feezinco depf avva winna
> Asilef mewellinin bittyhad fost,
> Isor swowee cwymbina stip-swoppy neesigh
> A wittihoss puwina catwoady wogs
> An stwidinsy datewy wivtwan keedecowum,
> Asmo pesan cwutchee the weinsofa hoss,
> In ovywaj boot sanna shot cotty shipskin,
> In ovysigh zmitten
> Za ti kneewee man.*

* From a poem by Nikolai Nekrasov: "One day in the freezing cold depths of the winter / As I left my dwelling in bitter-hard frost, / I saw, slowly climbing the steep-sloping hillside / A little horse pulling a cartload of logs / And, striding sedately with tranquil decorum, / A small peasant clutching the reins of the horse, / In oversized boots and a short coat of sheepskin, / In oversized mittens, / A tiny, wee man."

Nyura looked at Vadik, listened, smiled, and stroked her stomach, which wasn't all that big yet, but already discernible to the attentive eye. There was a little creature growing in there too, she'd like it to be a boy who might, perhaps, be as lively and bright as Vadik. Maybe she would call him Vadik, but then Ivan was better, after all. Let him be Ivan Ivanovich. And then, just like Olympiada Petrovna, Nyura would read her little Vanyusha, Ivan Ivanovich, poems about a little peasant boy.

12

THE BLIZZARD ENDED UNEXPECTEDLY and a calm, bright day emerged, so sunny you could go blind if you didn't squint. Early in the morning, wearing her old light coat and newly darned felt boots, Nyura ran off through the sun and the snow to Dolgov. Although she was pregnant, she ran lightly along the track made by the early wood sledges.

A whole heap of mail had piled up. There were four letters for Ninka Kurzova alone—three from Nikolai and one from her female cousin in the Penza region. There were two parcels as well. Nyura took one of them—for Grandma Dunya from her grandson—but she didn't take the other—for Alexander Plechevoi's wife from Lyushka in Kuibyshev—because the plywood box was too heavy. She borrowed a bottle of kerosene from Katka. She bought bread for a week on her ration cards—just over six pounds—and it was still warm. She picked little pieces off it as she walked along, unable to stop herself. When less than half of it was left, she stuck the remainder down as deep in her bag as she could and started walking faster, trying not to think about food.

The sun was still high in the sky and the glinting of the snow in the sunlight made her eyes smart. Even though it was clear that winter was already on the way out, the frost nipped at her nose, and come the evening (so they said at the post office) it was going to turn cold again. The old coat, cut out of her mother's warm plush jacket and her quilted coat with the sheepskin collar, was poor protection against the frost, but Nyura ran swiftly with her heavy load, like a horse with the scent of home in its nostrils; she ran easily, for the road had already been flattened for her, smoothed by sledge runners (it had a deep, rich gloss on it). Her legs carried her along, she only had to lift her feet in time.

Nyura wanted to deliver the post without going home so she would have time to feed Borka before dark, but as she ran past her own house she saw Olympiada Petrovna come out onto the porch without a coat, wrapped in a flannelette sheet that she was holding close to her throat.

"Anna Alexeevna!" she shouted, waving her free hand. "Come home quickly, you've got a visitor!"

Her heart started pounding, her legs went weak, a queasy feeling started rising in her throat: could it really be Ivan?

But why in the middle of winter, in the thick of the war? Unless he was wounded. She hoped it wouldn't be serious. But even if it was serious, even if he'd lost an arm . . . or a leg . . . or even if he had no arms or legs left at all . . . Already expecting to find a limbless stump, she went running into the hut—and stopped dead in the doorway with her mouth hanging open.

Sitting on the bench by the window was a little old man with stubbly cheeks and the hair on his bumpy head cropped short, wearing a tattered old NKVD uniform with faded collar tabs. His cheeks had collapsed into his face and his eyes were popping out of their sockets—he was a really frightening sight.

Nyura recognized the visitor and was surprised and disappointed— she hadn't been expecting him.

When he saw Nyura, the visitor got up and moved toward her, but after the first step he staggered and started waving his arms about grotesquely, trying to keep his balance.

"Pappy!" Nyura shrieked. She dropped her bag and dashed to her father, ashamed of her first feeling. She just managed to catch him and hold him up. Then she wrapped her arms around his small head, as solid as a block of wood, and started crying silently. The tears rolled down her cheeks, falling on the stubbly crown of his head, and her father, so little, with the body of a ten-year-old child, nestled against her breasts, with his thin arms dangling like sticks. Then he stirred slightly.

"Let go, child," he wheezed from under her elbow. "You'll smother me. I'm weak."

Nyura hastily released him and sat him down on the bench. She looked into his face and started crying again, loudly this time.

"Pappy, dearest Pappy," she wailed. "What has this damned war done to you!"

"People are more terrible than any war, child," her father said in a low voice, closing his weary eyes.

She went down into the cellar and picked out the best potatoes she could find in the dark, washed them, filled the pot with water and put it in the big Russian stove.

Her father was sleeping with his head resting on his hands.

In the next room Vadik was dragging a galosh about on a string and panting and hooting—pretending to be a locomotive. She asked him to hoot a bit more quietly and ran off around the village with her bag.

When she got back, she heard the noise while she was still outside. Pushing open the door, she saw the pot overturned on the table with the water spilled out and the potatoes scattered across the tabletop. Her father was grabbing them and wolfing them down greedily, stuffing a new one into his mouth before he'd even finished chewing the one before.

"Alexei Ivanich," said Olympiada Petrovna, who was fussing around him, "what on earth are you doing? What a thing to do! Anna Alexeevna, take the potatoes away from him, he'll give himself a twisted bowel."

Nyura rushed over to her father and pulled him back by the shoulders.

"Pappy, why are you doing that? Stop it! It's all for you. Wait, I'll give you a bowl and bring you some oil."

She tried to drag him away, but he was delirious and he kept breaking free, grabbing a potato, and sticking it in his mouth, snarling and panting and smacking his lips: he glanced into the empty pot, fumbled around in it with his hands, and collapsed onto the bench, completely drained.

In the evening Nyura lit a lamp and started making up the beds. She let her father have the stove to sleep on and threw a heap of old rags on the bench for herself. Olympiada Petrovna called Nyura aside and whispered in a tragic voice.

"Anna Alexeevna, please, I implore you. Do something about his clothes. It's quite unbearable, such a horrible sight, and we have a little child here."

"I don't understand, what do you mean?" Nyura asked politely, with a smile.

"Surely you can see?" said the lodger, throwing one hand up in the air. "Why, it's about to crawl away on its own." She pointed to the greatcoat hanging on a nail. Nyura raised the lamp to it and recoiled in horror: the greatcoat was completely covered with a teeming layer of white lice, as if it was woven out of them. Nyura had never seen anything like it in her life. Squeezing her eyes shut, she grabbed the coat between her finger and thumb, carried it outside and threw it on the snow by the porch. She went back in, found a set of underwear left over from Chonkin in a chest and gave it to her father. The underwear he took off, which stank like old footcloths, she first took outside, and later boiled in a big cauldron until three in the morning. After catching a short nap, while it was still dark she heated up the bathhouse so hot that the beams started cracking and oozing resin, filling the air with the smell of summer in the forest. And while she was stoking the fire, the new day arrived, calm, sunny, and frosty again. She went to get her father and lugged him to the bathhouse—he could barely drag his feet along.

In the bathhouse there were two barrels—one with hot water and one with cold—and beside them a swollen wooden tub, black with age. Nyura splashed plenty of water into the tub with the wooden scoop, splashed it about with her hand, and turned to her father.

"Take your clothes off, Pappy!"

Her father got undressed as far as his underclothes, pulled off the undershirt, and stood there, shifting from one bare foot to the other.

"Are you going to get washed in your drawers?" Nyura asked him. "Get them off."

"It's not right, Nyura, it feels awkward, like!"

"Stop acting stupid, Pappy," she said angrily. "Come on, get them off!"

She scrubbed him gingerly with the bast fibers, afraid of rubbing right through him.

He lived with Nyura for several days, incapable of communicating properly; he just ate, drank, went to the privy, and slept. He slept with his eyes open. Nyura walked up to him, looked and listened to see if he was breathing. And when he started coming back to life, his dreams became more and more disturbed. He ground his teeth in his sleep, groaned and shouted out, leapt up and gazed around wildly for a long time, unable to understand where he was and what was wrong with him. Gradually, however, he recovered and eventually gathered enough strength to tell Nyura what had happened to him.

13

"REMEMBER, NYURA, I WENT AWAY TO THE CITY. And I married a divorced woman. Lyuba, she was called. She worked as a secretary for our boss, Roman Gavrilovich Luzhin. And through her I got a few special perks. We lived well right up until the war. And we had a child, a daughter. Lyuba called her Vika, after the city fashion. She was a good little girl, always laughing. Then the war started and some of the staff were transferred to the army in the field. But they kept me because I was so old, and then again, because Lyuba petitioned Roman Gavrilovich especially. So then I'm moved to being a warden in the remand prison. Good work, quiet, and decent food. I'm getting by all right. Well, suddenly the big boss himself sends for me, Roman Gavrilovich Luzhin. I go to see him, and he comes out from behind his desk and shakes my hand, and calls me Alexei Ivanich, real polite: Hello, Alexei Ivanich, have a seat, Alexei Ivanich, would you like some tea, Alexei Ivanich, or some cognac, Alexei Ivanich? And he takes me across to his little table and sits me down on his leather sofa, and gives me a little glass of cognac, not a big one, of course, he hands me a little one, just a bit bigger than a liquor glass. And then he starts toing and froing; How's life, he asks, how are you managing moneywise? If you need, we can give you a hand, but we're in terrible need of some help ourselves. Of course, I say, why not? Always glad to help, any time, Roman Gavrilovich, I say. Not as I'm any good for brainwork, but if you need something fetched or taken away or some wood chopped, or a stove lit—then I'm eager and willing. Ah no, he says, that's not it. Fetching and taking doesn't need much brains, but there is one bit of business that takes a strong character, a firm will, and a steady hand. Right now, he says, there's a battle to the death going on, and our enemies have to be eliminated without mercy, so what do you, Alexei Ivanich, think about that, then? At first, like a fool, I thought it was the usual thing. Why, I says, Roman Gavrilovich, I've no need to think about it, I thought I was too old, but if that's what's needed, then like every other citizen, no matter what, I'm always ready to lay down my head for the homeland and motherland. Especially since there's nothing much of any great value in my head, no bright ideas ever hatch out in it, about the only thing it's good for is wearing a size fifty-four cap.

"Roman Gavrilovich laughs at that. What's all this you're saying, Alexei Ivanovich, joking with me, are you? We're not sending you to the front and we don't want you laying down your head for nothing either, no matter what it's like; on the contrary, we'll make other heads bow down to you.

"I was too stupid to catch on at first, but he started explaining to me, and when I realized what it was, Nyura, my hair stood right up on end, I really mean it. He offered me a job as a military executioner, shooting enemies of the people, that is. And the conditions are good, he says, and we'll raise your pay, and sort out your accommodation problems, and upgrade your rations to two pounds of bread and a quarter of a pound of butter a day, and a glass of vodka and a sandwich after every event.

"But I say, no, no, Roman Petrovich, offer me mountains of gold, shoot me if you like, but I can't do that. And I can't, Nyura, you know that, because I never raised a hand against any living thing, I could never even kill a chicken, I used to call the neighbor round. Everyone used to laugh at me about it: a country man, they said, and he goes weak at the knees.

"So I tell Luzhin about the chicken, and he frowns at that and says a chicken has nothing to do with the case, a chicken's a harmless creature, but an enemy of the people is no chicken, he's worse than any ravening wild beast. And anyway, he says, this is a huge expression of confidence in you, and you go getting awkward about it. You go now, he says, and think about it good and hard. Well, I get home, and my wife's there, and our daughter's crawling about on the floor, this way and that. I told Lyuba, and she says: What are you thinking of? Life's hard, she says, with one room in a barracks building, and we haven't got enough food to feed that little one properly, we've no money to buy firewood, and you go turning your nose up. What makes you so sorry for them anyway? You've been told, they're enemies of the people, and if you don't kill them, they'll find someone else to do it, they're not going to live anyway. And she started nagging at me: what kind of man are you? she says, you're not a real man, a walking disaster, that's what you are, I don't know why I ever took up with you, and so on, and more of the same. She ate me, skinned me alive, and I thought and thought about it all night long, scratched the back of my head bloody. Well, I think, after all, a job's just a job, and someone's got to do it, especially with them being enemies of the people, and even if they aren't enemies, like they say, there's no way I can help that. It's not me that condemns them, I'm just the tool, I just press the trigger, and someone's going to do it anyway. Well, I think, all right, I've never tried it, but if I squeeze my eyes shut and don't get up close . . . So anyway, in the morning I go to the boss. Well then?—he says. All right, I say, I agree. That's right, good man, I never had any doubts about you, he says, because you're one of ours, root and branch, and I believe your devotion to our cause is boundless. And concerning these little people you'll have to work with, you know, don't you, we don't go shooting anyone for nothing here, and if it's come to that, it means he's done a monstrous amount of damage to our motherland and people. And you don't feel sorry to kill someone like that. You can feel sorry for a fly, you can feel sorry for a cockroach, a chicken, and all the rest, but not for an enemy like that.

"All right, then, so they made me the military executioner, and nothing really changed that much. Except that I started getting more time off. I used to do twenty-four hours, then have two days off, but now it was three. And sure enough, they started upgrading my rations, and our turn for an apartment came up straightaway. Roman Gavrilovich went with us himself and showed us the apartment—you wouldn't believe it, three rooms right in the center of town, with furniture, too. And that furniture . . . when we walked in there, we couldn't believe our eyes: it was walnut or that birch . . . Korean is it? I don't have a clue about all that, but even I can see it's expensive wood. To tell the truth, it's all the same to me, a stool's as good as a chair, as long as there's something to sit on, but Lyuba's eyes light up and she wanders round the rooms, groping at everything with both hands like she's playing a piano and she asks, is that chandelier crystal? And the leather on the sofa, she asks, is that real? And the cupboard, she says, what wood's that made of? And there's a balcony there, and a bathroom too, and you know what that bathroom was like? You wouldn't believe it, there's this thing like a great big chamber pot, a toilet bowl it's called, a little tank of water and a handle hanging on a chain. You pull the handle and it washes everything away. And a bath, too. So big it's like a trough, and these two faucets. Twist one faucet and cold water runs out, twist the other one and hot water runs out. And naturally, Lyuba touched everything and twisted everything, and when she saw the bathroom she went crazy altogether. The bed was as wide as from here to there, with carved end boards, with animals' heads, and feather pillows as well, and a satin sheet and a lacy counterpane. Lyuba almost lost her mind altogether. Is all this going to be ours? she asks. And why not? says Roman Gavrilovich. Of course it's going to be yours. Why can other people live like this and you can't? And he turns to me: how about you, man of the house, he says, do you like the apartment or not? And I say, how could anyone not like it? Why, I tell him, it's sheer luxury, it's a real palace, I suppose some real bourgeois folk must have lived here. Why yes, he says, they did, first White bourgeois and then Red ones, but we caught them out, both kinds. Well, if they were caught out, they were caught out, there's nothing I can do about that either. I glance into the third room and I see a portrait: some kind of top brass general, two pips on his collar tabs, but no cap on. His head's shaved—just like Roman Gavrilovich's, by the way—and he's sat this little girl on his shoulders and the two of them are laughing. And the little girl's exactly like my Vika. I ask him: Who's that? Ah, says Roman Gavrilovich, that's the very same Red bourgeois who used to live here, getting monstrously fat at the expense of the workers and the peasants. And then straight off he says, yes, I completely forgot, there's a little job lined up for you tomorrow. So you take it easy today, relax, have a bit of vodka if you like, and tomorrow morning at nine go straight to the prison governor, Comrade Peshkin. Is that settled, then? he asks. And I look at Lyuba running round the apartment with her eyes popping out of her head and I say, all right, that's settled.

"And I don't even give it much thought. And then when I got home and I remembered, my heart stopped dead. Lyuba, I say, did you hear what Roman Gavrilovich said? She says, I heard, what of it? And she's sorting out her clothes, thinking what to throw out and what to keep for the new apartment. And that night she sets out her plans for me: We'll move the bed into the corner, she says, but we'll put the table out in the middle of the room. I'll grow flowers on the balcony, she says. She just doesn't understand that right now I can't be bothered with tables or flowers or anything like that. I tossed and turned the whole night long, didn't get to sleep until almost morning. And in the morning Lyuba woke me up. Get up, she says, they're here already, asking for you. So all right, I get up, get washed and dressed and have breakfast, but I can't think straight at all. And Lyuba says: I can see you're not yourself, I think I'll go along with you. So she gets dressed, puts on her lipstick, takes hold of my arm and leads me off. And we turn up like that to see the prison governor, and Luzhin's there already, with the public prosecutor and the prison governor Peshkin and the head warden Vasilii Popov, and another two wardens and another two men I don't know. And Luzhin asks, why have you both come? So then Lyuba took him on one side and started whispering to him. I found out later she was asking him to let her be there too, to support me, that is. And seeing as she was one of their own, Luzhin agreed, even though he was reluctant. Then he comes over to me and gives me this revolver and he says, there, Belyashov, that's your weapon, and this revolver has already fired many bullets into the enemies of our revolution, our power, and our people, and today it has been entrusted to you to use in your work. I don't say a word, I just take the revolver and put it in the holster, but my hands are like cotton wool, with pins and needles sticking into them all over.

"So then they take me to the death cell, and I feel like it's me they're taking to be shot. Well, I knew where that cell was before, the lads showed me, but I'd never gone anywhere near it. But I went all the way there this time. It's not really one cell, it's two. First there's something like a lobby; a cement floor with a slope, and a little hole in the middle of it like a mouse's burrow. And beyond the lobby, at the back, there's an iron door with a peephole. I walk over and look in and I see the little lamp's on, and there's a man there, sitting on a stool, reading a newspaper. He still looks strong and sturdy, and his head's shaved, of course. He must have sensed someone was looking through the peephole. He turns his head toward me, and I look, and oh my God, it's the same man who was there, in the portrait! So you can imagine the way I feel then!

"And Luzhin takes his watch out of his pocket and looks at it. Well then, comrades, he says, let's get started. Open up, he tells the warden. The warden walked up and put the key in so quiet so you hardly even hear it. Then the door swings open all of a sudden and we all burst into the cell, like wild beasts. I look at the man with the shaved head: the moment he saw us his face turned as white as chalk all over and he started trembling and made this terrible stink. And then they suddenly stick this black bag over his head. They twist his arms behind his back and drag him out at the double into the first cell and press his head against the little hole. And I stand and watch, like in a movie, as if all this has nothing to do with me.

"I hear someone shouting my name, but that's like a dream, too. Then I look, and Luzhin's running toward me, all red in the face, why are you just standing there, you this and you that, and someone shoves me in the back. I took the pistol out of the holster, put it against his head, and I hear this quiet voice from under the bag: 'Please, make it quick.'

"I only wish I could make it quick, but my hand's jerking this way and that, and my finger's numb, like it's wooden. Luzhin shouts, shoot, fuck you, you fucking bastard, but I just can't, I can't, my hand's shaking and my finger won't bend. Vasilii Popov grabbed the revolver from me. With your permission, he says, Comrade Chief. No, shouts Luzhin, no. Let him learn. And if he can't do it, then let his wife show us which one of them's the man and which is the woman. I gasped at that, what sort of thing is that to get a woman to do, and I shout: Lyuba, Lyuba! And Lyuba, with this smile on her face, just imagine it, she says:

"Why not? I can do it.

"You can? says Luzhin. Here!

"He takes the revolver from the warden and gives it to Lyuba. Lyuba takes the revolver, asks how to hold it and what to press, puts it against the condemned man, then turns round and asks where to shoot him, in the temple or the back of the head.

"Even for Luzhin that was too much.

"Shoot, he shouts, hell and fucking damnation! And he called her a female dog.

"And she turns to him and answers back with the same smile:

"What are you getting so nervous about, Comrade Chief?

"And she put the gun back, stretched her arm right out and moved out of the way, lifted up her skirt so it wouldn't get splashed, and then squeezed her eyes shut, after all . . .

"I didn't hear the shot, I'd fainted already. I came to in the corridor. Vasilii Popov was pouring water in my face and slapping me on the cheeks.

"And after that, what do you think, they moved me back to being an ordinary warden and they took her—can you believe it?—as the military executioner. And we got that apartment. And we slept together in that bed. And that was when I got sick. When I came home, I didn't know where to put myself. If I sit on a chair, I jump up straightaway, that man who was shot used to sit there. I lost my appetite, every bite stuck in my throat. And I can't sleep at night, I keep dreaming about that man. And he keeps saying the same thing, over and over: please, make it quick. I used to wake up screaming every time. And Lyuba says to me, what's wrong? what is it? And sometimes she starts sweet-talking and making up to me to get her pleasure and I wouldn't mind either, but then I remember her standing there with the revolver and holding up her skirt, and I start feeling sick, not just in a manner of speaking, but really sick, once I didn't even get to the bathroom and I puked in the corridor.

"And that was how I lived, without any pleasure in life, and I wanted to do away with myself, and then they called me to this commission and told me, you're being transferred from your job temporarily to the defensive works. And they sent me to the Tula district to dig anti-tank trenches, and that was where they really finished me off. They stole my cap, they stole my mittens, I went round all the officers to complain and they told me, that's no business of ours, we can't assign sentries to guard your mittens. And they forced me to work. And that was when I got all frostbitten and caught typhoid, so they wrote me off altogether. You can go wherever you like, Pop, they said, maybe you'll even die at home. I could have gone back to Lyuba, of course, but when I remember, I can't bear it. So I came to you."

14

WHEN YOU THINK BY WHAT A SLIM THREAD the tiny, trembling bundle of our life hangs, you can't help thinking what a great miracle it is when that bundle manages to carry on hanging there for several years, let alone the several decades that have been allotted to you and me, my dear reader. For some, a lifetime is measured in days, but for others, nature seems to begrudge even a few short hours to allow them at least to see the sun shining and smile at their mothers' faces.

Fate was unkind to Nyura. As she ran down off the porch of the post office, she slipped on an icy step and fell, smashing the back of her head hard, and only felt the pain in her belly after that. A pain so terrible, it felt as if someone had stuck a pitchfork right through her. And the contractions started immediately. Her scream brought her friends at work running, and they carried her across the road into the dispensary. There, in the corridor, before she even reached the midwife, Alevtina Kuzminichna, she gave easy birth to a premature infant of the male sex weighing no more than two pounds.

The stunted child cried almost without stopping for three days and three nights, but failed to survive the fourth night. The dispensary had been eviscerated by the war. There were no doctors and no medication. If they had been there, perhaps he would have survived. And after that, everything could have been completely different. Perhaps he would have demonstrated exceptional intellect and talent, and he would have become a writer or a theoretical physicist, or even an opera singer. Or things could have been simpler than that: he could have finished five or six grades of schooling and graduated from a training course for tractor drivers or chauffeurs. He would have learned to play the accordion and attract the girls. He could have served his time in the army and got married before the war in Afghanistan. He would have married a woman with an ample figure and a warm heart, battered her a bit when he was drunk, but lovingly, not too hard, and she would have borne him one or two children, but no more. The way wages were here, he couldn't have coped with more than that. But all this is "could" and "would," and things could have gone differently again. He could have grown a bit, fallen into bad company, quit school, started drinking and smoking, injecting drugs, and stealing and ended up in jail or the loony bin, or else become a homeless bum, wandering around the garbage dumps. His fate could have taken any form at all. It could have made his mother regret that he was ever born or didn't die in infancy. But what's the point of guessing like this, the infant has died without ever seeing anything good, and without having sinned even once, so he deserves a place in heaven. He's dead and with this death, nature seems to have wiped away the final evidence of Nyura's bond to her missing sweetheart.

On the way home her legs wouldn't hold her up, she was so weak. It was a good thing that Taika Gorshkova came along with her horse and took Nyura the rest of the way.

It was already dark when Nyura climbed out of the sleigh and walked to the house. Before she even opened the door, she caught a smell she hardly even recognized, it was so long since the last time she'd smelled it. As she walked in, by the light of the kerosene lamp she saw her father, Olympiada Petrovna, and Vadik feasting at the table, grabbing boiled meat out of the pot with their hands and chomping loudly, like piglets.

"Enjoy your meal," said Nyura.

"Thank you," Olympiada Petrovna replied.

"Nyura! My child!" her father exclaimed, suddenly realizing who was there. "Thank God you've come back. Where have you been, what were you doing?"

"You mean you don't know?" asked Nyura.

"Why, how would I know, my daughter? Do you ever tell me anything? You don't let me know where you're going to and when you're coming back. What happened to you?"

"What happened was I gave birth to a child and it died. I hadn't even decided what to call it." She herself was amazed at the calm way she said it, as if she'd told them something quite ordinary.

"Oi!" her father gasped. "Oi, Nyura, how did that happen, how could it?"

"My God!" Olympiada Petrovna put in. "My God, what a terrible blow! Anna Alexeevna, how could something like that possibly happen?"

"It happened," said Nyura, and started taking off her coat.

Her father jumped up to help her, muttering: "Oi-oi, how awful, Nyurinka. But you know, maybe he'll look down from up there at the suffering we go through down here and say: Thank you, Lord, for letting me take the express train to heaven. You sit down, Nyur, have a bite to eat . . ." He pulled off her coat. "Sit down with us and have a bite to eat."

She was hungry, so she didn't make him ask again. She sat down at the table, grabbed a piece of meat, and sank her teeth into it.

"Good, eh?" her father asked. "It really is good. A bit on the tough side, but still pretty good."

It might have been tough, but she started tearing at it with her teeth. She was weak from hunger and she hadn't eaten meat for a long time. "Where did you get the meat from?"

Olympiada Petrovna got up and went to her room.

"Uncle Lyosha slaughtered Borka," said Vadik.

"Why do you go and say that?" Nurya's father rebuked him. "You know I can't even kill a chicken, never mind an animal." He turned to Nyura and said: "Plechevoi slaughtered the pig. I asked him to, and he slaughtered it. And he took himself a chunk like that. I say to him, how come you get so much, and he says, did you think I was going to sweat for you for nothing?"

Nyura stopped chewing and froze with her mouth open, like someone bewitched. She turned and stared at her father with the same expression on her face.

"What's up with you, Nyur?" her father asked anxiously. "What are you looking at me like that for? Don't you be angry, Nyur, there's no need. It's not a person, it's an animal. It runs round with no wits, like a dog, and people, Nyur, people, people are walking round hungry."

Nyura put her hand over her mouth and dashed out of the house, then puked for a long time beside the porch. She thought she was going to die, and she didn't try to resist death. She lost consciousness, but not for long, and when she came around on the same spot, her father was standing over her without any cap on his head and shaking her by the shoulders.

"What is it, Nyurok, what's wrong with you?"

"Ah, fuck your fucking mother!" Nyura yelled, jumping to her feet, and flung herself at her father, flailing with her fists. When he tried to run, she grabbed the rake and smashed it down on his head, but she didn't catch him with the metal part, only the handle, and that broke. Her father clutched his head in his hands and sat down in the snow, bleeding heavily. She took fright and sat down beside him. "Dear Pappy! Oh lord, what have I gone and done?"

Afterward she washed him and bandaged him and wept for him, and for Borka, and for her own life.

In the night her temperature rose and delirium set in. She was sick for three days, but on the fourth day she woke with a clear head and realized she would have to carry on living.

15

WHEN THE HARD FROSTS EASED, Nyura's lodgers moved to a room at the school. Olympiada Petrovna was given it on condition that she teach first and third grades. Nyura was left with her father, whose health was gradually improving. The skin on his face turned pink and his wrinkles smoothed out; he started shaving with a piece of glass every other day. In late April he received an unusual letter—not a folded triangle, like all the others, but in an envelope. Lyuba wrote in regular, curly handwriting to say that she was living alone, not letting any men near her, and leading a steady, quiet life. Vika was growing up to be a bright little girl, she already knew her letters and she could even write the word "daddy." And the boss, Roman Gavrilovich Luzhin, had asked after him several times and was sorry things had turned out like this. He promised to find Belyashov some light work to do if he came back.

After he read the letter, Nyura's father put it back in the envelope and put the envelope in the pocket of his military tunic. But later on, Nyura saw her father take the letter out again and again and look at it, moving his lips and thinking long and hard about something.

And afterward, Nyura and several of the neighbors began noticing that on warm days Alexei Ivanovich, wearing his quilted jacket and quilted trousers, would sit down on the porch, pick up a small stick, and aim it at people walking by, holding it like a revolver.

He was clearly intending to go back to Lyuba and preparing for a possible job placement. But, as it turned out, his practice sessions were wasted.

One day, as Nyura was feeding him cabbage soup made with frostbitten cabbage, his hand stopped in midair before the spoon reached his mouth and he suddenly started wheezing; his eyes stared wildly and he started shaking the spoon, spilling out the cabbage soup, as if he were about to hit someone.

"Pappy!" Nyura shrieked. "What's wrong with you?"

But he just wheezed, shook the spoon, and stared.

"Pappy," said Nyura, suddenly suspecting, "not going to die, are you?"

"Looks like I am," he said. And he died.

16

THE RUMOR SPREAD THROUGH THE VILLAGE: Ivan had sent Nyura a letter after all. The source of the rumor was Ninka Kurzova, Nyura's closest friend and confidante. She told Taika Gorshkova in secret, and she told Nadka Kosorukaya in secret, and Nadka—also in secret—told her female neighbors, close and not so close, that Nyura had gone to Ninka and read her a letter that she had supposedly just received. The letter looked like the real thing all right, with an address and an instruction to deliver it in person, and there was a postmark stamped on it, but Ninka knew for certain that the writing was Nyura's.

The women refused to believe it for a long time, then they decided that, after all her misfortunes, Nyura's mind had given out, and they started pestering her, some with an undercurrent of spite, and others out of simple-mindedness, saying: if your man has turned up and he's writing, then you could read it to us too, not just Ninka. Nyura wouldn't agree at first, but then she did.

On Saturday evening, after the bathhouse, the entire female population congregated at Nyura's house. Ninka came with her child, Taika came with two. Grandma Dunya came with a flask of moonshine. The numbers were made up by the young twins Manka and Zinka Chertov, Nadka Kosorukaya, and black-haired, swarthy Klavdia, one of the evacuees, who was nicknamed Blackness. They said that Blackness had done time in a prison camp for a criminal conviction, and she had various tattoos on her body from that time, of which the most important, on her stomach, read: "My darling lay here." She was a harmless enough woman, but differed from the local women in the way she looked and the way she moved, the way she always smoked fat, clumsily made hand-rolled cigarettes, and the way she expressed surprise with the word "wujeva." Which apparently meant "would you ever."

The women congregated in Nyura's house with polite, incredulous smiles, some intending to have a laugh later, some simply to pass the time pleasantly.

They sat wherever they could. Nyura wasn't being stingy with the kerosene, she'd lit the lamp with the seven-line wick and turned it right up to its brightest. She unfolded the triangle, smoothed it out carefully, looked around at her listeners, and began nervously:

> Greetings from the N command! Hello, Nyura! Good day or evening to you. This is your Ivan with a frontline army greeting. I'm sorry for not writing for so long, insofar as I have been busy anyhilating the German fascist invaders who attacked our country so trecherously. They kill the old men and women, rape and pillage and generally behave in a shameful way, like real swine. I have to wage unequal aerial battles against them, flying on all sorts of airplanes with machine guns blazing. In the time since we saw each other I have shot down several bombers in unequal aerial combat, as well as enemy personnel and tanks. But don't think that all I do is fly and shoot at bombers and tanks and enemy personnel and I never think about you. No, our beloved Nyura, while I fly in airplanes and wage fateful battles in unequal aerial combat, I always remember your figger, your eyes, and your little cheeks and your little nose, the way we lived and kissed and cuddled for our mutual happiness. And when I remember all this, my love for you, my sweet Nyura, rises up with even more ferosious strength, and so does my hatred of the fascist enemy. And I also think and am certain that subsequently you too have not forgotten me either as I wage battle here, and are concerned for my young life and well-being. And I am for yours, too. With that I conclude in cordial affection, awaiting your letter as the nightingale awaits the summer, and wish you all the best in the prime of your young life, your husband Ivan.

Actually, it only said "your Ivan," but as she approached the end of her rendition of the letter, she decided to reinforce the impression of the signature by reading out "your husband Ivan."

The women reacted differently to what she had read. Some believed everything straightaway. And there's nothing surprising about that. Most people who don't possess a well-developed imagination of their own cannot, by definition, imagine that someone else does possess one and can describe something that hasn't happened in real life. They can't imagine anything, but they are highly susceptible to the imaginings of others and therefore believe implicitly in everything that they read in novels and see in the movies. This allows them to experience everything they see with sincere, profound feeling, with joy and tears. But others, a minority, never believe anything, they have no imagination of their own and are deaf to the imagination of others, texts and pictures leave them unmoved, completely fail to touch them, neither evoking a smile nor jerking a tear. Anyway, Nurya's fellow village-women almost all believed everything immediately, especially since the letter looked just like a real one. Everything was right, with the address of the recipient, and the postmark, and it was hard to believe that Nyura could have made up something like that out of her own head. Others didn't completely believe it, but they were interested and wanted to hear the continuation. Perhaps only Ninka Kurzova, in her stupidity, didn't believe a single word and regarded what she had heard with total contempt. Ninka, however, decided not to tell Nyura that to her face, but behind her back she described her friend as "bonkered."

Regardless of how everyone reacted, next Saturday the women congregated at Nyura's house again, and they listened to the next epistle in a silence broken only by the scrunching of roasted peas and the whirring of a spindle.

> And in the briefness of my letter I can inform you, Nyura, that yesterday, no sooner than we sat down to breckfast, we heard our commander yell "alert!" and a green rockit notified us of the approach of enemy bombers, and the commander ordered us to engage them in unequal aerial combat. And I immediately got into my airplane and took it up into the air. There I am, dear Nyura, risen up higher than the clouds. And I see an entire kind of armada flying at us and then I flew close and started shooting at them from my machine gun. And when I slammed in the first berst of tracer shells, I saw one airplane berst into flames, and then a second and a third and a fourth, and all four fell down to the ground . . .

"Oh my!" Taika Gorshkova exclaimed excitedly.
"Wujeva!" Blackness declared.

> . . . It was hevvy work, Nyura. Some people think, Nyura, that shooting down enemy airplanes is easy. But it's not easy. Because

while waging battle, you have to perpetrate a few acrobatic aerial manovers and fly likewise in the normal position and wheels upward. And of course, you also have to think about how there are people like you and me sitting in those hostile airplanes, only they talk differently. And perhaps they have wives and children too, and parents and all sorts of other reletives, both close and distant, and sometimes they feel upset, too, when they get a condolences letter saying: "he died the death of the brave for the motherland and Hitler." But what can I do, Nyura, if there's a war going on and these people refuse to understand that I have someone too who is dear to my ardant warrior's heart? Saying who is dear to me, I mean you, of course, Nyura. And when I remember your eyes and your smile and what the German fascists did to you, taking away your cow, I start shooting those vultures with retrippled vigor. And I see the ones I've shot and the ones who have taken to their heels, but one brazen villain still carries on flying his plane, and my ammunition has expired and there's next to no gas, too. But then, with one last effort I caught that departing vulture, smashed him with all my might with my rum . . .

"What's a rum?" asked one of the twins.
"That's this kind of club they have on airplanes," Taika Gorshkova explained. "When the cartridges run out, they usually carry on fighting with their rum."

. . . So I hit him with my rum, and I see the airplane has burst into flames, and the pilot has grabbed his head and he's shouting kaput, kaput. And when I came back down to the ground, our commander came over to me and said, you waged battle in unequal aerial combat very well today, Vanya, and for that I award you the Red Order of the Military Red Banner.
    And so at night when sometimes I can't sleep after an unequal aerial combat, and supposing the bedbugs are biting and I'm thinking about all my past life, I think how there was a happy time when we met in the village of Krasnoye, and if not for these accursed Germans, we would have built our close and loving family and you would have had children and brought them up and I would have worked on the collective farm or else

in the factory. And I would have corted you forever with all my
cordial affection and respect.

Listening to this, both twins shed a tear, and Zinaida Volkova started
sobbing, then ran out of the house, weeping and wailing.

And so it continued. On Saturday the women went to the bathhouse,
and then to Nyura's place. Some came with their little benches and tools
and their needlework, and occasionally with some kind of treat to eat.
They congregated, scrunching roasted peas and drinking tea through
chunks of sugar when they could, or without sugar if they couldn't; some
knitted, some searched for nits in the hair of the woman next to them;
they listened, sighed, discussed, wept, talked about their own men,
remembered the old life, and thought about the future—from which,
it must be said, they were not expecting any great joy. And this became
such a regular occasion that they gathered every Saturday without even
being invited. They congregated, listened, discussed, and dispersed in
the hope that things would continue in the same way. For these women,
the weekly reading of Nyura's letters became almost as vital a necessity as
the regular consumption of television serials would be for future genera-
tions. They actually lived from Saturday to Saturday, from one episode to
the next. But for Nyura, the preparations for the next Saturday became
an everyday chore. It was fine for the other women—they listened for
fifteen or twenty minutes and then went home—but for Nyura it was
a hard daily grind, akin to the writer's trade. She lived those years in a
constant state of creative tension and her own fantasy was enriched by
elaborating the material she gathered. Things she read in the newspaper,
things she heard on the radio and from other people—she assessed it
all to see if she could use it. This was where the descriptions of various
heroic feats came from, and the night combat scenes, and the long-range
bombers, and the parachute jumps. And this fiction that she composed
became the only thing that gave meaning to her real, genuine life.

THE LONGER IT WENT ON, THE MORE JEALOUS Ninka Kurzova
became. And one day she said to Taika: "It's strange the way everyone
keeps on going to Nyurka's place. They all know she writes it all herself,

but they still keep going. Why bother listening to her fibs when they could come to me? My man's not made-up."

"He's not made-up, but he writes stupid letters. In poems. Some Pushkin he is! You don't even want to read it yourself. But the things her made-up man invents really set your heart swooning."

"Well, I never," Ninka marveled. "Set your heart swooning. What's there to swoon over?"

Ninka went about feeling jealous and envious all the time, and one day she went and wrote a letter herself, supposedly from Nikolai, only not in verse. She got the women together on Sunday, and even brewed up oatmeal kissel for them all. The women came, happily ate the free kissel, scrunched peas, twirled a spindle, listened politely, but no one cried or laughed even once. And the next time only Zinaida Volkova came, more for the sake of the kissel than anything else.

At first, before she got used to it, Nyura found it hard to make up a new story for every Saturday, but she gradually warmed to her task. As she went on and on, writing text after text, expounding the story of the heroic feats accomplished by Ivan and the medals he won for them, she gradually advanced her hero higher and higher up the ladder of military rankings. And in addition to all this, the theme of passionate love and responses to events in Nyura's real life always figured in her letters.

> Hello, Nyura, good day or evening to you, or maybe morning, like it is here! It's morning here all right. I woke up today because it was quiet here in our N command, and everything all round was so fine, and the sun was shining as if there wasn't any war and there never had been, and I woke up because I was woken by this feeling that I'm not alone in the world, there is another sole that's just like mine, and maybe not even a sole, but half a sole, half of it's mine and half of it's yours, and these halves reach out to each other and they stretch out in all directions like sheets, and they're so big and wide, they cover everything in the world. And when these two halves are drawn tight, when they fit together, that's the moment when I can die. Because the way I think is, the gratest happiness is happiness that people die from. And everything is fine and calm with us. Yesterday I went back flying a combat mission, and six, or maybe more, of their bombers attacked just me, and I shot them all down with my machine gun, but they hit me a cowardly

blow from behind, too, with their rum, and I had to descend by parachute. And the commander met me down below and said, congratulations, now you're going to be a captain. And with that I regretfully conclude my brief account and remain, loving you with amazing tenderness for all the long years and through the ages, your Ivan.

A true author must believe in what he writes. For a writer, the boundary between real reality and the reality of the imagination is unstable, easily blurring to fuse these two realities into one. If you had asked Nyura to say honestly whether she believed in her inventions or not, she couldn't have given a definite answer because she wasn't writing, she was taking down the words dictated to her by her imaginary correspondent. As she wrote, she saw her beloved there before her, quite clearly and distinctly, getting into his airplane, climbing out onto the wing and jumping down to the ground, leaning over a piece of paper and describing his life. While she was writing, she was occasionally aware that it was herself writing, but she picked up the completed letter as if it really had come from far away. And sometimes she would start reading it through and smile or cry. And reading it to the other women, she lived through it all again.

18

TAIKA GORSHKOVA RECEIVED A LETTER of condolence, and she ran out into the frost in nothing but her nightshirt and rolled about in the snow, yelling so loud the whole village could hear. Nyura suddenly felt awkward that she was the only one who was so lucky—her Ivan went on fighting without suffering any kind of unpleasantness. So by next Saturday a letter arrived from him reporting that he had been wounded in unequal aerial combat and descended on his parachute again and ended up in the hospital. And from there he wrote, "As soon as I came round to consciousness, I opened my eyes and looked, and I couldn't understand where I was and how I managed to get here. And now that I'm lying here with my eyes closed again, I think of you and remember the way you look, and your voice, and your breathing. And the nurses here are all beautiful, but there's no one more beautiful than you."

The letters contained various precepts for every possible occasion. Ivan asked Nyura to take good care of her health and her life, not to go running out of the hot house into the cold frost without wrapping up well, and not to rinse out the laundry in the river until the ice was completely firm. And these admonishments were followed by all sorts of detailed explanations about how to store potatoes, chop cabbage, or fix the porch. And for some reason the correspondent was also concerned with questions of nationality—he touched on them repeatedly, and always in the same vein.

"And some people say the Germans are a particularly melicious nation, but let me tell you, my dear Nyura, that the nations are all equal to each other, and the only difference is the color of their hair or their eyes, and they talk diffarently, but as far as everything else, they're all exclusively the same as us, apart from the Gypsies. Yesterday a letter came from Comrade Kalinin to tell me I've been awarded the Order of Lenin again."

There were reflections on the best way to arrange life in the given circumstances:

> And tell the women who listen to my letters that now their life
> is so hard, no talltale could tell it and no pen could write it, but
> there's no getting round it, that's the way it is in wartime. And
> after the war there's nothing good to luck forward to, because
> as the war goes on, the number of men like me is gradually
> being brought down, and what I think is, that if we brought in
> the Muslim rules at least for a while, they have six or even ten
> wives for one man, so then there are enough men for everybody.
> I don't say that because I'm for that kind of deborchery, Nyura,
> but I feel very sorry for all you women, so sorry that I could
> marry you all at once and take care of you all. But in reality
> there is no one and there can't be anyone for me apart from you,
> and with that I take my leave until my next letter, which will be
> written in a week's time.

From his concern for deprived women and household tips, he went back to describing his heroic feats and the state decorations and military ranks he was awarded for them.

19

BY THE END OF THE WAR, Ivan had been made a Hero of the Soviet Union and promoted to colonel. Nyura knew that the various generals' ranks came after colonel, but she thought it best not to elevate her beloved to such dizzy heights.

The inhabitants of Krasnoye greeted the end of the war with joy or with tears. The women whose men came back to them were overjoyed and those whose men didn't, felt their grief even more keenly. Nobody knew who would arrive and when, several woman went to the station in Dolgov as regularly as if they were standing duty there. And Nyura went with the others. She had come to believe so completely in her fiction that when she got to the station, she gazed into the face of every one of the rare colonels who showed up and sometimes, admittedly, she looked at men a rank below that as well.

Three men came back to Krasnoye from the war. The only one undamaged was Myakishev. As for the others—Plechevoi was missing an arm and Kurzov an eye.

Every day on her way to the post office, Nyura turned the corner toward the station to meet another train, jostling in the crowd, furtively examining the passengers getting down onto the platform, and then left feeling devastated. And eventually she wrote herself a short, dry notification: "We hereby inform you that your husband died heroically in unequal aerial combat with fascist vultures."

She had to add a signature, but first she wrote the position: "Commanding officer, N Command" and then the rank, "major-general," then she decided that was too high and corrected it to "lieutenant-general," then she thought that was too low, and wrote everything out again from the beginning, appointing the signatory "captain-general," but, unable to think of a name even then, she just added a scribble and burst into sobs.

20

IN THE LATE FORTIES JOBBING PHOTOGRAPHERS appeared in the villages. For a small amount of money, or payment in kind—that is, food—they enlarged photos and, if necessary, embellished and colored

them, making people younger and dressing them better. One such professional, in a long woollen coat right down to his heels and a hat with
a turned-down brim, knocked on Nyura's door with a big box balanced
on his shoulder.

"Right then, missus, how about doing some portraits?"

"What?" Nyura asked.

"I enlarge photographs. Turn a fly into an elephant, a small photo into
a big portrait. A single's fifteen rubles, a double's twenty-five."

He opened a folder and started showing her retouched photo-portraits
of various people and what they'd been made out of. Nyura had already
seen similar creations at someone's house and had thought more than
once about ordering something of the kind, but she didn't know where
and how. And now the opportunity had turned up. She invited the
photographer into the house and showed him the photos—hers and
Ivan's. The photo of Ivan, pinned to the wall, was small and it had faded.
The man shown in it was barely even visible and he looked like a convict:
a shaved head and large, staring eyes. The dedication was still on the
back:

> Oh, turn the gaze of your fair eyes
> Upon my printed copy here,
> May tender memories arise,
> And in your mind may I appear
> —To Nyura B., from Vanya Ch., in the days when our lives were joined.

"Your husband?" the photographer asked.

"Yes," she said, delighted by the question. "He was killed in the war.
He was a Hero of the Soviet Union, a colonel."

"I see," said the photographer. In his line of work he had come across
generals, never mind colonels. "So, maybe we'll show him in a colonel's
uniform, with his decorations?"

"Can we?" Nyura asked in surprise.

"We can do anything we like, ma," said the photographer. "Throw in
an extra ten, and we'll promote your husband to general, and for another
five on top of that, we'll make him a marshal. Agreed? Right then, do we
do him in a peaked cap, an astrakhan hat, or bareheaded?"

"Can you give him an airman's cap?"

"We can do an airman's cap, all right."

And so they agreed.

And a week later the portrait, produced exactly as ordered, appeared on Nyura's wall. Nyura herself in a short, severe black jacket and white blouse, with her braid coiled around her head. And beside her a dashing air force colonel in a cap with an insignia, gold shoulder straps with stars, decorations on both sides of his chest, and the Gold Star of a Hero of the Soviet Union above the decorations on the left. Perhaps the colonel didn't really resemble Ivan very closely, and even Nyura didn't look too much like herself, but she liked the portrait. And so Ivan Vasilievich Chonkin was buried and immortalized. But prematurely.

PART TWO

The Transformation

1

ON A BRIGHT, SUNNY DAY IN LATE JUNE 1945, a cart on high wheels bound with iron rims, harnessed to a pair of frisky, well-fed horses, trundled briskly through the cobbled streets of the small German town of Birkendorf. It was loaded with empty food crates and rattled so loudly on the uneven cobbles that the windowpanes jangled in the nearby houses and the inhabitants shuddered in fright, thinking it was another artillery bombardment. But on glancing out into the street, they immediately relaxed, and those who were inclined to laughter even smiled. Seated on the driving box, leaning backward slightly, with his legs set wide apart in their hastily wound-on wrappings and American boots that had not been cleaned for a long time, was a rather short, scrawny Soviet soldier. His head was bound up with a dirty bandage, the edges of which had fluffed up and were protruding from under his fore-and-aft cap. There was just one medal—FOR THE LIBERATION OF WARSAW—dangling on his chest. The liberator of Warsaw appeared to be in a good humor. Holding the reins tight in his widespread hands, he was singing loudly to the rattling of the crates and rumbling of the wheels—singing a song he had been taught just recently by the air base storekeeper, Master-Sergeant Kissel:

> *Komm, Paninka, schlafen,*
> And I'll give you candy,
> Canned meat and sweet soap,
> Just peel off your panties.

There weren't many people out on the streets, but if he did happen to come across a Frau who wasn't really old, even if she wasn't really all that young, the soldier beckoned to her with his hand and shouted: "*Frau, ficken-ficken!*"—he had learned these words from Kissel, too.

Suddenly there was an even louder clattering behind the cart. A T-34 tank shot out from around a corner, skidding slightly on the bend, so that it even rode up onto the sidewalk with one caterpillar track, almost felling a streetlamp, but then immediately skidding back down onto the roadway and setting off along the street, striking sparks from the cobbles. Without slowing down, it overtook the cart, enveloping it in a cloud of exhaust fumes. The soldier in the cart grimaced and held his nose.

"You stinking fool!" he shouted after the metal colossus and twirled one finger alongside his head.

The tank went flying on to the next intersection and suddenly braked to a halt with a long grating sound, crept backward, and nestled against the rough curb. The cover of the hatch flew open and a tank trooper wearing a dark jumpsuit with an Order of Glory pinned to it and a ribbed helmet climbed out. He took off his helmet, ruffled up his sweat-soaked mop of ginger hair, and waited for the cart to trundle up to him.

"Hey, you!" he shouted and twirled the helmet above his head. "Chikin, or whatever it is you're called!"

The soldier halted his horses and looked at the tank trooper with an air of expectant curiosity. "Chonkin's our name," he corrected the other man guardedly.

"Yes, like I said: Chomkin," the tank trooper agreed. "But don't you recognize me?"

Chonkin gazed at him. "From the looks of you, seems as we've met somewhere," he muttered uncertainly.

"Ha, seems as we've met!" The tank trooper jumped down onto the ground, took out a gold-plated German cigarette case with American cigarettes in it, and held it out to Chonkin. "Smoke!"

Chonkin took a cigarette with a dignified, unhurried gesture, kneaded it through the hem of his tunic (his fingers were dirty) and leaned down over the proffered cigarette lighter, keeping his eyes fixed on the tank trooper's face, as round as a pancake, with a nose stuck on it at random.

The tank trooper laughed. "Remember Krasnoye? You used to live with Nyura there, the postwoman."

"So?" said Chonkin.

"I'll give you so. I'm Lyoshka Zharov, the herdsman—I used to twist the cows' tails."

"Well now!" Chonkin exclaimed in amazement. "I looked, and thought . . . there now . . . seems like we've met." He jumped down off the cart and held out his hand out to Zharov. "Howdy!"

"Howdy yourself!" Zharov responded.

"So how's life in general?" Chonkin asked with a friendly smile.

"Life in general is okay, pretty agreeable," said Zharov. "What's wrong with your head? Wounded?"

"Nah," said Chonkin with a carefree wave. "Fell off a horse."

"You, off a horse? How come? A country man sits a horse the way a city man sits a stool."

"That's just it, I wasn't sitting on her, I was standing. In Berlin. When I was signing that Ragbag of theirs."

"Reichstag," Zharov corrected him.

"Yeah, right," Chonkin agreed. "That's the one. I drove up to it in the cart, and I wanted to sign it like everyone else, but there wasn't any room left. It had all been written on. Who'd been there, what town they were from, what division, who'd come all the way from the Volga, and who'd come from the Dnepr. I only wanted to put my name on it, but there wasn't any room. So I got up on the horse."

He had perched on the horse's back (he didn't bother to bore Zharov with all the details) and started tracing out his name with a piece of black tar. But he'd only written the first three letters, *Cho,* when even higher up, he saw the name Kuzyakov, or Puzyakov, which he remembered immediately. He'd seen that signature four years earlier in a cell in the Dolgov town jail, where it had been traced out in excrement that had turned rock hard, and the same writing material had clearly been employed here as well. Chonkin wanted to put his signature up even higher. He went up on tiptoe, but just then the horse jerked and he fell, striking his head a hard blow, and abandoned any further attempts to immortalize himself. His signature was left like that, unfinished. And people who later saw the signature *Cho* probably thought it had been left by some Soviet Chinaman or Korean.

"The things that happen!" Zharov commented sympathetically.

"Elephants fly sometimes," Chonkin agreed. "Is it a long time since you saw Nyura?"

"Since before you did," said Zharov. "They took me right at the start of the war. I haven't been home again since. Some others at least have had injury leave, but I've spent the whole time from the beginning driving round stuck in my tank, like in a tin can, and never got so much as a scratch, see. But I keep up a correspondence with my woman. And she writes that life in the collective has got harder than it used to be. They don't pay beans for the workdays now, she says, and if it wasn't for the goat, and the little vegetable patch, and the chicken, it'd be a total *kaput* altogether, but she's getting by more or less okay. And she tells me your Nyura's dating some officer at long distance by letter."

"An officer?" Chonkin echoed, shaken quite badly. "What officer?"

"How should I know, what officer?" Zharov said with a shrug. "All I know is, he's an airman."

"An airman?" Chonkin repeated with a painful twinge of jealousy. "What d'you mean, an airman?"

Since Chonkin parted from Nyura, very nearly four years had gone by. At first he had suffered very badly, then the pain had gradually eased off. In recent times he had hardly remembered Nyura at all, and might not even have recognized her if he met her, but he was shocked and hurt by the news that she had proved unfaithful to him. And now he viewed the whole business as if he himself had behaved quite blamelessly in his love and devotion, as if he had been counting on going back to the promised life together, but she hadn't waited, she had been seduced by the faithless love of an officer, a ration certificate, and gold shoulder straps.

"Never mind that," he said, trying to get away from the subject. "Are you going to get demobilized or what?"

"Why, of course. I'll hand in this coffin for repairs, and I'm done. The company commander's asking me to stay on and do extra time, but not me. I'll go home and drive a tractor or a combine. How about you?"

"Who knows? I was promised they'd demobilize me, but you know how they are, say one thing today and another thing tomorrow. We'd like to let you go, Chonkin, they say, only there's no one to replace you."

"Don't you give me that baloney! No one to replace him! Stalin said no one's irreplaceable."

"Who said?" Chonkin asked.

"Stalin."

"A-ah, Stalin," Chonkin repeated respectfully, but he decided to object anyway. "Stalin said, so what? I won't deny that he's a big man, he's got two wives, but does he know anything about horses? He's probably never ridden a horse. Nowadays everyone's in a tank, or a towing truck, or even an airplane, and no one knows how to manage a horse. They think with a horse it's just pull the reins this way and that way, right and left, but when it comes to putting on a collar, for instance, or tightening a harness-strap, no major or colonel would have a clue!"

"That's true," Zharov agreed. "Our folk are really badly educated. They can all talk languages, all right, but they'd try to milk a cow by the horns. Listen," he said, changing his tone, "you're in the air force, right?"

"Right. So?" Chonkin asked.

"Can you get hold of some damping fluid?"

"Sure I can," said Chonkin. "You want to have a drink?"

"No, that's not it," Zharov said with a wave of his hand. He glanced around and lowered his voice, even though there was no one close by. "This evening, when it gets dark, come to the bridge by the railroad station, with the dampo. There's these two German women. Mighty respectable and all, in glasses, don't have a word of Russian, no need to talk to them. They guzzle vodka like horses. Will you come?"

Chonkin thought about it. It was a tempting offer, but not all that easy to carry out.

"This evening?" he said uncertainly, thinking out loud. "Ah, yes, the evening, that's right . . . I just have to be sure that louse of a master-sergeant won't catch me. You don't know what our master-sergeant's like—a dog, not a human being. Not even a dog, I don't know who he is, and he hasn't done any fighting, either. But he's always poking and prying, sniffing things out; he's dead set on stopping any AWOL. Are the German women fat?"

"As barrels," Zharov promised him. "Tits like this, and round the back—a parade ground. Red Square."

"Yes . . ." said Chonkin, turning thoughtful again.

The picture drawn by Zharov was tempting, but he was a bit frightened. Frightened, but tempted.

"Ah, all right!" he said with a nonchalant wave of his hand. "You wait and I'll be there."

THE CURIOUS READER CANNOT HELP ASKING himself where Chonkin has been all this time. How, after being condemned to death at the beginning of the war and escaping from prison, did he come to be back in an air force unit? And not just any air force unit, but the one under the command of that same Opalikov, who had started the war as a lieutenant-colonel and finished it as a colonel, having in the process added the Gold Star of a Hero of the Soviet Union to his numerous decorations?

If we related the entire route traveled by our hero along the highways and byways of war, and all his adventures, our story would be altogether too long. So we shall follow a dotted line, skipping from point to point.

After Chonkin and Klim Svintsov found themselves alone together in the Dolgov district, they spent the late autumn and early winter in the forest, moving through it aimlessly like insomniac bears, and were taken for animals by the local inhabitants who went out into the forest to collect mushrooms, berries, or firewood. At that time rumors were rife among the rural population of the area that partisans had appeared in the local forests, along with a considerable number of bears, forest spirits, and monkeys. And tattered, hungry, and cold as they were, Chonkin and Svintsov really did come to resemble wild beasts of some kind. Chonkin was still recognizable, the sparse Tatar-style beard that he had sprouted didn't conceal the basic features of his face, but Svintsov was smothered right up to his eyebrows in a filthy ginger fleece so thick that he had to part the wool with his hands before he could make anything out properly. Some people, however, did not take our fugitives for animals but for wild partisans. They had no interest in guerrilla warfare, though; all they wanted was to avoid getting picked up either by our side or the Germans, and to feed themselves somehow. Anyone else in their place would have soon croaked from starvation, but they were men who had grown up in the bosom of nature and been a part of it, and they also happened to have a rifle and cartridges. So they fed themselves somehow. They shot a bird, or picked a mushroom, or gathered cranberries. To make a campfire, they used the ancient method of flint and steel. Somewhere they found a rusty German helmet from the First World War, with a bullet hole in it. They plugged the hole with a scrap of foot-wrapping and turned the helmet into a saucepan. The rag got wet and didn't burn. They boiled up mushroom soup (from honey fungus; so many sprang up that year, the ground was thick with them), compote, and herbal infusions. They slept on the damp ground without taking their greatcoats off. They managed to get by like that, until one night there was a slight frost, and in the morning when they looked, all the honey fungus mushrooms had turned black and wilted. The hummocks of grass were covered with a thin crust of ice; the cranberries under it looked like museum exhibits behind glass. Chonkin had only been in a museum once, when the commandant's company had been driven into town and shown the fangs of extinct animals, ancient spearheads, and the decorations worn by the people of those times—all behind glass. And he remembered there were beads there too, just like cranberries, and they lay there, glinting under the glass. Winter was setting in, and the main problem now was to survive it somehow. They tried to dig a dugout, but the most suitable tool they had was a bayonet. Fate, however, was more or less favorably inclined to them. One day, as they were gathering kindling for a fire, Chonkin and Svintsov came close to a thick clump of bushes, and suddenly there was a stirring of leaves and something shaggy emerged.

"A bear!" Svintsov exclaimed, staggering back and dropping the rifle.

However, it wasn't a bear, but an extremely strange creature covered with a coat of long fur, with a bald patch at the base of its spine. It darted out of the bushes and went dashing away. Svintsov, who had almost turned into an animal himself by now, went darting off after it. The creature reached the nearest tree and flew up it, working all four paws nimbly, all the way to the top, and from there it gazed uneasily at the men who walked up.

Standing the rifle by his leg, Svintsov asked Chonkin: "What kind of animal's that, do you know?"

"I don't," Chonkin said in amazement. "Looks like a monkey."

"What do you mean?" Svintsov objected. "Have you ever seen monkeys?"

"Yes," said Chonkin. "Last year they took us to the menagerie. First the museum, then the menagerie. And there was one exactly like this, with a bare backside."

"Ugh!" said Svintsov and spat. "But how would they get here? We don't have any like that in the taiga. Bears, wolves, squirrels, and sables, we've got them, but there's no monkeys."

"Well, how could there be any?" asked Chonkin, remembering what Gladishev had said. "When they've all turned into people."

"How's that?" Svintsov said disbelievingly. "Like werewolves, you mean?"

"Yes something like that," Chonkin confirmed.

"It happens," Svintsov agreed. "In our village squint-eyed Varka used to turn into a cat at night. She sucked the milk of other people's cows. But my brother Seryoga caught her in the cowshed one night and chopped her paw off with his axe . . ."

While he spoke, Svintsov kept his eyes fixed on the creature sitting in the tree, screwing up first one eye, then the other, and the creature responded by screwing its eyes up in the same way.

"And what did he do with the paw?" asked Chonkin.

"Nothing. He wrapped it up in a rag and put it on the stove, and in the morning there was a human hand there instead of a cat's paw . . ."

"Well, and then what happened after that?" asked Chonkin, eager for a continuation.

"After that was what came next," said Svintsov. "What do you reckon? Can you eat monkeys?"

"Who the hell knows," Chonkin said thoughtfully. "I never have, but then why not, they're made out of flesh and bones too."

"Then," Svintsov reasoned, "since it hasn't turned into a person, it's the same kind of animal as, let's say, a pig. So first we'll scorch off the fur on a fire."

"Are you stupid?" asked Chonkin.

"Why, what?"

"What what?" said Chonkin. "Why scorch off the fur? We'll make mittens out of the skin and sew ourselves caps."

"Good idea," Svintsov agreed, rubbing his frozen ear. "Have you ever eaten kebabs?"

"What's that?"

"What's that?" Svintsov mimicked. "A real tasty treat, that's what it is. You cut meat up into pieces, thread them on a stick, put them in the fire and turn them so they cook evenly on all sides. What, why, I'm telling you, whoa-a-a, that's really . . ." he said, lost for words. He picked up the rifle and pulled on the handle of the breech.

"Don't shoot!" the monkey shouted in a human voice. "Don't shoot, I surrender."

"Well, lookee!" Chonkin said in amazement. "It's turned human already."

"Yes," said Svintsov, lowering the barrel disappointedly. "You know, I can kill a man, but I won't eat human flesh. I'd be sick. All right," he told the monkey, "get down here on the ground. And don't be afraid. If you don't run, we won't kill you."

The monkey raced down and stood in front of Chonkin and Svintsov, almost on two feet, only supporting itself slightly on a fallen tree with its front limbs.

Although it was covered from head to foot with long fur, Svintsov made out the badge of the male sex in among the thickets and asked the newly descended creature strictly: "Who are you and what nation do you belong to?"

The descended creature said nothing and trembled like a sheep before slaughter.

"Tell us who you are!" Svintsov growled and clicked the breech.

"Don't shoot!" the creature implored them again and started nodding its head rapidly. "I'm Russian. Orthodox," he added, evidently uncertain that this characteristic would count in his favor.

"You're lying!" Svintsov said distrustfully. "There's no such thing as Orthodox monkeys. Or aren't you a monkey after all?"

"Hey!" said Chonkin, nudging Svintsov. "What if he's a wood-goblin?"

"Ha!" exclaimed Svintsov, astounded by the very idea. "Answer, what are you?"

"I don't know that myself," said the creature, starting to cry. "I was a man, but maybe now I'm a wood-goblin."

"Do you live in the forest?" asked Svintsov, continuing the interrogation.

"Yes."

"Could you find something to eat?"

"For you," said the wood-goblin, "for you I'll definitely find something."

"Well, take us to your place. Only no witchcraft and don't even think of running off. Remember, a bullet runs faster."

They went in a straight line, through the thickets. The wood-goblin ran at the front, helping himself along with his front limbs. Svintsov and Chonkin couldn't keep up with him, but he kept stopping to wait, and then running off again, like a dog leading a hunter after the scent.

They went down into a ravine and crossed a slimy green stream on stones. They cut across a small clearing and stepped over the trunk of a large pine tree, lying there like a corpse. The bushes behind it were knit tightly together. The wood-goblin hesitated at the bushes, and Svintsov grabbed the lever of the breech just in case.

"We're here," the wood-goblin said in a tired voice.

"Where's here?"

"It's this way," said the wood-goblin and vanished into the bushes.

Svintsov darted after him, thinking he could choke him if he really had to, and then cried out in surprise: "Good grief! It's a den!"

The wood-goblin was already clambering into the den on all fours, with his bare backside glinting white. Svintsov clambered in after him and Chonkin followed. The den was a long passage that sloped gently downward and turned to the right. After they crawled a few meters along it, there was no light visible behind them any longer, and they felt firm ground under their knees. "Don't be surprised," they heard the wood-goblin's voice say, then a match scraped, flared up with a hiss, and lit a kerosene lamp.

"Yahoo!" Chonkin cheered and Svintsov added something to do with his mother.

They crawled on, with light now.

Beyond a narrow bottleneck there was a corridor that gradually grew wider and higher. The floor was spread with straw, and the corridor ended in something like a round room, quite well furnished, with a carpet on the floor, a mattress, and two piles of books, but what astonished the visitors most of all was the portrait leaning against the wall, showing a bearded man in an old-style uniform with shoulder straps and shoulder cords.

"And who's that?" Svintsov asked respectfully.

"Why that's . . ." the master of the den began and hesitated, "that's, how should I put it . . . ? That's His Imperial Majesty Emperor Nicholas the Second."

"Oho!" Chonkin gasped involuntarily.

"And pardon me, but who would you be, then?" Svintsov asked even more timidly and politely.

"Why," said the wood-goblin, "I'm Vadim Anatolievich Golitsyn."

And he told his guests his story. Vadim Anatolievich was a real Prince Golitsyn and a landowner in those parts, who later served in the retinue of His Majesty. He had been with the tsar in Yekaterinburg, but escaped just one day before the royal family were shot. He managed to get back to his home territory and settled in the forest, waiting for the end of the Bolshevik regime. However, he had to wait too long. As time passed, he grew a coat of fur and turned completely shaggy. He lived like a wild beast. He fed on mushrooms, berries, and roots. He caught hares and birds with his own hands and eventually became so much like an animal that the real beasts of the forest were afraid of him. He lived out in the open until he stumbled across the den and drove out the bear that was sleeping in it.

After that the bear became an insomniac, wandering through the forest, walking out onto the road, attacking horses and people, but it was afraid of the creature that had seized its den.

Living in the den, Golitsyn started his gradual return to human life. At night he crept up close to the villages and stole chickens, eggs, flour, and anything else he could lay his hands on. Eventually he acquired a kerosene lamp, a mattress stuffed with straw, a spade, an axe, a hacksaw, and other small tools, and used them to deepen and widen the den, turning it into a relatively comfortable underground dwelling. And just before the war he even acquired a library of his own, by chance. The driver of a mobile village reading-room crashed his van on the road and smashed himself up into the bargain. The library that the drunken driver was transporting had once belonged to Golitsyn, and now it had come back to him, in part. The part that he now recovered included the novels of Dostoevsky and Danilevsky, a children's edition of Turgenev's *A Hunter's Notes,* a deluxe edition of Pushkin's *Eugene Onegin,* three out of five volumes of Gogol, half of the publisher Marx's edition of Chekhov, the book *A Journey Down the Yenisei,* the myths of ancient Egypt and ancient Greece, and Scottish ballads in Zhukovsky's translation. In addition to these, the den now also contained *The Short Course in the History of the All-Russian Communist Party (Bolsheviks),* Stanislavsky's book *My Life in Art,* and a set of political agitator's notebooks for the second half of 1940. But the greatest asset acquired had been the lithographic portrait.

They moved into the den and lived there in great comfort. Someone somewhere was fighting for something, but Chonkin, Svintsov, and Prince Golitsyn sat it out in the bear's den.

Luck attracts luck, just as money attracts money. No sooner had they settled the problem of accommodation than luck came to them in the hunt. They shot a wild boar and two hares. They roasted the meat on a campfire, drank tea made from various herbs gathered by the wood-goblin, and in the evenings they listened to their host retelling marvelous novels from the old days. At times Chonkin thought: If only I could bring Nyura here, I could live all my life like this.

CHONKIN DALLIED IN THE FOREST like this for an indefinite period of time until one day, while collecting kindling, he was seized by a group of partisans and ended up in a large band of Red Army men who had

broken out of encirclement. Having thereby successfully avoided individual investigation, he was attached, along with the others, to the brigade commanded by a person already familiar to our readers—Aglaya
Stepanovna Revkina, the widow of Andrei Revkin, the secretary of the
Dolgov District Committee of the All-Russian Communist Party (Bolsheviks). She took Chonkin to serve her as a kind of orderly. The Germans didn't last long in the Dolgov district, and so the brigade under
Aglaya's command had no opportunity to distinguish itself in battle. It
only had time to plunder several of the nearby collective farms (Aglaya
still remembered how to do that from the old days of "surplus appro-
priation") and plant a mine under the wooden bridge across the Tyopa
River just outside Dolgov. It was a delayed action mine, so it exploded
after the district had already been liberated from the invaders, just as the
herdsman Innokentii had led his herd of cows onto the bridge. Two cows
were killed, one had its tail torn off, and Innokentii himself went slightly
deaf, and that was all. While the brigade was preparing for decisive battles, Chonkin looked after Aglaya and her horse, carried water from the
nearest stream, chopped firewood, lit the stove, cooked food, sometimes
swept the earth floor, and somehow it just happened that he took practically no part in any battles.

Aglaya's dugout was spacious and divided into two sections. She herself lived in the inner section. She had a simple pine table, three stools,
a trestle bed with a straw mattress, a washstand in the corner, and a tin
basin with two handles. Chonkin occupied the anteroom, separated off
from the inner chamber by a tarpaulin sheet, and he slept simply, on an
armful of straw tossed onto the floor. Once he was wakened in the middle of the night by a bright light and saw Aglaya standing over him in her
linen nightshirt, with her hair hanging loose, holding a kerosene lamp
in her right hand.

"Get up and come in," she ordered him and went back into her inner
chamber . . .

He obediently got up, shook the straw off himself, and went in. Aglaya
was already lying on the trestle bed, under a blanket that revealed her
naked shoulder. The lamp was standing at the head of the bed, on a stool.

Aglaya raised herself up on her elbow and told him: "Come closer!
Closer than that!"

He stood facing her bed while she examined him for a long time, and
then came another order: "Get undressed!"

He didn't understand. "What?"

"Don't you understand? Get your tunic off!"

Bemused, Chonkin did as he was told.

"Now the trousers!"

Chonkin didn't dare defy her this time either.

"Phew, your drawers stink. Get them off as well!"

He turned shy at that.

"Come on, what did I tell you?"

After looking him over from head to foot, she told him to lie down beside her. She put her arms around him and started kissing him, letting her hands wander.

He was in shock at first, he couldn't bring himself to understand what she wanted straightaway, and when he did understand, he felt frightened that he wouldn't be able to satisfy her desire. To begin with, it looked as if he really couldn't. But he was young, with adequate reserves of testosterone, he didn't require any additional means of stimulation as yet, and as a matter of fact, he pictured Nyura to himself, and even in imaginary form, she was immediately a great help. And so it all worked out in the best possible style, and more than once.

Early in the morning Aglaya, already dressed, woke him up and ordered him, in the same tone as the day before, to perform the same actions in reverse, that is, to get dressed. He was still winding on his leg wrappings when she stuck her Walther under his nose and warned him: "Mind now, Vanka, you spill the beans and I'll shoot you."

So a new duty was added to Chonkin's workload, one that he performed diligently, willingly, and even with a certain degree of satisfaction, although he never experienced the same state of self-abandonment that he had known with Nyura. Owing to the limited capacity of his small mind, he was, of course, unable to analyze his own feelings, but if he could have, he might have come to understand that intimacy with any woman can become a source of pleasure and enjoyment, but only love raises this intimacy to the level of sublime bliss.

Once recruited into the brigade, Chonkin lost all contact with his friend Klim Svintsov and Prince Golitsyn, the master of the bear's den. It emerged later that Golitsyn left the forest himself and surrendered to the Germans, who took him with them as they retreated in order to hand him over to the Berlin Zoo. There he was put in a separate cage as proof that representatives of the lower races, even those of the very highest social origins, were not yet far enough advanced along the road of evolutionary development to prevent them from turning back into monkeys under the right circumstances. As for Svintsov, in his case evolution appears to have taken a step backward. The legend has persisted in the Dolgov district, and even further afield, that, during and after the war, people encountered an abominable snowman in the forest and found his tracks, looking like unbelievably huge human footprints.

CHONKIN'S AIR BASE WAS LOCATED on the left bank of the river Elbe and was called Birkendorf after the little town to which it was adjacent. And there was another air base on the opposite bank, adjacent to the little town of Eichendorf, but it wasn't ours, it was American. The air bases looked like each other: the same temporary buildings, command posts, general stores, and fuel depots. At first glance, the only difference between the Soviet Il-10 fighter-bombers and the American Airacobra fighters was that the former had their third wheel in the tail and the latter had it in the nose section. And the two planes had different stars, too.

Although the Soviets and the Americans were still considered Allies, they regarded each other with a wary caution that was the policy of the two high commands, but the lower ranks treated each other with friendly curiosity.

The road that Chonkin usually took to the air base ran along the riverbank. As he rode along, he examined the American planes and the personnel hanging about around them. On occasion, his journey coincided with the movement along the other bank of an American soldier, also driving two horses. Everyone at the air base knew him and they used to say "There goes the American Chonkin!" And the American really would have been very much like Chonkin if he had not been black. That, however, did not prevent our Chonkin, entirely free of racial prejudice, from greeting his colleague joyfully by waving his arms and yelling in Russian: "Hey, John, howdy!" To which the hypothetical John would howl in reply: *"Hi, Ivan! How are you?"* and show off his white teeth. Chonkin thought that John really did know his name, but the American called him that because he didn't know any other Russian names. And Chonkin, in turn, called the other man John because he didn't know any other American names. And he hit the bull's-eye, because the black

Chonkin really was called John. When their journeys coincided for a long enough distance, Ivan's and John's exchanges went beyond isolated phrases; they commented on the weather and expressed interest in each other's personal lives, each speaking his own language—and each was convinced that he understood the other.

On this occasion, Chonkin said the weather was wonderful today, and if he only had a chance to sunbathe, he would soon be as black as John. John asked Chonkin what he fed his horses, oats or hay. Chonkin showed him a five-liter aluminum kettle and said he was going for some hydraulic damping fluid. John replied that his horses didn't drink tea, but he gave them a treat of chocolate every day. Chonkin informed him that he needed the hydraulic fluid for seducing the German girls he was going to see tonight, and John protested that the scenery in South Carolina was far more picturesque than it was here. After talking in this way, they both turned off—Ivan to the left and John to the right; Chonkin drove his horses toward the air base fuel depot, but where John trundled off to, we don't know, and we're not really interested.

Damping fluid, dampo, or "chassis liquor" was what airmen called the hydraulic fluid for the piston-engined airplanes of those days: a mixture of glycerine (70 percent), pure alcohol (10 percent), and water (20 percent). (In later times, distinguished by more advanced achievements of engineering and aviation's transition to jet propulsion, the quality of the mixture improved noticeably, becoming far more acceptable to the human stomach: 60 percent glycerine, 40 percent pure alcohol, and no water at all.) This whitish, semitransparent liquid was normally stored in two-hundred-liter metal drums beside the air base fuel depot.

The store office, which Chonkin now approached, was located in a small wooden trailer on sled runners. Master-Sergeant Konstantin Kissel, wearing an old singlet with a hole over his left nipple and an identical one under his left shoulder blade (as if a bullet had passed right through it), was sitting in front of the trailer in the shade of a tent that he had rigged up himself out of the canvas of a plane cover. One edge of the canvas was nailed to the wall of the trailer, and the other was spread-eagled across two poles hammered into the ground. The sergeant's chair was an old airplane seat adapted for earthbound use, with the parachute niche full of rags, and his table had been assembled out of four shell crates with a door laid across them. The door had bronze corner plates and a bronze handle in the form of a dog's head which, for some strange reason, had not yet been removed.

The canvas was tattered, with many holes, and the sunshine seeping through them dappled Kissel's prematurely bald head with numerous little patches of light, giving him a partial resemblance to a leopard. Having masses of free time on his hands, Kissel had set out two trophy notebooks in front of himself and was nibbling on the nails of his left hand as he copied out a text in capital letters from one to the other. The text was a novel in verse, *Eugene Onegin*, by an unknown author, who introduced himself to the reader as follows:

> I am no Pushkin, no, not I—
> An unknown member of the chosen,
> Repairing engines by the dozen—
> But my soul lives for poetry.
>
> No works have I had printed yet
> The state has not seen fit to publish,
> No talent have I to astonish,
> But I can promise you a treat . . .

This was only the introduction to the novel proper, which began with an unexpected event.

> My uncle, a most honest knight
> When illness rendered him too weak,
> Got stuck inside the cook so tight,
> That we could hardly pull him free . . .

Spotting the five-liter aluminum kettle that Chonkin was holding, Kissel didn't even bother wondering what it was for, and he certainly didn't think Chonkin had come to drink tea with him. Without asking what was going on, he just reached down, pulled a short rubber hose out from under the table, and waved his hand.

"Over there, siphon it out of the second drum."

"Okay, I'll siphon it off," said Chonkin, "but listen, there's this important piece of business I need to discuss with you."

"Well, go on," Kissel told him.

"You see, I had this woman before the war."

"Only before the war? You haven't had any during the war?"

"Nah, that's not it," Chonkin said with an impatient gesture. "The thing is, she's dating this officer. Listen, now, I'm here and she's there with an airman, and I need to dash off a little letter, you know, to say this is all wrong, how can this man be, you know, and . . . how can you be doing . . . something like that, eh?"

"So what's the problem? Write it. Write," Kissel repeated categorically. "Write: Why, you shameful bitch, here I am spilling my blood for the motherland and Stalin, and you, you great whore without a single shred of shame, go tumbling in the hay and looping the loop with your airmen. You shameless hussy, you've gone into a tailspin and you can't pull out of it!"

"Right!" Chonkin said delightedly. "That's what I need, just like what you said, only a bit gentler. She's not tumbling in the hay because they're only dating by letter."

"Well then, that's different, then write a bit gentler."

"That's just it, though, I'm no great shakes with a pen. I know pretty well all the letters for writing, but I can't cobble a proper letter together, no way. You write it for me and I'll give you this."

He handed Kissel a cigarette lighter that he'd got from a German at a flea market in exchange for a piece of soap.

Kissel twirled the lighter in his hands, examining it in surprise. It was made in the form of a naked female figure. When he pressed the hands together, her legs parted and a flame flared up between them.

"All right," said Kissel and put the little figure in his pocket. "Sit down, and we'll write our Letter to the Sultan of Turkey. What's her name? Okay, so we write: Hello, Nyura! Right?"

"Right," Chonkin agreed.

"All right. Next: I'm writing to you, then what? Well, something like: What else is there for me to do? What else can I say? And there really isn't anything else you can say. Then after that, first of all let's appeal to her conscience. Nyura, how could you do it, how could you swap me for some officer, even if it is only by letter? Someone you've probably never seen and never will see. Of course, I understand that he's got gold shoulder tabs and more money than I have, and better rations, but he's an officer, he can't be trusted, he's only interested in getting his own satisfaction, but as for the idea of founding a strong Soviet family for a whole lifetime, he hasn't got that in his head, no matter what he's got in his pants . . ."

The entire letter took no longer than an hour. And then Chonkin filled up his kettle and Master-Sergeant Kissel went back to the novel by the unknown author about the air mechanic Eugene Onegin's friendship with the motor mechanic Vladimir Lensky, how they worked together and their friendship was strong and true . . .

> All seemed true concord and affection,
> But bitter Fate, our life's true ruler,
> Assigned to them a new technician,
> A recent graduate from Tula . . .
> Tatyana, private super-class,
> Was voted by the regiment
> A perfectly configured lass,
> And eyed with obvious intent.
> How many eager words they spoke
> Of her beneath each airplane wing,
> With majors' faces all aglow
> And sergeants' eyes a-glistening.
> Even the regiment's commander
> Did oft with stubborn hope exclaim
> That love would recognize no hindrance,
> And simple age was no restraint.

IN THE OPEN-AIR MESS to which Chonkin usually delivered firewood and provisions, he mooched two cans of American stewed pork, a packet of dry crackers, and a slab of chocolate from the chef. All this was carried to the stable and hidden under the hay in the cubbyhole where spades, rakes, forks, and the implements for cleaning horses were kept.

In the barracks, Chonkin arranged with his friend, Private Vaska Mulyakin, that when the evening roll-call got as far as *Ch,* Vaska would answer for him. And then, if need be, he would put a "dummy"—a greatcoat stuffed with something—in Chonkin's bed.

Naturally, they marched to supper in formation, to the strains of the song "The Cossack Galloped Through the Valley." Sometimes they tried singing "Indomitable and Legendary," but somehow they struck up a jauntier stride riding through the valley with the Cossack. After supper, Chonkin told Master-Sergeant Glotov that he had to clean the horses and went to the stables. He really did scrub the horses down quickly, brushed out their manes, and even gave each of them a lump of sugar. One of them was called Daisy and the other Semyonovna. Chonkin had learned their names from the groom Grishchenko, who must have thought them up himself. The horses were docile with Chonkin, but their ears were still getting accustomed to their names, and they thought first before responding when called, clearly still dubious. They were captured German horses, and in their previous life they had been called something quite different.

Chonkin gave the horses a farewell slap on the withers and went to his secret cache. He stuck the canned meat, crackers, and chocolate in the front of his tunic and picked up the kettle. He went around behind the stables and then made his way through the bushes to the hole in the fence that let him off the base.

It was getting dark.

The little town of Birkendorf had survived the war relatively intact. The local inhabitants were very quiet, and in the evenings it was as if they had died out altogether; Chonkin didn't meet anyone on his way to the station, apart from a skinny lamplighter as black as an imp of hell. On his high bicycle, with his blazing torch on a long pole, the lamplighter moved from post to post along the sidewalk, first screwing open the little spigot at the bottom and then touching his torch to the top of the post. The lighted lamp sprouted a dim, uncertain bluish flame that lit up nothing but itself.

The railroad bridge that Zharov had mentioned was immediately beyond a small church at the junction of Tulpenstrasse and Rosengasse streets. The start of the crossing was lit up by two streetlamps, and Chonkin really didn't want to stand underneath them, since a patrol could show up at any moment—although it was almost impossible for it to appear suddenly, since military boots could be heard tramping across the bridge from a long distance away, especially if they had steel tips. But in fact Chonkin didn't have to waste any time standing about here. As soon as he approached the crossing, the figure of a lanky soldier with a big stomach emerged from behind a massive advertising column with the commandant's orders glued to it. It was Zharov.

"Did you bring it?" Zharov asked in a whisper.

"Yes," whispered Chonkin.

Zharov hadn't come empty-handed, either: the front of his tunic was bulging with something. They wound their way for a long time through narrow cobbled streets immersed in twilight, and Chonkin was amazed at how well Zharov knew the town. They cut across an absolutely dark park, squeezed through between the bent iron bars of the fence, and found themselves facing a small house adjoining a large mansion that had four columns and a tall porch with a pair of mangy stone lions sprawling peacefully, one at each side.

Zharov knocked on a closed shutter and walked up to the door. At first there was silence behind the door, then they heard a rustling sound and a woman's voice asked quietly: "*Wer ist da?*"

"Mashuta, it's me, Lyokha," Zharov said in a low voice, with his mouth up close to the keyhole.

The door opened and a woman's figure in a white dress with short sleeves appeared in the doorway, lit up by a faint light from one side.

"Lyok-kha!" she exclaimed joyfully, and hung on Zharov's neck.

"Let me introduce you, Mashuta," Lyokha said to the figure after it climbed back down. "My friend Vanya Chikin, an airman. Wounded in aerial combat. Look, a shell split his head wide open, and he's as right as rain. He's not exactly tall, it's true, but you know a stunted tree always grows big in the root."

"*Gut, gut,*" said Mashuta, giving Chonkin a kiss on the cheek. First she closed the door, then switched on an electric flashlight and led her guests down a long corridor to the room at the end, which was lit up by two kerosene lamps standing in the corners on special bases in the form of human figures holding trays. The walls of this spacious room were covered in greenish wallpaper with rectangular patches left by pictures that had once hung here, but had now been taken down by someone and carted off to parts unknown. There was only one large canvas left, depicting an old castle, a pond, a pair of swans on the pond, a plump young woman on the bank, and a roe deer sticking its face out of the bushes. Chonkin had seen something like it before. There were two iron bedsteads with brass knobs and high pillows standing in the far corner of the room, forming a letter L, and the center was occupied by a heavy square table covered with a sheet for lack of a tablecloth. A blonde with curled hair, wearing a yellow knitted jumper with short sleeves, was laying the table with settings unlike anything Chonkin had ever used for dining in his entire life: porcelain plates, silver knives and forks, crystal goblets.

"Hi there, Ninukha!" Zharov said to the blonde.

"Gud eefning!" she replied with a strange accent, but in a language that Chonkin understood, which took him by surprise, because he had believed what Zharov had said about neither of the German women speaking any Russian. Lyokha gave her a hug and a kiss too, and a slap on the backside. She wasn't embarrassed at all and slapped him back on the same spot.

She held out a plump hand to Chonkin and said: *"Janina. Jestem polka. Rozumiesz?"* (which was close enough to Russian for Chonkin to understand: "Janina. I'm Polish. Do you understand?")

She shook his hand firmly and looked into his eyes, which got Chonkin's hopes up straightaway. He remembered the excerpts Master-Sergeant Kissel had read him from his album with explanations of the signs women give when they meet a man: "She shakes your hand—she loves you; she shakes your hand firmly—her love is strong; she shakes your hand firmly and looks into your eyes—she will gladly grant you her caresses forever."

Janina wasn't exactly a barrel, but there was enough of her to get a good grip on. Her large breasts thrust out her jumper, and the proportions of her backside were seductive. In general, she had everything in the right place apart from her four front teeth, which were missing. She remembered this and tried not to laugh, and if she couldn't resist, she put her little hand over her mouth.

Chonkin put the kettle and the provisions he had brought on the table. Zharov also emptied out the front of his tunic, discharging onto the table a loaf of rye bread, a can of sardines, a lump of fatty bacon, and four packs of American cigarettes with a picture of a camel on them.

"Matka boska!" ("Mother of God!") Janina gasped and grabbed the cigarettes. Lyosha clicked his trophy lighter.

"Co ty takoi blyady?" ("Why are you so pale?") she asked as she took a light.

"Who?" Lyosha asked in reply. "I'm not *blyady*. You're the one who's blyada."

"Ai! Ai!" said Janina, shaking her head. *"Mislisz, ja ne rozumliu, co po-vashemu 'blyada,' to jest kurva?"* ("Do you think I don't understand that in your language 'blyada' means whore?")

"You understand?" asked Lyosha, embarrassed. "But I only said it just for a joke. You say I'm *blyady,* and I say you're 'blyada.' For a joke, understand? I wouldn't say it if it wasn't a joke. Come on now! I wouldn't, would I? Never! Do you believe me?"

"It doesn't matter," Janina said dismissively. "A whore's a whore."

While Chonkin opened up the cans with a German clasp-knife, Lyokha removed the spirit glasses from the table as unnecessary and started filling the crystal goblets with damping fluid.

"See," he said to Chonkin, "they live here on their own. The rich owners ran off, but where can our girls run off to? So they stayed. Then one day a whole company of ours started raping both of them right here in the yard. And I happened to be out on patrol with Major Kazakov. We were walking along the street and we heard some kind of rumpus and glanced in over the wall, and I see they've tied Mashuta to a plank and put a beam under it, and one of them, a sergeant, is rocking it with his foot and another, a private first-class, he's getting his fill. And when I saw that, my insides started boiling right up. Because I understand everything, we're all hungry after this war, mad for a woman's body, but you just ask her nicely, she needs the same thing, she'll always let you have it, she won't refuse, and if she doesn't, another one will say yes! But no, they have to go and use force. The moment I saw it, I grabbed my assault rifle and the major says: what's that you're doing, stop that, let's get out of here, we haven't seen anything. But I pushed him off with the shoulder stock and I fired this burst over their heads, and then that sergeant, who was rocking the plank, took out his pistol and I said to him: I'll shoot you, you filthy swine, and then—would you believe it?—he dropped his pistol, the lousy bastard, and ran off, taking these long leaps, like a goat. No, I tell you: I've got nothing against putting it round here and there, but you can do it nicely, can't you? Eh, Mashuta, what do you think about all this?"

"*Gut, gut,*" Mashuta replied.

They took their seats at the table. Lyosha and Mashuta facing Chonkin, with Janina beside him on the left. Chonkin looked at the tableware warily and watched to see what their hostesses would do. It might seem strange to some people, but he had never eaten with a fork in his life, and he wasn't even sure what it was needed for. A spoon was quite enough for him, but sometimes he hadn't even had a proper spoon. Spoons of all sorts—wooden, tin, and aluminum—often had no handles, so when he used them, he had to dip his fingers in the cabbage soup or the boiled grain. And Chonkin couldn't see how the goblets that Lyosha was filling were superior to an aluminum mug that stood solidly on the table, had a handle, and didn't break.

"Well now, right then, shall we have a drink?" Lyosha suggested, raising his goblet. Mashuta took hold of her goblet, looked at it against the
light, sniffed it, and frowned. "*Was ist es?*"

"Don't you worry about it," Lyosha reassured her. "You won't get poisoned. Russische liqueurisch. Sweet, tasty." He took a sip and smacked
his lips to show how good it tasted, filled his goblet up to the brim and
raised it for a toast.

"Right, girls, may we be as healthy as cows! *Essen, trinken, kumsen,
bumsen. Gut?*"

"*Gut,*" Mashuta agreed again. She said a few words in German to
Janina, and they both laughed in anticipation of what had been promised.

After trying the drink that had been brought, Mashuta winced and
looked at Janina, who took a sip and also put her goblet down.

"What is it girls, don't like it?" Lyosha asked anxiously.

Without answering, Mashuta went out to the next room and came
back with a matte green bottle and a corkscrew. She handed both of
them to Lyosha:

"*Mach auf!*"

Before he opened the bottle, Zharov raised it to the light and started
examining it.

"Ivan," he said, "can you read German?"

"Me?" Ivan asked in amazement.

"All right, then," said Lyokha. "But I can savvy a bit. They've got lots
of letters the same as ours. Look here, this one's an 'm', the same as ours,
and an 'o' . . . Mosyol."

"*Mosel,*" said Mashuta.

"Aha, Mosel," Zharov agreed. "From the year of 1922, and they haven't
drunk it yet."

While he was opening the bottle, Janina changed the goblets. Lyosha
poured the wine, tried it, and started spitting.

"God almighty, what garbage! What's wrong with you, girls? Surely
you're not going to *trinken* this, are you? What we brought is sweet, but
this is only good for spraying bedbugs!" Chonkin didn't like the wine
either, and they decided that the men would stick to their liqueur, and
the girls could drink slops, if that was what they liked.

They drank some more and sampled the hors d'oeuvres. Chonkin held
his fork like the handle of a shovel, but he managed by helping himself
out with one finger of his left hand.

When the drink went to Zharov's head, he decided to add a bit of sparkle to the gathering with a discussion of subjects of common interest.

"There, you see, girls," he began, pouring another glassful, "that's our life for you. It has lots of what you might calls twists and turns, to and fro. There's just been a brutal war, but what for, who needed it? Our political officer tells us: Lads, we didn't fight for Stalin and the motherland, but for Russia, for freedom and a better life. A life where there won't be any more war, and people can work, earn money, and buy themselves a thing or two. A pair of shoes, coats, caps, and all the rest of it. Where men and women marry each other and live together with their children and, as time moves on, with their grandchildren. When there's war, what's that good for! Listen, Vanya," he said, turning to Chonkin, "Mashuta here had a husband, but he was killed at the front. Mashuta, what was he called, that man of yours?"

"*Wie bitte?*" Mashuta asked.

"Your Mann," said Zharov. "That man of yours? What's his *vorname*? Kalus?"

"Klaus," said Mashuta.

"There you see, Klaus," Zharov repeated respectfully. "He was a decent man, worked at the post office. You can see what a beautiful girl he married. And think about it, what did he want with this war? He's not Hitler, he's Klaus. The same as you and me, except that he's German. Well, they herded him off too, for the motherland, for Hitler, *zurück* and *hände hoch*. And now you see, he's left his woman a widow. Do you think he wanted his woman to be left a widow and enter into sexual relations with thickheads like you and me? Do you think she would ever have got in between the sheets with a Russian? No, she wouldn't. Because you and me, Vanya, are uncouth clods, and our language is plain, and with them it's all *guten morgen, danke schön*—you can see what they drink, and they don't even bat an eyelid."

Chonkin was not following Zharov's line of thought very conscientiously, because his body was luring him into different actions, and he didn't know why he should postpone them. He reached his hand under the table and started feeling Janina's knee under its thick woolly skirt. She didn't move her knee or push his hand away, and he took that as an indication of permission to carry on. He carried on stroking her knee and started pulling up her skirt, meanwhile nodding at Zharov and agreeing with everything, even though he wasn't following. Finally advancing under the skirt, he felt his hand run up against devices of some kind for holding something up, but carried on, amazed by the cumbrous, labyrinthine complexity of these devices. He'd only just begun to make out the structural details when Janina jerked his hand back out.

"What's up?" he asked, resentful and surprised.

"*Ne tszeba spesit*" ("Don't be in such a hurry"), said Janina and reached for a cigarette. She took a drag and blew out a cloud of smoke straight into his face. Caught by surprise, he started coughing. Janina laughed.

"Why are your teeth missing?" asked Chonkin.

"*Kobyla vyperdovala*" ("A horse farted them out"), she joked, stubbing out the cigarette, and reached for him. And he couldn't even remember what happened after that. All he did remember was kissing her hard and reaching his tongue in through the gap in her teeth, and her pushing his hand under her jumper. Then they rolled around the floor in each other's arms, and he tore at her suspenders, and she squealed and laughed and hit him on the hands, but not hard, not angrily. They rolled in under the table, and there he finally managed to pull her underneath him, and he started hastily twisting his own buttonholes open.

"*Pocekai*," Janina told him. "*Ja skoro prszidu*." ("Wait a moment. I'll be back soon.")

She slipped out from underneath him and dissolved into the darkness, and he turned over on his back, put his hands under his head, and froze in anticipation. At first he couldn't hear anything for the sound of his own breathing, then he made out a creaking of springs and loud slobbering and voluptuous sobbing, no doubt from Mashuta, and a deep, hollow droning, no doubt from Zharov. Chonkin got excited and tried to get up to go and look for Janina, but after making the first movement, he felt like he didn't really want to go anywhere. "It's all right," he thought, "she'll come back on her own." And with that thought he turned over on his side, put his fist under his cheek, and drifted into a different space where there was a warm summer and a meadow covered with daisies, and he was lying in his light cotton uniform, buried in a haystack, with Nyura in a red silk summer frock. Nyura stroked his hair, kissed his eyes, and reproached him gently, with a smile, for forgetting about her and not even writing any letters, but the airman wrote, and that was why she had fallen in love with him. He started making excuses about living in a bear's den where there wasn't any paper or ink and he'd forgotten how some of the letters were written.

"In a bear's den?" she said. "Then let's sleep like bears."

She hugged him even tighter and started pressing her warm body against him, and he was close to taking her when suddenly enemy planes appeared over the meadow, flying across the sky without making a sound. They even seemed to be flying past, but Chonkin knew they weren't flying past, they were looking for him and Nyura, and as soon as they found them, they'd drop all their bombs on them. But even so his desire to possess Nyura was as strong as ever, he held her even tighter, but she started pushing him away, whispering in his ear that they had to get up and run, because it was her airman, he'd found them, and he was going to kill them. And then one plane separated off from the others, went into a dive and started dropping things, only they weren't bombs, but stools and chairs, and when they landed they smashed with a terrible crash. Nyura grabbed hold of Ivan's shoulders and started shouting at him: "Chikin! Chikin!" He wanted to say to her I'm not Chikin, what do you say that for, Nyura, I'm not Chikin, I'm your Vanka, Chonkin. But she kept on shouting: "Chikin! Chikin!" and he unglued his eyes, and he saw Lyosha Zharov's face in front of him and Lyosha was shouting at him: "Chikin, alarm stations, a patrol!"

"What?" asked Chonkin, shaking his head and trying to understand where he was, what was happening to him, and where Nyura had gone.

Meanwhile, the rumbling and crashing continued, but it wasn't planes or falling chairs and stools, but someone hammering on the door with boots or, more likely, gun butts.

"Chikin!" Zharov yelled despairingly one last time and made a dash for the window. He managed the catches deftly, and the bushes were already cracking under his weight when the door flew open, torn off its hinges, and the military patrol (a first lieutenant with a slanting haircut who looked like Hitler and two sergeants in helmets with machine carbines) came running into the room.

CHONKIN WAS DELIVERED to the garrison guardhouse where, in addition to him, fifteen men were awaiting their fate in a common cell. It was a small cell, damp, and its walls were covered, in the customary fashion, with various inscriptions, both legible and illegible and, moreover, in two languages, German and Russian. And just like in the Dolgov city jail, which Chonkin had not forgotten, the inscriptions were of various kinds: verse and prose, sentimental, philosophical, inane. Some men had simply signed their names, others had indicated their places of origin (Leningrad, Kuibyshev, Chelyabinsk). Chonkin found some inscriptions more astonishing, and some less so, but he was astounded most of all by a signature that he had already seen twice, left by a certain Kuzyakov or Puzyakov, and once again rendered in the same writing material, only this time on the ceiling.

While our hero contemplates this signature that accompanies him through his life, while he ponders the properties of the writing material used to create it, let us make a change of geographical location and acquaint ourselves with certain other individuals who, as yet, have nothing to do with Chonkin.

THAT SUMMER PROFESSOR VOVICH, Comrade Stalin's personal physician, took his family out to a dacha at Malakhovka, but he himself was very rarely there. Rising early and retiring late, he preferred to stay in Moscow. He most often returned home after midnight and, after drinking a glass of vodka, collapsed into his bed, sometimes without even getting undressed. On this particular occasion, however, he happened to find himself free unusually early and decided to drive out to join his family. He arrived at the dacha, changed into his flannel house pajamas and light leather slippers, ate dinner or supper (depending on your point of view), and started building a railroad with his four-year-old grandson. Before they'd finished building it, the grandson was taken off to bed. After he was taken away, the professor thought it would be a good idea for him to catch forty winks as well, and he went to his bedroom. An hour and a half later, he emerged from the room with a crumpled face and tousled hair. He had just sat down on the terrace to drink tea when two other "murderers in white coats" appeared—the pathologist Samuil Drappoport and the otolaryngologist Moisei Goldmann, who both lived on the next street.

In those patriarchal times, people could simply drop in on each other without any particular reason, without informing anyone first by phone or email. In any case, Goldmann and Drappoport didn't have phones at their dachas, and as for email and the Internet, they had absolutely no idea what they were, even though they were professors. Vovich himself did have a phone, but on this particular evening, no one had called him on it.

Well, of course, if friends have called round with a bottle, you have to go down into the cellar. A refrigerator's better, but at that time a refrigerator was as far beyond even Professor Vovich's reach as the Internet. Of course, it wasn't the professor himself who went down into the cellar but his housekeeper, Klasha, from the village of Beryozovo in the former province of Orlov. Klasha brought back up a lump of fatty bacon, a jar of mushrooms, a basin of salted cucumbers, and something else, and the standard Russian drinking session, a custom common to all Russians (including Jews) started up. They drank and they talked. They didn't talk about work, they avoided political subjects, told humorous stories from life and argued about the science of genetics, which they had heard something about, even though it was still prohibited then.

Drappoport said that in a certain American journal, which had come into his hands in some manner unknown, he had read an article about this so-called science that was not recognized at all by our scientific community. The authors of the article claimed that the inherited characteristics of a living organism, from a string bean to a human being, were determined by the genes that made up that organism. And that in each gene there was a specific number of chromosomes. The possibilities that would emerge when mankind learned to control this mechanism defied the imagination. Specifically, before someone was even born, it would be possible to endow him with the very finest of human characteristics by improving his genetic makeup: give him strength, stamina, great intellect, and a range of various talents. It would also become possible to prolong human life indefinitely by growing spare organs, that is, a heart, a liver, arms, legs, eyes, and ears. Then the poet Antokolsky arrived and read them a poem about his son, and soon after that Margarita Aligher turned up and read them a poem about Zoya Kosmodemyanskaya. In other words, they had a fine, interesting, very satisfying evening.

The visitors left after midnight, and then the professor worked in his study for a while and went to bed after one in the morning. But at about two, someone started hammering loudly on the door. The doctor assumed the worst, and he was almost right. Running out into the hallway in his underpants, he came across a tall military officer (Klasha had let him in) wearing full uniform and a cap with a blue band. The officer raised his hand to his cap and inquired politely if he had the honor of seeing Professor Vovich in person, after which he requested that the professor get dressed and accompany him to his car. The professor was afraid, he turned pale and broke into a sweat at the same time, and Klasha just stood there, also pale, not even noticing that she had come out to a strange man in nothing but her nightshirt. The military officer maintained his very polite tone, and when asked where they were going and why, he replied that he would tell the professor that on the way. The professor asked which of his things he ought to take with him, at which the officer smiled and said: nothing, apart from his passport.

This reply revived the professor's spirits—he had heard that if they were taking you to That Place, they always suggested taking certain things with you. The professor's fears are easy to understand, but, at the risk of getting ahead of ourselves, we can say straightaway that they were premature and the professor was not as yet in any danger. Nonetheless, of course, he was trembling with fear as they drove him into Moscow and around Moscow in the captured Opel automobile. However, the place he was taken to was not the Lubyanka, as he had been expecting, but the restaurant Aragvi. The officer politely opened the car door and gave the professor his hand to help him out. Then he showed him into the restaurant. They walked through the main hall, went up to the second floor, and found themselves in a small room where Lavrentii Pavlovich Beria in person, wearing a dark suit, was sitting in the mysterious half-light with a napkin tucked into his shirt collar.

"Here you are, Comrade Marshal, I've brought him," Vovich's military escort reported.

"Have a seat, professor," Beria said without any greeting, but also without any display of hostility. "Would you like a bite to eat? No? You've already had supper? It's my policy never to force anyone. Well, professor, let's get started straightaway. I wish to talk to you about a matter that is very serious and, as they say, highly confidential. If anyone should find out about it . . . well, you understand. I won't give you any more warnings. I have invited you here because I am very concerned about the health of your patient. As you no doubt realize, I am not a sentimental individual, but recently I have noticed that Comrade Stalin looks tired, he is pale, drinks too much, eats too little, and drags his left leg as he walks, and not only I, but everybody who is close to him has noticed that he becomes drowsy too often. He sometimes falls asleep even at the most important meetings, and yesterday he slept through a performance of *Swan Lake*. What do you think is wrong with him? Is he in need of urgent treatment? Perhaps even hospitalization?"

Professor Vovich felt alarmed. Recalling the Hippocratic oath, he was on the point of stammering something about medical confidentiality but, glancing at the other man, he realized it would be best to forget about Hippocrates. Even so, he attempted to avoid giving a direct answer.

"It is hard for me to answer your questions, Lavrentii Pavlovich, because Comrade Stalin is not a simple patient."

"It would be strange if he were simple!" Beria laughed.

"Yes, of course," the professor agreed. "But if you will permit me to speak frankly . . ."

"Speak frankly, and only frankly."

"Then I will say this. Comrade Stalin is used to working very hard. He himself says that he works like a horse. He became accustomed to superhuman workloads, especially during the war. But at that time he was supported by the awareness of his immense responsibility. It gave him additional strength. However, now that the war is over and the deadly danger to the country has passed, Comrade Stalin's body has involuntarily relaxed, and is no longer capable of bearing its former load, but it appears to me that Comrade Stalin is not aware of this and is still trying to work according to his former regimen, which is now beyond his strength. He works at night, drinks too much, smokes, eats heavy food."

"And in your opinion, how much longer can he carry on?"

"Eh?" Vovich asked and hesitated, not knowing what to say. Although he was a materialist and a professor of medicine and had no doubt that all human beings were mortal, as a Soviet man he simply could not imagine that Stalin would also die, like everyone else.

"I'm sorry," he said, perplexed, "I can't answer your question so directly."

"Why not?"

"Because I can only judge the state of Comrade Stalin's health from indirect signs: he looks unwell, he doesn't eat enough, he tires easily. But in order to give a professional opinion, I need to examine the patient thoroughly."

"Well then, examine him!" Beria exclaimed, rather too hysterically, as it seemed to the professor.

"I can't," said Vovich. "How can I, if Comrade Stalin refuses even to have an X-ray photograph taken or provide samples of blood, stool, and urine?"

"Yes, that is a problem!" said Beria, becoming thoughtful. "Well, for us intelligence officers, there are no problems that can't be solved. We'll get Comrade Stalin's stool and urine for you. But the blood . . ."

"I need the blood, too. From a vein. Or at least from a finger."

"Ah, at least from a finger!" the marshal exclaimed, suddenly brightening up. "The doctor needs blood from his finger. Won't blood from his ass do?"

The professor was completely disconcerted by this. Let us repeat, he was a Soviet man, and he knew very well that the combination of the two words "Stalin" and "ass" was shockingly inappropriate and could easily come under Article 58 of the Criminal Code. He started hiccuping and throwing out vague interjections, but Beria became really jolly, slapped the professor on the shoulder, and said: "Don't worry, professor, we're among friends here. You know, the old man has hemorrhoids, and sometimes there's copious bleeding."

THE DAY AFTER THIS CONVERSATION, the design office of the famous builder of airplanes, Andrei Nikolaevich Tupolev, received an urgent and absolutely secret order from the People's Commissariat of State Security. The operations of the Soviet intelligence service required the development, in the shortest possible time, of a special device which, being secretly installed in a toilet bowl, could collect samples from the specimens of human discharges passing through it, for subsequent delivery to a special laboratory. When he heard that the Ministry of State Security intended to divert his entire design team, Tupolev swore loudly in front of witnesses. He shouted that he was a designer of airplanes, not, as he put it, of shit gatherers. That he and his entire design office were working without any days off on the creation of the T-4 strategic bomber, the Soviet flying fortress, which the Soviet Union needed as a matter of absolute urgency, and he had no intention of redirecting his efforts to any kind of stupid trash. But Lavrentii Pavlovich phoned him in person and inquired if the recent ex-convict, Andrei Tupolev, had forgotten what prison gruel tasted like. Of course, Tupolev had not forgotten, and he didn't ask for another serving.

We can inform the reader here and now that the collective headed by Andrei Tupolev, the Hero of Soviet Labor, coped brilliantly with the task set for it. The device required was developed and tested successfully. The entire staff of the Tupolev design office and Tupolev himself tried it out and passed it fit for use. And a short while later a medical assistant with a pistol on his hip brought Professor Vovich a small zinc box like a casket, containing three test tubes in hermetic packaging. Trembling in anticipation, Vovich unpacked everything, took the test tubes to the laboratory, and performed the necessary analyses himself, not trusting them to any assistants or laboratory technicians. He himself smeared the substance under analysis on the glass slide, dropped the reagents on it, and pressed his eye to the microscope. He found the composition of the urine and the stool rather surprising, but when he reached the blood he simply couldn't believe his eyes, and when he did believe them he was dumbfounded and started twirling the disc of the phone rapidly. When he got through to some secondary figures, he demanded to be connected with the primary figure, and then demanded an immediate audience with the primary figure, went straight to him at the Lubyanka, tossed the sheet of paper with the results of the analyses onto his desk and said: "You should be ashamed of yourself, Lavrentii Pavlovich, playing tricks like this on someone who's getting on in years."

Lavrentii Pavlovich frowned. "What does this mean? Who do you think you're talking to? Do you realize where you are?"

"Yes, I realize," the professor replied defiantly. "I know you can have me arrested or even shot, but I won't allow anyone to play jokes like this on me."

"I can have you shot, of course," Lavrentii Pavlovich said with a polite smile, "but I need to have at least an approximate idea of what for. What is the problem? Why are you so agitated?"

"You don't know?"

"No, I don't."

"If you don't know, then your subordinates who cooked up this stupid joke must. The specimen you gave me to analyze is not Comrade Stalin's blood. It's not human blood at all, but the blood of some animal."

"An animal?" Lavrentii Pavlovich echoed. "Which animal?"

"I don't know, I'm not a veterinarian. Most likely a horse."

"Uhu," Lavrentii Pavlovich said thoughtfully and starting chewing on his nails. "A horse? Are you sure of that?"

"That it's a horse—no; that it's not a man—a hundred percent."

"Good. You can go back home and sleep soundly. But if you've tried to make fun of me, or even made a mistake, you'll regret it very seriously."

After his conversation with the professor, Lavrentii Pavlovich summoned and questioned the agent who had obtained the material for analysis. The agent swore to God that he had done everything according to the instructions he had been given and the material presented for analysis had been obtained as a result of Comrade Stalin answering nature's larger call.

Beria ordered a second sample to be taken and sent it to the veterinary academy, without indicating the source. The specialists there, having conducted a thorough analysis, were extremely surprised and stated that the composition of the specimen was similar to horse's blood, but it contained components that had not previously been observed in known breeds of horses.

Lavrentii Pavlovich became very thoughtful indeed. But then he remembered something and ordered several works by the biologist and traveler Grigorii Grom-Grimeilo to be delivered to him.

THE GUARDHOUSE DID NOT MAKE a very frightening impression on someone like Chonkin. In this place a man was supposedly punished by being deprived of his freedom, but these men called soldiers had already been deprived of it as a matter of course. The food here was not at all bad, better in fact than what the prisoners had consumed when they were still nominally free. The chefs who dispatched the containers of food to the "slammer" felt sorry for them and tried to make things a bit easier by sending them the thickest soup and the choicest tidbits. The company here was interesting in its own way, too: bandits, hooligans, and men who had gone AWOL. They had all broken laws, regulations, and rules of behavior, some of them repeatedly, so they had a certain freedom-loving air about them. And that made them interesting, while law-abiding individuals generally arouse a feeling of respectful tedium and set people's teeth on edge.

The conversation, arguments, and speculation in the cell were the same as in any barracks at that time. They discussed openly whether there would be a general demobilization or they would be let go by year of birth, with men up to '26 being allowed home while those from '27 kept on, because men who were born in '27 had only now reached the draft age and their previous time in the forces didn't really count. They argued about what life would be like after the war: Would the collective farms be disbanded? Would ration cards be abolished? They argued about Germany and what the standard of living was like there. They expressed amazement that the Germans had turned into such ferocious beasts. They told stories about a famous marshal who only a few days earlier had sent back to the homeland six railroad cars of trophies, including two automobiles, a concert grand piano, furniture for his city apartment and his dacha, and several more containers of old clocks, dinner services, chandeliers, candelabras, door handles, diamonds, fur coats, lengths of woollen cloth, and other items absolutely essential for a marshal's household. They said: Serve the bastards (the Germans) right, their führers like Goering plundered lots of stuff from all over Europe, too! They tried to guess what would happen to the leaders of the Third Reich. They talked about how, before Goebbels and his wife committed suicide, they first poisoned their six children. At that time only Stalin and the military interpreter Lena Rzhevskaya knew that Hitler was no longer alive—so in the cell they argued about whether he was alive or not, what would happen to him if he were caught, and what each participant in the discussion would do to him if he could. There were various plans, from shooting to hanging, to putting Hitler on display, naked, in a menagerie and then driving him round cities in his cage so that people could spit on him and say all sorts of things to him. From Hitler they naturally moved on to Stalin, and here there were no arguments, only admiration. Smart, brilliant, and great. He's in control of everything, knows everything, and what's more, he reads five hundred pages of a book every day and hardly ever sleeps, he's always thinking about us.

Chonkin's bunkmate was the artilleryman Vasya Uglov, who had previously served in Stalin's bodyguard in the Kremlin. He had been taken on because he was tall and had been dismissed for being drunk. It had only happened once, in fact, but in the Kremlin guard, once had been enough. In the cell, just like everywhere else Vasya had been, they started asking him if he had seen Stalin in person.

"I saw him, lots of times," Vasya replied with dignified pride.

"With your very own eyes?" asked Private First Class Mitiushkin, who, like Chonkin, had ended up in the slammer for going AWOL.

"Yep, with my very own," Vasya confirmed. "When I was on duty at the john, he used to walk past me several times a day."

"What for?"

"What d'you mean, what for?"

"What did he go to the john for?"

"Are you stupid, or what?" Vasya asked in amazement. "What do people usually go to the john for?"

"That's people," protested the private first class, "but this is Stalin!"

"What a bonehead!" commented Sergeant Gavrilov. "D'you reckon Stalin's not a human being, then? Even Marx said: Nothing human is alien to me."

"Did Marx go to the john, too?" asked Mitiushkin, even more astonished.

"No," said Vasya. "Marx used to shit his pants."

And then everyone in the cell started laughing at Marx and Mitiushkin and asking the private just who he thought the leaders of the proletariat were if they didn't enjoy such natural pleasures. Mitiushkin started sulking and declined to continue the conversation, but that night he shook Chonkin awake and asked:

"Do you think Stalin goes to the john, too?"

Chonkin, recalling that he had once got his fingers badly burned over the matter of Comrade Stalin's personal life, replied evasively that he didn't think anything at all about Stalin. In the morning Mitiushkin's three days of detention came to an end. Once back with his unit, he immediately requested a meeting with the political deputy commander and submitted a report that Vasilii Uglov, currently under arrest, was spreading libellous assertions that Comrade Stalin went to the john. And the arrestee Chonkin, he added, proudly claimed that he thought nothing at all of Comrade Stalin. The political deputy commander was a sane individual, he regarded the discussion in the cell as no more than a piece of nonsense, but this was a political denunciation, he had to respond to it somehow, even if only formally. So he advised Mitiushkin to contact Colonel Gunyaev of the counter-intelligence service SMERSH.

Colonel Gunyaev would also have preferred simply to ignore the three fools. Almost every night just recently they had been picking up dozens of soldiers who had gone AWOL and harmless gossipers. They were reported to their own direct superiors, who decided how much time each of them should be given. However, not all the superior officers were vicious brutes, many of them understood just how much the soldiers had had to put up with and how much they had seen during the war. So what if they had eased back on the brakes, gone on a spree, had a bit of fun with German girls or grannies, or even blurted out something they shouldn't have? They deserved at least a bit of indulgence for what life had put them through. So the officers were reluctant to stick their men in the slammer, and if they did stick them in, they only gave them moderate sentences.

10

CHONKIN, TOO, AFTER SPENDING A FEW DAYS in the guardhouse, would probably have gone back to his own barracks and his little horses, Daisy and Semyonovna, and been demobilized soon afterward, if only another stroke of bad luck had not befallen him. Just when he decided to go AWOL for perhaps the only time in months, an order on the strengthening of discipline in the forces was issued by the Supreme Commander in Chief and circulated to all units. The order stated that since the Soviet Armed Forces had ceased active fighting, signs of moral degeneration and a slackening of discipline had been observed in military units. Among the soldiers of the occupying forces there had been instances of refusal to obey unit commanders, frequent cases of drunkenness, hooliganism, looting, rape, pillage, and the sale of army property and weapons. Special mention was made of the dangers of increasingly frequent contact with the local population, which led to infection with venereal diseases, of desertion, of the revelation of military secrets, and—most terrible of all—of ideological corruption. The order enjoined commanders of all units, large and small, and also the officers of SMERSH, to take decisive measures to reinforce discipline and punish all those who violated it by slacking or going absent without leave.

There was an order, and there was also a clarification. To deter violators of discipline, a number of show trials should be arranged. Cases tried by a traveling court martial should demonstrate to all slackers that punishment would be inescapable, severe, and swift.

When the order and the clarification reached the air force division in which Chonkin was serving, the head of SMERSH, Colonel Gunyaev, called the commandants of the division's garrisons and asked them to present lists of all men arrested for going AWOL. In one of the lists he came across the name "Chonkin," already familiar to him from Mitiush-kin's denunciation. Chonkin's case was the most suitable for a show trial. Absence without leave, drunkenness, contact with the local population, and the expression of dubious opinions. Gunyaev even thought that the very name Chonkin was suitable for a court case, it was so easy to re-member. The colonel summoned the chairman of the military tribunal, Suknodyorov, and ordered him to prepare Chonkin's case for hearing. The chairman knew his job very well: it had never, even once, occurred to him to consider himself an independent judge; on the contrary, in conversation with his superiors he always emphasized that he never issued any independent verdicts except in the most trifling cases, and had no intention of ever doing so. And when Gunyaev expostulated with him from time to time, reminding him that he was a judge and answer-able only to the law, Suknodyorov would reply that for him the wishes of his superiors were the law, and he obeyed it. Although he would im-mediately add I'm joking, I'm joking.

"What kind of stretch are we going for?" asked Suknodyorov.

"Give him a couple of years, that's enough," said Gunyaev. "I feel sorry for the lad." He sighed, raising his eyes to the heavens. "After all, he is a front-line veteran."

The investigator Pleshakov took the case and for form's sake sent inquiries concerning Chonkin's past to the appropriate agencies. And then—just imagine it, my highly esteemed and patient reader!—every-thing that had happened before happened all over again! The inquiry made the rounds of the agencies' addresses, certain faceless and mute individuals with duck-waddle walks carried it in folders along corridors and round offices, then glanced into the archive catalogues and wrote their résumés. With moderate speed, the inquiry assumed the guise of an operational report, which determined that Ivan Vasilievich Chonkin-Golitsyn, born 1919, Russian national, non-Party member, unmarried, formerly a private in armed forces unit 249814, had been tried in 1941 for desertion, betrayal of the motherland, armed robbery, and an attempt to detach a section of Soviet territory, transfer it to the enemy, and declare himself tsar. He had been convicted but, taking advantage of the confu-sion of wartime, had somehow managed to avoid punishment.

Of course, when all this happened, the lower-level staff of The Right Place realized that the fish they had caught was far too big for them to decide its fate themselves. Colonel Gunyaev actually thought there might even be a glimmer of a chance that he would reach the rank of general early. And therefore he embellished this case in fine style, employing all his literary talents, which were quite real (unbeknownst to his comrades-in-arms, he wrote poems, and rather good ones too, about the motherland, nature, and love for domestic animals, and he subsequently became a member of the U.S.S.R. Union of Writers). Having framed the case neatly, Gunyaev dispatched it upward, and the people at the top sent it on to people who were even higher, and eventually, the case rose to such a great height that it reached the most important individual of all in The Right Place, that is, once again, the self-same Lavrentii Pavlovich Beria.

11

LET US IMAGINE THAT ONE SUNNY SUMMER MORNING Lavrentii Pavlovich has awoken after a wonderful night with a beautiful stranger picked up by his adjutants on Gorky Street. At first, before she grasped what was happening, this beautiful stranger wept and implored him: "Oh, mister, my mom will give me hell!" But later, when she realized just who this mister was, she went wild with delight and in the middle of sex she shouted out: "Oi, just look who's poking me! When I tell Lyuska, she'll never believe it!" Lavrentii Pavlovich was himself delighted by these outcries and he laughed. But in the morning, after giving her twenty-five rubles out of his own wallet (he was an honest man and he didn't spend state money on his personal requirements), he warned her: "If you tell Lyuska, you'll disappear, and your mom will never know where your grave is." Following which he took a cold shower, wrapped himself in a silk robe, and sat down to breakfast.

His breakfast was modest, consisting of orange juice and boiled rice with medallions of the choicest tender meat. His food was served to him by his housekeeper, a kind of butler in a skirt. Before she got the job, Kapulya, as Lavrentii Pavlovich called her, had been subjected to severe and extremely lengthy checking. The special services had sought to establish who her mom and dad, grandmas and grandpas were, whether she had ever been put on trial, taken prisoner, or located on occupied territory, and whether she had ever been registered as psychiatrically ill or had any relatives abroad. She had given exhaustive replies to every question, presented the necessary documents, demonstrated how long she had worked in the system of The Right Place before the war, and eventually had become the most trusted of Lavrentii Pavlovich's servants. She was his secretary and housekeeper and waitress, and from time to time she carried out personal assignments of a clandestine nature for her boss. And as yet probably not a single living individual, apart from Allen Dulles, the head of American intelligence and also, naturally, the author of these lines, was aware that the name Kapitolina Goryacheva was a mask for a double-dyed female spy, formerly a German citizen, but now the American Katalina von Heiss.

While breakfasting, Lavrentii Pavlovich read the latest issue of *Pravda,* then glanced through the minutes of several interrogations, taking great pleasure in his reading. He was especially amused by the confessions of major Party members and state officials who had once been fat, smug, and arrogant but were now paltry and pitiful, only too willing to admit that they had inflicted damage on the state, plotted assassination attempts against Comrade Stalin and other members of the Soviet leadership, sabotaged various items of machinery, poisoned wells, and hidden microfilms with espionage reports for their transatlantic masters in the hollows of trees or garbage cans. When he read these minutes, Lavrentii Pavlovich could easily picture to himself how such confessions had been obtained, and this picture gave him a warm glow inside. In such cases he often laughed soundlessly and Katalina von Heiss would glance over his shoulder and also laugh quietly, delighting in the way that the Communists were destroying each other.

Beria's meal and his reading were punctuated by telephone calls. Among others, he received a call from the head of state, Mikhail Ivanovich Kalinin. Formally speaking, according to the State Constitution, Mikhail Ivanovich held the supreme office of the state and could appoint anyone he chose to a high position, remove him from it, confer distinctions on him, and sentence him to death or pardon him. Formally speaking, he could even remove Stalin from his post or deprive him of his title of Generalissimus. But in fact, Mikhail Ivanovich was an entirely powerless individual with no rights and he could not even protect his own wife against arrest. He did, however, permit himself to petition on her behalf and this time he was calling yet again to grovel and plead. "Lavrusha, dear fellow, please release her. After all, you know she's not guilty of anything."

"Misha," replied Lavrentii Pavlovich, "you're the head of state, not some ignorant little nobody. You understand perfectly well that we don't put anyone in prison for nothing. You know that there are many things I would do for you, Misha. I'm a very kind man, I'm soft-hearted, you can ask my wife. But Misha, when it's a matter of enemies of the people, my heart turns very hard. And I would advise you, Misha, not to petition for enemies of the people—a people that has entrusted you with the highest office in our state."

While he was talking to the head of state, known among the common people as the All-Union Elder and among his comrades-in-arms more simply as the Old Goat because of the style of his beard, Kapulya whispered in his ear that the individual he had summoned was waiting outside the door. When he hung up, Lavrentii Pavlovich asked for this individual to be shown in, and when he appeared, instinctively leapt to his feet, because the person who came in was Iosif Vissarionovich Stalin, although he was dressed very unusually. Not in his quasi-military field jacket, not in his marshal's uniform tunic, but in a double-breasted suit and a tie, an item that Iosif Vissarionovich had never worn in his life.

At this point we ought to insert a double space between paragraphs and switch to something else, following the rules of counterpoint. Distract the reader's attention, let him suffer the agonies of uncertainty for a while as he wonders exactly why Iosif Vissarionovich has turned up to see Lavrentii Pavlovich so early in the morning although, as everyone knows, he never got up that early. Everyone knows that he worked without respite, sometimes until the first cockcrow, but he never got up earlier than noon. So why has he shown up at the crack of dawn to see Lavrentii Pavlovich, and not summoned Lavrentii Pavlovich to come to him? We shall not keep the reader in suspense for long, however, but reveal the plot to him immediately: the individual who has arrived in person to see Lavrentii Pavlovich is not Iosif Vissarioniovich Stalin, but Goga, i.e., the actor and People's Artist of the U.S.S.R. Georgii Mikhailovich Melovani. This Melovani was so like Comrade Stalin that sometimes when he appeared, Comrade Stalin himself would jump to his feet, afraid that perhaps this was the real Comrade Stalin and he, the real Comrade Stalin, was perhaps not entirely the real Comrade Stalin.

And so, at the apparent appearance in the dining room of Comrade Stalin, Lavrentii Pavlovich also instinctively leapt to his feet, but in fact immediately realized his mistake and, after reuniting his buttocks with his chair, gestured invitingly to his visitor and said:

"Hello, Goga, *gambardjoba*,* dear *genatsvale*,* come in and sit down facing me. Kapulya, serve him a couple of meat cutlets. Eat, my dear *kunak*,* eat. This is good meat. From a young mammal, you understand. Pour him some wine, Kapulya, no, don't pour him wine, make him a Bloody Mary. That's a good drink. Personally I find, don't you know, that a Bloody Mary arouses a powerful feeling of lust."

They drank a mixture of vodka and tomato juice, accompanied by supremely tender cutlets that literally melted in their mouths. And while they ate they had a conversation in broken Georgian so that Kapa (one of their own, but even so . . .) would not understand what they were talking about. But Kapa, of course, knew Georgian, Armenian, and, in particular, Azeri, as well her own native tongue. Since she didn't have a pocket dictaphone to hand (it hadn't been invented yet), she remembered everything that was said word for word and that very evening, together with the garbage, she put out a coded message for her chief Allen Dulles concerning the proposal made to Georgii Mikhailovich by Lavrentii Pavlovich.

The gist of this proposal was as follows. Comrade Stalin, having reached a certain age, had begun to tire under the burden of the numerous responsibilities entrusted to him, and it was already hard for him to be present everywhere he needed to be present, sometimes at one and the same time: in the Politburo of the Central Committee of the CPSU, in the Council of Ministers, at General HQ, at the Peace Council, at the Stalin Prize Committee, and at all sorts of sessions, meetings, briefings, and emergency consultations. And therefore Beria had a request or, rather, a top secret Party assignment to present to People's Artist Melovani: to exploit his exceptional resemblance to Stalin in order to take Comrade Stalin's place occasionally, standing on the platform of the Mausoleum or attending presentations of credentials by ambassadors.

As had been expected, Melovani was initially taken aback by this proposal and gasped:

"Oi! Oi! Lavrentii Pavlovich. But how could I? I'm only a stage artiste, Lavrentii Pavlovich. I can only play someone else in the theater or the movies. But actually take the place of the genius of humanity at state functions? How could I possibly? Lavrentii Pavlovich, I am a simple man, Lavrentii Pavlovich."

---

* Georgian words: *gambardjoba*—"welcome" (literally, be victorious); *genatsvale*—"respected friend"; *kunak*—"friend" (buddy).

"But Comrade Stalin is a simple man, too. And Lenin was a simple man. And you are not only an artiste, you are also a Communist and you should realize that the Party's suggestion is an order. Do you realize that, *genatsvale?*"

And the *genatsvale,* of course, had realized that straightaway, but he took the opportunity to put forward a request on his own behalf. Since he would now have to develop an even better feel for the image of Comrade Stalin, he would like to be provided with approximately the same living conditions as Comrade Stalin himself.

On hearing that, Lavrentii Pavlovich frowned slightly and muttered: "Ah, how materialistic you are." However, he promised that the request would be considered.

"But watch out," he warned Georgii Mikhailovich. "If anyone discovers our secret, I'll have you buried alive."

12

HAVING LET THE PEOPLE'S ARTIST GO, Lavrentii Pavlovich was intending to rock for a little while in his wicker rocker and read another set or two of minutes, and perhaps take a brief doze, but at this point a courier arrived with certain documents, and when Lavrentii Pavlovich glanced at them, he first whistled in surprise, then said *"vai-vai"* in Georgian and then clapped his hands. We should perhaps observe in passing that this was a habit of the leaders of that time—clapping their hands. A clap of their hands magically summoned someone to appear before them, an individual or individuals immediately ready to do whatever their bidding might be. The moment Lavrentii Pavlovich clapped his hands, his indispensable housekeeper appeared before him again, holding up in one hand a white shantung silk suit and a cream-colored shirt on a wooden hanger. After changing rapidly, Lavrentii Pavlovich strolled out onto the sun-drenched porch, carrying a thick briefcase. He squeezed the briefcase between his knees and brought his palms together once again in another clap. Immediately a long black ZIS-101 automobile rolled up to the porch, its polish gleaming like a brand-new rubber galosh, its tires rustling gently, and a little red flag fluttering on its hood. While it was still moving, a security officer leaned out the front door and opened the back one, grabbed the briefcase from Lavrentii Pavlovich, and thrust it into the back seat. Lavrentii Pavlovich himself dived inside, grabbed the briefcase, sank back into the deep, soft seat, and said in a quiet voice: "To Kuntsevo!"

Half an hour later he was outside a pair of inconspicuous green metal gates with a lacy openwork design along the top. The gates opened, allowed the automobile through, and closed again, and the automobile stood there, blocked in between the first set of gates and a second pair, like a barge in a canal lock. Two uniformed officers immediately emerged from a building at the side and asked the passenger to get out of the car, show them his ID, and present the briefcase to be searched. While one of them sorted through the contents of the briefcase on the hood, the other asked Lavrentii Pavlovich to turn to face the car, place his hands on the roof, and spread his legs wide apart, which Marshal Beria did without expressing even the slightest dissatisfaction, for this was normal, routine procedure. This was not the first time the marshal had been checked like this, and the procedure was the same as ever. He was groped thoroughly but civilly, with no vulgarity, from head to foot, especially under the arms and in the groin, after which he was permitted to proceed into the grounds of the dacha on foot.

Lavrentii Pavlovich picked up his briefcase and set off along a path covered with pink gravel. Despite its routine nature, he had found the search to which he was subjected unpleasant, but it had not spoiled his mood, and the marshal's mood was very good indeed, so good that he almost skipped along, occasionally jerking his neck to one side and whistling the tune of a Georgian song that he liked because the senior comrade he was on his way to meet liked it. The pink path first wound between tall pine trees, then emerged into an open area in front of a modest-looking dacha with peonies, dahlias, gladioli, and large white roses growing in separate beds on each side of it. The dacha really was modest in appearance, a single story with no superfluous external decorations or internal luxuries. These days any New Russian would be ashamed to put his yard keeper in a dacha like that, but in those days even some of the high and mighty gloried in their power while remaining extremely modest in their own requirements. The occupant of the dacha was standing by a rose bush, wearing a pair of threadbare linen trousers with baggy knees, a washed-out gray shirt with short sleeves, and sandals on bare feet. His left hand was clad in a canvas mitten and in his right he was holding a large pair of pruning shears. This amateur gardener was, of course, Iosif Vissarionovich Stalin.

In recent times Iosif Vissarionovich's health had deteriorated seriously. He was only sixty-five years old—a considerable age but, with good nutrition and general care, not so very extreme. Other people at that age follow a very active lifestyle: they do their exercises in the morning, do a full day's work, and sleep with their wives, while the liveliest among them even sleep with other people's wives. But despite high-quality nutrition, good living conditions, and excellent care, such joys were beyond Stalin's reach: he had had his wife shot a long time ago, he had sent Rosa Kaganova packing, and other women gave him no pleasure. He experienced pleasure of a special, even sexual, kind when he eliminated his enemies and his brothers-in-arms, making them turn numb with terror, squeal in pain, and beg on their knees for mercy. Unfortunately, all of this, even coupled with good living conditions and a sound digestion, was insufficient to compensate for the damage inflicted on his body by the extreme stresses of the war years, the burden of immense power that he bore on his shoulders, and a persecution complex that grew steadily stronger with the passage of time. The great power for which many people strive so irrationally requires a constant and sometimes intolerable and exhausting effort. And power that is uncontrolled and employed lawlessly at the ruler's own vicious whim arouses in him the constant fear of possible vengeance. Stalin, as we know, was terribly cruel and therefore everyone feared him, but his fear was even greater, because he feared everyone. He never slept in the same room two nights running, but one thing always remained the same: none of the rooms in which he slept had any windows. No one was supposed to know which room he was actually sleeping in, but his bodyguards and their commander General Nikolai Vlasik knew everything and kept mum. They knew, because they often heard snoring coming from the room where the individual under their protection was sleeping—a strange inhuman sound, more like a horse snorting than anything else, and sometimes they definitely heard a horse's neigh.

Although the guards heard all this, they couldn't discuss the phenomenon even in a whisper—they didn't even dare to glance at each other. But the Generalissimus snorted and neighed like that because very often he had almost exactly the same dream over and over again—an idyll that merged into a nightmare. He was a little sorrel foal that had gotten separated from the herd grazing on some mountain pasture, and at first everything was fine. The sun shone gently, butterflies and dragonflies flitted about, the grass under his hooves was deliciously juicy,

with a tangy, sour taste. Everything was fine, but suddenly, out of nowhere, wolves appeared. He tried to run away but discovered that he
was hobbled; he tried to tear his bonds apart but he couldn't, and the
wolves were getting closer, and then he saw that they weren't wolves, but
Beria, Khrushchev, Malenkov, Molotov, Kaganovich and—sometimes—
Voroshilov and Budyonny, with their wolfish jaws gaping wide, reaching
out for him from all sides. He remembered that he had bodyguards and
he called out (that was when the guards heard the strange neighing), but
it was pointless, no one came hurrying to his rescue. On occasions like
this he jumped up and gazed around, not immediately realizing where
he was. He felt the walls, checked that the bolts were secure, lay down
again and then jumped back up in horror. His basic feelings in recent
times had been depression, fear, and suspicion. Mistrust of absolutely
everybody and of every word they spoke was draining the Generalissimus's strength and undermining his health. At the age of sixty-five he
looked eighty: his face was wrinkled, his hands dark, his arms flabby,
with feeble muscles, and his chest hollow and overgrown with gray wool.
The look in his eyes was always wary. When he worked in the garden,
however, his mood improved.

"Look, Lavrentii, see what I'm doing," said Stalin, smacking his
cracked lips. "I'm snipping off what's superfluous. To keep this bush
beautiful, healthy, and luxuriant I have to make resolute use of the shears
and snip off everything superfluous. Do you take my meaning?"

"Indeed I do, dear Koba.* Oh, indeed I do. I spend all my time snipping off what's superfluous. Sometimes it can be a superfluous head," he
said, to be more specific, and laughed loudly, holding his pince-nez so
that it wouldn't hop up and down on his nose.

"Oh, the things you say, Lavrentii!" said the gardener, wincing. "You're
quite incorrigible! Why do you have to imagine something so disagree-
able when I'm talking about the beautiful? Just look at this rose. Doesn't
it seem to you, Lavrentii, that a rose is a wonder of nature? Eh, Lavrentii,
doesn't it seem so to you?"

"It does, it does, dear Koba," Lavrentii assured him ardently. "That's
exactly how it seems to me. It seems to me that a rose is truly a very great
wonder of nature."

"Does it seem to you to be so, or is it really so?" Iosif Vissarionovich
asked and looked at Lavrentii Vissarionovich with the sly smile that

---

* Stalin's nickname within the Communist Party comes from the fictional hero Koba in a Georgian novel of 1883, *The Patricide*, by Alexander Kazbegi.

everyone knew, which made many feel uneasy, and even gave some heart attacks and strokes.

"It seems to me to be so and it really is so," replied Lavrentii Pavlovich. "A rose is a remarkable wonder of nature, perfect in every respect. But you, I think, are an even greater wonder of nature than all the roses in the world."

Stalin made a wry face.

"Don't be sycophantic, Lavrentii. You know I don't like flattery. But I am glad that you agree with me about roses. I don't like flatterers, but I like those who disagree with me even less. And the perfection of this flower, Lavrentii, consists in the fact that it is not only insanely beautiful, but also prickly. Dostoevsky said that beauty will save the world, and I agree with him. However, beauty can only save the world, and save itself, if it is prickly. Do you understand that, Lavrentii?"

"Precisely so," Lavrentii Pavlovich agreed, nodding his head. "I understand that, I understand that very well."

"You don't understand anything!" Stalin exclaimed, flourishing his shears. "You don't understand very much in general, and therefore you can never be a great politician. You can only be someone who serves someone else, but you could never lead a state, especially a large state, especially a state like our state."

"And I don't want to, Koba," Lavrentii Pavlovich said earnestly. "I have absolutely no desire to. A great state must be led by a great man. And I am not a great man. But I am the kind of man who, when he is devoted to a great man, can help that great man lead a great state successfully."

"Well, all right, all right," said Iosif Vissarionovich, satisfied. "The thing I admire about you, Lavrentii, is your modesty. Do you have something to report to me, or did you just come to take a look at my roses? If you wanted to look at the roses, you've already looked at them and you can go, but if you have business to discuss, then tell me about it."

Lavrentii Pavlovich told him. About various bits of current business, both trivial and important. The important business included a report from the intelligence services that the Americans had tested some very big bomb in the desert in Nevada. Lavrentii Pavlovich told Iosif Vissarionovich about the possible use of the bomb in the war against Japan and showed him coded messages received from secret agents and a note from the academician Igor Kurchatov, in which the information received was described as credible and the intentions of the United States as very serious. Kurchatov reminded Stalin that the atom bomb, as had already been reported to him on several occasions, was a highly promising weapon, it would possess a destructive force beyond all comparison with anything else, and a future war would be won by the side that possessed such a weapon. Iosif Vissarionovich heaved a painful sigh. He had heard about this bomb several times before but had regarded the rumors about it with distrust. Now he had come to believe in it very seriously and regretted his previous attitude. In a few days' time he was planning to attend a conference of the heads of government of the victorious powers, at which he intended to demand a few things from Harry Truman and Winston Churchill, but if the Americans really had such a terrible bomb and it worked as well as planned, he would have to tone his ultimatum down a bit.

"What an abominable man you are, Lavrentii!" Iosif Vissarionovich said with real feeling. "Why do you always tell me about things that make me feel depressed? Is there nothing at all in your swollen briefcase except all sorts of nastiness?"

"Oh, yes indeed there is!" Lavrentii Pavlovich declared cheerfully. "There is, my dear Comrade Koba, there most certainly is." He stuck his hand into the briefcase and pulled out a slim blue folder. "Remember, during the initial period of the war, we dealt with the case of Prince Golitsyn? He was arrested and sentenced to be shot."

"Well?" Stalin asked expectantly.

"Well then, as it happened, the sentence was never carried out and the prince managed to escape his just punishment. But my people did not forget about him, they kept searching for him throughout the war, and now, just imagine, dear Koba, they have found him in the bed of a German whore."

Iosif Vissarionovich snipped off a rose, turned around, and held it out to Lavrentii Pavlovich.

"Here, take it. It's for you. For distinguished service."

Lavrentii Pavlovich realized that this was mockery, but nonetheless he said:

"Thank you, Koba, for valuing my modest efforts so highly."

"How could I possibly not value them?" asked Iosif Vissarionovich. "The KGB try to catch the same man several times, and every time they build it up into a case, and every time they earn appointments, ranks, and decorations for it. And what's more, I am absolutely convinced that of course this case was concocted entirely out of thin air, crudely cobbled together with rusty nails, and could never hold water. But I won't let you have this Golitsyn now. I need him for other business."

"What business is that, if it's not a secret?" asked Lavrentii Pavlovich.

"I won't hide it from you," said Iosif Vissarionovich. "I have received a report concerning Russian émigrés. As a result of our victory, what I would call a very serious patriotic mood has developed in émigré circles, especially among those with once-proud names. During the war there was a great upsurge of patriotic spirit among the émigrés, but we have certain people, certain, I would even say, perhaps, enemies of the people, who are willing to serve a great state even in mere supporting roles as long as they can cause as much harm as possible. And these same potential—you understand—enemies of the people possibly deserve to be dealt with like this."

Iosif Vissarionovich jerked his hand suddenly. The shears glinted in the sun and Lavrentii Pavlovich felt his nose squeezed tight between the two blades. But squeezed carefully and not yet cut.

"You know," Iosif Vissarionovich said sadly, without removing the shears, "I would really like—providing, of course, that it is possible—for this prince to be here tomorrow, at approximately this spot at approximately this time. What do you think, is that possible, or simply impossible?"

Lavrentii Pavlovich was afraid to move, but nonetheless he was obliged to reply.

"Tomorrow?" he asked with a distinct nasal twang. "In twenty-four hours? From Germany?"

"Do you think it not very possible?" asked Iosif Vissarionovich.

The shears, fortunately, were not very sharp, but they squeezed the nose tighter as he spoke, and Lavrentii Pavlovich was obliged to open his mouth to breathe.

"It . . ." he said, with his tongue sticking to the roof of his mouth. "It . . . I think it will be possible."

"You think so?" Iosif Vissarionovich opened the shears and lowered them. "I also think that it is possible, and I also know that for a friend like you, nothing is impossible. And I think that as a good friend, you could even do the impossible for me."

"My dear Koba!" Lavrentii Pavlovich replied agitatedly, pretending to adjust his pince-nez as he felt one side of his nose and then the other with his little finger. "For you I will do anything, possible or impossible."

"Good, my dear friend," Iosif Vissarionovich said in a warmer, paternal tone of voice. "Perhaps now that is all you have for me?"

"No," said Lavrentii Pavlovich, wagging his entire body. "There is just one little question, but I'm not sure if it is worth bothering you with it. You know, the actor Goga Melovani, who has played you in our very best films, is constantly working to improve his skills, and he claims he can play you so well that no one could tell you apart."

"Oh, yes?" Stalin replied. "No one could tell us apart? And what does he need for that? Perhaps he needs good makeup?"

Sensing a sudden wariness in Stalin's tone of voice, Lavrentii Pavlovich decided for the time being not to expound his basic plan for using Melovani in a way that would serve his own purposes. He set the question aside and merely said that the actor Melovani himself believed that in order to feel his way completely into the image of Comrade Stalin, he needed to have living conditions approximately the same as the conditions appropriate for Comrade Stalin, and therefore he was asking if he could perhaps live for a while at one of Stalin's dachas, at Lake Ritsa, say?

"Feel his way into the image of Comrade Stalin?" Stalin put on a puzzled expression and started shaking his head to left and right, as if he were discussing the possible options with himself. "Comrade Melovani wants to feel his way into the image of Comrade Stalin and live like Comrade Stalin for a while? But Comrade Stalin is so fed up with living like Comrade Stalin that perhaps he would like to feel his way into the image of Comrade Melovani and live the carefree life that Comrade Melovani lives?"

He dropped the shears on the ground, pulled off his canvas glove, took his pipe out of his pocket, and started filling it. He spent a long time filling it without speaking. He took out his matches and lit it, his hands shaking as he did so. He puffed a few smoke rings at Lavrentii Pavlovich's nose (Lavrentii Pavlovich drew these rings in through his open mouth, with an expression of unmitigated pleasure). "So," said Stalin, "feel his way into the image of Comrade Stalin . . . Well, all right," he continued, nodding. "If he wants to feel his way into the image of Comrade Stalin, let him start with exile in Turukhansk."

Iosif Vissarionovich escorted his visitor almost all the way to the gates and as they said good-bye, he reminded him:

"At this time tomorrow you will be here with that prince, or I'll snip your nose off."

He repeated:

"At this time tomorrow."

13

SOMETHING LIKE THIS HAD HAPPENED to Chonkin before. He was stuck in the guardhouse, but wasn't feeling particularly oppressed by that. If he was worried at all, it was only about who was looking after his horses. He knew nothing about the danger of a show trial hanging over his head, and the prospect of spending a few days in the slammer didn't bother him. So life felt pretty comfortable. But that evening he was suddenly moved to a solitary cell—not an ordinary one, either, but an officers' cell. It had a spring bed with a mattress, a pillow, and fresh starched sheets (Chonkin had never slept on sheets like that in his life). Beside the bed were a stool and a nightstand that contained the guardhouse regulations and the *History of the All-Union Communist Party (Bolsheviks),* which was said to have been written by Comrade Stalin himself, who out of modesty hadn't put his name to it.

For supper they brought him boiled rice and two meat cutlets, with white bread, butter, and even jelly as well. Chonkin was surprised and started wondering what all this could mean. And with the logic of a simple mind he thought that if the higher-ups had decided to pamper a little man like him in this way, it wasn't likely to lead to anything good. But even so, in the morning he enjoyed his mashed potato with fried salami and was just about to drink his cocoa with American crackers when the door opened abruptly and three men walked into the cell: the head of SMERSH, Colonel Gunyaev, the sergeant of the guard, Liubochkin, and an officer he didn't know with four stars on his shoulder straps. They strode in so briskly and ominously that Chonkin cringed, thinking an execution was in the offing. Then he jumped to his feet and stood to attention. The men who had come in looked at him and he looked at them. Suddenly Gunyaev smiled strangely and asked a question.

"What?" Chonkin asked.

"I asked: how did you sleep?" Gunyaev repeated.

"Just fine," said Chonkin with a shrug.

"He says he slept just fine," said Gunyaev, turning to his companions and smiling as happily as if he were the one who had slept well. "But you finish up your cocoa, and then . . ." he snapped his fingers and a soldier Chonkin didn't know appeared from the corridor with a pile of clothes, which he put on the bed, and then stood a pair of boots beside it.

"We'll go out," said Gunyaev, "and you finish your drink. Then get changed. Well, you've got about another five minutes."

He backed out, smiling all the while and looking at Chonkin strangely. The others walked out, too, and they closed the door quietly behind them. Chonkin looked at the clothes, unable to believe that they were all for him. New shorts and singlet. Breeches, tunic, cap—all officer's clothes, but with a private's shoulder straps. Shiny leather high boots instead of shoes, and socks instead of puttees. He was surprised, but after thinking for a moment, he started putting it all on, forgetting about his cocoa.

"Now then," Gunyaev said after he reappeared and ran his eye over Chonkin like a tailor. "That's good. The cap's a bit too big, but don't pull it down so tight. Let it sit loose. But all the rest could have been made to measure. Oh yes, where's your medal?" he said, suddenly remembering. "Here it is, what were you thinking . . . let's move it from the old blouse to this one. For the Liberation of Warsaw—a minor decoration, but an honorable one, everyone knows that the battle for Warsaw was far from easy. And why haven't you got a Guards badge? We're a guards regiment. Wait. Here." He took off his own "Guards" badge and pinned it on Chonkin's chest, and then stepped back and looked at Chonkin as if he were a picture.

"Well, all right," he said rather uncertainly. "Now we'll take a walk. That is, we'll take a ride. First we'll take a walk, then we'll take a ride." He seemed to think that he had made a joke, and he laughed.

They walked outside to where a Willis automobile was waiting. The driver put it in gear and it started up, lurched over the cobblestones of the road, trundled out of the town and fifteen minutes later rolled up to an aircraft parking area, where the regimental commander Opalikov, wearing a leather jacket and a com helmet, was standing beside a fighter-bomber with its covers removed, together with two generals whom Chonkin didn't know (he didn't actually know any generals at all) and the mechanic Leshka Onishchenko, who was so dumbfounded by what had happened that when Chonkin said "hello," he shouted back: "Good morning, Comrade . . ."—and then stopped, unable to imagine what rank might be applicable to Chonkin now.

But then, the others were also surprised, astounded, and stunned after hearing that Private Chonkin had to be dispatched immediately to Moscow on the personal orders of . . . how could you possibly imagine it? . . . some Chonkin or other . . . on the personal orders of the Supreme

Commander in Chief! Everyone was mystified. What could Comrade Stalin possibly want with such an unusual cadre? But the army is the army, a place where you don't ask unnecessary questions, and carry out orders unquestioningly.

In view of the exceptional importance of the order, its implementation had been entrusted to the most experienced airman, Colonel Opalikov. At this stage Opalikov was a Hero of the Soviet Union. He had actually shot down enough planes to be awarded the title twice over, but he hadn't been awarded it a second time because he persisted in expressing his admiration for the conquered Germans' standard of living. In the restaurant where the airmen celebrated the Victory, he had said the Russian people could live just as well as the Germans if it wasn't for the collective farms. And in addition, citing the authority of some relative of his, he had claimed that the character of Soviet Man was not molded by society but by certain particles in the living cell that were passed on by inheritance. These statements by the colonel had reached the ears of the head of SMERSH, and he had immediately accused Opalikov of anti-Soviet propaganda, adulation of all things foreign, and being under the clear influence of false Western doctrines alien to Marxism-Leninism. The commander of the division, Lieutenant-General Vasilii Prosyanoi, had tried to hush the matter up, but Opalikov had been refused his second star and transferred from fighter planes to ground attack aircraft. But the head of SMERSH had not let things go at that: he wrote an eloquent report to Moscow, denouncing the unhealthy mood in the air force division concerned, in which certain members of the command personnel took the liberty of passing anti-Soviet remarks while others of even higher rank protected them. The SMERSHovian's efforts had not yet been crowned with success, but no one could say that that would continue to be the case.

General Prosyanoi was also a Hero of the Soviet Union, and a very handsome man, with a fluffy mustache on his dark-complexioned face and black arched eyebrows which, according to some people, he applied every morning with a black pencil. Many women went weak at the sight of him, and he himself went weak at the sight of Opalikov's wife, Nadezhda, and apparently there was something between them. This something was, perhaps, the second reason why Opalikov and not someone else had been chosen to deliver Chonkin to Moscow. As for Opalikov, he understood very well the reason for the great trust that had been placed in him and he had prepared a response to this meanness which, in the spirit of a later age, could have been called asymmetrical.

While Prosyanoi discussed the route of the flight with Opalikov, jabbing his finger at the map case lying on a wing, the other general, a short man with a big belly and gold teeth, sidled up to Chonkin, shook his hand, and introduced himself.

"Major-General Novikov."

"Aha," said Chonkin, and felt frightened that now he would get a dressing-down for not answering correctly, but he didn't know how to answer correctly in such cases, because no general had ever introduced himself to him before.

The general, however, was peaceably inclined.

"Well now, Comrade Chonkin, do you already know where you're flying to?"

"I've got no idea," said Chonkin.

"Well now then, you'll find out," the general said with a smile. "You'll soon find out."

Meanwhile Prosyanoi was briefing Opalikov.

"So," he said, running his finger across the map. "You fly with four landings: Zagan—Chenstokhov—Belostok—Orsha, and the refuelling there will last you as far as Moscow. Are you listening to me at all?"

"Yes, yes," Opalikov responded.

In fact he was listening, but not hearing anything. And in his thoughts he was plotting an entirely different route.

Eventually they finished discussing everything and walked over to Chonkin.

"So, has the comrade been prepared?" Prosyanoi asked, only now looking at Chonkin. "Well, soldier, not afraid to fly, are you?"

"No," Chonkin said tersely.

"Why should he be afraid, he's flown before," remarked Opalikov.

"Well all right then," said Prosyanoi. "In that case, as they say, a soft landing to you."

Chonkin had been transported on a plane four years earlier, only then he had been facing the pilot's back, and now he was facing the tail and the machine gun, but he had been warned not to touch that.

The colonel climbed into his seat. The mechanic spun the propeller with a forked lever. The appropriate commands followed.

"Contact! Stand back!"

The engine sneezed, cracked like a pistol, spat out a jet of black smoke, and started throbbing regularly and confidently. An eddying stream of air, swirled into motion by the propeller, flattened the tall grass against the ground. Holding his cap on with one hand so that it wouldn't get blown off, the mechanic dove under one wing and pulled the chocks out from under the wheels. General Novikov saluted, but Prosyanoi simply waved. The engine roared and the plane started moving. Opalikov didn't taxi toward the runway but tore off smartly across the airfield toward the river flowing nearby and took off, leaving a cloud of dust behind him.

"One of Stalin's falcons!" Prosyanoi laughed with a shake of his head and glanced at Novikov. He was surprised when he saw the expression on the major-general's face.

"What's wrong?" he asked.

"Y-y-y!" the major-general groaned, reaching out his hand toward the plane that had taken off.

Prosyanoi looked in the same direction, and a certain well-known Russian phrase concerning mothers, intended exclusively for the expression of very strong feelings, burst out of his throat.

14

AT THAT MOMENT, IN THE COMMAND POST of the American air base on the opposite bank of the small river, there were two majors on duty—Bill Hunter Jr. and Michael Pogarek. They were sitting in the little wooden house on wheels with big windows that gave a very good view of the Soviet air base. Following the American habit, Hunter Jr. was leaning back with his feet up on the desk, smoking a fat Cuban cigar, puffing out his cheeks and blowing plump, tidy smoke rings up at the ceiling. Pogarek, leaning over the desk with his head propped on his hands, was struggling against drowsiness. Neither the Americans nor the Russians had any flights today, and the majors were discussing the recent news about the progress of the war in Japan. Hunter recalled his period of service in the Philippines, where he had had an affair with a Japanese woman. He had actually wanted to marry her, but the command had objected violently. He had been warned that if he did marry, he would have to move from the Air Force Special Units to some other branch of the service. He had even been prepared to sacrifice his career, but that had been prevented by the unfortunate death of his fiancée in a car accident. Yawning into his fist, Pogarek said that he also really liked Japanese, Chinese, Korean, and Filipino women, but he would never marry a woman of a different race—not because he was hostile to other races, but because that kind of mixing had a bad effect on the children. He himself was a result of the mingling of Anglo-Saxon and Polish blood, and he could constantly feel two different personalities struggling with each other inside him. The Pole was always blustering, urging him to commit various acts of folly, while the Anglo-Saxon was always trying to persuade him to be reasonable.

"Michael," Hunter interrupted him, "doesn't it seem to you that those Russians over there are bustling about as if they were going to do some flying today?"

"That's strange," said Michael, yawning. "Since the war ended, they haven't usually flown on Mondays. They're all superstitious, and Monday's a tough day for them. On Sunday they drink damping fluid and on Monday their heads ache, so they study Uncle Joe's biography."

When Hunter Jr. took down the binoculars hanging on the wall and raised them to his eyes, he was even more surprised.

"Listen, Michael, there really is something unusual going on across there. Two generals hanging about beside the same plane. Right . . . now they've started up the engine, taken away the chocks . . . Michael!" Bill exclaimed excitedly, grabbing for the microphone. "Look at what he's doing!" And he shouted nervously into the microphone: "Attention, duty squad. Come in!"

The radio responded in the voice of Captain Richard Thorndike.

"Dick," Hunter said to him, "the Russians are displaying suspicious activity. Start your engines and be ready to take off."

"Yes, sir!"

The solitary aircraft on the other side of the river dashed across the airfield, leaving a cloud of dust in its wake.

At the same time the two engines of the duty squad's plane roared into life.

"Michael!" said Hunter.

"Bill!" said Pogarek, finally becoming alarmed.

And then both of them fell silent, gazing entranced at the Soviet plane as it took off and rose no more than twelve yards into the air, leaving its undercarriage down, then lined up to land on this side of the river.

"We're taxiing out, sir!" Thorndike's voice said from the radio.

"Wait," Hunter interrupted him. "It's too late to taxi out now."

It had all happened too fast to make sense of anything or take any kind of decision. The plane with the red star on its tailfin had already driven off the runway and was taxiing toward the command post at a speed which suggested it was about to ram it. Vehicles from all the air base services were dashing toward it from various directions: a fire engine, an ambulance, and a military police jeep.

When majors Hunter and Pogarek came darting out of their hut, one of the Soviet airmen had already killed the engine and jumped off the wing onto the grass, but the other was hesitating. To make quite certain that he wouldn't try to take off, the military police jeep halted right in front of the aircraft's nose. Six soldiers with the letters "MP" on their helmets tumbled out of the jeep and held their weapons at the ready. The airman was forty-something years old, dressed in blue breeches and a maroon leather jacket that was half-open, revealing a military blouse decorated with the Gold Star of a Hero of the Soviet Union.

When Hunter and Pogarek approached, the Soviet airman saluted and spoke first.

"Major Hunter?" he asked.

"Hunter Junior," Bill corrected him with enough dignity to suggest that he was really Hunter Senior. "And are you Colonel Opalikov?"

When they spoke by radio, the airmen of the two sides referred to themselves by numbers, but the commanders of the American and Soviet units knew each other's names.

"What happened to you?" Pogarek asked in Russian.

"I sick," Opalikov replied in English.

"You are sick?" Pogarek asked and switched back to Russian. "Do you mean to tell me you are ill?"

"Nou," the colonel protested in English. "I sick for political asylum." And then he repeated that in Russian.

The Americans exchanged glances and thought for a moment. Hunter said:

"Let's go in here."

They withdrew into the command post. They didn't ask Chonkin to join them. He stayed with the plane and, since he didn't know what to do, he decided to guard it. Although how could he guard anything without a weapon? Nevertheless, he took up a position between the propeller and the police jeep. The six large Americans with the letters "MP" on their helmets stood between him and the jeep, with their automatic weapons trained on him, but he just gazed at them, determined not to surrender.

At that moment a cart drawn by two horses, with a black soldier on the driving seat, trundled up to the site of the incident. There was clearly nothing for this soldier to do here, he had simply been attracted by idle curiosity.

"Hey, John!" called Chonkin, brightening up at the sight of him. "Howdy! How's it going?"

15

LAVRENTII PAVLOVICH SHOWED UP at Iosif Vissarionovich's dacha like a beaten dog. Once inside the gates, he took off his hat as he walked along, then stooped over very low and mopped his bald patch—not because it was unbearably hot, but because he invested these movements with a very specific repentant and self-deprecatory significance.

"Why are you alone?" Iosif Vissarionovich asked him sternly. "Did I invite you to come alone?"

"Koba, dear fellow!" Beria appealed in a tearful voice. "Something entirely unforeseen happened. The airman who was supposed to deliver our prince turned out to be a traitor. He turned out to be the kind of skunk that you couldn't even imagine. *Vai-vai-vai!*" Beria shook his head and rolled up his eyes to indicate to Iosif Vissarionovich that he was far too pure-hearted and trusting to even imagine the kind of skunk that this damned flyer was. "Can you imagine it, a fighter pilot, a major, a Hero of the Soviet Union. A nephew of one of our major academicians—and a traitor."

"What academician?" inquired Stalin.

"Well, you know, there was this academician called Grom-Grimeilo."

"Grom-Grimeilo?" Stalin repeated with a frown. "He's Grom-Grimeilo's nephew, and you let him get away? Stop trembling like a dog, will you? I'm not killing you yet. Not yet." He sat down on a bench and folded his fingers, as flaccid as sausages, across his stomach. "Tell me about it."

Beria thought it best not to sit down beside him and told his story standing. He told Stalin how Colonel Opalikov had flown across into the American zone and requested political asylum.

"How did he explain his request?"

"Dissatisfaction with the internal policies of the U.S.S.R."

"Ah!" For some reason Stalin was reassured by this information. "Dissatisfaction, that's all right. I am also dissatisfied with the internal policies of the U.S.S.R., and the foreign policies too, as a matter of fact."

"But actually," Beria continued, "the head of SMERSH told me that Opalikov did this to spite General Prosyanoi for sleeping with his wife."

"Well now, that's understandable," Stalin said magnanimously. "I would have defected too in that case. Although no—in that case, first I would have shot my wife and General Prosyanoi and then defected. By the way, have that general removed from his post and demoted. And tell me, did this Opalikov not put forward any third reason for his defection?"

"Apparently not," said Beria.

"Aha, all right then. Now tell me about Prince Golitsyn. Did he defect, too?"

"No, Koba, he didn't defect. He became a defector against his will. Colonel Opalikov was supposed to deliver him to you, but instead he took him into the American zone."

"But he stayed there."

"He stayed there. But, my dear Koba, he's not worth all your trouble. My people have discovered that he isn't a prince at all, but a simple army private who used to be nicknamed the Prince. In reality he has worked in stables all his life as a groom or a driver. And he's also a very ludicrous kind of soldier, the butt of constant jokes."

"And what is he called, this ludicrous soldier?"

"I don't recall exactly. Something beginning with *Ch.*"

"It wouldn't be Chonkin, would it?" asked Stalin, recalling the hero to whose health he had once drunk with general Drynov.

"Ye-es," said Beria, very greatly surprised. "Do you know him? The Supreme Commander in Chief knows the names of every one of his soldiers? Koba, don't take this as flattery, but you're a genius."

"Perhaps I am a genius, but who are you, I'd like to know. Why, no matter what task I set you, does everything always go wrong? I tell you what, my dear friend. You get me this Chonkin anyway. I give you three months. Four. Five. If he's not standing here in six months, right here on this spot, you'll be lying in your grave. Do you understand me, Lavrentii? You know, Lavrentii, that I never make idle threats. That's all. The audience is over. I'm tired of you. Now push off and don't forget what I told you."

16

NATURALLY, THE DEFECTION OF TWO MEMBERS of the Soviet armed forces in a secret airplane of a new design gave rise to friction between the Soviet and American authorities, who were still pretending to be Allies. Since they were still pretending, the Soviet Union Telegraph Agency (TASS) initially put out a relatively mild announcement, which began with the words "As already known." This agency was in the habit of beginning all its angry international declarations with the words "As already known," especially in those cases concerning something that no one had actually heard about before. "As already known," TASS declared, "a few days ago an aircraft of the Soviet Air Force made a forced landing at a military airfield in Eichendorf in the American occupation zone of Germany. The crew of the aircraft consists of two men: the captain, Colonel S. P. Opalikov, and the gunner and radio operator, I. V. Chonkin. The Soviet government hopes that the American authorities, acting in the spirit of the alliance, will not obstruct the return of the aircraft and its crew to the Soviet side."

It goes without saying that the hope expressed by the authors of this declaration was entirely illusory. It was clear that the Americans would not hand back the plane or the crew, and therefore the top Soviet intelligence agents in America, Germany, and other countries of the West received coded instructions to find the former members of the Soviet armed forces, Opalikov and Chonkin, eliminate Opalikov, and take Chonkin alive and transport him to Soviet territory. These instructions were signed by Comrade Lavrentiev (that was Lavrentii Beria's pseudonym).

17

AFTER READING THE STATEMENT FROM TASS, however, the Americans did ponder briefly. They didn't want to sour relations with the Soviets, so handing over the defectors was not entirely ruled out, but they were really curious to find out about this new Il-10 assault aircraft and how it differed from the old Il-2, and what the top-secret navigational system installed in it was like, not to mention the absolutely brand-new "ours-theirs" recognition system for approaching aircraft.

And apart from that, Colonel Opalikov had stated under interrogation that the flight had been arranged on specific instructions from Comrade Stalin and that Chonkin was not a gunner and radio operator at all but a simple wagon driver—that is, he drove horses, and the colonel couldn't even imagine what Comrade Stalin could want with him. So obviously the Americans felt it was important to find out exactly why Uncle Joe really wanted this "simple driver" (they put those words in quotes).

18

MEANWHILE, ON THE SOVIET SIDE, the staff of The Right Place conducted a search at the quarters of the defectors. In Chonkin's nightstand they discovered a letter from him to an obscure woman by the name of Nyura. Analysis of the letter failed to produce any conclusions, and the absence of an address made it impossible for them to locate this Nyura. However, in Opalikov's quarters they discovered adequate proof of the premeditation of his actions. The main clues were a textbook of English for beginners and notes based on it, which, among other phrases, included the following: "I am a Hero of the Soviet Union, Colonel Opalikov. I seek for political asylum. I hate the Soviet system. I love the American government and personally President Truman." There was a separate folder containing cuttings from popular science magazines. One included a concise biography of General Przhevalsky with his portrait, which looked very much like Stalin. The investigators paid attention to the article "The Myth of the Centaurs" only because there was a note in Opalikov's handwriting in the margin: "She always was a whore and still is." Under interrogation the colonel's wife testified that she knew nothing about her husband's plans, she had absolutely no idea and she didn't notice any suspicious preparations because lately their relationship had deteriorated so badly that they were practically strangers.

Nonetheless Nadezhda Opalikova was sentenced for involvement with a traitor to the motherland (in complete accord with the laws of those times) to five years of exile in distant regions of Siberia. Vasilii Prosyanoi was also punished for lack of vigilance and involvement with the wife of a traitor to the motherland; he was demoted from general to colonel and sent to Turkmenistan as deputy commander of a divisional flying unit.

19

THE AMERICANS DRESSED OPALIKOV AND CHONKIN in civilian clothes (khaki-colored pants and jackets) and housed them temporarily in a small wing of the soldiers' barracks. The wing was divided into two parts and had separate entrances on different sides so the individuals under guard could not contact each other. They lived there, each of them in a separate room with a shower and a flush toilet. Their household needs were attended to by John, Chonkin's long-standing acquaintance. They were fed separately: Opalikov in the officers' mess and Chonkin in the privates', but only after the principal diners—the Americans—had left.

For the first few days Chonkin was left in peace: the Americans were too busy with Opalikov. But his turn came, too. One warm, damp morning, he was escorted by two black guardsmen to the old villa occupied by American intelligence. The villa stood under old lime trees on Spiegelstrasse, behind a lacy ironwork fence with main gates and a wicket gate. One of Chonkin's escorts pressed a doorbell and a quiet, squeaky voice from a concealed radio device asked a question. The escort leaned down and answered, the wicket gate immediately opened with a gentle whisper, and the heavy door of the villa opened simultaneously. A short chubby gentleman appeared in the doorway, wearing a three-piece suit with a gold chain across his round stomach. He skipped down from the porch with a joyful smile, took a step toward Chonkin, held out both hands and started talking in fairly good Russian, but with a strange lisp.

"Hello, hello, dear Ivan Vathilievich! Abtholutely delighted to thee you."

He took Chonkin arm-in-arm as if he were a woman he desired, and they walked up together onto the high mossy porch and into the house, leaving the escorts outside. They made their way into a spacious hall containing several cupboards, a sideboard with tableware, and a low broad round table with four green leather chairs standing around it.

Chonkin's host led him over to one of the chairs and put his hand on Chonkin's left shoulder, inviting him to sit down. "Have a seat, have a seat. Make yourself at home."

Chonkin obediently plonked himself into the armchair, which felt uncomfortably soft to him. He was used to sitting on something a bit firmer: a stool, a driver's box, or a shell crate. But here his backside slumped toward the floor and his legs jerked upward. He squirmed about for a while, trying to find a position that felt more natural.

His host sat down facing him and felt just fine. But then, he always felt just fine in any position, perhaps because he was a born spy and could adapt instantly to any conditions. He was a second-generation American of Jewish-Hungarian extraction. His former surname was Perelmuter, but his father, a dealer in fur goods, had followed the custom widespread among Americans and reduced it to a single syllable that was pleasing to the ear.

"I am American Army Colonel George Pearl," said the master of the villa, introducing himself with a strange kind of smile that appeared and disappeared and appeared again. "George Pearl," he repeated, "but Russians usually call me Georgii Ivanovich. Would you like something to drink?"

The question was superfluous. Chonkin was always ready to have a drink, a fact that he expressed with an indeterminate movement of his chin and a convulsive reflex jerk of his Adam's apple.

The soft armchair was clearly not the most comfortable of seats even for Georgii Ivanovich, because before getting up, he turned over on his stomach, braced his hands against the thick, springy cushion and pushed, thereby eventually reaching a standing position, and then made a movement with his hands as if he were brushing dust off them. After that, he walked over to the sideboard and opened one of its doors to reveal a two-story bar: tumblers, wineglasses, and shot glasses up above, and dozens of bottles of various colors with bright labels down below.

"What would you like," Georgii Ivanovich asked, presenting the choice: "American whiskey, scotch, Madeira, vermouth, Calvados, Campari, Pernod? Colonel Opalikov told me that Russian aviators prefer damping fluid to anything else. I'm sorry, we don't have any at the moment, but I can order it."

From the assortment offered, Chonkin chose the only drink that he had heard anything about—whiskey.

"Scotch or bourbon? If you've never drunk it, I advise scotch."

Chonkin agreed to scotch.

"Straight, with water, or with ice?"

Chonkin agreed to straight. Pearl made himself a whiskey and soda with ice. He rang the little bronze bell standing on the table and a black girl appeared out of a secret door at one side, carrying a tray with fresh grapes, bananas, and mandarins and a bowl of roasted peanuts. She blinded Chonkin with her brilliant white smile, put the tray on the table and left, wiggling her prominent backside. Chonkin watched her go with a lingering glance. Pearl caught that glance and laughed.

"Tell me, Ivan Vasilievich, have you never slept with any black women?"

"Na-ah," Chonkin admitted. "I haven't."

"Well, you should," said Pearl. "Very feisty ladies, don't you know. It can be arranged, if you like."

Chonkin didn't say anything, but he put on a grimace obviously intended to indicate that he was shy, but it would be interesting.

"Everything can be arranged," Pearl repeated. "If you behave yourself."

He stood his glass on the palm of his left hand and supported it with the fingers of his right. His fingers were white and flaccid, with well-manicured nails. The ring decorating the ring finger had a large black stone. Pearl raised his glass to his mouth, but he didn't down his whiskey in one, merely took a little sip. In order not to appear a complete savage, Chonkin did the same.

Pearl studied Chonkin through his glass, wondering how to begin the interrogation. Pearl's superiors, having received a report from him on the interrogation of Opalikov, wanted to know who Chonkin was and what use he could have been to Generalissimus Stalin. In case they might be helpful, the suggestions put forward by various people had been summarized: perhaps Chonkin wasn't actually Chonkin but Stalin's son Yakov Djugashvili, who had been hiding behind this name until the Soviet special services tracked him down; or perhaps he was one of the prominent Nazis who had gone on the run. At that time UFOlogy was still poorly developed, or perhaps it didn't even exist, but there was already a rumor that one night, somewhere in the Soviet occupation zone or, to be more precise, in the vicinity of Dresden, something had landed that was unlike anything ever seen before, or perhaps like a big flat griddle-cake, and this gave rise to the short-lived hypothesis that this Chonkin might possibly be an alien. A certain political analyst with a Polish name had put forward an absolutely fantastic conjecture. He said that Stalin was probably annoyed by the fact that his daughter Svetlana always chose Jews for her lovers and had decided to marry her off to a man of pure Russian stock, and no better candidate had been found for the bridegroom than Chonkin. If that had really been the case, the author himself would gladly have grasped at this thread, because it offers the glittering prospect of a genuinely fabulous twist in the plot: Ivan the

Fool marries the princess! But the author, being an unswervingly consistent adherent of the realist school, decisively rejected this theory, and it was eventually disproved by information gathered by both the Soviet and American intelligence services.

So, Chonkin sat there, facing Colonel Pearl, and Pearl sat there, watching him through his glass and grinning. None of the theories proposed seemed even slightly plausible to him, and he still hadn't come up with a way to conduct the interrogation, or a goal to achieve with his subject.

"Would you like to smoke?" he asked unexpectedly.

Chonkin had no objections to a smoke either. An open pack with a picture of a camel on it immediately appeared in front of him, together with a lighter bearing a picture of the same animal and an ashtray likewise adorned. Pearl took a small wooden box out of his jacket pocket and extracted a thick cigar and a small knife from it. He trimmed off both ends of the cigar and lit it with a match. He smacked his fat lips together and breathed out a cloud of smoke that concealed his face for a moment.

"Well then?" he said, smiling his strange smile as he emerged from the cloud. "How's life in general, Ivan Vasilievich?"

With a twist of the lips, a roll of the eyes, and a shrug of the shoulders, Chonkin indicated that in general life wasn't bad at all, thanks, he'd never had it so good: all on his own in a bright room with a spring bed with a soft mattress, a personal privy and shower, and three meals a day.

"You don't suffer from nostalgia?"

Chonkin decided that must be something to do with the nose and replied that he did have a cold.

"Well yes, yes," said Georgii Ivanovich, nodding eagerly. "In some people nostalgia starts as a cold but passes off quickly. In others, as Tsvetaeva wrote: Yearning for the homeland is a hocus-pocus that was exposed long ago. But that's a lyrical diversion, Ivan Vasilievich, and I'm not really interested in lyrical questions. I'm sure you'll tell me everything immediately without trying to keep even the slightest thing back. I hope very much that you won't try to be cunning with me, play cat and mouse, pretend to be a simpleminded fool, because that is quite simply useless. Well then, let me ask you the first question, the one most important for me: Who are you, Mister Chonkin?"

After pronouncing this strange phrase, Pearl looked Chonkin in the face with a tenacious, unblinking stare, and his own face immediately became harsh, unsmiling, and unfriendly. Chonkin was so surprised by the abruptness of the change that he goggled back at Pearl, staring straight into his eyes without blinking. And in this game of stare he proved the stronger, because Pearl was acting out the ruthless toughness of a military man, but Chonkin wasn't acting at all. He was simply surprised by the question and waiting for what would come next. Pearl lost the game of silent stare and so, trying to buck himself up, he repeated his question in a more nervous voice.

"Well, I asked you a question: Who are you, Chonkin?"

Chonkin sighed.

It wasn't the first time in his life that someone had asked him about something similar and demanded a straight answer with no dissembling or evasion, but experience had not improved his ability to find the right answers. Once again he was all at sea, but he tried to explain.

"Who am I, who am I. Why, Chonkin, of course!"

"Chonkin?" Pearl asked again. "Simply Chonkin and no one else?"

Not knowing what answer to give, Chonkin simply shrugged.

"All right. But then tell me why Generalissimus Stalin summoned you?"

Chonkin repeated his previous answer with the same movement of the shoulders.

"How is that possible?" Pearl asked, bewildered. "Let us accept that you don't know. But you might have a few ideas. Think for yourself, how could you have been useful to Stalin? Well? Do you have at least some kind of inkling in your head? What did he want from you?"

"How would I know what he wanted?" Chonkin protested ardently. "How could I know? I don't know him. I've only ever seen him in portraits, never in person."

Chonkin spoke sincerely, and George Pearl found his answers entirely convincing. But all the same, all the same, all the same, something had aroused Stalin's interest in Chonkin, and it wasn't possible that he didn't have any ideas of his own about that.

THE FIRST INTERROGATION SESSION went entirely successfully for Chonkin. Not only was he given whiskey, but they fed him lunch in the next room. A swanky lunch. They sat at a table covered with a starched tablecloth, with equally crisp napkins tucked onto their collars. And he and Georgii Ivanovich were served by Jessica, the same young black woman whom Pearl had promised to Chonkin, hinting that he wasn't making the promise for its own sake, but in return for a frankness which so far he had apparently failed to discern in what Chonkin had told him.

In the afternoon Chonkin, well fed and slightly tipsy, was taken back to the place where he lived. And in the morning he was brought to Mr. Pearl again. But this time Mr. Pearl greeted him sullenly, acted like a stranger, didn't offer him any whiskey, and spoke harshly, with threats and hints, something like this:

"Some people think that we Americans are freedom-loving, democratic, and humane, that is, too kind-hearted. Unfortunately not. We used to be very kind-hearted, but we saw that the world around us was cruel and unfriendly. We've made allowances for that. We've learned a thing or two from the Germans." This final phrase was a veiled threat, but it went unnoticed by Chonkin, because he took it to mean that Pearl had learned German from the Germans. It should be explained that the change in Pearl's mood was not fortuitous, but entirely deliberate, in accordance with the concept of good cop, bad cop. First the bad cop shouts at the subject of interrogation, threatens him with various unsanctioned methods of persuasion, and sometimes applies them. The subject becomes fearful and embittered and he clams up. Then the good cop comes in. The subject relaxes and opens his heart to him. So Pearl was good cop and bad cop in a single person. He had used this method on many people he had interrogated, with some considerable success. Good today, bad tomorrow, good again the day after tomorrow. That was how he behaved with Chonkin. One day, when Pearl was good, he fed Chonkin drink, gave him cigarettes, showed him pornographic postcards with pictures of other girls, and promised that they could be available to Chonkin in the flesh. And the next day he was bad, unapproachable, didn't give Chonkin any treats, and intimidated him with threats of appalling punishments. On one of these days, when he was bad, he put Chonkin through a lie detector test.

Chonkin passed the test easily, but that didn't convince Pearl of anything. From his experience with Soviet spies and defectors, he had learned that, having grown up surrounded by lies since they were in diapers, they could deceive any lie detector without the slightest effort. On the other hand, as soon as they tried to tell the truth, the detector immediately overheated and broke down. Naturally, the search for the truth was not limited to the interrogations conducted by Georgii Ivanovich. The answer to the question Who is Chonkin? was sought, on Pearl's orders, by dozens of American secret agents. They uncovered certain facts from Chonkin's previous life—in particular, the records of Chonkin's trial at the beginning of the war at which it had been alleged that this name was a cover for a Prince Golitsyn. George Pearl was delighted by this discovery, but it was soon demolished by the real Prince Vadim Anatolievich Golitsyn. After being liberated from the Berlin zoo by the Americans, the prince testified that he was personally acquainted with Chonkin, had shared a home with him in the forest, knew of the legend that had ascribed the title of prince to him, and knew the origins of that legend. It derived from the fact that during the Russian Civil War, a certain Lieutenant Golitsyn had been quartered with Chonkin's mother, from which fact idle gossips had later drawn certain conclusions. But the problem was that the lieutenant was Vadim Anatolievich's cousin, Sergei, who couldn't possibly have been Chonkin's father. That possibility was absolutely excluded by a wound he had suffered at the front. Vadim Golitsyn's testimony was implicitly corroborated by the former Soviet chairman of the court martial, Colonel Dobrenky. After the Victory he had been discovered in the army of General Vlasov, and was later handed over to the Soviet authorities and hanged. But until the Americans handed him over, Dobrenky had tried to oblige them. He had testified that Chonkin's case was an absolute fake, invented from beginning to end by the prosecutor Evpraksein, and that Chonkin's princely origins had not been confirmed by any facts. The only authentic fact was that Chonkin had worked in a stable before, during, and after the war. Colonel Opalikov also had insisted on that, and what he said had been confirmed by a surprise witness from the American side—the driver John, with whom Chonkin used to converse across the river and who was now attached to Chonkin in the capacity of something like a chambermaid.

Eventually Georgii Ivanovich was left with no doubts that Chonkin was Chonkin, a simple country lad, a driver and groom, and no one else. But even so, Mr. Pearl was tormented by the riddle that remained unsolved, and every now and then, not during interrogations but in what might be termed friendly conversations, he suggested that Chonkin think about what Stalin might have wanted him for. But what could Chonkin say? Nothing. For a long time he made a conscientious effort, but he couldn't think of anything cleverer than the conjecture (which he himself realized was absurd), that perhaps they needed someone in the Kremlin who could take care of horses.

21

CHONKIN'S CONJECTURE AMUSED MR. PEARL greatly, but it didn't seem so funny to Colonel Opalikov. It was perfectly possible, he told Pearl, that Stalin had required a qualified groom and that was what Chonkin was, if you stretched the meaning a bit.

"What for?" asked Pearl, puzzled. "What would your Stalin want a groom for? If he wanted a groom, he could have made Marshal Budyonny his groom."

"Very witty," said Opalikov, "but my reasoning is based on a premise that I won't reveal to you now, because you wouldn't understand it."

"Why wouldn't I understand it?" asked Pearl, almost offended. "It seems to me that I'm not that stupid. If I were very stupid, I would hardly have been accepted to work in intelligence."

Opalikov didn't say anything to that, but he chuckled to himself. In the course of his life he had met Soviet, and now non-Soviet, intelligence and counterintelligence agents, and he didn't think very highly of the intellect of any of them. Nonetheless, George Pearl was the person whom Opalikov informed that he wanted to address the American military and the world community with an announcement that would astound them all.

"What kind of sensational announcement could that be?"

"A genuinely sensational one," Opalikov confirmed. "But I can't tell you any of the details yet."

"No? Why not?"

"Because it will sound like nonsense to you and your secret service will shelve it or, even worse, classify it so strictly that no one will ever find out about it."

"And whom do you want to find out about it?"

"I," Opalikov said firmly, "want everyone to find out about it. The whole world."

"That's impossible," Pearl objected. "Before we can make your discovery public . . ."

"It's not mine."

"All the more so, then. Before making it public, we have to study it ourselves, have it run through by experts, and decide if it's worth revealing."

"It's worth it," Opalikov said firmly. "And I'm going to reveal it with you or without you."

"As you wish," Pearl agreed. "But even so, if you're counting on our support, can't you tell me what it's about, what it concerns?"

"All right," Opalikov agreed, "I'll give you a hint. It concerns the mysterious parentage of Joseph Stalin . . ."

"So that's it!" Pearl leaned back in his chair and put his hands behind his head. "And just what is so mysterious about the parentage of your Stalin? Everybody knows that he's the son of a shoemaker and a simple Georgian woman . . . I've forgotten what her name is."

"That's what you think."

"That's what everybody knows."

"But I know something about this which, I assure you, will astound the entire world."

Naturally, Mr. Pearl didn't put a lot of faith in the seriousness of this secret that the former Soviet colonel intended to reveal to the world. Pearl wasn't interested in jaw-dropping, sensational revelations, but in the ordinary military secrets to which the colonel had access, that is, the number of the unit, the number of aircraft, their design, speed, load capacity, bomb load, armaments, and navigational equipment. These were the simple things that interested the intelligence agent George Pearl, and he had received exhaustive replies to his questions on these matters. The parentage of the Soviet dictator might perhaps arouse some people's curiosity, but it would be of no interest whatever to the intelligence service.

Owing to the nature of his work, Pearl had met many very different people in the course of his life, including madmen trying to promote their own discoveries and inventions, starting with perpetual motion devices and ending with the same. Opalikov, however, did not seem like a madman and therefore, despite certain doubts, Pearl sent a report of his conversation with the colonel to Mr. Allen Dulles in Washington. Sometime later he received approval to hold a large press conference devoted to Opalikov's announcement, with reporters from the major and not so major Western newspapers attending and also, by special invitation, biologists of the kind not yet called geneticists, who were nevertheless already investigating questions of inheritance.

22

NOT HAVING RECEIVED ANY RESPONSE from the American authorities, TASS issued a more serious statement which spoke in a distinctly unfriendly tone about the aircraft and its crew being detained by force. The American ambassador in Moscow, George Kennan, was summoned to the Ministry of Foreign Affairs, where he was handed a note of protest. Both sides tried not to fan the flames of scandal, but the tension caused between the U.S.A. and the U.S.S.R. was so serious that at the Potsdam Conference, Stalin appealed in person to the U.S. president, Mr. Harry Truman, to return the plane and its crew to the U.S.S.R.

The circumstances of this conversation, which is not recorded anywhere, were approximately as follows. During an interval in the proceedings of the conference, which the Americans called a coffee break, Harry Truman, with a cup of espresso in his hand, approached Joseph Stalin and suggested that they take a stroll around the park adjacent to the palace where the conference was taking place. Stalin readily agreed. They went out into the park, where low pine trees were growing, roses were blooming, squirrels were scampering about, and butterflies were fluttering through the warm air.

Here Truman took his colleague by the elbow and said: "Marshal Stalin, I have a little something to tell you that I think will not be pleasant for you to hear."

"Oh, come now!" Stalin assured him. "Conversing with such a great man as you brings me a pleasure that no unpleasant subject could possibly diminish."

"I thank you with all my heart," said Truman, setting his hand on his chest. "I can say the same about you, Mr. Marshal. But what I wanted to say to you is this. At the previous meeting I listened with immense gratitude to your declaration of preparedness to assist us in crushing the Japanese militarists. It was very touching. But I think that at the present stage there is no need for you to join the war against the Japanese monster. Your country has already suffered prodigious losses in the war with Germany. You face the huge job of restoring the destruction left by the war. Why would you want unnecessary casualties?"

Stalin listened to his colleague with a gentle smile on his face and his head bowed respectfully. "You are absolutely right," he said. "Our losses in the war have, quite frankly, been prodigious, but we Russian people value the brotherhood of the front line and our responsibilities to the Alliance, for our Allies we are prepared to give even more."

Truman took note of the words "we Russian people" and was slightly surprised, since he had heard from the deceased President Roosevelt that Stalin was Georgian. But Stalin's protests did not surprise him. He understood that it was not a matter of brotherhood or the obligations of an Ally, but of Stalin's desire to be involved in the final stage of the war with Japan—not in order to help his Allies, but in order to grab his own slice of the pie.

"Yes," thought Stalin, "we won't let you have our slice of the pie." And he imagined the pie in the form of a map of Japan showing the territories that it controlled: Manchuria, Port Arthur, the Kuril Islands, and the half of Sakhalin that was taken from the Russians in 1905. Naturally, Stalin understood what Truman was thinking when he tried to persuade Stalin not to get involved in the war, and Truman understood what Stalin was thinking when he insisted on becoming involved, but their conversation continued despite this.

"Believe me, dear Marshal, I value most highly your generous offer and the readiness of your people for further sacrifices, but at the present time there is no need for them. And by the way, I would like to share with you, in confidence, a piece of news which you might perhaps find interesting."

"That's curious," said Stalin. "It seems to me that I am a well-informed individual and know all the news that is worth knowing."

"I hope you don't know this news yet," Truman chuckled. "I won't beat about the bush, but tell you straight out: our scientists have invented and created a weapon of immense destructive power, and in a few days' time this weapon will be used against Japan, after which, I assure you, Japan will be brought to its knees immediately. So your sacrifices would simply be pointless. What do you think about that?"

"I think," said Stalin, unfastening the top button of his linen tunic, "that it is getting hot. Why don't we take a stroll along that avenue? There is more shade there."

"Very well," Truman agreed and added, jesting, "You see, I accept your proposals unconditionally."

They both laughed, after which Stalin said that he also had a little request, so little that he, the effective head of state, felt rather awkward asking the head of another state about it, but . . . "You have probably been informed that a Soviet plane made a forced landing at an American air base."

Truman, of course, lied and said that he had not heard anything about it. Stalin, naturally, did not believe him, but was obliged to pretend that he did, and he told Truman a brief version of the story, according to which a Soviet Il-10 plane had lost its bearings entirely by accident and made a forced landing at an American air base. The American authorities were holding the plane, the pilot, and the gunner-cum-radio operator illegally, so could Truman possibly intervene in this matter and return the plane and its crew to their homeland?

"Very well, very well," Truman promised. "I'll give orders for this matter to be looked into, but now I remember that I have heard something about this after all. I remember I was told that your plane, Mr. Marshal, did not lose its bearings and could not have lost its bearings, because it simply flew across a narrow river and, as I was informed, your pilot apparently requested political asylum from our authorities."

"So what?" said Stalin. "What does it matter who asks for what? Refuse."

Truman stopped and took hold of a button on Stalin's field jacket in a very familiar manner. Stalin did not like it. Nobody dared to treat him like that. Not even Churchill.

"Marshal Stalin," Truman said in an agitated voice. "Please understand me correctly. I cannot grant your request."

"Get your hand off my button," Stalin shrieked and snorted in indignation. Truman recoiled in fright. He had heard that Allen Dulles had received a report about a strange habit of Stalin's: in a fit of extreme indignation he sometimes snorted like a horse.

"Sit down," said Stalin, pulling himself together and pointing to the nearest bench. "Calm down and think what you're saying. You grant the pilot's request, but you can't grant mine? He's a nobody!"

"He," said Truman, "is a colonel of yours. A Hero of the Soviet Union!"

"So what? I'm a Hero of the Soviet Union too. What if I request political asylum?"

"You?" Truman felt disoriented and even broke into a light sweat at this suggestion, although he realized that it had not been made seriously. Of course, like any naive American (and all Americans, even presidents, are naive), he was certain that all non-Americans wanted to become Americans and would become Americans if the opportunity for them to do so should arise. And naturally, Marshal Stalin would also have liked to become an American, only he did not have the opportunity, because he would have to leave two children behind in Russia. But even so . . .

"If you were to apply for political asylum," Truman said with a smile that made it clear this was all a mere joke, "your application would probably be considered on a priority basis."

"I don't doubt it," Stalin agreed quite seriously, "but I am a patriot and I wouldn't swap my homeland for your hamburgers. Colonel Opalikov, however, is a traitor. You Americans are very fond of traitors and defectors who go over to your side. You don't understand that treason should never be encouraged. A man who has betrayed his own country will betray someone else's even more readily. Well anyway, all right. Take this traitor, you can even keep the plane, but I ask you, please, please return the gunner and radio operator."

Truman said that he would gladly return the plane, but as for the gunner, or whatever he was, although he had not requested political asylum, he didn't seem in a rush to go home either. Stalin started losing his temper and snorting again: what's the difference, he asked, whether he's in a rush or not in a rush, I'm asking you to hand him over, so hand him over. Truman apologized, laying his hand on his heart, and explained that the Constitution of the United States did not allow him to deprive a man of the right to political asylum. And if he violated the Constitution, Congress would interfere in the matter.

"Imagine," said Truman, "that you have violated your Constitution, what would the Supreme Soviet do to you then?"

"What would the Supreme Soviet do to me?" Stalin asked, and when he imagined what the Supreme Soviet would do to him, or what he would do to the Supreme Soviet, he started laughing and neighing, almost literally, and jerking his right foot as if he were trying to lash out and kick someone. Truman looked at the leader of the Kremlin and asked quietly if Marshal Stalin required medical assistance. The interpreter replied stiffly that Comrade Stalin's health was always excellent and doctors had no business going anywhere near him.

AT THIS TIME A LOUD BELL RANG in the palace where the conference was taking place and both leaders hurried back to the meeting hall, where they reached agreement on many things, but not on what they had discussed in the park. On that point no agreement was reached, so after the session they both hurried to their residences, and from his residence Truman sent an order to the U.S. Air Force to expedite the dropping of the atom bomb on Hiroshima, while on his part Marshal Stalin called Marshal Malinovsky and ordered him to make urgent preparations to advance against the Japanese army in Kwantung, which had to be routed before the Americans did it.

Despite all these events George Pearl, aka Georgii Ivanovich, spent a little more time on Chonkin, not interrogating him any longer, but simply acting as his mentor. And he grew strangely attached to him. He had spent so much time associating with wily, insincere individuals that the more he saw of simple, ingenuous Chonkin without a single devious notion in his head, the more he liked him.

24

ONE DAY, TOWARD EVENING, Pearl came to Chonkin's place carrying a large sack. He tipped its contents out on the bed. They included a new two-piece civilian suit with dark-gray jacket and trousers, and there were also a light-colored shirt, a maroon tie, and a pair of black shoes. The trousers had suspenders instead of a belt. Pearl told him to get changed immediately. Even in his wildest dreams Chonkin could never have imagined that someday he would try on classy clothing like this. His fingers, which could do so many things, fiddled with the buttons for a long time, and he had absolutely no idea what to do with the suspenders and the tie. He had to turn to Georgii Ivanovich for help, which Pearl gave him and then led him over to the large mirror in the hallway. Chonkin couldn't believe that the elegant young man he saw reflected in the mirror had any connection with him. Pearl was pleased, too.

"Well, Vanya, you're quite the prime minister! All right, let's go, they're waiting for us."

"Who is?" Chonkin asked.

"You'll see."

A large automobile with an American flag on its hood was standing outside the building. Pearl opened one rear door and let Chonkin in. He got into the back seat from the other side and told the driver: "Let's go."

They drove into the town, wound to and fro through a few streets, and stopped in front of a large gray building with rough walls and two white columns at the entrance. There was a crowd of journalists armed with cameras standing there. When they spotted Chonkin climbing out of the car, they rushed toward him like vultures to carrion. Flashlights flared blindingly and the air was filled with the smell of burned magnesium. Chonkin turned away from one flash and was caught in another. Simultaneously with the flashes he was showered with questions in English, which he didn't understand, and questions in Russian, which he was thoroughly sick of.

"Mr. Chonkin, who are you? What did Generalissimus Stalin want from you?"

"Mr. Chonkin, what do you think about human rights in the Soviet Union?"

"Mr. Chonkin, are you going to request political asylum?"

"Mr. Chonkin, are you a member of the Communist Party?"

"Keep quiet!" Pearl told Chonkin in a whisper. "Don't answer any questions."

Pearl went first, shouldering his way through the crowd and dragging Chonkin after him, like a tug towing a ship. Inside, at the entrance to a spacious foyer, two marines asked them to show their ID and open their briefcases and purses. Chonkin didn't have a briefcase or a purse, and Pearl showed some ID for him.

They pushed their way through into a large hall with a stage and rows of chairs sloping down toward it. There were sheets of paper with the word "Reserved" on them lying on the chairs in the front row. Pearl removed two sheets of paper from chairs in the center of the row, sat Chonkin down, and then sat down beside him. There was a table on the stage covered with red cloth, with a carafe and four glasses standing on it—it reminded Ivan Chonkin of his time in the army before the war, when they were herded into a hall almost exactly like this one (only smaller) on February 23, May 1, November 7, and December 5 to listen to yet another public holiday lecture. There was a table covered with red cloth there too, and a carafe on the table, and a lectern beside the table, and two portraits—on the right and the left of the stage. There were two portraits here too, only not of Lenin and Stalin, like there, but Stalin and Stalin. Which rather surprised Chonkin.

He had thought they didn't have much respect for Stalin here. It turned out that they didn't respect Lenin, they hadn't hung up a single portrait of him, but they did respect Stalin, and how! They'd stuck him up on both sides, so that people sitting on the right and people sitting on the left all had a good view. So they wouldn't have to twist their necks unnecessarily.

The public was allowed in and flowed down into the hall in two even streams from the doors at the back, filling it completely. There weren't even enough chairs for some and they took up positions in the aisles and on the false windowsills. But the stage remained empty and people in the hall started getting nervous, whispering impatiently and clapping.

Suddenly four men emerged from the wings and stood behind the table in a row: one in an American general's uniform and three in civilian clothes. Chonkin barely recognized the civilian standing in second place after the general as Colonel Opalikov. It was hard to recognize him because before, Chonkin had seen the colonel only in military uniform with his medals or in a leather flying jacket, and couldn't possibly have imagined him in any other kind of attire. In uniform he had looked like a substantial, large man, but in civilian dress he looked small and insignificant. The men who had walked out to the table paused for a moment and sat down, and then the gaunt man in a gray suit on Opalikov's left stood up again and spoke to the audience.

"Ladies and gentlemen, you will now be addressed by Mr. Sergei Opalikov, a former Soviet airman, a colonel, who, as you already know, flew across from the Soviet occupation zone into the territory controlled by the Allied forces. I don't know what he is going to talk about, but I hope you will not find it boring."

Opalikov got up from the table and stood at the lectern. His face was pale. He was clearly nervous, and that surprised Chonkin, too. Chonkin had always thought that important people like that never got nervous, but Opalikov was nervous. Probably if he'd been wearing his military uniform with the Gold Star of a Hero of the Soviet Union, he would have been less nervous. He spent a long time sorting through his papers at the lectern, and even from a distance it was obvious that his hands were trembling.

"Ladies and gentlemen," Opalikov began, and his voice wasn't commanding, the way it used to be, but quiet and not military at all. "As you obviously know, the soldier Ivan Chonkin and I recently flew from the Soviet occupation zone in Germany to the American zone in an Il-10 warplane. This fact was widely reported in your Western newspapers. Some elements of the gutter press, unable to find a logical explanation for my action, announced to the world that I had done this because my wife had slept with the commander of my air force division, General

Prosyanoi. But that, ladies and gentlemen, is absolute nonsense. My wife has slept with many people, and she is not the only person I have slept with, and such a trivial reason could never have been the motive for my dramatic decision. After all, if your wife sleeps with someone else, it is easier to change your wife than your homeland."

The audience liked this remark of the colonel's and responded with a double burst of applause: those who understood Russian applauded first, and then the others, who had waited for the translation.

"The respectable newspapers," Opalikov continued, "showed greater understanding of the crux of the matter by interpreting my defection, quite correctly, as a political act, as a sign of my profound disenchantment with the Soviet system. I do genuinely dislike the Soviet regime, because within it, under the leadership of Stalin, monstrous crimes are committed against the people. But this was still not the main reason for what I did. The main reason was a secret that I kept to myself for a long time, knowing that I must reveal it to the entire world or I would come to despise myself. The secret was revealed to me about ten years ago by my uncle on my mother's side, the well-known Soviet traveler, geographer, zoologist, and entomologist Grigorii Efimovich Grom-Grimeilo. Apart from his generally known works, my uncle Grisha also kept a secret journal, but in 1936 it disappeared, it was stolen from his safe. My uncle was terribly upset and afraid. He suspected that the journal had fallen into the hands of those people to whom he would least of all have wanted to show it. He invited me to take a stroll in the park and told me: 'Seryozha, my manuscript has disappeared. If it has fallen into the hands of . . . you're a grown-up now, you understand who I mean . . . if it has fallen into their hands, I don't have long to live. But if you ever happen to find yourself abroad, that is, beyond the bounds of the omnipotent power of these people I am thinking of, I ask you to publicize what I am about to tell you as widely as possible after my death.' A week after our conversation my uncle died under mysterious circumstances. I suspect that he was poisoned.

"His secret was genuinely so important and astounding that even then, when I was still a beardless youth, I started thinking about making my escape from the concentration camp called the Soviet Union. I became an airman with the idea that someday this profession might help me to get across to the West. And now, at last, I am here and can carry out my late uncle Grisha's request. The announcement that I am about to make may perhaps seem incredible and fantastic to you. But I beg you, before you say that it is impossible, think, assemble the facts, and only then decide to reject or to take on trust what I am about to tell you. But first of all, here is a question for all of you in the audience. Who is depicted in these portraits?"

Chonkin took another look at the portraits and said to himself: "It's obvious, Stalin."

The hall immediately started buzzing and droning, someone somewhere started laughing, regarding the very question as humorous, because the answer was so obvious. Then there was a scattering of answers, and some of the voices sounded irritated.

"Stalin, Stalin. Of course it's Stalin."

"Stalin," Chonkin repeated to himself. "Who else?"

"Right," Opalikov responded. "The portrait on the left really does show Generalissimus Stalin. But when you say the portrait on the right is also Stalin, you are mistaken. Look more closely: he's wearing the uniform of a tsarist general, not a Soviet generalissimus, and that is not a joke by the artist. Because the person depicted here, ladies and gentlemen, is not Stalin, but my uncle Grisha's teacher, another well-known traveler, geographer, zoologist, and natural scientist, General Nikolai Mikhailovich Przhevalsky."

"No, really?" someone exclaimed in the hall.

"That just can't be!" someone else protested.

"Ah, but it can!" Opalikov replied. "There's absolutely no doubt about it. Let me tell you immediately, ladies and gentlemen, that the unusual similarity between Stalin and Przhevalsky was noticed by some people a very long time ago, this is no incredible new discovery of mine. Since long ago many researchers have expressed, even in writing (you can find it in the appropriate publications) the idea that the Soviet dictator's real father was the Russian general Przhevalsky, and not the Georgian shoemaker Djugashvili. There is a huge amount of direct and circumstantial evidence to support this view.

"It is well known that some time before Stalin's birth General Przhevalsky passed through the town of Gori on his travels and could have entered into a relationship with the young mountain woman Keke Djugashvili (her maiden name was Geladze). However, there are certain things that don't fit in this theory. The dates of Przhevalsky's presence in Gori and the date of Soso Djugashvili's birth don't match up. The difference between them is a little over a year. Some Soviet researchers have explained Keke's year-long pregnancy by the fact that such an unusual man as Stalin could not be carried to term in the standard nine months, and nature made an exception for genius. Serious scientists realized that this was nonsense. But although they realized that, they couldn't find the answer to the riddle.

"Although that answer was obvious, no one but Grigorii Efimovich Grom-Grimeilo had the courage even to approach it. In fact, my uncle understood very well what would happen to him if he revealed his secret prematurely. That was why he entrusted it to me, hoping that someday..."

At this point Opalikov started coughing and apologized to the audience, saying that he had a tickle in his throat. Some kind of attendant, who looked like a secretary bird, promptly appeared beside the lectern, handed the speaker a glass of water, and walked away without making a sound, bending the knees of his thin legs at right angles, like a cricket.

"Well then," said Opalikov, "my uncle Grigorii Efimovich Grom-Grimeilo..."

The author thinks it appropriate to interrupt Colonel Opalikov's talk at this point and warn the reader that the colonel's stories about Grigorii Efimovich Grom-Grimeilo and Nikolai Mikhailovich Przhevalsky have not been confirmed by any proofs or documents known to the world of science and therefore any doubts concerning their veracity are entirely justified. Perhaps the colonel was a dreamer, perhaps he had gone mad, or it is perfectly possible that he was playing to the gallery. Perhaps he was simply trying to arrange a bit of PR for himself, as they say nowadays; we can only guess, but we cannot conceal from the reader the theory proposed by the colonel, so let him speak.

"Well then," said Opalikov, "my uncle Grigorii Efimovich Grom-Grimeilo, having visited the places that Przhevalsky had passed through before him, after studying Nikolai Mikhailovich's diaries and questioning numerous witnesses, became firmly convinced that General Przhevalsky, and not the shoemaker Djugashvili, was indeed Stalin's father."

"But so what?" shouted a dishevelled individual, jumping to his feet in the middle of the hall. "So he became convinced. You yourself said that other people already knew that before your uncle."

"Yes," Opalikov confirmed, "other people did know that before my uncle. But my uncle's discovery was that Stalin's mother was not Keke Djugashvili, no, not Keke at all, but a horse, a horse, a horse," he repeated, like a scratched gramophone record, "a Przhevalsky horse..."

At this point everybody noticed that something rather unpleasant was happening to the colonel. He suddenly turned as white as a sheet, which could be seen even from the back rows. Large drops of sweat suddenly sprang out on his forehead, which was already glistening, and rolled down across his face, which jerked and twisted into a strange grimace. The colonel started foaming at the mouth and his fingers started tapping rapidly on the lectern, as if he were beating out a drum roll. He grabbed hold of his own throat as if he were trying to strangle himself and started slithering down behind the lectern, as if he were concealing himself behind it in a game of hide and seek. But suddenly he tumbled out from behind the lectern onto his side and froze. At first no one understood a thing. Then the hall erupted into a general hubbub, with everyone jumping up off their seats. The men at the table ran across to the man lying on the stage. The general leaned down over him. He straightened up and asked the audience if there was a doctor in the house. Immediately three men who said they were doctors climbed up on the stage. They bent down over the motionless body. One felt the pulse on the colonel's neck, another slapped him on the cheeks, and the third lifted up his eyelids. Finally the oldest of them, with a little gray beard, got up off his knees and, turning to the hall, announced in a loud voice:

"This man is dead."

25

MANY YEARS LATER, while collecting material for this book, the author rummaged through the archives of the Hoover Institute and read old newspapers in the Library of Congress. He leafed through the bound copies or examined the microfilms of almost all the respectable newspapers of those days: the *Washington Post,* the *New York Times,* the *Times,* the *Guardian,* and *Le Monde,* as well as several less respectable newspapers; and he came across the story of Colonel Opalikov's public talk and death.

Concerning Stalin's origins, all the respectable papers without exception mentioned the theory proposed in Opalikov's talk—if they mentioned it at all—with a certain irony softened, perhaps, by the fact of the speaker's death. But all the newspapers of what we call the yellow (or gutter) press dwelt on the subject and informed their readers, as an absolutely incontestable fact, that a horse had given birth to the Soviet dictator Stalin. They even found a photo of a Przhevalsky horse somewhere and compared it with portraits of Stalin, discovering many similarities.

They claimed that in full face he looked like his daddy, and in profile he was like his mommy.

These same newspapers, which regard the checking of facts as an optional extra, also claimed in one voice that the colonel had been poisoned. Here are some of the headlines: "Death of a Defector," "The Long Arms of the Kremlin," "The Kremlin Stamps Its Hoof." Why the colonel was poisoned and on whose orders was not hard to guess, but who actually poisoned him? Of course, they remembered the man resembling a secretary bird who handed Opalikov a glass of water during his talk. But no one had any idea who he was, how he got into the wings of the stage, where he got the water from, and where he himself went afterward—and the police failed to discover anything. The serious publications, afraid of publishing unverified facts, merely informed their readers that the colonel's body was subjected to a post mortem by a group of forensic pathologists led by Professor Fisher. The doctors' conclusion was that death occurred as a result of a heart attack that could be explained by the agitated state of the deceased during his unusual lecture. Naturally, the author of these lines, being a highly depraved individual, was inclined to believe the yellow press rather than the red press or any other but, like all other depraved individuals, the author had no proof until 1954, when the *Süddeutsche Zeitung,* under the title "I Killed Opalikov," published an interview with a Soviet spy who had defected.

This man told the story of how Lavrentii Pavlovich Beria in person had handed him an ampoule containing a highly toxic liquid with no color, taste, or smell that had been developed by the chemists of the NKVD, and told him to "kill the creep." Dissolved in a glass of water, the poison caused immediate paralysis of the heart and instantly decomposed, which was what had misled the forensic scientists who performed the colonel's autopsy. Since Opalikov had been dead for ages and the entire story was lost in the mists of time, the defector's confessions failed to make much of an impression on anyone. But one newspaper at least did comment that since Opalikov had been poisoned while telling his sensational story, it meant that the subject was not to someone's liking, which meant there was something in it that deserved special attention. But even this suggestion was only made very tentatively by the journalist. And in general, the entire theory was somehow left hanging in the air and I too did not believe it for a long time—not the poisoning, that is, but the reason for it, that a horse could give birth to a man, even such a ghoulishly abhorrent man as the late generalissimus had been.

Imagine, then, my amazement . . . By the way, I really dislike that overused, threadbare phrase "imagine my amazement," but my amazement was indeed so great that it seemed to be quite boundless. It overwhelmed me in the archive of the Hoover Institute, where I came across a bundle of letters from someone unknown to someone else unknown. They were battered, yellow sheets of paper with damaged edges, held together by a rusty paper clip, with a strange text written in a bad hand with an indelible pencil, that is, with a writing instrument the very existence of which is only remembered nowadays by old men like myself. The letters of the text, originally purple, had faded very badly over the period of the manuscript's existence. I never did find out for whom these letters were intended, and there is no certainty concerning the author's identity. I can surmise that he was in fact our great scientist Grom-Grimeilo. But I would not be surprised if serious scientists, applying the latest research methods such as graphology, spectral analysis, and other little tricks that modern science has up its sleeve, were to discover that this manuscript is nothing more than a skillful forgery.

In Russia, thank God, we are well used to forgeries like that. Let us recall *The Lay of the Host of Igor, The Appeal of Daniil Zatochnik, The Legend of the City of Kitezh.* If these things were, as some scholars assert, forged by someone, then why not forge the letters of Grom-Grimeilo? Especially since the person who might do that would presumably have a more serious reason for it than the forgers of ancient manuscripts. Hatred of a tyrant could have driven the unknown author to extreme lengths of artifice and invention.

But if this is the case, it must be admitted that the forger possessed an absolutely remarkable imagination and great talent. His story is filled with details that seem to me quite impossible to invent. And also, if we decide, after all, to trust the author and assume that he was indeed Grom-Grimeilo, we should not forget that he was a younger contemporary, follower, and biographer of Nikolai Mikhailovich Przhevalsky. He went to the places where Przhevalsky had been, which are described in the above-mentioned letters. One argument for the letters' authenticity was that they contained many of the author's own scientific observations, which I shall simply omit and tell you about the part that so amazed me.

In describing Przhevalsky's journey through Mongolia and northwest China, the author of the letters makes several acute remarks concerning the famous traveler's personality. "Przhevalsky," he writes, "despite his noble origins and corresponding education, was a blunt individual, sometimes even coarse and despotic. He felt uncomfortable in human company. He did not like people of his own social level because, so he claimed, they were all mired in depravity. Unlike the majority of his contemporaries, who had read too much Nekrasov, he was not fond of the peasants either, regarding them as drunkards and idlers. His education was one-sided. He was fascinated by the natural sciences and history, but he was indifferent to music, painting, and the theater, he didn't read stories, novellas, or novels and absolutely hated women. He loved animals, but only wild ones. He despised domesticated animals that served man, ate from his hands, and meekly offered up their throats to the knife. But he respected wild animals for their free, independent temperament, for the fact that they obtained their own food and didn't swap their freedom for the scraps from man's table. At the same time, from the days of his youth he had been inclined toward a romantic view of reality. In his childhood he read the Greek myths with fascination."

The myth of the existence of creatures that were half-man, half-horse, that is, centaurs, made an especially deep and lasting impression on him. His childhood drawings were devoted to this creature spawned by the imagination of the ancient Greeks. When he was already a famous traveler, geographer, zoologist, entomologist, and God only knows what else, he maintained an unflagging interest in the problems of hybridization of living creatures, above all the creation of a hybrid of man and one of the higher mammals, to which he devoted numerous experiments.

At one time here in Russia, great, indeed excessive, emphasis was laid on the general precedence of Russian science, on how Russians had invented everything before anyone else. These assertions were so obsessive that they gave rise to numerous jokes and sayings, such as "Russia is the motherland of elephants." It was taken to absurd lengths—supposedly X-rays had been invented by the fourteenth-century Russian peasant who told his wife: "I can see right through you!"

"But I," writes the author of the letters, "do not have the slightest doubt that in the field of hybridization Nikolai Przhevalsky far outstripped his Western contemporaries."

At that time the Austrian monk Gregor Mendel had only just conducted his first hesitant experiments in crossing lentils with beans, and the words "genetics" and "chromosome" had not entered scientific usage, but our great scientist set about conducting experiments to create a hybrid of man with a higher mammal. Science was still in an undeveloped state and even artificial insemination was a thing of the future.

The experiments had to be carried out using entirely natural techniques, which the reader can imagine for himself. At first the general wanted to involve his orderly Ferapont in this work, but he proved to be too religious, high-strung, and conservative. When the suggestion was made, he became hysterical and started waving his hands about.

"Holy God! No, Your Excellency, you can do what you like: flog me, shoot me, but I'll never agree to commit sins like that."

The general was forced to set his own hand to the plow, so to speak. And in total secrecy, because he was afraid of the consequences if he were found out. (Let us note in parentheses that the society of that time was still dominated by backward views on the matter of sex and governed by imperfect criminal legislation. Nowadays, of course, people take a broader view of things. In the more advanced countries, single-sex marriages are already permitted and I am sure that in the near future mixed families of humans and animals will be legalized and granted equal rights. Beginning with the very highest animals, and then with the others, including fish, reptiles, and insects. But when Przhevalsky was alive, so-called bestiality was regarded by everyone as a terrible sin and a crime, and it was severely punished. So in conducting his experiments, Nikolai Mikhailovich was risking not only his personal reputation in society, but his freedom.) For him, however, the claims of science were always uppermost. He took the risk and copulated selflessly with all the species of wild animals that he discovered. With a female coney-eating bear, a wild she-ass, and a female wild camel, but always remembering the centaurs, he concentrated his efforts on the wild horse to which he gave his name.

The general discovered the Przhevalsky horse in the steppe, in the border region between China and Mongolia. There was a small herd of wild and aggressive horses that would not allow any other animals to approach them. One filly Nikolai Mikhailovich especially liked was cut from the herd and captured with some difficulty. Przhevalsky called her She-Eagle for her large eyes and impetuous character, and the way she flew over the steppe as if on wings. She was a very beautiful, free-spirited, wild, and skittish creature. At first she clearly didn't find the general attractive. Driven into a special stall, she tried to break free, bucking, biting, and snapping the ropes. Nikolai Mikhailovich had no respect for females of the human species (although he enjoyed great success with them). But he courted She-Eagle very gallantly, fed her the finest oats, gave her Swiss chocolate as a treat, bathed her, combed out her mane, and decorated her with wild flowers. He spoke tender words to her, thereby indicating that he did not at all consider her a lower creature than himself, and eventually he melted the proud animal's heart. And his own was completely melted, too.

In his intimate diary he confessed that his scientific experiments were bringing him ever greater pleasure. She-Eagle also became attached to the general. She greeted him with a joyful whinny and no longer tried to break out of the pen where she was kept to prevent her from being covered by some passing stallion, which would invalidate the experiment. The diary entries mention that the lead stallion of the herd, Maurice, who was jealous over She-Eagle, constantly hung about near the pen, and one day at dawn even smashed out the bars, but he was driven away in time by the groom Mironich. In fact, for a while it was not clear if he had been driven away in time or not. Maurice might have managed to ruin the experiment while the groom was still sleeping (Mironich never admitted to having been asleep). In any case, the stallion died shortly afterward. Driven insane with jealousy, one day he attacked Przhevalsky and the general shot him in self-defense (or perhaps also out of jealousy).

Some time went by and She-Eagle was found to be pregnant, which excited the experimenter greatly. Could the event he had dreamed of with such passion really have come to pass, was she really pregnant by him? Was she really carrying his child? But there was still a lingering suspicion that Maurice might have been responsible, during his single break-in. We should remember that a mare's pregnancy usually lasts about a year. In those days people had no conception of ultrasound, there was no way to check in advance what was maturing in the mare's womb. We can only imagine the state of agitation in which the general passed that year. And then, finally, it happened . . . at night. Ferapont woke up the general with his cry:

"Your Excellency, the lady's in labor!"

"What lady?" the general asked drowsily.

"The lady, your little mare-wife, Your Excellency."

The general dashed to the stable, even forgetting to fasten on his sword. He got there just in time to deliver the child. The newborn fell straight into the general's hands and he started examining it with hasty curiosity. No, it definitely wasn't a foal. Not even a centaur. It was a normal male human child, but covered with an unusually thick coating of hair . . . It also had one other distinguishing feature: its toes were fused together and its heels were hard and horny.

26

THE LAST OF THE LETTERS supposedly written by Grom-Grimeilo was left unfinished. What happened subsequently is also unknown. But I have heard somewhere that shortly after the birth of the colt-child, She-Eagle was transferred to the Askania-Nova wildlife reserve, where they tried to pair her with various stallions, but she resisted desperately and, if she had been a human being, her general condition could have been described as depressed. She started pining. When she was driven out to pasture, she didn't nibble the grass and kept apart from the herd. They tried to feed her oats, but she wouldn't even go near them and soon died—we could say that she pined away.

The general, having acquired such a strange heir, did not know what to do with him. He was reluctant to acknowledge him as his son, because there would inevitably be unsavory rumors and they could reach St. Petersburg. The general didn't give a damn about St. Petersburg, but he was concerned that the petty, malicious people there might—indeed, definitely would—convey these rumors to the ears of the sovereign, and that would not be good. Przhevalsky would not have cared a whit for the tsar's opinion either, if he had not been hoping for support from the treasury for further expeditions and experiments.

In short, Przhevalsky decided to unburden himself of the infant by placing him in good hands—but temporarily, not forever. During a journey that the general made to the Caucasus at that time, he happened to find himself in the town of Gori, where he became acquainted with a local shoemaker, Vissarion Djugashvili, when he called on him to have heel plates put on his boots. They fell into conversation. The shoemaker complained that his wife, whose name would have been Ekaterina in Russian, but who was Keke in Georgian, was a fine woman in every way, but she bore him only girls. The local folk mocked him, asking: What a botcher you are, Vissarion, can't you produce anything but twin-barrel jobs? To put an end to these spiteful jokes, he was even willing to adopt a little boy from somewhere. That would stop the jokers' mouths and, if he couldn't ensure the continuation of his line, he would at least have someone to inherit his shoemaker's booth.

When he heard that, Przhevalsky realized he had just been handed the solution to his problem. He ordered Ferapont to bring the child from the covered wagon and show him to the shoemaker. The child was brought, set down on the large bed, and its diapers were unwrapped. Vissarion liked the child, he even thought that it looked like him. Of course, he did have a few doubts, but they were offset by the general's promise to give him a thousand rubles every year for the child's upkeep—and the first installment was paid on the spot. For a shoemaker in the remote provincial town of Gori a thousand rubles was an immense sum, he could never earn even half as much in his entire lifetime. So there was temptation, but there was also hesitation. He called his wife to ask her opinion.

"Look here, Keke," he said. "Let's talk this over between us and adopt this little babe. You keep giving me girls all the time, but I need a man in the house to continue the trade at least, if not the family line, so there will be someone to inherit our shoemaker's booth and the secrets of my remarkable skills. Look what a fine little lad he is."

Keke looked at the little lad and burst into tears.

"What's wrong with you?" her husband asked. "Don't you like the child?"

"I do like him, but why is he so hairy, and what's wrong with his feet?"

"His feet are all right," the general reassured her. "The kind that give you a firm footing. And as for the hairiness, well . . . All the Caucasian men I know have a thick covering, it's an obvious sign of virility."

"But he's not a man, he's still a little boy."

"Yes, a little boy," the general agreed, "and already a man."

"And what's his name?" asked Vissarion.

Przhevalsky hesitated for a moment, because he still hadn't thought of a name for the child and simply referred to it as "he." But he had to answer quickly, and said: "Stallion."

"Is that a Russian name?" the shoemaker asked in surprise.

"No," said Nikolai Mikhailovich. "It's an English name."

"And what does it mean?"

" 'Stallion' is the English word for a stud horse," the general explained.

"That's no good!" said the shoemaker. "Are we supposed to call the boy a stud?"

"Well, certainly, he's a boy now, but later he'll be a man. And a man can't be compared with anything more flattering than a stud. Isn't that so, my esteemed Keke?"

Keke didn't dare object and she didn't want to. She agreed with the general, but the Caucasian notion of chastity prevented her from expressing her agreement. She said nothing and blushed furiously in embarrassment.

"Well then," said the cobbler, "my wife and I have consulted and decided that if you add another two hundred to the thousand rubles . . ."

"I'll add three hundred," Przhevalsky interrupted.

"All right, then we'll take our little Stalin. Hey," he said, leaning down over the child. "Hey, Stalin! Sweety pie!"

But little Stalin suddenly kicked out and caught his new father right on the nose, so hard that a narrow thread of blood trickled out of it.

"Well, how about that!" said Vissarion, startled. He put his hand to his nose and looked at the blood on his palm. He reached into his pocket for a handkerchief. "What do you think you're doing, my darling? So little, and already fighting. Like some kind of animal, not a child."

"That's because you got his name wrong. He's not Stalin, but Stallion," Przhevalsky remarked.

"What difference does that make, my dear fellow, Stallion or Stalin? We'll just call him Soso anyway. Hey, Soso!" he said to the child, prudently leaning back as he spoke.

Three months after the general's departure, the shoemaker, his face set in a false smile, informed his neighbors and relatives of his son's birth.

"What?" the neighbors and relatives exclaimed in amazement. "Where? How? Keke's last labor was only four months ago. Is it some kind of premature abortion?"

"It's not premature, it's a rapidly developing fetus," Vissarion protested. "Premature babies are little, but my Soso already weighs more than sixteen pounds."

And that, according to the information gathered by the author of these lines, is how the future Father of the Peoples, Leader of the World Proletariat, and Luminary of all the Sciences began his long life, in the course of which many legends would be composed about him with no more claim to authenticity than ours. I admit that the story of a mare conceiving and giving birth to a human requires rather more conclusive proof than has been adduced in these pages. Yes indeed, it is hard to imagine that Stalin was the child of a wild mare, but the author finds himself overwhelmed by even greater doubts when he wonders how such a monster could possibly have been produced by an ordinary human mother.

27

THE SOVIETS HAD DONE FOR OPALIKOV, but for some reason they wanted Chonkin alive, which George Pearl still found perplexing—it made him think he must have overlooked something after all. One afternoon he showed up at Chonkin's place in the Willis, told Chonkin to get changed quickly, and drove him to the commandant's headquarters. Two American officers and two Russian men in identical civilian suits were waiting for him there. The Russians were both short and extremely chubby—they had clearly not spent any time in Leningrad during the blockade or in Auschwitz. Georgii Ivanovich introduced them.

"Now, Ivan, these gentlemen or comrades are members of the Soviet consular service, they want to talk to you. Did I understand you correctly?" he asked the Russians.

"That's exactly right," one of them replied. Judging from his manner, gray temples, and obtuse expression, he was the senior member of the duo.

"Vanya," Georgii Ivanovich put in. "Let me remind you that you are on territory controlled by the United States of America and under the protection of American law. You have the right to decide your own fate. The way you want."

"I protest," said the senior Russian. "You are exerting pressure on a citizen of the U.S.S.R."

"I am not exerting pressure," Georgii Ivanovich retorted, "I am explaining his rights to him. Vanya, while you are here with us, you have nothing to be afraid of."

"We have long arms," the junior Russian remarked in a low voice, apropos of absolutely nothing, apparently talking to himself as he studied a modest landscape on the wall.

Surprised, Chonkin looked at the man's arms and thought to himself that he was lying, they weren't really that long.

"Gentlemen," said Georgii Ivanovich, intervening again, "take your seats, you two over there and you here . . ."—he pointed to opposite sides of the table. "You may address Mr. Chonkin, but without any threats."

"Yes, yes, of course," the senior Russian muttered and turned toward Chonkin. "Comrade Chonkin, we have come to see you on the instructions of the Soviet leadership. We know that you found yourself in the American zone against your own will, as a result of the treacherous actions of your commander Opalikov. You know what happened to him after that. The sensation-seeking Western newspapers claim that we poisoned him. But it wasn't us. I think it was done by the special services of the West in order to cast suspicion on us."

"Don't talk rubbish," said Georgii Ivanovich.

"We," continued the senior Russian, "reject terror as a means of attaining political goals. We act exclusively through the method of persuasion. We did not kill Opalikov."

At that point the second Russian started winking at Chonkin, as if to say: We killed him all right, we took him out, and we'll do for you too, you bastard.

"We have long arms," he said, as if he was talking to himself.

"Here, Ivan, sign this," said the senior Russian, putting a sheet of paper with some text on it in front of Chonkin.

"What's that?" Georgii Ivanovich asked warily.

"A statement for the press."

"If you don't mind!" said Georgii Ivanovich, picking up the statement and starting to read it. "Gentlemen of the press, as is already known, owing to the traitorous actions of my commander, the former Colonel Opalikov, I, Ivan Vasilievich Chonkin, a guards regiment private soldier in the victorious Soviet Army, found myself in the American occupation zone of Germany, where various forces hostile to the Soviet Union have attempted to induce me to betray my motherland. I am obliged to assert with the firmest possible resolve that these gentlemen's efforts are a complete waste of time. Although I am not a Party member, as a Soviet man I am a patriot of my country, devoted with all my heart to our Communist ideals and to Comrade Stalin in person. Perhaps you gentlemen educated in a different system of values cannot understand my feelings and my actions, but I am going back to my motherland."

"Uhu," said Georgii Ivanovich when he finished reading. "Powerfully expressed. And what do think about this, Vanya?"

Ivan pondered. At this point, given a chance, the reader will ponder too. What reply could Chonkin give in these circumstances? Should he meekly accept his fate and move from an American camp for displaced persons to a Soviet one for enemies of the people? No, dear readers, of course Chonkin had never been known as a great thinker, indeed some people saw him more as something of an Ivan the Fool, but then even Ivan the Fool was only a fool at the beginning. When life taught him a thing or two, he learned his lesson and achieved something in life.

Chonkin did likewise. After listening to the suggestion that he go back to his motherland, he thought hard and tried to imagine what his motherland meant to him, and the faces that arose before his mind's eye belonged to Sergeant Peskov, Captain Milyaga, Lieutenant Filippov, Colonel Dobrenky, Prosecutor Evpraksein, and other functionaries of the same ilk, and they all had long arms, and those arms were reaching for his throat. Certainly, Nyura's hazy image also appeared somewhere in the background. But it seemed to him that Nyura's hands, her eyes, and the expression on her face were all signaling to him: Don't do it, Vanya, don't agree, they won't let you see me and they'll make your life hell.

Seeing Chonkin hesitating, Georgii Ivanovich said: "Gentlemen, I can't take the decision for Mr. Chonkin, because Mr. Chonkin is a free man and free to manage his own life as he chooses, but it seems to me that this is a serious matter and it would only be fair to give Mr. Chonkin some time for thought."

"What for?" the senior persuader asked in surprise. "What's there to think about? Ivan, let me remind you once again that your motherland is giving you a chance to atone for your guilt and earn the forgiveness and trust of our people through honest labor. Any man who has even a scrap of conscience and love for his motherland would immediately take advantage of this offer and fly as if he had wings, crawl on his stomach . . ."

"We have long arms," the junior Russian reminded Chonkin.

"Vanya," said Georgii Ivanovich, interrupting the visitor, "let me remind you that you are a free man and have the right to act as you wish. You can crawl on your stomach or you can stand on your own two feet and tell these gentlemen where they can go."

"Where they can go?" asked Chonkin. "To hell, you mean?"

"To hell or even further, if you like," Georgii Ivanovich confirmed, "I'll stop my ears."

"Careful, Chonkin!" the senior Russian exclaimed in sudden fright. "Don't you dare be abusive. I'm a general."

"Ah, a general!" muttered Chonkin. "Ah, a general!" he repeated, remembering the general who had ripped the medal off his uniform blouse. "Ah, a general," he repeated for a third time, and suddenly he felt an absolutely insatiable desire to do what Georgii Ivanovich had suggested.

"Well, general, you can . . ." said Chonkin.

Georgii Ivanovich really did stop his ears, just as he had promised. He didn't hear the continuation of the phrase and therefore could not be a witness to the abuse of Soviet negotiators in the performance of their official duties. And when he took his fingers out of his ears, he heard a quite different conversation.

"Look here, Chonkin, look here," the senior Russian said in a voice filled with anger and resentment. "I spoke amicably to you. I spoke like an older comrade, like a father. I warned you what a deep chasm you were falling into. I thought you had got into a difficult situation uninten-tionally and I offered you my hand . . ."

"We have long arms," the junior Russian declared yet again.

"But you have rejected my hand. That means you have made a con-scious decision to sell out your motherland, the Party, and Comrade Stalin in person. And why? What for? What have they seduced you with? Coca-Cola? Gin and tonic? They're mollycoddling you now, but soon, when they don't need you any longer, they'll lose interest and dump you on the garbage heap. Very well, live as you like . . ."

"For the time being," the junior Russian put in.

". . . but know that your motherland will never forgive your treason."

The general looked disappointed—miserable, in fact. Possibly when he came here he had been hoping to convince this stupid soldier and thereby earn some kind of bonus in the form of another decoration or permission to transport some of his war trophies back to the mother-land. Chonkin had shattered his hopes, and it cost him a serious effort to make this speech. As he uttered it, he broke into a sweat and started mopping his plump cheeks and fat neck with a handkerchief.

"Have you said everything you want to say?" Georgii Ivanovich in-quired politely. Without waiting for a reply, he concluded: "Well then, gentlemen, the audience is over."

"But we will report to our superiors," the senior Russian warned him, "that our so-called Allies are encouraging our servicemen to commit treason."

So saying, he turned around, and his comrade turned around, and they strode toward the double doors, stamping their feet loudly, for some reason. At the doors the junior comrade looked back and reminded Chonkin once again about their long arms, although he didn't sound very confident.

28

WHEN GEORGII IVANOVICH, that is, George Pearl, realized his mission had exhausted its raison d'être, he handed Chonkin over to his friends at a White Russian émigré organization, the People's Labor Alliance (PLA). At first they wanted to take him into the propaganda section so that he could address Soviet soldiers through loudspeakers and call on them to turn their weapons against the odious Bolshevik regime. Naturally, these people at the PLA could have been depicted satirically, like any others, and they fully deserved to be treated in that manner, but we should remember that Soviet writers have flexed their satirical muscles so many times already in relation to these particular individuals that it is probably best for us to remain silent. Let us note, however, that some of these people were possibly the last Russian idealists who dreamed of a benign and bounteous Orthodox Russia. But their vision of what it should be like, this benign and bounteous Orthodox Russia, was as vague as the vision of the well-known heroine of a certain well-known book, who saw a benign and bounteous Russia in a dream.

In hopes of smashing the Soviet order that they hated, these people printed leaflets inviting Soviet soldiers to cross over into the American zone, where the embraces of their comrades-in-arms and young women of easy virtue awaited them, as well as anti-Soviet literature, pornographic magazines, and strong liquor, with snacks in unlimited quantities. But all these efforts at the expense of the American taxpayer proved futile. The Soviet soldiers didn't see these leaflets, and those who found them by chance were afraid even to read them. They demonstrated vigilance; that is, they took the leaflets to their political deputy commander or the special section, where they were always glad to accept these offerings. The leaflets were vivid proof of the fact that postwar Germany was saturated with anti-Soviet elements, and battling against them offered a chance for effective and safe advancement with the acquisition of higher ranks, Soviet decorations, and German marks.

Unfortunately, very little information has survived concerning the time spent by our hero in the ranks of the PLA, among people who defined themselves by the stupid word "solidarists." One of the leaders of the People's Labor Alliance, Vladimir Dmitrievich Poremsky, whom the author of these lines once had the good fortune to meet, did vaguely recall that there was someone like that, clumsy and awkward, whom Poremsky's colleagues tried to employ for their work.

"He tried," Poremsky told me, "but without any—how can I put it?— individual spark. Every assignment he was given was an external demand for him. And our principle was to accept into the organization only those who regarded our cause as their own, of vital importance to them, those who were prepared to sacrifice everything, even their lives, to liberate Russia from the Bolsheviks."

This reminiscence, which, you must agree, lacks a certain clarity, is perhaps the only one that exists about that period of Chonkin's life. Almost no other reliable information about this period has survived, and therefore we shall omit it.

YOU MIGHT HAVE THOUGHT that everyone would be thoroughly fed up with this Chonkin by now, but apparently there were still some people who thought about him more often than he did about them. In particular, that self-same Lavrentii Pavlovich thought about Chonkin a lot, because circumstances obliged him to do so. Although Lavrentii Pavlovich had come across the name Chonkin before, he simply hadn't noticed it. He had paid attention to the name Golitsyn, of course, because that wasn't just any old name but a princely one. Coming from a place where almost half of his compatriots were princes, Lavrentii Pavlovich had taken his own commoner status very hard and envied everyone who could trace his family line from someone older than his grandfather, from some noble *djigit** ancestor whose portrait with a mustache, a Circassian jacket with cartridge pockets, and a dagger hung in the drawing room. And therefore there was no way the name Golitsyn could escape Lavrentii Pavlovich's attention. But Chonkin . . . Lavrentii Pavlovich would not even have bothered to hold that name in his head. These days, however, Stalin (what a pest!) never ended a single conversation, either in person or on the phone, without the question: "Well, what about Chonkin? What are your people doing? When are you going to get him for me?" And sometimes he reminded Beria: "Remember, Lavrentii, your time is running out together with my patience."

* Literally, "skillful horseman" (Georgian).

Realizing what this reminder meant, Lavrentii Pavlovich tried his best, but he was fatally unlucky. He had failed to get hold of Chonkin by persuading him to return voluntarily. Two attempts to kidnap him had also failed. A certain highly experienced intelligence agent, sent to catch Chonkin, was caught himself when he tried to get through the checkpoint of the unit where our hero was being held. The agent had been provided with remarkable identification documents issued in the name of a sergeant of marines of African American origin, Bill Andrews. He had also prepared himself remarkably well by rubbing boot polish on his face. But if he had really been as experienced and smart as he was thought to be, he would have noticed, as he approached the spot where he was to carry out his mission, that people walking toward him were casting very surprised glances his way. In fact, he did notice these glances, but decided that those casting them were admiring his new American uniform and the bearing acquired in the Higher School of the People's Commissariat of State Security, and thinking: What a remarkably handsome fellow that soldier is! At the checkpoint he presented his ID to a sergeant of approximately the same color as himself. The sergeant examined the documents at length, comparing the face with the photo and the photo with the face.

"Do you have a problem with something in my ID?" our secret agent asked in modern English with a certain degree of defiance and a barely perceptible Alabama accent.

"Everything's in order, sir," said the sergeant, pressing the button to summon the guard. "Or almost everything. You just forgot to wax your ears."

Our poor spy was arrested and convicted by an American court martial. Many years later, when there was no more Stalin or Beria, he was exchanged for some eminent Soviet dissidents. The second agent sent into the enemy's lair by Lavrentii Pavlovich decided not to tempt fate: he surrendered without waiting to be exposed, thereby economizing on boot polish. At that point Lavrentii Pavlovich decided to play his last card.

"Listen, Kapulya," he said to Kapitolina one day as she was serving him breakfast, "I've heard that you know German and English very well."

"Me?" Kapitolina asked in amazement.

"Come on, stop pretending," said Beria. "I know all about you and I know who you work for. But right now I want you to work for me."

"What do I have to do for you, chief?"

"You have to seduce Chonkin and deliver him to me. If you do that, I'll give you access to the kind of secrets that will make your boss and my friend Allen Dulles promote you to general."

Lavrentii Pavlovich checked in person how well Kapa would cope with her assignment by holding a rehearsal with her, unaware that he had just acquired the clap from his latest street beauty.

The outcome of the plan hatched by Beria was that one morning when Chonkin came back to his room after breakfast, he found a white woman there making up his bed. She was very easy on the eye, which made him want to get to know her better. Chonkin was by no means a racist, but he found the white Russian woman more attractive than black John, who had performed the duties of housekeeper before her. They introduced themselves: Katya—Vanya. And then they launched into a relationship that drove him insane, and for two whole days he was willing to follow her to the ends of the earth, even to his motherland, which, as she assured him, was waiting for him impatiently. Katya and Vanya worked out a subtle plan for him to trick the guards at night and crawl under the fence behind the garbage container in the corner of the compound. Katya promised to be waiting on the other side of the fence in a car with Soviet diplomatic number plates and dimmed headlamps. However, that evening he began suffering unbearably intense, sharp cramps in a certain place, and instead of a Soviet vehicle with a diplomatic number plate, he ended up in an American vehicle with a red cross on it. At the hospital he was diagnosed with suppurating gonorrhea and total blockage of the urinary canal, which cooled his feelings for Katya and his motherland substantially.

Having failed in her assignment, Katya decided not to return to Moscow and became yet another defector, although in her case this could hardly be called a precise definition. Lavrentii Pavlovich was left without Katya and without Chonkin, but still with the clap—and with the anticipation of consequences even more lamentable than clap could cause.

Left without any hope of carrying out his leader's orders, Lavrentii Pavlovich realized that his fate was sealed. Stalin, vindictive and bloodthirsty, would never forgive such failure. And he, Lavrentii Pavlovich Beria, would die in the prime of life unless he could come up with some unexpected, paradoxical, ingenious way out of the situation.

He thought all night, and by morning he had come up with an answer. And the sensation was so euphoric, he actually felt as if his clap were gone.

ON DECEMBER 7, 1945, Beria summoned People's Artist of the U.S.S.R. Georgii Mikhailovich Melovani to his home, regaled him with French cognac, and asked, as he polished his pince-nez, "Tell me, Goga, what would you say if you found out that our country was being run by a horse?"

When he heard that, Goga was taken aback and even broke into a light sweat. The question was unexpected, but if it had been asked by someone else and not the man who had asked it, he could have laughed it off, or recalled some historical examples—about the horse that used to sit in the Roman Senate, for example. Or called on his knowledge of literature and cited Swift, and even brought in Lenin, who had promised to teach, not a horse, of course, but a cook to run the state. But if a cook could do it, why wouldn't a horse be able to manage? All of this flashed through Melovani's mind and he opened his mouth to reply, but then closed it again, realizing that that would be best. When a question was asked by a man like this, you had to think hard before joking, citing, or adducing analogies. If you told him that, yes, a horse could run the state, naturally he would take it to mean that he, in his own opinion a great statesman, could be replaced by a simple horse from the collective farm stables. Melovani was not such a very wise man, but he knew that when people like Lavrentii Pavlovich Beria asked such strange questions, it was best to take your time in answering, because the wrong answer could cost you your head. So he thought for a long time, then laughed, on the assumption that the best thing to do was treat the question as a joke, but when he started laughing, the cold, unsmiling glance he received from behind that pince-nez pierced him to the very soul.

"I think," he said, "I think . . . I think . . . Lavrentii Pavlovich!" he cried out despairingly. "I don't know what to think! Tell me what I ought to think and I'll think what you tell me."

"Very well," said Beria, "very well. Stalin has ordered you to be arrested." He paused before assembling his second sentence. "And exiled to Turukhansk. Do you realize what that means, arrest and exile to Turukhansk? Do you know where Turukhansk is, eh?"

Goga didn't know exactly where Turukhansk was, but he could easily picture to himself the boundless, snowy steppe, a long column of hungry, freezing convicts and himself at the back of the column, shuffling along in wooden stocks, a miserable, pampered urbanite, unaccustomed to such deprivations, stumbling and collapsing in exhaustion. Having pictured all this, he turned terribly pale and started trembling. He pushed away his glass and could barely find the strength to ask:

"What for?"

Beria set his pince-nez on his nose and walked across to the mirror to see how it sat there.

"If it was *for* something," he said, pressing the pince-nez down onto the bridge of his nose with his forefinger, "he would have you shot." And he laughed—a cackling kind of laugh: "Kha-kha-kha-kha! But then," he said when he stopped laughing, "Stalin could have you shot anyway."

"But I haven't done anything wrong. I love Comrade Stalin. Tell him that I love him very much."

"Well now, I believe you, I believe that you love him," said Beria. "But what's important is whether he believes you. We'll go to see him tomorrow, and you can show him how much you love him. Do you remember what we spoke about last time? Last time you and I spoke about how you could take Comrade Stalin's place. But you have to replace him, you have to play his role in real life, not in the cinema, so well that no one, not even the people who are close to Comrade Stalin, will suspect that it's not him. Can you act like that?"

"Yes, I can," Melovani said with a confident nod. "I, Lavrentii Pavlovich, am an artiste. I'm a very good artiste. But even so I would hesitate to take on such a responsibility."

"I will take on this responsibility for you without any hesitation. And you can imagine what will happen if you fail to justify my trust. But first I have a question for you: is your mustache real?"

"Certainly not, Lavrentii Pavlovich, it's a false mustache. I glued it on to give you an idea of how I will play Comrade Stalin. But I never go outside in the image of Comrade Stalin, so that no one will think I am impersonating Comrade Stalin."

"Good," said Beria with a nod of his bald head, "tomorrow we'll go to see Comrade Stalin. Give me the mustache. I'll take it with me and you'll glue it on when I tell you."

31

THE NEXT DAY THE ZIS AUTOMOBILE of the People's Commissar of State Security was back once again at the familiar green fence. This time there were two passengers: the Commissar himself and People's Artist Melovani. The Commissar was wearing a long coat of wool cloth with an astrakhan collar and an astrakhan fore-and-aft cap; the artiste had on a dark blue suit with a polka-dot tie. Both visitors went through the usual search-and-check procedure, which was rather superficial on this occasion: the guards didn't even pay any attention to the false mustache in Lavrentii Pavlovich's briefcase, perhaps because it wasn't a firearm or an item for cutting or stabbing.

Fortunately, Stalin was in a good mood and greeted his visitors cordially in the entrance hall. He was wearing a marshal's uniform tunic with two gold stars on the chest—for the decorations of Hero of the Soviet Union and Hero of Socialist Labor. It wasn't the formal uniform tunic, by the way, so it looked reasonably modest.

Stalin and Beria embraced as they greeted each other and then Beria introduced Melovani.

"Look, dear Koba, I've brought you the People's Artist who, as you know, plays the role of Stalin, that is, of yourself, in many films. I recall that you liked *The Fall of Berlin* very much."

"Not *very* much," Koba protested, offering his hand to Melovani. "Not *very* much," he repeated, looking into the artiste's eyes, which made Melovani cringe. "I didn't like the film *very* much . . ." He paused. "I liked it, but not *very* much. So," he said, addressing Melovani directly, "you want to feel your way into the image of Comrade Stalin and live in more or less the same conditions as Comrade Stalin?"

"I only wanted . . ."

"I understand," Stalin interrupted. "You wanted. Everybody wants. I suggested that you start with exile in Turukhansk, but I heard my suggestion didn't go down too well, as they say."

The People's Artist took fright again. He thought that if he said that Stalin's suggestion had gone down well, then Stalin really would exile him to Turukhansk. But if he said it hadn't gone down well, Stalin would get angry and send him to Turukhansk, or even further, anyway. He also thought that leaders, despite his great love for them, were best seen in portraits and not in the flesh. "Oh no," he said, trying to explain himself. "I wanted . . . I want everything that you want to want . . ."

"It's all right, don't make excuses," Stalin interrupted. "As the Russian people say, you can make your excuses in the militia station. I'm joking, I'm joking. But meanwhile let's go in here."

Stalin pressed a button on the wall and a door that had been invisible before swung three-quarters of the way open to reveal a small room about three meters by four. A plain iron bedstead, standing with its head end to the wall—not nickel-plated, but painted with green gloss paint, like one in a prison. A straw mattress covered with a gray woollen army blanket. There was even straw sticking out of the pillow. A modest bracket lamp above the head of the bed. A simple pine night table beside the bed, with two books on it: *The History of the All-Union Communist Party (Bolsheviks)* and *Crime and Punishment*. On a wall covered with colorless wallpaper, several pictures cut out of the magazine *Ogonyok* and nailed up.

Stalin said, "There, that's how Comrade Stalin lives. Do you want to live in conditions like that?"

"Comrade Stalin, for you," said Melovani, pressing his hand on his chest, "For you I would sleep on anything! Even on nails!"

"Oh," said Stalin, smiling, "on nails, that's not necessary as yet. That's for Lavrentii Pavlovich, he's a well-known tormentor of the flesh; he could lay a man out on nails. Me, put such an artiste on nails . . . no, no. Unless you were going to rehearse the part of Rakhmetov."

Melovani felt an immense relief. So immense that he even dared to ask why Comrade Stalin had pictures from *Ogonyok* when he could take works by Repin or even Rembrandt from the museums, at least temporarily.

After he asked, he cringed, frightened again that Comrade Stalin might get angry. But Comrade Stalin didn't get angry. Comrade Stalin said:

"You know, *genatsvale,* if I start pilfering pictures from state museums, then all my ministers, marshals, and Regional Party Committee secretaries will pilfer everything from the museums and take it home. So I'm not going to set them a bad example."

"Above all, Goga," Beria added, "you must understand that Comrade Stalin is a very modest man. And his modesty makes him great. And you should also know that Comrade Stalin works very, very hard. Too hard, unfortunately. He's wearing himself out, but we must not simply accept that. Koba, dear fellow," he said to Stalin, "the comrades and I have consulted and decided that you work too hard. We must ease your burden. That's why I've brought Comrade Melovani to see you. Do you see how closely Comrade Melovani resembles you? When he puts on his mustache, he resembles you so closely that your own mother couldn't tell you apart."

Stalin frowned at the words "your own mother." He suspected that Keke Djugashvili wasn't his mother, but he didn't know who had really given birth to him. Nevertheless, whenever his mother was mentioned, it gave him an unpleasant feeling, although he couldn't say why.

He frowned, but Beria, who usually noticed every change in the leader's mood, didn't notice anything this time and continued with the inspired exposition of his plan.

"So, dear Koba, we thought: Why couldn't our great artiste stand in for you in your work? Perhaps at some not very important sessions."

"How do you mean, he could stand in for me?" asked Stalin, knitting his eyebrows together above his nose.

"Well, like this. He would put on your clothes, the field jacket, the breeches and boots, glue on his mustache, or even grow one, and sit there, taking notes, sometimes clapping his hands, sometimes passing a few remarks."

"All right," Stalin said approvingly. "And what am I going to do all this time?"

"You'll be doing a bit of gardening. Pruning the roses. Resting. Lying down. Reading Marx's *Capital* . . ."—he squinted at the night table . . . "*The History of the All-Union Communist Party (Bolsheviks), Crime and Punishment . . .*"

"Hmmm," Stalin said in response and started thinking. He got up. Walked across the room. Lit his pipe that had gone out. Walked from corner to corner again. He seemed perfectly calm. Meanwhile, however, there was a storm raging inside him, but he was so good at hiding his feelings that even a subtle psychologist like Beria didn't notice anything.

"So," said Stalin thoughtfully, "so, you've decided that Comrade Stalin is tired, have you?"

"Well, yes," Beria confirmed. "Yes. You really have got a bit tired. Forgive me, my dear old friend and comrade-in-arms, I know how tough you are, you work night and day, like an ox, or a horse. But even your strength has some limit, my dear Koba! A high limit, very high, but it does have a limit. Of course, during the war, when the fate of our country was being decided, when you bore an incredible burden on your shoulders, like a giant, like Hercules, like that . . . well, I don't even know who . . . but now, when, under your brilliant leadership, we have totally routed the fascist hordes, when the red banner flutters proudly over their capital, why should you not transfer at least a few of the less important responsibilities to the shoulders of some simple man, to bear them like a simple ass . . ."

Comrade Stalin completed another assault dash from one corner to the other. He puffed on his pipe and smacked his lips. "Comrade Stalin is tired," he agreed sadly, "Comrade Stalin has grown old and decrepit, he's no good for anything any longer and he can be replaced by absolutely anyone, even an ass. Do I understand you correctly?"

"But Koba . . ." Beria tried to protest.

"No, no, I don't mind," Koba went on. "It's a good idea, but it needs a little thought. I'll give it a little thought. When I've given it a little thought and I realize that you want to exclude me from important business little by little, I'll let you know what I think of this entirely obvious device . . . But in the meantime we'll go and sit down peacefully—for the time being—and have a modest bite to eat."

Once out of the room, Stalin pressed the push button again. The door closed soundlessly and merged into the wall, leaving no visible joint at all. Two guards with Shpagin automatics were standing in the corridor facing each other—silent, motionless, unblinking. Stalin walked between them without speaking and pressed another push button on the wall. A more spacious, oval-shaped room was revealed. It contained a table covered with a white tablecloth and laid with drinks and hors d'oeuvres. Two waiters, as mute as the guards, were standing to attention by the wall. They were wearing white suits and black bow-ties, with large starched napkins over their arms.

"You can go," Stalin told them as he walked into the room. Then, more for Melovani's sake than theirs, he added: "I'll serve my guests myself."

The waiters left. Stalin pressed a push button and the room was transformed into a closed space with no exit. Stalin moved out a chair for Melovani and said: "Have a seat, artiste. What will you have to drink? Vodka? Wine? Cognac?"

"What will you have?" the artiste asked.

"I'll have Khvanchkara."

"And I'll have Khvanchkara."

"And so will I," said Beria.

It is well known that when he needed to, Stalin could drink robustly and he rarely got drunk. Beria knew how to drink too. And Melovani was also no novice where drink was concerned. They drank, they drank a lot, proposed toasts to the great leader, to state security, to art in general, and to the art of dramatic impersonation in particular. They also spoke a little Georgian and sang Georgian songs, and Melovani sang especially well (an artiste is an artiste, after all). The conversation turned to various concerns of the day which it would be boring to retell here. Suddenly Stalin recalled the airman Opalikov, who had not only defected, but also taken with him that finest of Russian soldiers, the hero Ivan Chonkin.

Remembering that, he flew into a rage. "You," he said to Lavrentii Pavlovich, "what did you tell me? You assured me that you'd get those two. Did you get them?"

"Oh, did I!" Lavrentii Pavlovich declared gleefully, chewing on a mouthful of Olivier salad. "I got one of them already and I'll get the other one too, and very soon. Soon, I assure you, dear fellow, I'll get the other one soon."

"How did you get the first one, and what exactly does it mean to say you got him?"

"This is what it means," said Lavrentii Pavlovich. He rummaged in his briefcase and took out a folder of newspaper cuttings. There weren't many of them, about fifteen, but they were all about the death of Colonel Opalikov. "There, Koba, these are the English newspapers, these are the French ones, and these are the German ones. They all say more or less the same thing. They talk about the long arms of the Kremlin. And we really do have long arms, Koba. So long that we can get anyone we like wherever we like."

"And how did this unfortunate colonel die?" Stalin asked in a warmer voice.

"He took a drink of water," said Lavrentii Pavlovich, slicing off a piece of his steak.

"Water?" Stalin queried. "Plain water?"

"What good is plain water? Mineral water," Beria said with a throaty chuckle. "Plain mineral water. No fizz."

"What about Chonkin. Wasn't he given the same water?"

"Of course not, dear Koba. You wanted to see him alive, so we'll get him for you alive."

"When?"

"Soon."

"You've been promising it will be soon for ages. All right. I'll wait a bit longer. A tiny little bit longer, Lavrentii. I hope my meaning is clear?"

"Absolutely clear, Koba," said Beria, bowing his head. "I'll do whatever's necessary," he added, investing his promise with a different meaning than Stalin had in mind. "And by the way, what's that picture you have up there, Koba?"

"Where?" asked Koba.

"Up there, right in front of you."

"That one?" Stalin asked in surprise. "What an ignoramus you are, Lavrentii! The people think you're a leader and carry your portraits at demonstrations, but they have no idea how ignorant and illiterate you are. That's a Russian classic! *The Hunters at Rest* by the remarkable Russian artist Vasilii Perov!"

"Ah, so that's it!" said Lavrentii, as if he really had only just recognized *The Hunters at Rest*. But to himself he thought: "I might be an illiterate ignoramus, but you've just shown what a real dunce you are."

And he had good reason for this opinion about his brother-in-arms, because Stalin, who was always wary and extremely vigilant, had been caught out by a primitive thief's trick: he had allowed his attention to be distracted. After looking up, he had spent no more than ten seconds gazing at Perov's picture, but those seconds had been quite enough for Lavrentii Pavlovich to drop something into the other man's glass—a tablet that dissolved instantly in either water or wine and had no taste or smell.

"Well then," said Stalin, raising his glass. "Let's drink to Private Chonkin and to all the soldiers without whom no generals or even generalissimuses could have prevailed over a powerful enemy!"

Stalin stood to drink to Chonkin for the second time. And People's Commissar of State Security, Lavrentii Pavlovich Beria, and People's Artist of the Soviet Union, Georgii Mikhailovich Melovani, stood with him to drink to Chonkin.

The wine that Stalin drank had an odd aftertaste.

It also made Stalin feel odd. He suddenly felt dizzy. He looked at his drinking companions and he seemed to be standing in the center of a circle, a strange merry-go-round, with his companions sitting on cardboard horses and galloping around him.

"You, Lavrentii," Stalin began, trying to fix his gaze on Beria. "You, Lavrentii." He wanted to say something to Lavrentii, but Lavrentii was whirling past him faster and faster, getting smaller and smaller every time he came around, until he shrank to the size of a fly and then dissolved completely in the rarefied air. And with that the light went out in Comrade Stalin's eyes and Comrade Stalin lowered his head onto the table, only not into the salad, as some people might have expected, but beside his plate.

Silence filled the room. Melovani sat there pale-faced with his mouth open and a piece of suluguni cheese suspended halfway to it. Beria, on the other hand, carried on eating as if nothing had happened.

"Why aren't you drinking, Goga?" he asked after a while.

"Me?" said Melovani. "I . . . I don't want to."

He pushed his glass away, moving it cautiously, as if he were afraid the liquid in it would splash up into his face of its own accord.

"Well don't, if you don't want to," said Lavrentii. "But I think I'll have a drink."

He picked up Melovani's glass and drained it in large gulps. He looked at Stalin and shook his head. He looked at the artiste, who was sitting there as pale as a sheet and trembling rapidly, the way a dog trembles when it's led away to be put down.

"Listen, my dear fellow," the People's Commissar said to him, "what's wrong with you? Are you feeling unwell?"

"No, no," Melovani said hastily. "I feel fine. And I didn't see a thing. I didn't," he repeated, "see anything at all."

"I didn't see a thing, I didn't see anything," Beria repeated hastily, but with a hint of humor. "You didn't see anything, and I didn't see anything, and he still can't see anything now. Why are you trembling? Do you think I poisoned him? My senior comrade and brother-in-arms, a faithful follower of Lenin and the leader of all the peoples, do you think I poisoned him? I just gave him a little something to help him sleep. Because, let me tell you, he, Comrade Stalin, is tired, he needs rest, and I, as an old friend of his, as one Communist to another, gave him a bit of help. Sit here and don't budge. I'll just be a moment."

Beria darted into the bathroom adjoining the dining room and emerged holding a large glittering razor of the kind that used to be called a cutthroat.

At the sight of this object Melovani jumped to his feet and dashed to the door, but it was closed. Then he huddled back against the wall and started trembling even more violently. Beria approached Stalin with the razor in his hand. Melovani recovered his wits slightly and found the strength to ask, in a voice shuddering with horror: "Pardon me, but are you going to slit Comrade Stalin's throat?"

"Oi," said Beria, wincing as he adjusted the napkin he had tucked into Stalin's collar, "what kind of dull, muttish fool are you, what kind of asinine dolt? Why do you always have stupid ideas like that, thinking I've poisoned him and I'm going to slit his throat? Who do you take me for? As if I would slit the throat of the leader of the international proletariat, the father of the peoples! What's the matter with you? I just want to shave him, to make him as handsome as you are. Then glue the mustache on you, to make you as ugly as he is. Go into the bathroom and bring the shaving brush and soap. And pull yourself together. You are about to demonstrate your art. Now we'll see what kind of an artiste you are. You're going to play the most important role of your entire life, and if you play it badly, you and I will be left headless."

Some time later the door of Comrade Stalin's dining room opened and Comrade Stalin walked out into the corridor with his two guests, Lavrentii Pavlovich Beria and Georgii Mikhailovich Melovani. Although to say that Melovani walked out would be incorrect. He had his arms around Lavrentii Pavlovich's neck and was literally hanging on him, muttering something incoherently and dragging his feet across the floor.

"Look at that," Stalin complained, pointing to Melovani with his pipe. "A People's, would you believe, Artist and the swine gets as soused, would you believe, as a herring. Vlasik!" he said when they came across the head of the guard. "Tell your men to help Comrade Lavrentii Pavlovich carry the artiste to the car. I'm going to my room, don't disturb me again today."

History's a tricky business, a kind of chest or camera obscura, filled with secrets so scorching hot that when you discover them, even just a few, it leaves you breathless and dizzy and parches your throat. And you shake your head and think: No, that simply cannot be. Ah, but it can. It can. Very easily.

EVENTUALLY THEY REALIZED IN THE PLA that the chances of turning Chonkin into a valuable colleague were slim. He was sent to a small town, the precise name of which I forget, but I think it was somewhere near Munich. Or Mannheim. Or perhaps Münster. Anyway, somewhere beginning with the letter *M*. Since it was a small town, it had no strategically important industrial or military targets in it, so it had escaped being bombed and was as quiet, clean, and green as before the war. There were two churches there—Catholic and Protestant—three schools, six shops, two gas stations, one movie theater, one repair shop for automobiles and tractors, one slaughterhouse with a butcher's shop attached to it, and a small open market. In those difficult postwar days, part of the market site was occupied by a flea market where people tried to sell whatever they had: a piece of bread, a pair of old galoshes, American cigarettes, SS service caps, Third Reich decorations, knives and forks, and anything else that might come to hand.

The only military target there—which had not been bombed by the Allies, because they kept it for themselves—was the barracks of the former artillery college. Two of the two-story red-brick barracks buildings were now occupied by American soldiers, and the other four bunkhouses had been converted into a camp for so-called displaced persons. This was where Chonkin ended up. Immediately after the war, there was an entire international community here: Americans, Englishmen, Frenchmen, Italians, and so forth, but everyone on this list promptly left for home, where they were received with great honors, leaving behind a group including Poles, Bulgarians, and Romanians, but with a majority of Russians or, rather, Soviet citizens of various nationalities who occupied the whole of bunkhouse No. 4, with its double-tier iron bunks.

These men were in no hurry to get home, because what was waiting for them there, in the very best case, was a camp for repatriated Soviet nationals, in the intermediate case—a corrective labor camp and, in the worst case—a firing squad. They were former Ostarbeiter, prisoners of war, Polizei, Vlasovites, and others guilty of something, or perhaps guilty of nothing but having been born in Russia. For the most part, whether Russian or not, they were simple men like Chonkin, passive and submissive to their fate. When they were driven on to face bullets, they faced bullets; when they were taken prisoner, they surrendered. When they surrendered, they didn't even think about whether they were traitors or not. They simply wanted to live, but the Soviet state and Stalin regarded this desire as reprehensible. Their numbers also included several of the numerous women who had been abducted and taken to Germany, where they worked in military factories. The local plant had now been closed and everyone in it transferred to this camp. Chonkin slept in an upper bunk and his "downstairs neighbor" was an engineer from Kiev, an individual of Uzbek extraction who called himself Usman Usmanovich Usmanov. He had been taken prisoner in July 1941 and spent the entire war in a camp. The Germans had noticed that he was circumcised and suspected him of being a Jew. The camp commandant, an SS officer who didn't believe him when he said that he wasn't Jewish, summoned him for regular interrogations and tried to catch him out in lying, as well as taunting him and urinating in his mouth, but the commandant was unable to prove anything and let him live. The bunk next to Chonkin was occupied by a Vlasovite officer who had miraculously escaped being handed over to the Soviets, and on the other side, snoring ferociously in his sleep at night, was one of the twenty-eight heroes from General Panfilov's division. He had been awarded the Gold Star of a Hero of the Soviet Union and the Order of Lenin posthumously, thanks to the rampant imagination of the journalist Krinitsky.

Krinitsky had once invented these twenty-eight heroes who supposedly fought the Germans in unequal combat at the Dubosekovo railway junction. In actual fact, as we have mentioned earlier, there was no engagement at Dubosekovo junction. Most of the twenty-eight supposed heroes listed were still alive, and when Kalinin was signing the decree awarding the posthumous title of Hero of the Soviet Union to Chonkin's neighbor, this particular hero was working as a Polizei in Smolensk. There were various different kinds of men here. Most of them missed their friends, relatives, parents, wives, and children. They both yearned for their motherland and were afraid of it. There were rumors that the Americans and the British were handing over former Soviet citizens to the Soviet authorities, and those who were handed over could expect, at best, prison and, at worst, death. A horrendous example was set for all of them by the fate of General Krasnov's Cossacks, who fought as part of the German forces. Stunned by the devious cunning of the British, the Cossacks shot themselves or threw themselves under the train. There were rumors, perhaps exaggerated, that those who traveled as far as the first Soviet station on the railroad were shot there and then, beside the goods sheds, and their wives and children were sent to Siberia. This was terrifying, and while most of the camp's inhabitants were homesick for their own country, they feared a reunion with it like death itself.

The left wing of the bunkhouse was occupied by several men who were distinguished from the common mass by their education and intellect.

Some of the inhabitants of the right wing referred to them as "academicians." This group of "academicians" included the same two Thinkers whom we have described at the very beginning of our narrative. This is both surprising and unsurprising, because such Thinkers show up unfailingly wherever an accumulation of people exceeds a certain critical mass and they are in the mood and have the time to argue about something. You may ask: Who are they, where are they from, what age are they? And I will reply that they have no age. These people have always existed and always will, they always *are*. If one generation of them succeeds another, then the process is imperceptible, because the new arrivals are in no way different from those who have departed. They are always arguing furiously among themselves and never reach any agreement. If one says yes, then another is bound to say no. But if, in a sudden impulse of magnanimity, the one who said yes agrees and says no, you're right, of course it's no, then the one who thought it was no will immediately change his point of view. They were constantly embroiled in learned discussions, in the course of which they decided the fate of countries, nations, and individuals. One of them thought that Germany should be disarmed and left in peace. The other felt that it should be completely dismembered, not into occupation zones but into its separate *Länder,* and divided up among Holland, Poland, Czechoslovakia, and Italy, as well the Soviet Union, America, Britain, and France. They argued with each other over who was worse, Stalin or Hitler, and one of them concluded that Hitler was worse, but the other objected that in fact Stalin was. An especially large-scale argument blew up over the destruction of the city of Dresden. One called the bombardments by the Allies barbarous. "You should fight against the army," he said, "not against the peaceful civilians."

"Don't talk drivel!" the other replied heatedly. "In this war there weren't any peaceful civilians. It was fought with systems, countries, and nations. In this war it was the fighting spirit of the nation at war that was important. When the Germans attacked us, they knew that the German people was standing behind them, that they had the blessing of their fathers and mothers, brothers and sisters, for their heroic effort. And apart from that, they were encouraged by the hope that there would be no retribution. When a German airman dropped his bombs on the inhabitants of Kiev, London, or Coventry, he himself was prepared to die, but he was sure that no bombs would fall on his mom and dad, his wife or his kids. The scum was counting on the nobility of his enemies . . ."

"And he was right to count on it, he was right," the First Thinker objected. "We people of the Christian civilization should not emulate the barbarity of the barbarians."

"That's precisely what we should do. In order to defeat German fascism, it wasn't enough to win a victory at the front, the will of the German people had to be broken. All the Germans had to be shown that if the soldiers to whom they had given their blessing were going to destroy cities and kill peaceful citizens, then we would not recognize the immunity of the rear either. Dresden was a lesson intended to intimidate the German people."

Chonkin listened to both Thinkers from a distance, and when one spoke, in his mind he agreed with him, but when the other one objected, Ivan found his arguments convincing. The two Thinkers also argued about whether for them the motherland was simply a place where you happened to be born, or something more than that. One of them said bitterly: "We are exiles"—but the other, citing some poetess or other, objected confidently: "No, we are envoys."

The first said that his motherland was the Russian language, but the second said that he had brought Russia with him on the soles of his boots.

The next day Chonkin looked at the Second Thinker's feet and thought what a liar he was. His boots were new. American. There was no way he could have brought Russia with him on those soles.

WHEN CHONKIN MOVED TO THIS CAMP, he had brought some food with him just to be on the safe side. Some canned goods and salami. Even a loaf of bread wrapped in the German newspaper *Neuer Beobachter*. The First Thinker spotted him unfolding the newspaper and asked if he could read it.

"Take it," said Chonkin, "only it's all in something foreign."

"It's all the same to me what language it's in," said the First Thinker, spotting the heading of an article: "Stalin—the Son of a Horse?"

He started reading. The newspaper was old, the issue that had reported on Colonel Opalikov's talk, his strange announcement, and his mysterious death.

After reading the article, the First Thinker became highly excited and announced to the entire bunkhouse that Stalin was apparently the offspring of a Przhevalsky horse.

"Now what nonsense are you spouting?" exclaimed the Second Thinker.

"Ah, but it isn't nonsense!" protested the First Thinker. "Look, it's all here in black and white . . ."

"Will you look at this man," said the Second Thinker, shaking his head, "he still believes the printed word."

"I wouldn't have believed it, but there are facts here, facts. Listen. General Przhevalsky, while traveling through Northern China . . ."

"I don't even want to listen," said the Second Thinker, demonstratively placing his hands over his ears. "Tell me," he said, turning to Usman Usmanovich Usmanov, "you're a sober individual who thinks realistically, an engineer, can you believe that Stalin was the offspring of a horse?"

"Certainly I can," said Usman Usmanovich. "When it comes to people like Stalin or Hitler, I'm willing to believe that they are the offspring of jackals, hyenas, polecats, or scorpions."

"Ha!" said the Second Thinker, spreading his arms wide. "Believe me, I hate these two villains every bit as much as you do, but the conscience of a scientist will not permit me to sacrifice the truth to suit my personal bias."

"Are you a scientist?" Usman Usmanovich asked in surprise. "In what discipline, if you don't mind me asking?"

"I'm an encyclopaedic scientist," the Second Thinker explained vaguely.

"So am I," said the First Thinker.

"We are both universal scientists," the Second Thinker confirmed, "but we take very different views of things. However, there is someone here among us who is more competent to resolve our dispute. Savelii Felitsianovich," he said, turning to a scientist sitting by the stove who bore the strange surname of Devochka, that is, "little girl" in Russian. "You're a biologist, aren't you? Tell him that a hybrid of a human being and a horse is impossible in nature."

"You know," Savelii Felitsianovich said thoughtfully, "I was hoping to keep out of your argument, but if you insist that I become involved, then I have to tell you that in nature everything is possible. Everything that appears in accordance with its laws and as a result of its mistakes. Of course, nature has provided all the plants and animals with mechanisms for protecting their species. But sometimes, for some reason, these mechanisms fail, and then anything can happen. We know of masses of plant or animal hybrids that have been bred artificially or exist simply as nature's jokes. In ancient times these jokes used to happen more often. Living organisms were still only developing then. I began my career in science as a convinced Darwinist. And even now, generally speaking, I think that man is descended from a monkey. But other animals might have been mixed up in it, too. At that time there weren't any laws or morality or established aesthetic ideals. The males and females of various species, including man, entered into chaotic sexual relations with each other. Sometimes a massive attack on the weak defensive systems of a species produced a result, and then creatures appeared among people who looked perfectly human, but with indications that they were carrying inherited characteristics intrinsic to other representatives of the animal world."

At this the Second Thinker rolled up his eyes and flung his arms wide. "Well, if even a biologist can talk such drivel . . ." he said.

"Drivel?" said Devochka, offended. "Tell me, have you ever been to Lake Titicaca?"

"Where?" asked the Second Thinker.

"In Peru."

"Well, what do you think? How could I, a Soviet man who has been in exile, ever get to Peru?"

"But I, also a Soviet man, went there on a scientific expedition. We visited several floating islands and worked in Lima for a while, studying the results of several archaeological excavations. We found masses of clay figures made by members of ancient Peruvian tribes. These figures, which clearly attempted to reflect reality accurately, were often devoted to the sexual life of the people of those times. Well then, many of these small sculptures depict sexual acts between a human being and an animal, most often with horses or asses, which produced little centaurs whose images are also captured in clay. Most of these hybrids are more like horses, but some are closer to human beings. My current theory is that many people, who basically derive from monkeys, also carry characteristics inherited from other animals, which are definitely reflected in their character and, naturally, their behavior."

"All right then," said the Second Thinker. "I won't argue with you. Let's assume that something of the sort could have happened a very long time ago, but in our time the species' defense systems have probably improved, haven't they?"

"Undoubtedly," Devochka agreed. "But what I said still holds true: even now nature is still capable of anything. Of even bigger mistakes."

Chonkin listened to this conversation attentively, thinking not about distant antiquity, but about his own childhood and boyhood in a village. At that time and in that place there were also men who copulated with anything and everything. His cousin Mitka Chonkin slept with his mother. Filipp Trofimov slept with his wife and his four daughters, and there were some who didn't draw the line at animals. The groom Grigorii used to sleep with a mare and didn't try to hide it, the goatherd Ignat employed a she-goat for the same purpose, and they said that Manka Deliukina, who had no nose, used to console herself with her dog Rex. Chonkin didn't think there had been any offspring from these couplings. Kuzma Gladishev had told him that the gelding Osoaviakhim had miraculously been transformed into a man, but at the time Chonkin had taken that as idle gossip. Now, however, after listening to these learned scientists, he thought how true it was that in life anything could happen.

DURING THE LATE 1940s, a rumor ran round the islands of the Gulag Archipelago or, in the people's vernacular of that time, "the shit spread," that the Man in the Iron Mask had moved into the basement of the Lubyanka. In other words, that the KGB prison now held an extremely mysterious prisoner whose face was concealed behind a mask of iron, like his predecessor in seventeenth-century France who had been held in the Bastille. (It is perhaps worth mentioning in parentheses that the face of the seventeenth-century original was actually covered by a mask not of iron but velvet, which would seem to us likely to have made his life rather less terrible, but such is the nature of the public— worldwide, not just in Russia—that it thirsts for horror in its pure form and finds half-horror insufficiently titillating.) As for our Soviet prisoner, according to the rumor, his face was definitely concealed by an iron mask and, while various opinions were expressed concerning his identity, the general consensus was that he was Stalin, who had been kidnapped by his enemies and secretly replaced by a People's Artist of the Soviet Union. This Artist, or Artiste, was a mere puppet in the hands of

Stalin's enemies. He nodded his head and clapped his hands at meetings, but in reality everything was controlled by Stalin's enemies, who were exterminating the finest part of the Soviet people in his name. There were definite grounds for this rumor, deriving primarily from the fact that the people's profound faith in Stalin, their belief that he was boundlessly wise, humane and just, simply could not be reconciled with the atrocities that were being perpetrated on his authority.

So if you were to assume that the author has concocted the entire story about Stalin being replaced by the artiste Melovani, you would be mistaken.

Nonetheless, to get back to the mask, I myself will make bold to assume that it never existed, in either iron or velvet form. There was, however, a solitary cell, not in the basement but on the first floor, where prisoner number 37/14 BSh, who had no name pro tem, was held. No one knew his real name apart, of course, from People's Commissar Beria. A certain Ivan Spiridonovich Lapochkin, born in 1921, who has survived to our times, was working then as a warden in the Lubyanka Prison. Now that he is allowed to speak, he has opened up and recently made a statement on TV in connection with this legend. He said that during the winter of late 1945 or early 1946 an elderly man of Caucasian appearance was delivered to the corridor that he guarded and as the man was being locked in his cell, he kicked out and shouted: "Let me go! I'm Stalin! I'll have you all shot!"

"But tell me," the presenter asked Lapochkin, "did this man really resemble Stalin?"

"Oh, no," said the former warden, "certainly not! Nothing like Stalin. I'd seen Stalin in his portraits and in the flesh, too. When we were led round Red Square on a demonstration he was standing there, up on the Mausoleum, with all the others, you know, Voroshilov, Molotov, Kaganovich, and all the rest of them. I saw him standing there, so don't you tell me I wouldn't have recognized Stalin! Stalin was a fine figure of a man! But this was a shabby little guy, his face looked like it had been blasted with peas. And he didn't have a mustache either."

"But once in the cell," asked the presenter, "did he start behaving calmly then?"

"Calmly, you must be joking!" Lapochkin exclaimed excitedly. "He hammered on the door with his feet, yelled, cajoled, and swore at everyone. 'You,' he said to me, 'you fascist pig, if you let me out, I'll make you a colonel, and if you don't, I'll have you shot.' And he carried on creating a racket like that until I couldn't stand it anymore. I'm a Chekist, so I know how to restrain myself, but I'm not made of iron."

"Do you mean to say that you beat him?" the presenter asked.

"Well, what does that mean, beat him? I whacked him a couple of times across the neck. What could I do, if he wouldn't listen to normal straightforward talk?"

Naturally, in trying to reconstruct the details of this mysterious story, we did not rely solely on the testimony of the old man Lapochkin. We also questioned other witnesses of those events, but there are not many of them left now. One former political prisoner, whose memory does not inspire confidence, told us that Stalin was not held in solitary at all, but in a mass cell, in fact in the same mass cell where he himself was held. This cell was inhabited by a motley crew of individuals, including Socialist Revolutionaries, Trotskyites, rootless cosmopolitans, currency speculators, and a bandit by the name of Khan Baty. Of course, the new occupant was placed in the cell without a name, under the number indicated above, but no one had forbidden him to introduce himself. Which is what he did. When he walked into the cell, naturally they paid attention to him and asked who he was. He said: "I am Stalin."

Probably he was hoping to create a great stir with his announcement, perhaps even start a revolt among the prisoners, but nothing of the kind happened. A prison isn't a loony bin, but in those times especially there were plenty of people with delusions of various kinds, or who pretended to be loony.

"Fair enough," said Baty, "when I was doing my last stretch, I met Lenin. Since you're a new boy here, Stalin, you'll sleep by the can. You'll move up later, if you make an effort."

"In here," remarked the former black marketer Dusik Dorman, "it's pretty much the same as out in Sovietland; non-Party members live on the floor by the gash bucket, and the Party members have the bunks."

I asked the person who told me this story: "Didn't any of you realize that Stalin *was* Stalin?"

"Well no," he said, surprised at that himself after all those years. "But how could we have guessed? He didn't have a mustache. And a Stalin without a mustache isn't Stalin. And then there was the other Stalin, with a mustache. The one that sat in the Kremlin with his mustache, and stood on the Mausoleum, and spoke at all the especially important meetings and celebrations, and stood for election as a deputy of the Supreme Soviet . . ."

It goes without saying that I did not limit myself to the testimony of two old men, but my attempts to gain access to the Lubyanka archives ended in total failure. I regretted not having tried to do it in the early nineties of the previous century, when many things were more accessible and for fifty dollars you could carry off half an archive, but now . . . Ah well, it can't be helped. We have been obliged to reconstitute the events of the past on the basis of sources that are not entirely reliable, comparing contradictory claims of fact and employing our own intuition to extract our story lines from the inexhaustible source of thin air.

35

THE DAY WAS DECLINING TOWARD EVENING and thick, gray snow was falling outside the windows of the Lubyanka when two wardens—Lapochkin and Ivanov—delivered prisoner No. 37/14 Sh, with no mask and no mustache, to the office of the People's Commissar of State Security. The prisoner's white silk shirt was crumpled, his shoes had no laces, and his trousers had no belt or buttons. To prevent them from falling down, the prisoner had to hold them with both hands, which is what he did.

He was a pitiful sight. He had hardly slept at all the whole night long, shivering in the freezing cold and thinking that he was going to be shot. When he occasionally did fall asleep, he immediately started dreaming that the door of the cell was opening soundlessly to admit a prosecutor, a doctor, and the men who would carry out his sentence. He cried out and was woken by his own cry. Only the day before he had imagined that he was the leader of the nations, a great general and scholar, a luminary of all the sciences, and ruler of one sixth of the world's land surface, that is, something rather like an emperor.

. . . The buttons had been cut off his trousers to make him feel wretched and pitiful. And indeed, how can a man not feel pitiful when he has to use both hands to hold his pants up? He can't help it. Only the day before, with a single word, a gesture of his hand, or a movement of his finger, he could set in motion immense armies and entire nations, force them to migrate thousands of kilometers from one place to another, make them dig canals and build dams, he could have any number of people shot or starved to death, and start a world war, but now he couldn't do anything except hold his pants with both hands to stop them from falling down.

The escorts led him into the office and stood him in the center of it a meter and a half from the desk, then left immediately on Lavrentii Pavlovich's instructions. Beria sat at his desk, the prisoner stood in the middle of the office. Beria looked at the prisoner and smiled benevolently, the prisoner looked at the floor, but sometimes cast a glance filled with burning hatred at Beria.

After a long silence, Beria said: "Hello, Goga!"

The prisoner shuddered involuntarily and gave Beria a surprised, questioning look.

"Goga, didn't I just say hello to you?" said Beria.

The prisoner paused and then asked, "Why are you calling me some stupid name?"

Beria protested. "Why is it a stupid name? It's a very good name, Goga. Georgii, Goga, what's wrong with that?"

"There's nothing wrong with it, but you know it's not my name."

The voice of the People's Commissar of State Security turned flinty. "I call you Goga, and if I call you Goga, that means you are Goga. Do you understand me, Goga?"

The prisoner didn't answer.

Beria scooted out rapidly from behind his desk, walked up to the prisoner and held out his hand. "Hello, Goga!"

"Take your hand away," said the prisoner.

"Hello, Goga!" the People's Commissar repeated and smacked the prisoner so hard across the face that he fell over onto the floor, let go of his trousers, and grabbed hold of his head, expecting to be kicked. But he wasn't kicked.

Beria stood over him and said, "Get up, Goga, get up."

The prisoner got up off the floor with a great struggle and grabbed hold of his pants again to stop them from falling down.

"There, you see, Goga," Lavrentii Pavlovich said to him in a gentle, paternal tone of voice. "I think you're already getting used to your role and your name. Is that right, Goga?"

The prisoner didn't answer.

"Goga, I asked you if you are getting used to your role and your name. You must always answer my questions, Goga. Because if you don't answer, I'll have to ask other people to help, people who, as you know, can help anyone to answer, just as long as he's still alive. You yourself taught me, Goga, that if we wish to obtain some kind of confession from someone and we try very hard, we can reduce even the strongest man of iron to a whimpering lump of meat, and in the end he will tell us what we want to hear anyway. Think about it, Goga, and tell me that you understand me."

The prisoner thought about it. He knew what Lavrentii Pavlovich's assistants were capable of, and as a man with a realistic cast of mind, he realized it was better to agree with Beria here and now than after he had been reduced to a whimpering lump of meat. Of course, he hoped that Beria's scheme would fail. He believed that people who were devoted to him, perhaps Marshal Zhukov, or Marshal Konev, or someone else would understand that a monstrous substitution had taken place, and then . . . Then he would have to think how to make the death of this traitor and scoundrel as slow and agonizing as possible. But while he was still in the hands of this blackguard, the blackguard could do whatever he wanted with him. In these circumstances it was simply stupid to ask for trouble. What was needed above all now was a cool head and prudent action. He mustn't give them any reason to maim him.

"Yes," he said with a nod and added in a barely audible voice: "I am Goga and I understand you."

"That's good!" said Lavrentii Pavlovich, delighted. "That's just wonderful. Now that we've agreed that you are Goga, we can discuss a few other things as well, Goga. Have a seat here, in the armchair. Make yourself comfortable."

The armchair was standing beside the conference table that abutted on the desk of the People's Commissar. Beria sat down facing him and clapped his hands. In our text various highly placed individuals clap their hands very often. But it can't be helped. In those days a clap of the hands was a device widely used to attract attention to yourself or something close to you. Beria clapped his hands and two generals appeared in the office. Beria asked them to get something done, they passed on the instructions, and the table in front of Stalin was set with a bottle of Khvanchkara, a dish of pies, a plate of suluguni cheese, a bowl of fruit, and a box of Herzegovina Flor *papyrosas*. Beria gave a sign and the generals disappeared. Beria poured wine for himself and his guest and said with a grin:

"Don't worry, it's not poisoned. We can swap glasses if you like. Your health!" He held his glass out toward Stalin, who held out his own reluctantly. They clinked glasses. Beria broke off a piece of suluguni.

"Right then, dear fellow," he began, "this is what I have to say to you. You, of course, are a great man, I won't argue with that. But you are an extremely cruel tyrant who will stop at nothing for the sake of his own personal power. You have exterminated and continue to exterminate very many people, often using me to do it. And many people think that I am the one who is so cruel, that I do it all and you are a good man, you sit in the Kremlin and know nothing about it. While in actual fact I only carry out your commands. By nature I am a very kind man. Yes, of course, I am a womanizer, but not a butcher. You made me into a butcher. You drove millions of people into the collective farms and turned them into slaves without passports. The people live in constant fear, the country is in a state of profound stagnation, and nothing can change while you are in power. I have decided to set things right. At the risk of my own head, I kidnapped you and replaced you with the actor Melovani. He is a very good actor, in fact a better actor than I had expected. He plays you so well, nobody has an inkling that he is not you. Neither the members of the Politburo, nor even the commander of your own guard, General Vlasik, have noticed anything. And now the country is really run by me. He plays the part, I direct him, and you are superfluous. What should I do in this situation? I know what you would do with me, if you were in my place. But I won't do that. I could also dispatch you to some stable and attach some Private Chonkin or other to you, to make you haul water and beat you with a whip. But I won't do that either, if you accept my proposal. I think you have no choice and you must accept, Goga. You're an intelligent man, you're one of the most intelligent men on earth, you understand that if you do what I say you will live, and live rather well. If you don't do what I say, I shall have to do to you what you would do to me or, in an act of supreme mercy, have you sent to a stable and fed on oats. Do you understand me, Goga?"

"Tell me your proposal."

"It is simple and will be good for you. You will not merely live, you will live well. The burden of responsibility that you have borne for so many years will drop from your shoulders . . ."

"Be more concise."

"I will be concise. The artiste Melovani is playing the role of Stalin in the Kremlin, and you will play the role of Stalin in the theater, but your name will be Georgii Melovani. Eh? What do you think about that? Why are you staring at me like that?"

Stalin gazed fixedly at Beria. Then he started shaking all over. He grabbed hold of the edge of the table and started slowly getting up, glaring at Beria with a gaze of wild hatred that seemed about to reduce the other man to ashes.

"Stop! Stop!" shouted Beria and leaned over the table, putting his hands on the shoulders of his former leader and teacher and pushing him back down onto the chair. "Listen, dear fellow," he said, not calling Stalin Goga anymore. "Before you start getting angry and objecting, just think. You'll never go back to the Kremlin now, you understand I can't allow that. So you have a choice. On the one hand, you know what. On the other hand, you remain alive and well and play the same part, not in the Kremlin, but in the theater, there's no great difference. You'll still come on, as usual, with your pipe, and you'll say a few words, the dramatist Pogodin will write them for you."

"What are you talking about?" Stalin sighed. "How am I going to act? I'm not an artiste. My memory's failing, I won't be able to remember the words that your Pogodin writes for me."

"*Vai-vai-vai!* What a great disaster that is! If you can't remember, don't bother. Just say anything. Say the same—pardon me for the expression—benign bullshit that you do in real life, your beloved people will applaud every entrance and exit. And shower you with flowers."

Stalin reached out to the Herzegovina Flor box to take a *papyrosa*. As he took it, his fingers cramped up and the *papyrosa* broke. He took another one. His hand was trembling. Beria held out a lighted match for him.

"But tell me, Lavrentii," said Stalin and started coughing. "But tell me, Lavrentii," he repeated and waited for the lump in his throat to pass before continuing. "What will you do if I address the people from the stage, or somewhere else, and say that I am not the actor Melovani, but Stalin? Can you imagine what the people will do to you? They will sweep you away, they will tear you into little pieces. Or will your fine fellows shoot me to prevent me from doing that?"

"*Oi-yoi-yoi!*" Beria exclaimed, clowning. "How could you ever imagine anything like that? Who would ever allow my fine fellows to shoot such a great actor? No, dear Goga, I won't allow anyone to fire at you. And what's more, you have my permission to say anything you want. But before you decide to appear before the people and tell them that you are Stalin, think what the people will think about you. And what our psychiatrists will say about it. Have a good think about that, dear Goga."

Stalin finished his *papyrosa* and lit another one from the match that was obligingly held out. "Ah, Lavrentii, Lavrentii!" he said quietly. "You're an even bigger bastard than I am."

THE FOLLOWING MORNING had been chosen by Lavrentii Pavlovich for the second step in the implementation of his grand design, a task that he thought would not be very difficult. After breakfast he sat on at the table for a while, picking his teeth with the pointed end of a fingernail, and thinking about the pleasant things in store for him. He smiled to himself, clapped his hands, and set off once again to the nearby dacha in his gleaming limousine. Here, to his displeasure, he was searched in exactly the same way as before, as if nothing had happened. "Well, but that's right," he thought. "They mustn't know that anything has happened." General Vlasik in person escorted him to the dacha, where the artiste Melovani, who looked so much like Stalin, was sitting in the corner chair in the parlor with his extinguished pipe in his hand, wearing the uniform tunic of a generalissimus.

"You can go," Melovani said to Vlasik, then turned to his visitor and said: "Sit down!"

And he indicated the chair facing him with a movement of his chin, not making the slightest attempt to get up himself. Beria was unpleasantly surprised once again: Why was he behaving in such an insolent fashion? After all, when there were no witnesses, he ought to remember the real line of seniority.

"Listen," said Beria, "I've prepared a few little decrees, and you can tell that old goat Kalinin to promulgate them immediately."

"Some little decrees?" Melovani asked. "What are they?"

"Here," said Beria, holding out a sheet of paper to him, "this is the draft for a Party Central Committee Plenum decree to rename the Council of People's Commissars the Council of Ministers. The second one is to appoint me chairman of the Council of Ministers."

"And is that all?" asked Melovani.

"No. Here," said Beria, holding out another sheet of paper, "this is the draft of a Central Committee Plenum decree concerning my election as General Secretary. And here also is the draft of a decree concerning the election of Comrade Stalin, that is, you, as Honorary Chairman of the Party. It's a very good position. You'll live in ideal conditions, receive a large salary, and do nothing."

"Interesting," murmured Melovani. "Very interesting. You know what the difference between simply a chairman and an honorary chairman is,

Lavrentii? It's like the difference between the words 'sire' and 'sir.' Well, sir, I do not accept your draft decrees."

Melovani tapped the sheets of paper against his knee to align them neatly. Then he tore them up.

"What's the meaning of this?" Beria shouted. "Listen, *genetsvale*!" He was overwhelmed by two feelings: indignation and bewilderment. "You seem to have felt your way too deeply into your role. I didn't put you in this position so that you could decide what to accept and what not to accept for yourself. I put you here so that you could *pretend* to control things. But in fact I am going to control everything. All you have to do is listen to my cues and do as I tell you."

"So that's it!" the artiste Melovani exclaimed, seeming offended. He got up off his chair, lit his pipe, and started walking across the room. "So, you say I've felt my way too deeply into my role?" He paused and blew out three smoke rings. "Well let me tell you, *katso*,"* he said, using a form of address more insolent than the previous one. "You're right, I really have felt my way into my role. I've felt my way so far in that now I feel that I *am* Stalin. And you are only Beria. So I will manage things, and you will do what Stalin tells you to do, like before. That is, what I tell you."

"Why, you sly bastard!" Beria exclaimed, fuming. "What do you mean by imagining anything of the sort! Why, I'll . . . I'll . . . I know what I'll do to you! I . . ." He reached into the pocket where he usually kept a small Walther lady's handgun, forgetting that it had been taken from him at the checkpoint. But while he was fumbling in his pocket, Melovani clapped his hands (another handclap—evidently these people simply couldn't manage without this gesture)—and General Vlasik instantly appeared in the doorway. He looked attentively at the person he thought was Stalin, then at Beria, who immediately pulled his hand out of his pocket and started brushing stray crumbs off his jacket.

"Is there something you would like, Comrade Stalin?" the general asked in a thin, ingratiating voice.

"There is," Stalin confirmed. "Tell them to serve us two cups of Turkish coffee. With cognac. Georgian cognac. No, better Armenian. Or even French."

And he waved his hand lavishly.

From that time on, right up until March 5, 1953, the state of the U.S.S.R. was controlled by the People's Artist G. M. Melovani, and he

* "Man" or "my man" (Georgian).

did it so skillfully that absolutely no one at all noticed the substitution. Neither his comrades in the Politburo, nor the members of his guard, nor even his own children, Sveta and Vasya. Admittedly, it is well known during this particular period, that is, from December 1945 to December 1949, the children were not allowed to see their dear papa on a variety of pretexts. But other people close to Stalin didn't notice the substitution at all, as we have already said, because the state machine continued to operate as before. Just as they had before, the miners dug up coal, the steelmakers made steel, the cooks made soup, the collective farmworkers were paid in labor days, children went to school, military men studied the biography of Comrade Stalin, and the personnel of the Right Place sought, found, and eliminated enemies of the Soviet regime and of Comrade Stalin in person. Some people, of course, won't believe this, they'll say it's impossible, they'll say: How could a simple artiste who hadn't graduated from any special courses manage the state? But my answer to that is: a bad business is easy to manage, as experience has shown. States, even very big ones, have been managed by all sorts of surprising people. From time to time there have been sovereigns of some intelligence, but most rulers have been fools, cranks, madmen, halfwits, semi-educated dolts, schizophrenics, and paranoiacs. In Soviet times the most highly educated of them had studied at the university but never completed his course, while his successor had not completed his studies at a seminary, and they were followed by people who could barely even pronounce the words needed for their speeches, such as "communistic" and "intensification of production," unless they were under hypnosis. These people proved that, as Vladimir Ilich Lenin cynically foresaw, even a cook could manage the state, and we have grounds to believe that a horse could, too. Georgii Melovani was, after all, neither a cook nor a horse, but a People's Artist; he had a gift for dramatic impersonation and was a talented man in general. Many years later in America another artiste governed the country, also entirely successfully. Of course, you might have expected that Georgii Melovani, as a representative of the liberal arts who had found himself in the supreme post by chance, would have wished to encourage a certain softening of laws and procedures. And at first he did intend to encourage this. But once he had donned, figuratively speaking, the Cap of Monomakh, he immediately developed severe megalomania and a persecution complex. He was obsessed by the fear that someone would notice the substitution. In his struggle to conquer this fear, he started eliminating people who had been too close to Stalin and had known him too well. When he discovered that the commander of Stalin's guard, General Nikolai Sidorovich Vlasik, kept a regular diary in secret, Melovani ordered the diary to be obtained for a short period and glanced into it. The diary was devoted entirely to the life of Comrade Stalin. The almost daily entries were about when Comrade Stalin woke up, what he ate, whom he received, what instructions he gave, what he talked about at table, and the jokes he told. All the texts were imbued with a spirit of great piety, but the recent entries included these lines:

> It sometimes seems to me that in recent times Comrade Stalin has changed for the better—he has become younger and his appearance has improved . . . Yesterday Comrade Stalin called me dear fellow. He said: "Dear fellow, do you think you could bring me a glass of kefir?" It's strange, he has never drunk kefir before, or called me dear fellow. The other day he inquired for what offense Mikhail Ivanovich Kalinin's wife had been imprisoned and asked me if I thought she could be released. It seems to me that in recent times Comrade Stalin has not only improved on the outside, but also begun to show a certain softening of attitude toward his enemies that is untypical of him.

After reading this entry, Stalin, that is, Melovani, immediately re- moved Vlasik from his post and decided not to show any more softness, in order not to arouse anyone's suspicions. And indeed, he was a match for the person he had replaced, in the sense that he was just as terrifying, even though, as far as we are aware, his family line was not known to include any wild animals. However, no one knows (science has not yet developed that far) exactly how animal characteristics are manifested in a man's character, although this process is especially typical of vain, power-hungry individuals who wish to rule states, nations, and armies as if they were swarms, droves, flocks, or herds. When I look at people like that, I wonder: What do we know about their origins? I don't mean their close relatives, their grandmothers and grandfathers, or even their great-grandmothers and great-grandfathers, but those human forebears from the depths of time who have left us no written records of their ex- istence. How did they live, with whom did they mingle, into whom did they discharge their seed, and whose did they accept into themselves? Darwin once explained to us that a monkey could turn into a man. But how did he know that? Who told him? As certain pieces of research—

scientific, pseudoscientific, empirical, and other—have shown, according to the laws of large numbers, in distant antiquity the mass copulation of everybody with anybody could have produced the most varied and surprising results. Including the phenomenon of a highly varied range of hybrid creatures. This is hard to prove and practically impossible to refute, but if you look at individual representatives of the human species, it is possible, when considering the characters of those who wish to rule us, to discern something vulpine in some, something equine in others, and something jackalish in yet others, while in the character of those who wish to be ruled there is something from other, more docile animals. It was of them that the great poet wrote:

> By honor's battle-cry unstirred,
> Ye peaceful nations, browse in peace!
> Freedom means nothing to the herd
> Meant to be slaughtered or be fleeced.
> A yoke with tinkling bells will be
> Each generation's legacy.

However, let us set this subject aside for the time being and leave the artiste Melovani in his new role in his new walk of life and remember the real Comrade Stalin, who has been obliged to play the role of Georgii Melovani. At first this actor felt the position in which he found himself to be extremely humiliating. Even though on stage he played the part of the leader of the peoples, in the theater he was just another actor. He had to go to rehearsals, learn scripts, and listen to all the director's comments, which were sometimes offensive.

The director, Alexei Bocharov, was a polite man in everyday life, but at rehearsals he shouted at the actors and called them all sorts of names. Melovani felt the sharp edge of his tongue especially often.

"You must realize," Bocharov impressed on Georgii Mikhailovich, "that you're not playing yourself here, but a great man. Try just a little bit to imagine yourself in his place. In the place of a man on whom the fate of all mankind depends. But you're playing some kind of office manager with an affected Georgian accent and fussy gestures. I realize how hard it is for you to rise higher, but make an effort."

Some of the actors took offense at Bocharov, but Stalin-Melovani put up with him. Strangely enough, he had developed an attitude of tolerance—previously quite untypical of him—for human failings, weaknesses, and vices. As he gradually grew accustomed to his role, he even began taking a special kind of satisfaction in it. He played Stalin in all the productions that included the role of Stalin, he earned a good salary, was rewarded with thunderous applause, and bore no responsibility for anything; the day came when he even decided that this kind of life suited him perfectly well. But sometimes, when he had been drinking, he would blow his top and start shouting at anyone who happened to be nearby: "I'm Stalin! I'm Stalin!" Some people laughed at him and said: "Look what it does to a man, constantly playing a role like that!" Or "Look where drinking has gotten him!" Everyone, however, regarded him as a harmless mad- man. But there were times when he yelled such outrageous things in the street that he was picked up and carted off to the slammer or the loony bin. However, once they had established who he was, they immediately apologized because, although he might not be Stalin, he was a People's Artist who played the role of Stalin, that is, the kind of individual it was better not to get involved with.

37

EARLY IN THE SPRING OF 1946 it was announced at the camp for displaced persons that farmers had come from America to recruit work- ers—in other words, agricultural laborers. About a hundred men lined up in front of the bunkhouse. Those who were familiar with agriculture were asked to take a step forward. The entire hundred took that step, including the "academicians" and both Thinkers, although some of them couldn't tell a harrow from a spade and only knew what a cow looked like from the wrappers of Moo-Cow candy. What motivated them to take that step was not the desire for a closer relationship with agricul- ture, but for a more distant one with their motherland.

The group of farmers was led by a raw-boned, stooped man with a stiff leathery face, a droopy mustache, and a wide-brimmed leather cow- boy hat, who spoke in a mixture of Russian, Ukrainian, and English and evidently already had experience dealing with individuals aspiring to work in American agriculture. He peered at every man who claimed to be a peasant and flung out tricky questions at random. What's the differ- ence between autumn-sown crops and spring-sown crops? What's the difference between a winnower and a thresher? How many teats does a she-goat have? And so on in the same vein. Chonkin was surprised when he heard it.

One of the Thinkers failed at the very first question, for not knowing why a collar was used on a horse and a yoke was used on an ox.

"Because a collar won't fit over the horns," the questioner explained, promptly losing all interest in the Thinker.

Everybody was nervous as they waited for the questions, but Chonkin felt nervous for a different reason. When the questioner reached him, he said:

"Howdy, Pan Kaliuzhny!"

Starting at being addressed with the Polish for "Mr. Kaliuzhny," the man gave Chonkin a very searching look.

"How do you know my name?" he asked.

"Why shouldn't I?" Chonkin exclaimed, puzzled. "We were in the slammer together, shared the same bunk."

"In the slammer?" the farmer repeated. "What's that, a slammer? I was in jail? On a bunk? You were inside with someone as looked like what I do, called Kaliuzhny?"

"I was inside with you," Chonkin insisted, unable to understand why Mr. Kaliuzhny was being so stubborn.

"No," said Kaliuzhny. "You weren't inside with me, that was my brother Stepan. But I'm Petro. Him and me's twins. I fled out of Poland at 1930 and then into America. And they put him inside for me. And pinned some kind of Protskyism on him, they did. When was it you saw him? At forty-one? And I haven't heard anything about him since the thirties. Well, what do you say, will you go in America?"

"Sure I'll go," said Chonkin, without even the vaguest idea of what America was and where exactly it was located. So Chonkin got into the chosen group practically without any exam at all.

PART THREE

Chonkin International

1

THE JOURNEY FROM HAMBURG TO NEW YORK was long and wearisome. Chonkin sailed on the deck of the *Santa Monica*—which seemed a very big ship to him but was actually an average-sized steamship of prewar design. The steamship shuddered with the strain, but plowed on stubbornly toward its distant goal, leaving a wake of white broken water and puffing out smoke through its three tall smokestacks. The smoke first rose up in a black column, then curved over in a tight loop, sinking right back down to the water and trailing behind the ship in an endless plume.

Although Chonkin had heard of the existence of seas and oceans, he could never have imagined that there were spaces somewhere so vast that whichever way you looked there was water, more water, and nothing but water. They had rough weather several times on the journey. The vessel swayed from bow to stern and back again. As if it were riding a gigantic swing. Another passenger on the *Santa Monica,* a former Soviet sailor, told Chonkin: "When it's like this, we say it's swilling. Water pouring into the hold and out through the smokestack." The passengers had been given paper bags to be sick into, but they were all used up in the first few days of stormy weather, and then all three decks and the stairways between them were covered in vomit. All the passengers waited impatiently for dry land to appear, like members of Magellan's or Columbus's expeditions. But the dry land also received the travelers inhospitably. They were put ashore first on Ellis Island, known as the Island of Tears to those who had visited it. Here the people who had money were allowed through without any unnecessary formalities, but the ones without money were questioned very intensively: Were they former Nazis or Communists, did they intend to engage in subversive activity, were they hoping to work unofficially and avoid paying taxes?

Many were turned back without any explanation of the reason, and that was why this was the Island of Tears. But Chonkin was lucky. With Mr. Kaliuzhny's help, he passed the test and soon found himself on a corn-growing farm in the state of Ohio.

FIFTEEN YEARS WENT BY . . . Chonkin's life had changed dramatically. For those who have not experienced the kind of changes our hero went through, it is hard to imagine how someone so Russian to the marrow of his bones could put down roots in a country as alien to him as America. But that was what he did. And very successfully, too. Just as the American potato adapted to the soil of Russia, so the Russian man Chonkin adapted to the soil of America. In his previous life, no matter how hard they tried to teach him, he hadn't been able to master the art of standing to attention or making a left about-face (why not a right one?), he couldn't remember what the GOELRO plan was, and even what posts Comrade Stalin held. But here he found himself in circumstances that were entirely natural for him and figured out what was what very quickly. Perhaps it was only here that he came to feel like a full-fledged human being.

Previously he had never been trusted to do anything except drive a horse. Mr. Kaliuzhny didn't have a single horse, but he did have two tractors, two combines, and two automobiles. Constantly surprising himself, Chonkin mastered all this equipment and even developed a distinct self-respect—within reasonable limits, naturally. As for the English language, certain researchers have calculated that the average peasant gets by with a vocabulary of three or four hundred words. Chonkin eventually mastered approximately this number, too. And since he also knew three or four hundred words of Russian, by the standards of his neighbors, he could have passed for a polyglot. Especially since in his speech these two languages amalgamated and coexisted.

There were three of them living together: Mr. Kaliuzhny, his wife Barbara, whom he had brought from Canada, and Chonkin, who was allocated a section of the house with its own entrance, toilet, and shower. He also had his own kitchen, but they ate together. Their meals were filling and monotonous. In the morning Barbara prepared an omelette, or

cornflakes with milk, or red grapefruit baked in the oven, and decaffein-
ated coffee. In the daytime the men took with them plastic boxes containing sausages or hamburgers, generously doused with ketchup, and
in the evening at home they ate corn grits with milk or farmer cheese.
They didn't drink any alcohol at all. At mealtimes Barbara served plain
water with ice. In the summer they worked from dawn till dusk, in the
winter they allowed themselves to relax, and in the evening they played
cards. And when TV appeared, they sat down in front of the screen with
popcorn and chewed it as they watched the old films.

On Sundays they drove twelve miles to the church, where Father
Michael (who had a day job as a fireman) read sermons and led prayers
without the slightest concern for any canonical sacraments or rules.
The prayers dealt with the affairs and concerns of his parishioners, their
health and the health of their relatives, friends, and acquaintances, and
the health and welfare of their beloved animals, including dogs, cats,
cows, goats, sheep, and horses.

Chonkin integrated so well into American life that it soon came to
seem like the only natural and normal life to him. Russia became a distant place for him, and not only in the geographical sense—as time went
by the spiritual bond with his motherland grew weaker and weaker. He
thought of Russia less and less often, especially since reasons to think
about it were few and far between. They had a radio in the house that
mostly broadcast only local news, from fires and accidents to murders
and suicides. True, murders and suicides happened extremely rarely, because the folks who lived here were simple, healthy in mind and body,
not given to depression, and with a sound moral code assimilated from
birth. Not all the farmers read the Holy Writ, not all of them could for-
mulate the rules of their behavior, but they all had consciences that told
them it was wrong to kill, to steal, to lie, or to bear false witness, and they
were not tolerantly inclined toward adultery. In the American provinces
of those times (and it even happens sometimes nowadays), they didn't
lock up their houses, and they couldn't even imagine that someone might
come in and take what wasn't theirs. Chonkin's life revolved around the
local people and the local interests, he knew nothing of what was happening in his motherland. But he heard about Stalin's death, when it
came, from the farmer Timothy Parker, who had been told about it by
Jessie Clark, a regular reader of the newspaper *The Village Voice*. Then
Chonkin himself heard about it on the radio and felt surprised that even
people like Stalin sometimes die.

Stalin's death was deeply mourned by the entire Soviet people. It gave rise to the fatal crush on Trubnaya Square and enlivened the camp of the Sovietologists, who bet against each other on who would take Stalin's place: Beria, Malenkov, or Molotov? Several of them expressed the suspicion that the Soviet overlord had not died a natural death. The suspicions that arose then are still expressed even today, and the prime suspect is, of course, Lavrentii Pavlovich Beria. With good reason. He feared the living Stalin—in both versions—more than the others did and possibly had greater hopes than the others of seizing the throne when it became free. Some researchers believe that apart from Beria, certain of his brothers-in-arms also had an interest in the Soviet leader's death, including Molotov, Malenkov, Kaganovich, and Khrushchev. There is also the theory that the possible participants in the assassination were acting not only to save themselves but to save the entire world. Some scholars assert that there are grounds for believing that by the beginning of 1953, Stalin, or the person who sat in the Kremlin and called himself by that name, had developed a profound paranoia and, realizing that his life was coming to an end, had determined not to depart alone but to take as many other people with him as possible. Perhaps even the entire world. To achieve this, he had devised a plan to plunge mankind into World War Three. The first step toward war was to be the deportation of the Jews, planned for March 5, 1953. It would have provoked international indignation, triggered a sharp rise in international tension and mutual threats, and the threats could have been followed by action. We won't get into a discussion of how serious these theories are, but we have an additional theory of our own, which does not refute any of those listed above.

IN ORDER TO PRESENT OUR ARGUMENTS CLEARLY, it is necessary to recall a visit that Stalin, or the pseudo-Stalin—in other words, the Stalin who was actually in control of the country at that time—paid to the Moscow Drama Theater (MDT) on February 28. On February 27, he had watched *Swan Lake* yet again, and was due to watch the film *Retribution* the next day with his comrades-in-arms. But on the way back from the Bolshoi Theater to Kuntsevo, he changed his mind after being prompted by Lavrentii Beria, who was riding in the same car with him.

Since these two men had clarified which of them was the boss, Beria had accepted that he had no other option but to go back to his customary role as Comrade Stalin's devoted friend, brother-in-arms, and confidant. While he continued to weave his plots, he did so with greater caution than previously. Melovani trusted Beria even less than the real Stalin had, and to be on the safe side, he transferred the Ministry of State Security into the hands of a certain Ignatiev, while Beria was put in charge of the atomic energy industry, which Stalin regarded as the same kind of disaster area as agriculture. However, Melovani was, after all, only an artiste, with insufficient understanding of intrigue at its most complex level. He didn't realize that Ignatiev had been planted on him by Beria, as had Ivan Khrustalev, the replacement for the unfortunate General Vlasik, who was slandered, removed from his post, and eventually imprisoned on criminal charges. Of course, the real Stalin would have spotted what Beria was up to, but the pseudo-Stalin remained an artiste at heart and therefore allowed the wily villain to stay at his side.

And so, on February 27 Lavrentii Beria offered to see Stalin home after the performance, in order to discuss with him the forthcoming deportation of the Jews and the anticipated storm of national fury that would follow it. But, on seeing that Stalin, after the ballet he had watched, was in too benign a mood for such a discussion, he decided to postpone the subject and continue talking about art. Especially since a good excuse for doing so turned up. As they drove along Arbat Street, Beria spotted a poster and drew Stalin's attention to it. The poster informed the public that tomorrow at the MDT there would be a performance of the play *Stalin in October* by the Stalin Prize–winning dramatist Mikhail Pogodin.

"What's this?" pseudo-Stalin asked with a frown. "Has the cult of my personality sunk to such demented depths that they replace Lenin with Stalin in a well-known dramatic work?"

"No, no," Beria protested. "Nothing of the kind. *Lenin in October* is Lenin in October 1917. But this is about October 1941. Of course, you do remember what happened in October 1941, don't you, Koba?"

"Yes, of course," said Koba, brightening up, "of course, I remember very well. In October 1941 I was in Kuibyshev, and I met this little singer . . ."

"Pardon me, dear Koba. Permit me to interrupt you. I think you are getting things slightly confused. The actor Melovani was in Kuibyshev but you, Comrade Stalin, with the courage so typical of you, remained in Moscow and by your personal presence inspired our glorious warriors defending Moscow to feats of great heroism."

"Ah, yes, yes, that's right," Koba agreed hastily, "while the actor Melovani was chasing singers deep in the rear, I, Comrade Stalin, with the courage so typical of me . . . Can you perhaps remind me exactly how it was?"

"Why me?" Beria asked with a shrug. "It's Saturday tomorrow. You can take a little break from your daily labors and amuse yourself by watching how that time is portrayed by the dramatist Pogodin, the artistes of the MDT, and our principal, so to speak, People's Artist."

Stalin reacted rather tensely at first as he tried to figure out if Lavrentii's suggestion was a cover for some kind of trick. He looked at Beria closely. Beria replied with the unblinking gaze of an honest man.

"Why not?" said Stalin, and his eyes glinted mischievously. "Let's take a look at what our People's Artist is doing there. Shakespeare said: 'All the world's a stage, and all the men and women merely players.' But it's one thing to play a part in life and quite another to play it on the stage. Not everyone can even play himself convincingly. Just imagine that they've let you out on stage to play the part of yourself, Beria. Do you think you could play it? No. The way you'd play it, everyone in the audience would say: No, that's not Beria."

"But why do you think that, Koba?" Lavrentii Pavlovich asked resentfully. "How can you tell, Koba, that the world has not lost an actor of genius in me?"

"No, Lavrentii," said Stalin, shaking his head. "The world hasn't lost anyone in you. You're a villain. And as Pushkin said, genius and villainy are not compatible. But tomorrow we'll take a look at another villain and decide if the great poet was right or not."

The outcome of this conversation was the appearance at the MDT next morning of certain men in civilian clothes who threw the entire place into turmoil. They examined all the entrances and exits, decided that one of them was superfluous, and ordered it to be boarded up. They checked the list of everyone involved in the performance, including the assistant director, the theater manager, the usherettes, the lighting crew, and the stagehands. They ordered the director of the production to be temporarily suspended from duty because of his Jewish surname. They gave instructions to reserve thirty front orchestra seats for security men. The director, frightened to death, held a special meeting with the company and then spoke separately with the actor playing the lead role.

"Georgii Mikhailovich," he said agitatedly. "I beg you, please, not a drop to drink and take this business very seriously. I know that Comrade

Stalin thinks very highly of you as an artiste, so please, I implore you, try to justify Comrade Stalin's confidence in you. Today you must act so that Comrade Stalin believes in the image you create, believes that you are him."

"I assure you," chuckled the pseudo-Melovani, also extremely agitated, "Comrade Stalin will certainly believe that I am him."

Although only a quarter of the tickets were sold at the ticket offices, the theater was a hundred percent full, thanks to secret agents and so-called front-line production workers herded in from the Hammer and Sickle plant—that is, people who worked on the production line very rarely because the management placed special trust in them and they were regularly sent to government meetings, demonstrations, conferences, hearings, and consultations, where they expressed the people's joy at, for instance, the overfulfillment of production plans, or fulminated against the international imperialists for still being alive.

ON THAT DAY THERE WAS A HEAVY SNOWFALL and several special machines worked into the evening, clearing away the snow in front of the theater. Exactly five minutes before the performance several long black limousines rolled up to the stage entrance, one after another. Stalin, Beria, Khrushchev, Malenkov, and Bulganin got out of them. They were shown through to their box and the show began immediately.

First they showed a large airplane. An engineer and a motor mechanic were preparing it for a flight. The motor mechanic said he had heard that the plane was going to take someone very important to the rear, perhaps even Stalin himself. The engineer objected that Stalin was not the kind of man who would abandon our capital to the whim of fate. The motor mechanic recalled Kutuzov, who had abandoned Moscow to the French and destroyed them by doing it. The engineer agreed, but he reminded the mechanic that first, in 1812 Moscow was not the capital and, second, Kutuzov was only one of the tsar's generals, but Stalin was the unique and irreplaceable leader of the whole of progressive mankind.

The scenery was changed and different people appeared on the stage—members of the State Defense Committee. They talked about the critical position on the front, about how the Germans had reached the very gates

of Moscow, about evacuating factories and state institutions to Kuibyshev, and Lavrentii Beria (the artiste Kvanturia), who was leading the
discussion, suggested that first of all they should get Comrade Stalin out
of Moscow since he was their greatest treasure. All the members of the
State Defense Committee agreed with Beria and voted to ask Comrade
Stalin to leave Moscow immediately. At this point Comrade Stalin himself appeared and was supposed to listen to the proposal and then reply
proudly, with a slight Georgian accent, that Comrade Stalin didn't leave
the field of battle when the going got really tough. But he wasn't given
a chance to listen to anything or say anything. The moment he walked
out on stage the audience went wild. Everyone in the theater jumped to
their feet and started applauding his entrance furiously. In the box the
other Stalin's companions looked at him and also jumped to their feet.
Fired up by them, even he stood up. The applause in the auditorium was
so loud that the walls of the theater seemed about to collapse. There were
shouts of "Bravo!" and "Hurrah for the great Stalin!" And then the audience spotted the other Stalin in his box and turned to him, then back to
the Stalin on the stage, then back to the one in the box, and they kept
swinging back and forth like that, whooping hysterically in a spontane-
ous outburst of mass schizophrenia.

Then the performance continued. Stalin strolled around the stage,
smoking his pipe and uttering a few tedious words, the airplane stood
there, waiting in vain for its passenger, the home militia lined up at the
army enlistment offices, then marched across Red Square and directly
to the front, singing "Arise, immense country!" and Comrade Stalin saw
them off, standing on the Mausoleum. Every time he appeared the audience greeted him with a storm of applause, exploding into shouts and
shrieks, pounding their hands together and flying into hysterics, then
turning toward the box and directing their ecstasy in that direction.

If that long-forgotten play were shown to a modern theatergoer, he
would probably leave before getting halfway through the first act. And
even in those days the public wasn't exactly breaking down the doors to
get in. However, the presence at the performance of two Stalins, the real
one and the one playing the role of the real one (the public, fed on various rumors, couldn't tell which was which, but it applauded them with
equal fervor) was the reason for the mass insanity. When the onstage
Stalin made his entrance to deliver the final monologue, the audience
greeted him with yet another burst of stormy applause and turned to the
box once again. But there was no one there.

The other Stalin, followed by all his brothers-in-arms, had left the box so quietly that no one had heard them. They put on their coats in the office of the theater manager, who asked with a guilty smile:

"Comrade Stalin, didn't you like the performance?"

"I did like it," replied Comrade Stalin. "But I didn't like it a lot."

"But would you like," asked the theater manager, screwing up his courage, "to make any comments to the actor Comrade Melovani?"

"No," said Stalin, "I don't want to tell him anything in person. But you tell him that he plays well. Convincingly. He has felt his way deeply into the role. He acts so well that even I can't tell which of us is real."

His entourage broke into loud laughter. He gave them a somber look and they fell silent, realizing that although he was joking, he was in a dark mood and it was best to keep their distance.

His mood really was as black as it could be. On the way to Kuntsevo he kept prodding the driver in the back and shouting: "Step on it! Step on it! Step on it!"

This was strange. He usually took good care of his life and didn't like to drive fast. Previously he, or rather, they—both the first and the second Stalin—had always driven through Moscow with ominous, unhurried majesty. Boris Slutsky described this in one of his poems, "God Rode in Four Cars." There were far more cars now, because his four were followed by the cars of his brothers-in-arms—each with his own bodyguards. The tires whispered, the dry, early-spring snow swirled in the air, the militiamen couldn't turn off the traffic lights fast enough and blew hysterical blasts on their whistles.

He tried to settle himself on the rear seat, feeling unusually agitated. The theater had stirred up a storm in his heart. He felt that he had made a fatal, irreparable mistake in his life by undertaking to play a role that was beyond his powers and not to his taste. Although he had had no choice but to undertake the role, that swine Lavrentii had pushed him into it. And at the beginning he had been seduced by it, too, wondering if he had the talent to play it so convincingly that no one would ever know or suspect. It had turned out that he had, and that had flattered his vanity. He had wanted to savor the delight of power. He had savored it and become intoxicated by it, but as soon as he took the burden on himself, its oppressive weight became unbearable. And every day it bore down on him more heavily. "Heavy are you, oh Cap of Monomakh!" He had thought that was just a dramatic turn of phrase. Now he realized it was much more than a phrase.

His power was unlimited. He could decide the fate of individuals and millions of people on a whim, and as time passed, he made ever more frequent use of this capability. He didn't like it, and it plunged him into despair. With a single word, hint, movement of his finger or nod of his head, he could set in motion masses numbering millions. He could elevate any of his subjects to celestial heights, cast him down, reward him for nothing, or have him killed for nothing. He distanced his brothers-in-arms from himself and jumbled them together in the Central Committee with individuals whom no one knew. He replaced the man who had been the head of his guard for many years, encouraged the persecution of the Jews throughout the country, and was planning to deport them on March 5. But the more widely he employed his power to do evil to people, the more he felt the effects of evil on himself. The fear that he would face vengeance for everything that he had done penetrated into his very soul and took complete control of it.

He was afraid of shots from around corners, poisoned food, the judgment of the peoples of the world—and he didn't exclude the judgment of God. This fear became more and more impossible to bear. It tormented him ceaselessly day and night. At night, if he didn't sleep, he seemed to see someone incorporeal entering his room, intending to kill him, strangle him, drown him. And if he slept, he was harassed by nightmares after which he rose exhausted and yellow-faced, with a feverish gleam in his eyes and the desire to tear someone's liver out.

At this same time the real Iosif Vissarionovich Stalin, having played himself yet again, went to his dressing room. He took a bottle that had already been started and a pickled cucumber out of a locker. He poured himself a full tumbler of vodka. He drank it, ate the pickle, washed off his makeup, and took off his false mustache and put it in the little drawer under the mirror. He got changed. He took another swallow of vodka, said good night to the other characters in the play, and set off up Gorky Street in an exalted, philosophical state of mind, remembering the arrival at the theater of his double and the entire camarilla, the members of which people regarded as leaders, men endowed with great power. But in actual fact, as was quite obvious to an outside observer, they were the most pitiful and powerless of men. Lickspittles. The man who was regarded as their leader could humiliate any one of them, insult him, fillip him on the nose. He could have any one of them imprisoned or executed, or send his wife to a prison camp. No other man, not even the very simplest, lived as terrible a life as they did. They stood on the platform of the Mausoleum, their portraits were on display right across the country, people thought that they were leaders, demigods, but they were simply nobodies. Mere lice. Pitiful slaves and groveling toadies. They hovered around their boss, hanging in awe on every banal word that he uttered. They laughed loudly and almost naturally (they could have played on stage) after every feeble joke that he made. But really (this was visible even from the stage) they hated him and were only waiting for him to kick the bucket. And even he was essentially a slave of circumstances. He always had to be on his guard, he could never trust anyone in his circle of closest deputies, never trust their words, their intentions, their gestures, and their smiles. His fate was always to observe vigilantly, to make sure they didn't come together, didn't conspire to shoot him, poison him, strike him down with an ashtray, smother him with a pillow. But how could he tell what they had on their minds, each one separately and all of them together? When Stalin was in the Kremlin, he had been tormented relentlessly by unresolvable doubts, which had given rise to a persecution complex. He had been liberated from that when he was transformed from a leader into a play actor. Now he was free of power and its terrors.

He walked along the street and he wasn't afraid of anyone, no one wanted him, and that was happiness—not to be wanted by anyone!

IT WAS AFTER TEN WHEN THE LINE OF BLACK AUTOMOBILES drove up to the gates of the dacha that we have already described. Men tumbled out of the automobiles, all of them equally well fed, wearing dark coats with gray astrakhan collars and caps of the same fur. The master of the dacha got out, wearing a marshal's greatcoat and a peaked cap.

The commander of the guard reported that everything at the dacha was in order and the guard was on duty in full force.

"Good," said the master and turned to the men who had arrived with him. "What have you come for? Where do you think you're going?"

The other new arrivals were thrown into confusion. They huddled against each other, not knowing how to behave and what to say. Naturally, Lavrentii Pavlovich was bolder than the others. He came forward.

"Dear Koba, you yourself invited us to supper."

"I've changed my mind," said the false Koba. "I'm sick of your lousy faces. And your mug especially, Lavrentii. Clear off."

His brothers-in-arms knew their place. And they knew how to behave in situations like this. They immediately went back to their cars and disappeared into them, closing the doors silently. And one by one the cars disappeared stealthily into the darkness, as if on tiptoe.

Inside the house, Stalin tossed his greatcoat onto a trunk standing in the hallway and walked over to the door of one of the bedrooms. The new commander of the guard, Ivan Khrustalev, came skipping up to him.

"What are your instructions, Comrade Stalin?"

"Clear out, all of you!" said Stalin.

He locked himself in the bedroom. Nobody knows the details of what happened after that. The guards, left outside the room, heard him walking around inside with steps that were unusually fast. The door was closed tight, but a faint little strip of light and the smell of smoke from a Herzegovina Flor *papyrosa* emerged through a narrow crack up at the top. It was quiet. But at two o'clock in the morning the secret phone monitoring service set up by Beria recorded a conversation that would seem strange to us if we did not already know what was going on.

The call was from Comrade Stalin in Kuntsevo to the actor Comrade Melovani. Here is the full transcript of the conversation:

s: Good evening.

m [*annoyed*]: What evening? It's three in the morning.

s: I'm sorry, but I know that you go to bed late. So do I. Do you know who's talking to you?

m: It's not hard to guess.

s: Yes, I suppose not. I hope you still remember my voice from the old films.

m: Well, what is it?

s: I wanted to tell you that you acted wonderfully today.

m [*with irony*]: That's nice to hear from a professional.

s: You have only one fault. Your acting eclipses everyone else, and that's not right. In a harmonious production a highly talented actor should restrain himself and not excel the others by too much. But with your talent, you will always stand out.

m: It's not a talent, it's character. I always was a leader.

s: And do you still have the aspiration to lead?

m: I don't know. Perhaps.

s: Then tell me, please, how would you take the idea of us swapping roles again? [*A long pause*] Why don't you say anything?

m: Are you serious?

s: You can assume that I am.

m: I can assume that you are, or you are?

s [*after a long pause*]: I am very serious.

m: Then I'll have to think about it. You haven't changed the number of the direct line, have you? I'll think about it and call you back.

Half an hour later the phone rang in pseudo-Stalin's bedroom. The guards heard it. Stalin picked up the receiver and in response to his "hello" heard just one word: "No!"

WE KNOW EVERYTHING THAT HAPPENED AFTER THAT. Or we know nothing. Because there are many different accounts, but not one of them is entirely reliable. If we add the various elements together, then it went like this. Usually Stalin (genuine or substitute, it makes no difference) went to bed late and got up late. Therefore, when the door of his room had not opened at eleven or twelve or one or even two in the afternoon, nobody showed any concern. At four o'clock the commander of the guard Khrustalev and his deputy Lozgachev exchanged significant glances, but didn't say anything to each other. At five o'clock Lozgachev said: "Comrade Stalin seems still to be resting." He would never have said: "Comrade Stalin is sleeping"—since it was assumed that Comrade Stalin never slept.

The commander replied that Comrade Stalin had had a particularly heavy day yesterday: work, the theater, telephone calls.

They both sighed in sympathy for Comrade Stalin and said nothing for another hour. At ten minutes past six Khrustalev said to Lozgachev: "Ask Comrade Stalin if there's anything he wants."

To which Lozgachev replied: "You're the commander, you ask him."

To which the commander said: "I'm the commander and as my subordinate, you must implicitly obey any order that I give you."

To which the subordinate responded with a demand: "Then write me a written order to wake Comrade Stalin."

To which the commander objected; "Not wake him, ask him if there's anything he wants."

With which the subordinate agreed: "Write: 'if there's anything he wants.' And sign it."

At which the commander gave up and went himself to ask Comrade Stalin if there was anything he wanted. Instead of a reply he heard a strange bleating. The automatic door was blocked from the inside and the commander and his deputy had to open it from the outside with an axe. A terrible sight was revealed to their eyes. Comrade Stalin was lying on the bare floor in his own urine, bleating incoherently. An open bottle of Borzhomi mineral water was standing on the night table and Comrade Stalin was holding a glass in his hand. The stage was set for the actor Melovani to play his final role in the tragedy "The Death of Stalin."

All those who were in the country at the time, and even those who weren't, know that the funeral of the ostensible Stalin was the occasion of a horrific crush which resulted in dozens of people being trampled to death or dying under the hooves of the mounted militia's horses. Those who managed to reach the coffin observed that Stalin was lying there as if he were alive, looking much younger than his age and in general, resembling the actor Georgii Melovani in the film *Victory Day*. That was how many people remembered him. Afterward his admirers drove around with portraits of this Stalin on their windshields and carried them at demonstrations in the 1990s, and some still carry them to this day and will go on carrying them for a long time yet.

Of course, both the genuine Comrade Stalin and the fake are secondary characters in our narrative, and therefore, it seems to us that they are taking up rather too much space here. But since we have followed the fate of the fake Stalin all the way to the end, it is worthwhile relating, at least in brief, the end of the genuine Stalin's story. He heard the news of his double's death, the crush on Trubnaya Square, and the behavior of his comrades-in-arms with mixed feelings. After the nocturnal telephone conversation with Melovani, he bore him no ill will and now even regretted that this remarkable artiste had died so early, at the age of only sixty, and probably not from natural causes. If he had been working in the theater, he could have lived a bit longer. The real Stalin understood that Beria had been tricked and could never forgive Melovani for his deception. If he had forgiven him, he would not have been Beria. Later Stalin would hear the rumors of how his treacherous and dastardly brothers-in-arms had reacted. The moment the pseudo-Stalin breathed his last, Beria shouted triumphantly: "The tyrant is dead!" That famous phrase: "Khrustalev, the car" was the second thing he said. Stalin's suspicions about Beria and the others had been proved true.

THE DEAD PSEUDO-STALIN WAS STILL LYING in the Hall of Columns when Fyodor Rastoropny, an instructor from the Central Committee of the CPSU, showed up at the MDT to make a few changes. After watching the jaded old production of *Don't Get into Someone Else's Sleigh,* Rastoropny gathered a few people together in the theater manager's office, including the manager himself, the senior director, and several of the leading artistes, and told them that the theater's planned repertoire had to be changed.

"Here, for example," he said, jabbing his finger at a poster, "you're showing *Stalin in October* six times, even though it doesn't bring the audience in. It's not good box office."

"But," the manager tried to object, "it's a play about Comrade Stalin. And it has been nominated for a Stalin Prize, you know." But then he asked warily: "Has our attitude to Comrade Stalin changed, then?"

"It has," the instructor said firmly. "For us Stalin remains a statesman of outstanding importance but, as you yourselves understand very well, his services have been greatly exaggerated."

This conversation was the first occasion when the phrase "personality cult" was pronounced by a Party official. Everyone at this small gathering exchanged glances and started thinking hard: they were shaken. The artist Melovani was the only one who spoke up.

"Tell me, please," he asked with a stronger Georgian accent than usual, "this opinion that Comrade Stalin's services have been greatly exaggerated, is that your personal opinion or the opinion of the higher Party leadership?"

"What do you think, Comrade Melovani?" Rastoropny replied rather ironically. "Can you imagine that I, an ordinary Central Committee instructor, would dare to alter the policy of the Party?"

"So your opinion," the artiste continued, "is not your opinion, but the opinion of our highly respected leaders, the opinion of comrades Beria, Khrushchev, Malenkov, Bulganin, and so on."

"Absolutely right," Rastoropny agreed, "it's the opinion of the Polit-buro, that is, the opinion of the Party, which you and I should follow unswervingly."

You can imagine People's Artist Melovani's mood on his way home. Thinking about his erstwhile brothers-in-arms, he realized that his suspicions had been confirmed in the very worst way possible. As soon as their leader (that is, the man who they thought was their leader) gave up the ghost, they had not only rushed to divide power up between themselves (probably going straight for each other's throats—how else would they do it!) but also started to denounce him in the vilest terms possible before he was even cold. Only a few days earlier they had been hanging on his every word, acclaiming his every utterance, even the most banal, as an epiphany of genius and the very summit of human wisdom. He could do whatever he wanted with them. He had taken away Kalinin's and Molotov's wives and put them in prison camps. He had made Khrushchev dance the gopak. He had knocked out his pipe on Poskrebyshev's bald patch. He had grabbed Beria by the nose. Lacking any sense of simple human dignity, none of them had ever expressed even the slightest resentment. They had behaved like devoted dogs. They had sworn to him that they were willing to give their lives without the slightest hesitation. "Bastards," he thought, "scum, traitors, unprincipled toadies." It was a long time since he had felt any nostalgia for his previous position and omnipotence, but now he felt a passionate desire to return to his former post, if only for a day. One day would be enough for him to have them all shot, hanged, crucified. He would have them executed in the most appalling ways it was possible to imagine. But unfortunately, there was nothing he could do. He couldn't go back to the Kremlin, he couldn't have anyone shot or hanged. He could only get drunk.

That evening several people on Gorky Street noticed an old man who was weeping and wailing loudly as he walked along. They looked around in amazement at him, not recognizing him as either Iosif Stalin or Grigorii Melovani. Along his way he bought a bottle of vodka at the Jewish restaurant The Anchor. At home he drank almost all of it and fell asleep fully clothed. He woke in his bedroom at the Kuntsevo dacha at an indefinite time of day. Although there were no windows, the room was bright, but the light didn't come from the lamps on the ceiling or the walls, he couldn't tell where it came from. He was surprised, although not greatly, to find that he was not alone. Also in the room with him were Beria, Khrushchev, Malenkov, and Bulganin. Beria was standing

in front of the open safe, taking out documents one after another, looking through them, and throwing them on the floor, muttering under his
breath as he did it. Khrushchev, with his straw hat pushed to the back
of his head, was sitting in a wicker chair, gnawing on a corncob. He was
moving the corncob from side to side as if he were playing a mouth
organ, leaving messy trails on both cheeks and dropping occasional
grains on the floor. The sheer insolence of sitting in Stalin's bedroom and
gnawing on a corncob was outrageous enough in itself, but what out-
raged Iosif Vissarionovich most of all was that this usurper was sitting
there with Stalin's uniform tunic with the two gold stars casually thrown
across his shoulders. Malenkov was dictating a text to Bulganin, something about light industry, which had to be given preference over heavy
industry. They were all absorbed in their own business and didn't immediately notice that their leader had woken up. The first to notice was
Malenkov. He jostled Bulganin, Bulganin hit Khrushchev on the hand,
and the corncob went flying through the air and struck Beria on the
shoulder. Beria saw that Stalin had woken up, and at first he was dumb-
struck, but then he dashed over to him and started kissing his hand and
speaking very rapidly.

"Koba, dear fellow, you've come back! I knew you were alive, but they
all said: he's dead. I knew that you didn't die and you couldn't die, because you're immortal. But they started dividing up your posts. This one
became the chairman of the Council of Ministers, that one became the
minister of defense, and this corn-eater here seized control of the Party.
Can you imagine it, this semiliterate miner is going to lead the Party
that you and Lenin . . . See how dishonest and cunning they are, Koba!
They all told you that they loved you, but you can see what malicious,
power-hungry, underhanded scoundrels they are. I am your only selfless
and devoted friend. And I've acted like a friend, I've had them arrested."

And then Stalin saw the entire group in their underwear—ragged
undershirts and long johns that were falling down, with iron shackles
on their hands and feet. They stood in front of him, quaking in fear. And
his first thought was to subject them to some terrible, slow, excruciating
form of punishment. But suddenly his heart was pierced by an intense
feeling that he had never experienced before—a feeling of pity for these
men. He was very surprised, because he had never pitied anyone in his
life, apart from himself, but now he felt pity for these paltry individuals
quaking in fear.

"Let them go, Lavrentii," he said with a feeble gesture of his hand.

"What?" Lavrentii asked in astonishment, in no hurry to carry out the order. "How can I let them go if they have betrayed the man who is most dear to me?"

"What can be done, Lavrentii? That's the way people are. Even the apostles betrayed their Teacher."

"Only Judas," Lavrentii corrected him. "That son of a bitch sold out for thirty kopecks. He was such a bad man. He was like Trotsky. But the other disciples . . ."

"The others were the same," Stalin retorted. "You didn't read the Gospels very well, Lavrentii."

"I haven't read them at all," Lavrentii replied quickly. "I only read what you have written. *The History of the All-Union Communist Party (Bolsheviks)* and *The Fundamentals of Leninism.*"

"That's good," Stalin said approvingly, "but it wouldn't do you any harm to read the Gospels, too. If you had read the Gospels, Lavrentii, you would have noticed that when Christ was arrested in the Garden of Gethsemane, all his disciples fled. They all fled," he repeated. "So what can we really expect from these pitiful, insignificant men? Let them go, Lavrentii."

"As you wish," Lavrentii said with a shrug.

In a single gesture Lavrentii removed all the prisoners' shackles and, instead of expressing their gratitude, they threw themselves on Stalin, snarling horribly. Lavrentii was the first to grab him by the throat . . . and then Stalin woke up. He opened his eyes, but it took him a long time to come around and realize it had all been nothing but a dream.

A garbage truck was growling outside the window.

MR. KALIUZHNY GRADUALLY DEVELOPED such strong family feelings for Chonkin that he came to regard him as something of a son. Especially since he had no children of his own. Barbara, who was thirty years younger than him, was a fine woman in every way, but she was barren. Kaliuzhny even started thinking about adopting Chonkin, but that wish was not fated to be realized. In the early 1960s the old man started feeling a strange lack of energy and suffering intense stomach cramps and nausea. He put off going to the doctor for a long time, but eventually he went to the nearest town, Springfield. He came back pale and serious and told Chonkin his news without any superfluous emotion. Dr. Greenfield had told him that he had cancer of the stomach, with metastases in the lungs and the bone marrow. The situation was hopeless. Kaliuzhny had asked the doctor how long he had left to live and the doctor had answered: "About four months, if you're lucky."

After Kaliuzhny shared this with Chonkin, neither of them said anything. Chonkin wanted to say something about the situation, he knew that he ought to say something, but he couldn't think of what exactly to say, and that made him feel very awkward.

"I tell you what," said Kaliuzhny, when he had been silent for long enough. "I was going to adopt you, but now I've had another idea. When I go out there . . ."—he twirled his hand, as if he were describing some curly route of departure, corkscrewing upward—"I want you to marry Barbara. She's a good wife, her age is better suited to you than me, you can run the farm together, and as for bed, you can figure that out for yourself."

The doctor gave Kaliuzhny some tablets. Perhaps it was thanks to them that the patient felt relatively well for the first month. He showed Chonkin the ropes of the business and told him all the subtle points of the farming profession: how to tell what the weather would be like and what the prospects for the harvest were, and how to fix the combine, sell the grain, and keep the expense accounts.

Sometimes it seemed that the doctor had been wrong, but Kaliuzhny soon started wasting away and turning yellow. He took to his bed and died exactly four months after the forecast was made.

Chonkin's and Barbara's fate had been decided. After burying Pan Kaliuzhny, they didn't wait any lengthy set period for the sake of propriety. If they had remained formally single, they would have had to pay much more for medical insurance and taxes. In order to avoid that, they registered their marriage only three months later and had the ceremony in the church, where Father Michael made them both promise that they would stay together in good times and in bad, love each other, and support each other until death did them part.

BARBARA WAS PLEASED WITH HER NEW HUSBAND. He had a calm disposition, worked hard, wasn't fussy about his food, consulted her on all business matters, and proved to be indefatigable in bed. She was very keen on sex, and Pan Kaliuzhny, who didn't understand her yearnings, had neglected his obligations owing to his own age and thoughtlessness. But Chonkin fulfilled those obligations most successfully.

If anyone had asked Chonkin if he loved Barbara and he had been willing to answer truthfully, he could have replied in the affirmative. Life with her was calm and good. She cooked his food, washed his under-clothes and shirts, kept the house clean, and never refused him in bed. What else did he need? But if he had been asked if he had felt even once the same joy that possessed him when Nyura came home after being away for several hours, if the pleasure of copulation with Barbara was the same as the pleasure he got from his couplings with Nyura, he could not truly have answered yes. Some people, however, only experience that kind of pleasure once in their lives, and the majority never experi-ence it at all, but they get by well enough, taking their pleasure where it's available.

Barbara was very active in sex, she lifted her legs up high and she didn't gasp or moan, but laughed loudly and happily. As she approached the climax, she shouted out: "Oh Boy!" This "Boy" has a capital letter because Boy was what she called the Lord God.

Every now and then they went to the cemetery to visit Pan Kaliuzhny's grave. American cemeteries are not like Russian ones. They are kept clean and tidy, but they have an ascetic look to them. Small stone slabs, usually with nothing but a name and dates of birth and death, laid out in regular rows. One day Barbara crouched down by the stone and Chonkin heard what she said, but wasn't sure that he had understood it correctly. She said: "Thank you, Peter, for dying."

Chonkin was so astonished by these words that later on that night, he couldn't resist asking her what they meant. She kissed him and said: "If he hadn't died, I couldn't have lived with you."

10

ONCE, ON BARBARA'S SUGGESTION, they took a trip to New York. They visited the Metropolitan Museum, watched the musical *West Side Story* on Broadway, strolled around Times Square, stayed the night in a Holiday Inn, and set off home the next day. In one of the kiosks at the railroad station Chonkin saw a newspaper with Russian letters, which he hadn't seen since he left Germany. The newspaper was called *Novoye Russkoye Slovo* (*The New Russian Word*). Chonkin bought it and started reading it on the train. He had never been a great one for reading in any case, and now he found it really difficult. But he came across an article entitled "Two Stalins" that really caught his interest. He had always thought that there was one Stalin and he had two wives. But apparently there were two of him. So if there were two of him, how many wives did they have between them? Two each? Running his calloused farmer's finger along the lines, he started going through the text carefully, and rapidly became enthralled by what he read. The article began with the story of the generalissimus's parentage and the claim, with which Chonkin was already familiar, that Stalin was the offspring of Przhevalsky and a Przhevalsky horse. It described an event of which Chonkin had been an eyewitness, that is, the talk given by Colonel Opalikov, with its reference to the research of the scientist Grom-Grimeilo and the sudden death of the speaker. But then it moved on to a different subject. To be precise, it spoke of the real Stalin being replaced by the actor Melovani, and of Stalin taking Melovani's place on the stage. Effectively they both played the same role, only in different circumstances. The article spoke of how Beria spent ages making up to Melovani, who had deceived him so basely, and eventually got close enough. And when the pseudo-Stalin was dying, lying in a coma, and suddenly came to for a minute, Beria supposedly dashed over to kiss his hand, but really he didn't just kiss his hand, he whispered something at the same time. The other men standing around only heard the word "genius." This word was actually uttered, but in what context? In his diary Beria wrote: "I leaned down to his hand, pretending to everyone there that I was kissing it. But what I really wanted to tell him and did tell him was this: 'Now do you understand, you pitiful little actor, which of us is which? When you got into the Kremlin, you imagined you were a genius. But now you understand that I am the real genius!'"

As for the real Stalin living under the name of the artiste Melovani, he took the death of the artiste living under his name very hard. Although he had always been a realist and never entertained any illusions about anybody and, naturally, never trusted his brothers-in-arms, following his own supposed death he was stunned at what chameleons they turned out to be. How mendacious and hypocritical their words about his greatness, genius, and irreplaceability had been. How greatly they had hated him, and how artfully they had concealed their hatred. His distress was exacerbated by the fact that with the death of the false Stalin, his life immediately changed for the worse. After March 5 the play *Stalin in October* was only performed twice: once in that same month of March and once on April 22, Lenin's birthday. And that was all! In assigning the parts for other productions the directors politely passed over him. The general feeling was that this actor could play only the role of Comrade Stalin and nothing else. Sometime later, however, they put on a play based on the life of the First Cavalry Army and Comrade Stalin, that is, the actor Melovani, that is, in actual fact, Comrade Stalin, who was taken to be the actor Melovani, was entrusted with the role of Marshal Budyonny's horse. In this role he demonstrated immense talent. All the critics remarked on the remarkable naturalness of the artist's performance, saying that he played the part as if he had actually been born a horse. Some spiteful critics, however, commented that this was not so much a fleet steed as an old gelding fit only for the slaughterhouse.

By the time of the Twentieth Party Congress, he had no roles to play at all. Khrushchev's speech and the debunking of the personality cult hit him very hard. He agreed with the speaker about some things, but he couldn't help remembering how zealously Khrushchev had carried out all his instructions, often with even greater diligence than was required from him. That year Stalin was seized by the terrible fear that, in order to cover his tracks, Beria would want to put the real Stalin in the Mausoleum. Beria was actually arrested and shot soon afterward because he turned out to be a British spy, but the genuine Stalin's fear that they might replace the corpse lying in the Mausoleum with him never left him and seriously undermined his once sturdy health.

There is information to suggest that, never having been indifferent to hard liquor, in the final year of his life he drank more and more. With no roles to play, he effectively stopped going to work. He only went to the theater twice a month: on the day they paid the advance and the day they paid the balance of the salary, which he received regularly without fail.

Apparently he had other savings, but he blew them all on the races, to which he had become addicted in recent times. Habitués of the racetrack at that time remember that the artiste Melovani, who had aged greatly and was always a bit tiddly, always used to bet on his favorite—a mare by the name of She-Eagle. He was so fond of her that he used to visit her regularly with the permission of the grooms, to scrape her down and comb out her mane and tail. Witnesses whose testimony should be regarded with great caution claim that the drunken People's Artist used to share the secrets of his heart with She-Eagle, who by that time was heavily in foal. They say that he complained to her about all the members of the Politburo, calling them scoundrels and marauders. He was especially insulting about the new leader of the U.S.S.R., Nikita Khrushchev. The newspaper article said that by a strange coincidence of events, on Stalin's birthday, December 21, 1956, She-Eagle gave birth to a male foal, which the grooms named Generalissimus in honor of the date.

Testimony has also survived, although it is now classified as top secret, that People's Artist Gregorii Melovani was present when the foal was born. Supposedly he then got very drunk and said he was going home, but he was found dead on a pile of hay beside She-Eagle's stall the next morning, the day after the seventy-seventh birthday that was really his. The author of the article expressed certain doubts concerning the reliability of his own sources, but did not exclude the possibility that they represented the full truth.

After he read the article, Chonkin told Barbara what it was about and as she listened, she laughed loudly and exclaimed "Re-ally?" or "It's impossible!" She told him that in Canada many farmers lived with their animals too, but she had never heard of them producing any offspring.

CHONKIN LIVED EXACTLY TWELVE YEARS WITH BARBARA and he was happy. But after twelve years she died in her sleep of heart failure, and since she didn't have a single relative and there were no claimants to her estate, everything that had belonged to her and Pan Kaliuzhny went to Chonkin, including four hundred acres of land in the state of Kansas. The distance between the two properties was considerable and in order to travel between them, Chonkin was obliged to buy a small

Cessna airplane, which he learned to fly as he had learned to use all the other machines. At that stage he was having difficulty selling his produce, but the government told him not to try too hard and even paid for him not to grow any surplus. In the 1970s, however, new opportunities appeared. The Soviet Union started buying a lot of grain from the U.S., and Chonkin became one of the suppliers, a well-known figure in business circles and even on Capitol Hill in Washington, where his interests were defended by Congressman Walter Shipovsky.

In those years large trailers appeared on the roads of America, bearing the inscription:

CHONKIN INTERNATIONAL GRAIN PRODUCTION LTD. INC.

12

IN THE SUMMER OF 1989, at the very height of the harvest season, Chonkin got a phone call from Congressman Walter Shipovsky, whom he had supported in the latest elections.

"Hi, John!" said Shipovsky. "How would you like to visit your motherland?"

"What?" asked Chonkin.

"I mean Russia, the Soviet Union," Shipovsky boomed on the phone. "We're putting together a delegation of grain exporters, and I don't see how a team like that can manage without you. What do you think?"

"Hmmm," said Chonkin and started thinking. Then he remembered something: in the 1960s the Soviet leader of the time had made a whirlwind tour of the corn-growing states of America and even visited Pan Kaliuzhny. That bald-headed man . . . Chonkin couldn't recall his name, but he could picture him as if it were yesterday. In his embroidered Ukrainian shirt he had walked around a field with a large crowd of ministers, journalists, men with movie cameras, and bodyguards, breaking off the cobs that weren't ripe yet, biting into them to try the taste, and shaking them under the noses of his companions, who smiled joyfully and diligently wrote down his comments in their notebooks. After trampling an entire field, the visitors left, and afterward Pan Kaliuzhny told Chonkin that the Soviet leader had ordered the entire territory of the Soviet Union to be planted with corn.

Chonkin didn't know if the order had been carried out and what had come of it, and he hadn't tried to find out. During the years spent in America he had got out of the habit of thinking about his country of origin, in fact he had almost forgotten it, and he accepted willy-nilly the impression that people around him had of Russia as a wild expanse where it was always cold, where semisavage fanatics thought of nothing but Communism, worked a lot, and shared their wives.

True, he did dream of his motherland sometimes, but these dreams were strange and unpleasant. He dreamed many times that he had ended up in Russia as a result of some misunderstanding and was trying to come back, but insuperable obstacles kept arising. He went around various institutions to request permission to leave because he was an American citizen. But they laughed and told him: If you're an American citizen, you must have an American passport. And he said: I do have an American passport, and reached into his pocket, but he discovered that he didn't even have a pocket, let alone a passport, because he was completely naked. He started running to some place where he knew his passport was, but got stuck in a swamp, in a quagmire, and the harder he tried to scramble out, the deeper he got stuck. And then he opened his mouth to call for help, but no sound came out. He woke up in terror and gazed around for a long time until the joyful realization came that in the waking world he was very far away from the place he had been dreaming about.

After he said "Hmmm," Chonkin was silent for so long that the congressman became impatient and asked:

"Are you there?"

"Yes," Chonkin responded.

"Are you having doubts?"

"Yes," Chonkin confirmed. "I'm afraid they'll put me in jail."

And he explained that, as far as he was aware (someone had told him about it), he had been condemned by a Soviet court to be shot as a traitor to the motherland, and the sentence had to be put into effect as soon as he was discovered anywhere on the territory of the Soviet Union.

"All right," promised Shipovsky, "I'll check it out."

A few days later he called and said that everything was okay. President Bush had called Michael Gorbachev in person, and he had guaranteed the safety of all the members of the American delegation, no matter who they were.

13

IT WAS A STATE VISIT. Chonkin flew first class and had the right to drink French champagne, but he only drank water with ice. In Sheremetievo Airport they were met by an entire delegation that included the deputy minister of agriculture, the head of the agricultural section of the Central Committee of the CPSU, the assistant general secretary of the Central Committee of the CPSU, two female interpreters, and some other substantially built, well-fed individuals in gray suits. They all smiled amiably, even fawningly, but their eyes had a wary look and drilled inquisitively into the visitors, as if they suspected that the new arrivals were not who they made themselves out to be and their goal was not the one stated in the program but some other, secret one, perhaps even espionage and sabotage. And no one in the reception committee would have been surprised to learn that the visitors had microphones and miniature cameras hidden under their jackets and were carrying Colorado beetles in their baggage. From the height of our knowledge we can laugh at these poor people and the vigilance from which they had suffered, like a sickness, all their lives. It goes without saying that the farmers were not planning any sabotage, they didn't have any microphones under their jackets, weren't carrying Colorado beetles in their baggage, and were carrying their cameras quite openly. But nonetheless the delegation did include two CIA agents (why try to conceal the fact now?)—they were members of the group of experts who were supposed to determine the condition of agriculture in the U.S.S.R. and how stable the Soviet order was in general.

At the start of September the weather was warm and the crowns of the trees were only lightly tinged with yellow. The farmers were put up in the hotel Moscow, the best hotel in the city, so they were told. The windows of the two-room semideluxe suite that Chonkin was given looked out straight onto Manege Square, and the balcony had a view of Red Square, but going out onto the balcony was forbidden. A notice in two languages, attached to the doors with thumbtacks, warned guests that the balcony was in a dangerous condition and could collapse at any moment. This was the time when not only balconies were collapsing but the entire Soviet state—there were only two years left until it would fall apart completely.

The guests were fed in the buffet on the ninth floor. At breakfast in the morning Chonkin wanted red grapefruit and cornflakes with milk, but the buffet didn't have grapefruit or milk or cornflakes. What it did have were large, greasy meat cutlets with mashed potatoes and thick sour cream in water glasses. The spoons and forks were aluminum, and there were no knives or napkins at all.

The first evening they were taken to the Bolshoi Theater to see the ballet *Spartacus*. Chonkin really enjoyed it, especially since it was the first live performance of a ballet that he had seen in his entire life, and whenever he saw ballet on TV, he had always switched to a different channel. He found the saber dance particularly impressive. On the way to his room, he was stopped by the female attendant in the corridor, who asked if he had anything that needed to be washed. Seeing that the guest was favorably inclined to conversation, she went on to ask what his name was and introduced herself as Kaleria Maratovna. She questioned him about American life, inquired if there really were many black people there, if he had a car and what make it was, why the Americans wanted to fight the Russians, and what their religious faith was. Then she asked where he worked.

"On a *farm*," said Chonkin.

Failing to recognize this foreign word, she asked if he meant a pharmacy.

Chonkin didn't understand.

"Nah," Chonkin said peevishly, "I'm a *farmer*."

Even then she didn't understand properly. She thought he worked in a *ferma*, like the ones on collective farms, milking the cows and clearing away the dung. She was very surprised and didn't really believe him when he said he had almost 500 hectares of his own land and he cultivated it all himself.

Kaleria Maratovna was on duty for two days in a row, because she took another attendant's shift. The next day she brought Chonkin's washed and ironed underwear to his suite. He asked how much it cost, but she just waved her hand, as if to say: Don't bother about it—and asked if he could give her a Sony television.

Chonkin left the question of the television open, but he gave her ten dollars and then dipped into the collection of trifles that he had prepared in advance for such occasions and presented her with a pair of tights, a pack of Marlboro cigarettes, and menthol chewing gum, which delighted her greatly.

On Sunday the farmers were invited to visit the Tretyakov Gallery.

Chonkin declined the offer and set off to walk around on his own. What he found most surprising was the abundance of Russian. At first it seemed unnatural to him that everyone spoke that language, asked questions in it, answered in it, and understood each other. And although he had already tested his knowledge, it still felt strange that he could walk up to somebody in the street and ask in Russian how to get somewhere or other, and the person would understand him and explain to him in the same language and he would understand the explanation. He enjoyed asking questions and getting answers in Russian so much that he spoke to almost every person he met along his way as he gradually approached a round intersection with a tall pedestal in the middle of it and a cast-iron individual whom he didn't know standing on the pedestal, with a greatcoat, a thin face, a baleful glare, and a long goatee.

At the entrance to the metro station he walked up to a man in a leather jacket, said "Hi!" to him, and asked how to get to Red Square. The man said "Hi!" and replied in perfect English that he would get to Red Square if he walked this way, straight along October 25 Street.

14

THE LINE TO GET INTO LENIN'S MAUSOLEUM proved surprisingly short, and the sight was uninteresting. Lenin wasn't lying like everyone else did, with his arms crossed on his chest; for some reason he was holding them by his sides with the fists clenched as if he intended to fight a boxing match, and his head was exceptionally large, with a ginger beard and eyebrows.

Leaving the tomb behind him, Chonkin decided to take a look at what kind of people lived in Moscow and the way they lived. He walked past his hotel again and up along Gorky Street. Before the war he had heard many times about what a magnificent sight the capital of the Soviet state was, especially its central street. But a lot of time had passed since he had heard that. Thanks to a twist of fate more than forty years ago, he had been to Berlin, New York, Chicago, San Francisco, Los Angeles, and Paris. After those cities Moscow didn't seem so very big or so very magnificent to him. He saw it as scruffy and neglected. It was hard for a Moscow resident or a visitor to the city at that time to imagine how it would be transformed in fifteen years: what modern office buildings and apartment blocks, shopping centers and hotels would spring up here, how this megalopolis would be flooded with electric light and blossom with bright-colored advertisements, how the streets would be filled with Rolls-Royces, Mercedeses, and Cadillacs. But there was none of this yet, and Chonkin walked along, staring in amazement at the boring, color-less appearance of the streets, the drab sameness of the automobiles and the clothes, and the unhealthy-looking human faces. Trolleys and buses crept along the street one after another, grating and creaking, all old, dirty, and rusty. He tried to squeeze into one of them, but the crowd somehow swirled him around and spat him out, and the bus left without him. He tried again and the same thing happened.

He continued on foot and came across a military patrol: a senior lieutenant and two privates with red armbands. He noticed that they had picked him out and were exchanging comments. First they cast a few quick glances in his direction and then one of the privates, a small, bandy-legged man exactly like Chonkin had once been himself, sepa-rated from his comrades and moved to cut him off. An atavistic response that suddenly surfaced prompted Chonkin to cut and run, and he even took a step to one side, then recovered his wits, but not completely, and reached into his pocket for his passport.

The soldier was not only small, but scrawny too, with unhealthy look-ing, pimply skin.

"Hey, Pop," he said, "give me three rubles, I fancy a bite to eat."

Chonkin was startled. He had been expecting anything but that. All sorts of things had happened to him when he was a soldier, but he had never begged for handouts and never seen other soldiers do it, let alone in front of an officer. He reached into his pocket, this time not for his passport, but for money. He pulled out one of the bills by touch—it turned out to be twenty dollars—and handed it to the soldier.

The soldier took the piece of paper, started turning it over in his hands, and asked in amazement:

"What's this, Pop? What's this you're giving me?" and he held his hand out to give the bill back.

"Twenty bucks, isn't that enough?" Chonkin asked in surprise, re-membering that American beggars were glad to get a quarter, but then the officer came skipping over, took the bill from the soldier, and spoke to Chonkin:

"*Danke schön.*"

And all three of them tramped away rapidly.

Chonkin moved on, too.

Eventually he reached the Belorusskaya metro station. As he rode down on the escalator, he noticed that almost all the people coming up toward him had gloomy expressions on their faces, like miners coming back up to the surface after a heavy shift. He rode a rattling train to the next station, Novoslobodskaya. He saw a toilet and felt it would be a good idea to use it. He read the sign. It said: "PAY TOILET, Pissoir—20 kop., stall—80 kop. Heroes of the Soviet Union, Heroes of Socialist Labor, and Knights of the Order of Glory, third degree, are accommodated free of charge." At the entrance a woman in a blue cotton coat was taking the money and handing out a single square of toilet paper to those who paid for a stall. Walking out of the toilet, Chonkin turned a corner and found himself in some kind of yard with an astonishing sight: there were two large receptacles for garbage that hadn't been emptied for so long that they were overflowing, standing among the naked trees. Scattered all around them were cigarette butts, cigarette packs, scraps of newspaper, pieces of cardboard, old food cans, a rusty wheel from a child's bicycle, and a dead cat. The ground squelched underfoot and stank, but people walked through this filth with a rapid, matter-of-fact stride, not at all dispirited by it, although they had the same gloomy faces as people in the metro. Behind the garbage dump, standing on little columns built of bricks instead of wheels, was an old automobile, rusted right through, with holes and dents and no windshield. A man who obviously owned the car had laid out a piece of rusty tin plate on the dirt and was hammering on it with a wooden mallet.

Noticing the curious attention that he was attracting, the man looked up and asked: "Hey, Pop, you got a smoke on you?"

"*Sure,*" said Chonkin, taking out a pack of Camels and deftly shaking one cigarette into the man's dirty fingers.

"Oho!" the man said in surprise, "Where do you get cigarettes like that from, Pop, in the Beryozka shop, maybe?"

"Nowhere special," said Chonkin, not going into the details. He held his lighter up to the other man's nose. "Doing a *repair*?" he asked, using the English word.

"What?"

"You want to fix it up and drive it?"

"Not drive it, fly in it," the other man said and coughed. "Strong cigarettes. I'm going to fly on a cushion of air. I'll flatten out this plate and bend it into a nozzle. And the guys have promised to lift a compressor for me from the Zhukov plant."

"What are you going to fly in? You mean this?" asked Chonkin, pointing to the remains of the automobile.

"What else? This is a Victory, do you know what a Victory is?"

"We-ell," Chonkin replied evasively. He didn't know what a Victory was, because after the war he had ended up in a place where there weren't any Victories and similar automobiles were called Opel Kapitäns. But he didn't know that then, either, he was too busy with other things.

The other man simply couldn't imagine that anyone really didn't know what a Victory was. He had no doubt that this elderly man did know what a Victory was, but assumed that he had no idea of the great virtues of this automobile. So he started to explain.

"A genuine Victory is a real beast! It's thirty years old already, and still almost running. I'll beat out the body a bit and weld it up and it'll serve for another forty years."

When Chonkin asked where exactly he was going to fly, the owner of the Victory replied that he'd bought a little cabin up by Lake Seliger in the Kalininsky region, but he had no way to get to it. He couldn't use anything that rolled across the ground, even a tractor would get bogged down. So there was no way he could manage without a hovercraft.

Chonkin marveled at the inventor's talent and resourcefulness, shook another two cigarettes into his side pocket, and went on his way.

15

ON A BROAD STREET CHONKIN SAW A STORE that occupied almost an entire block, with the words FRUIT AND VEGETABLES spelled out on it in huge letters. The massive windows were half obscured with white paint, on which an artist had depicted cucumbers, tomatoes, cantaloupes, watermelons, cherries, apples, oranges, pineapples, and other abundance. Chonkin decided to drop in and buy himself a couple of red grapefruit for breakfast.

It was a big store and there were lots of doors leading into it, but they were all closed and one was even boarded up. Only one door at the end was open, and even then only one half of it, and in some miraculous manner customers flowed through this half in two streams. Those on the way in collided in the doorway with those on the way out, their stomachs thrust against each other and there seemed to be no way they could pass, but they performed strange rotational movements that had been perfected over the years and revolved their way into or out of the shop like two gearwheels. Chonkin also stood in this line and when he encountered a very well-fed woman coming the other way, he overcame the obstacle easily, because he himself was lean and his stomach was not a convex form but a hollow into which the woman's stomach fitted.

Once inside, he didn't find any grapefruit, not even yellow ones, and the store as a whole was practically empty, apart from something that was being sold in the far corner, but he couldn't tell what it was immediately, it looked to him like simple clumps of earth. The people stood behind one another in the line leading to the counter, which was built of wooden crates. Standing on the counter was an old-fashioned set of scales, the kind onto which you put weights on one side and goods on the other. A saleswoman wearing an old padded jacket, crimson fleece harem pants, and knitted gloves trimmed short to leave her fingers exposed, with a dead cigarette in her mouth, was taking money and counting out change, gathering lumps of earth into a plastic basin, weighing them, and tipping them with a rumble into the bags set down to receive them. Chonkin turned to an old woman standing behind him and asked why they were selling clumps of earth. She gaped at him in amazement and asked what earth, couldn't he see they were selling carrots? Chonkin looked closer and really did see something like carrots peeping out from under the dried dirt. He turned to the old woman again and asked why the saleswomen didn't wash the carrots before they sold them. That seemed to drive the old woman crazy and she started shouting: "What? Wash them? Maybe you'd like them to peel them too? And maybe boil them and feed them to you with a spoon?"

And strange to say, the entire line took the old woman's side and they all started shouting something, but the old woman was the most vociferous of all. "They want the easy life!" she shouted. "They've forgotten about the war. We lived in dugouts! We ate goosefoot! We survived the blockade of Leningrad!"

Chonkin was embarrassed by these shouts, feeling as if he were personally to blame for the blockade of Leningrad and them having to eat goosefoot, and in general suddenly feeling that he was too capricious and had forgotten about everything that mattered in the world. Seeing that the people were growing heated and might even start belaboring him around the neck, he huddled up and headed for the door without contradicting anyone, which only served to fuel the fervor of his accuser, who continued shouting after him: "Just look at him! An old man and talking such nonsense! They ought to wash the carrots! You go and give yourself a wash!"

Chonkin went out into the street and decided not to visit any more sales outlets, but when he came across a shop with a sign that said SAUSAGE, he couldn't just walk by. He remembered that he had once been treated to Odessa sausage brought from Moscow, and it had tasted so good he had remembered it ever since. So he decided to drop into the sausage shop after all. Especially since there was no sign of any line inside. But this shop also proved to be absolutely amazing. There were three saleswomen, one cashier, and no goods at all apart from gray paper packets displayed behind the glass of all three counters with the words "coffee drink" printed on them. The saleswomen who, to judge from their figures, fed on something more substantial than coffee drink, were busy discussing hypnosis sessions that they had seen on TV with some kind of psychic called Shapirovsky, but at the sight of Chonkin they fell silent and gaped at him in amazement. No one had even glanced into the shop for ages except for a few individuals who, perhaps in hopes of some fortuitous miracle, had opened the door slightly and stuck their heads inside, but on seeing very clearly that there was no miracle, had promptly pulled them back out again.

But this old man in jeans said "*Hai!*" when he walked in (he must be some kind of Ukrainian), walked across to the saleswoman opposite the door, and started reading what was written on a packet, moving his lips.

All four women gazed at this crank, not knowing what to expect. Finally the one he had walked across to couldn't take any more and asked him what he wanted.

"I'd like to buy some Odessa sausage," said Chonkin, suspecting that he was saying something wrong.

The saleswoman gave him a keen look, exchanged glances with her colleagues, looked at Chonkin again, and inquired politely, very politely indeed, "Is it definitely Odessa you want, granddad? Wouldn't Krakow suit?"

"Or Doctor's!" another saleswoman shouted from her counter.

"Or Special," put in the third.

"Or Chopped Ham," the cashier asked, bursting into laughter.

"You wouldn't have come from abroad, would you, granddad?" asked the first saleswoman.

"He's from America," the cashier put in. "Can't you see—an American in jeans."

They all doubled up in laughter then, and Chonkin became flustered again and walked out into the street with an embarrassed smile.

Chonkin hadn't noticed (and he didn't really need to) that he was accompanied on his walk around Moscow by at least four men on foot and another eight moving about in two automobiles and communicating with each other by radio. The result of their collective surveillance was an operational report on how a member of the farmers' delegation, Mr. John Chonkin, formerly Ivan Chonkin, aka Ivan Golitsyn, had visited the Lenin Mausoleum but declined to visit the Tretyakov Gallery. Instead of this he had taken a walk around the city. However, he had not shown any great interest in the architecture of the capital or its historical monuments, but focused his attention on the most unsavory alleys, yards, and garbage dumps. When he called into shops, he had drawn attention to the temporary absence of certain goods and criticized their quality, and in the sausage shop he had asked the saleswomen provocative questions.

Naturally, this report was sent to the bosses of the department that kept an eye on foreigners, and then even higher, to a place where people wearing generals' shoulder straps sat and pretended—or perhaps even thought—that they were occupied with the important business of defending the fatherland, whereas in actual fact, in terms of wit, intellect, way of thinking, and the range of duties that they carried out, they were perfect representatives of that human subspecies commonly known as the lame-brain.

These half-wits immediately gave instructions for U.S. citizen Ivan Chonkin to be thoroughly checked and kept under surveillance at all times. They had been informed beforehand that Chonkin was a member of a delegation invited in person by the General Secretary of the Central Committee of the CPSU, which alone was enough to make him almost untouchable, but they regarded even the General Secretary as not entirely untouchable and even that was only temporary.

16

ON MONDAY AND TUESDAY the delegation of American farmers visited the All-Union Exhibition of Economic Achievement and one of the model Moscow-region Soviet farms, where vegetables for members of the Central Committee of the Party of the Workers were grown without chemical fertilizers and cows for the exhibition were fed on butter. The small Soviet farm shop had all kinds of sausage, cheese, vegetables, and fruit—clean, washed, and laid out in separate trays. Even here, however, there was no red grapefruit. Nor were there any customers. The delegation was received at the Ministry of Agriculture by the minister himself and on Wednesday they were asked to dress more formally (not to wear jeans and sneakers) and taken to the Kremlin to meet President Michael Gorbachev.

They were shown into a huge hall with molded ceilings, bizarre crystal chandeliers, and large paintings showing Lenin or devoted to various historical events such as the storming of the Winter Palace, the GOELRO plan, the construction of the Dnepr Hydroelectric Power Plant, and the taking of the Reichstag.

The surrounding splendor had a strange effect on the visitors. Although they were supposedly free men, they suddenly turned timid and lined up in single file of their own accord, without any word of command. Eventually the doors opened and a man whom Chonkin recognized from his portraits came striding through them rapidly—bald, with a large birthmark shaped like South America on his head. Trotting along beside him was a well-fed young man who later turned out to be an interpreter and trailing behind him in single file came the ministers, heads of department, deputy heads, and deputy deputy heads. They all walked in a rather unnatural way, holding their arms as if they were superfluous appendages.

The farmers drew themselves up even straighter. Gorbachev walked up to the first one, Jerry McCormack, held out his hand, and said: "*Zdravstvuyte*."

The farmers started to introduce themselves, as they had been instructed to do, and every time Gorbachev turned his left ear toward the man speaking, spoke only a single word, "*Priyatno*" (the interpreter translated it "A pleasure"), and moved on to the next man. Gorbachev reached Chonkin and held out his hand. Chonkin said, "Chonkin."

"*Priyatno,*" said Gorbachev and moved on, then stopped when he was struck by some thought, turned back, and said to the interpreter: "Ask him what kind of name that is. It sounds Russian."

"I am Russian," said Chonkin.

"Aha," said the GenSec, nodding his head, "I thought there was a Russian kind of sound to it all right. Were you born in Russia yourself? Not from Stavropol by any chance, are you? No? A pity. I happened to know a Chalkin there, too. He was a fine lad, a tractor-driver and Young Communist but, you know the way of it, he overdid this business a bit." The GenSec flicked his Adam's apple with his finger to indicate the abuse of drink. "And then one day, you know the way of it, when he was drunk he fell down a well and drowned himself. Well now, to judge from your age you must be from the second emigration? Were you taken prisoner or what?"

"Things just happened," Chonkin said evasively.

"Yes," said Gorbachev, nodding, "that's been the way of it, the history, so to speak, of our century! Dramatic! It shattered lives, scattered our people all over the place. But we'll put the mistakes of the past right somehow. So now you're in agriculture, then?"

"I'm a *farmer,*" Chonkin said modestly.

The GenSec asked what kind of farm he had, how much land, and what was grown on it. Chonkin said: "About nine hundred acres."

"How much is that in our measure?" asked the GenSec, turning to the minister of agriculture and thereby causing him serious embarrassment, because the minister had moved straight to agriculture from general Party work and before that he had been in charge of culture. But he was rescued by the interpreter, who knew more than just the language, in fact there seemed to be damn near nothing that he didn't know.

"Approximately four hundred and fifty hectares," he said.

"And how many people work for you?" asked Mikhail Sergeevich.

"What?" asked Chonkin, puzzled.

"Well, I'm asking how big your collective is. How many tractor drivers, combine operators, agronomist technicians?"

Chonkin thought for a moment and said:

"I'm on my own."

"Well, that's something I just can't get into my head. How do you mean, on your own? I understand that you don't have Party committees there," the GenSec joked and everyone walking behind him laughed loudly. "But even without Party committees you have to plow, sow, fertilize, thin

the crop, harvest it, thresh it, winnow it, transport the grain to the eleva-
tor. And who does all of that?"

"I do," said Chonkin.

"All on your own?"

"When I had a *wife,* we did it together. But now I do it alone."

"That's not possible," said the minister of agriculture.

"Ah, but it is," Mikhail Sergeevich retorted sharply. "People there don't
work the way we do here. Wouldn't you like to come back here? We
could give you a collective farm about the same size, let's say, as your
farm, you'd be the chairman and you'd have another two hundred people
under you, or perhaps we could send a delegation to you for training?
Would you have any objections?"

Without waiting for an answer, Gorbachev moved on, but the ideological secretary following him stopped beside Chonkin and asked in a
quiet voice:

"Pardon me, but who makes the decisions on your farm?"

"What decisions?" asked Chonkin, mystified.

"The decisions on when to start sowing, when to start harvesting."

The GenSec was already shaking the last farmer's hand, but he turned
out to have very good hearing. He looked back and told the ideological
secretary:

"That question proves it's time for you to retire."

THE NEXT ITEM PLANNED FOR THE FARMERS was a tour of two
districts of central Russia, with visits to progressive collective farms and
Soviet farms. They traveled by train, in two-berth compartments. The
car was new, the curtains were clean, and the conductor handed out tea
with biscuits. There was a timetable of trains hanging in the corridor
and Chonkin started reading it for lack of anything else to do. He hadn't
realized to begin with that the train would travel through places that had
been so important in his life. But now he came across a familiar name—
Dolgov—and it took his breath away.

After all the years that had passed, he still sometimes remembered the
village of Krasnoye and the woman with whom he had lived so briefly
but happily, although his memory had become veiled in mist and the

distant image that arose in his mind's eye was blurred and indistinct, it didn't stir his soul. But now suddenly it all came flooding back.

He tossed and turned all night, sometimes falling asleep briefly, and then he dreamed very clearly and distinctly of Nyura—young and plump, smelling of fresh milk. She was smiling to him, enticing him with her arms and her legs spread wide. Just as he fell into her embrace, he woke up, feeling frustrated with reality because it didn't conform to his dream and angry with himself for having a stupid dream like that: if Nyura was still alive, how old would she be now? She was even older than him, after all.

When morning came he had hatched an idea and he went to discuss it with the leader of the group, Jerry McCormack.

After listening to what Chonkin had to say, Jerry told him he was a free man, a citizen of a free country, and free to act as he thought best.

"But I advise you to consider that here your actions might be misinterpreted."

They agreed that Chonkin would travel to rejoin the delegation on the same train the next day.

He stepped down onto the platform at Dolgov station, a gaunt elderly man with a weather-beaten, leathery face and porcelain false teeth, wearing jeans and a waterproof anorak, with a travel bag over his shoulder.

Two local gourmets were sitting on the bench under the monument to Lenin outside the station, washing down the dried sprats they were chewing on by taking turns to swig the locally brewed murky brown beer from a three-liter plastic container.

"*Hai!*" Chonkin said to them. "Where can I take a *bus* or something to Krasnoye?"

One of the gourmets replied that he played the trumpet in the local orchestra. But their bass was Kolka Zhilkin, who was unavailable just at the moment, because he was in the middle of a serious binge.

"Is it only the bass you need, Pop, or the full orchestra?" the trumpeter asked.

"*Nou,*" said Chonkin, "no orchestra. I need to go to Krasnoye village."

The gourmets explained that during the muddy season it was practically impossible to get to Krasnoye on any kind of vehicle apart from a tractor, and there wasn't any tractor, but it wasn't very far to walk.

"You go along this street until you get to Victory Square—it's got this kind of pimple on it. Stand with your back to the pimple and you'll be facing the District Committee and District Executive Committee, the gray building. Walk round it on the right and then on the right you'll see the Street of the Panfilov Division Heroes. Go down it and keep going straight on, and eventually you'll get to Krasnoye. Only don't put on too much speed," the trumpeter joked, "or you'll shoot straight past it."

When he reached the square that had been mentioned, Chonkin saw an empty pedestal in the middle of it, surrounded by a low little fence of interwoven iron rods. The pedestal was clearly the object that the trumpeter had called a pimple. A dishevelled old woman in a knitted jacket and with her head uncovered was sitting on a small wooden bench beside the pimple. She had a shopping bag lying at her feet, evidently containing groceries, and a quarter-liter bottle of vodka in her hand. From time to time she raised it to her lips, muttering something that didn't greatly resemble articulate speech. But if Chonkin listened closely, he could make out individual words or phrases like "damshitocrats," "faggots," and "shoot them all." Chonkin had the feeling that he'd seen this old woman before somewhere. Straining his eyes to take a closer look, he barely managed to recognize her as his former partisan commander, the indomitable Aglaya Stepanovna Revkina, who had once coerced him into cohabitation. Hanging on the front of the District Committee of the CPSU was a large Board of Honor with portraits of so-called leading production workers, and to the right of this board, standing in a row along a pathway that was called the Avenue of Glory, there were several stone slabs bearing the incised names of forgotten heroes of old battles who were buried there. One of the stones was dedicated to the head of the NKVD before the war, the smiling Captain Milyaga. According to the stone, he had been laid to rest here. In actual fact, as the reader knows perfectly well, Captain Milyaga was not here and the bones lying under the stone were those of the gelding Osoaviakhim, who had supposedly been intending to become a man. The stone protruding crookedly above this grave had been covered with mildew and moss for a long time. Neither the captain's face in profile nor the inscription on the stone could be made out, but some inexplicable feeling made Chonkin stop and stand there for about a minute and a half before he moved on.

The Krasnoye road really was impassable, but on one side, stretching along the edge of a field of winter crops, there was a path that was dry and well-trampled by people's feet. Chonkin walked through a landscape that didn't remind him of anything until he reached a low hill, and he recognized the view that appeared beyond it immediately: a village of crooked little houses with a steep slope down to the Tyopa River.

Other villages, those that stood along the paved highway or close to it had long ago been colonized by motorized urbanites and rebuilt so that they looked like moderately prosperous dacha communities. But because of the constantly impassable road, only the very poorest summer residents, those without cars, ever reached Krasnoye. They didn't buy up the houses and they paid poorly for lodgings, so the village had not developed but had remained almost exactly the same as when Chonkin, the future Mr. Chonkin, left it in the wartime autumn of 1941.

Walking down to the village, he met a man on a horse who was wearing high boots, leather breeches, a leather jacket, and a hat with a narrow brim turned down to his ears.

"*Hai!*" Chonkin said to him. To which the horseman replied with a doff of his hat and the words:

"Good health to you!"

"Gladishev?" Chonkin exclaimed in surprise. "Kuzma Matveevich?"

"Gladishev," the other man confirmed. "Only with one correction. Not Kuzma Matveevich, but Heracles Kuzmich. Kuzma Matveevich is lying at rest over there, in the cemetery."

"*Sorry!*" said Chonkin. "You look just like him."

"That's what everybody says," agreed Heracles Kuzmich, a qualified agronomist and the father of a small family. "So you knew my pappy personally?"

"We met a few times," said Chonkin, deciding that there was no point in explaining in detail. "Nyura Belyashova, the postwoman, she used to live here . . ."

"And she still lives here, in that house over there," said Heracles Kuzmich. "Only she's out at the moment. She went to Dolgov to get some bread."

This statement surprised Chonkin yet again: why go from the village to the town to get bread, and not the other way around? But then, when he thought about it, he remembered that he didn't bake bread on his farm either.

Without waiting for any more questions or comments from Chonkin, Heracles Gladishev told him:

"Well, good health to you!"

He touched his hand to his hat and smacked his lips. The horse understood this sound correctly and bore its rider onward at a leisurely trot.

18

STRANGELY ENOUGH, NYURA'S HOUSE had remained exactly as it was in that distant summer, except perhaps that it was a little bit darker and more crooked than before, and the paint had peeled off the carved wooden surrounds of the windows. There was the vegetable patch, and the porch, and even a hog lying in front of the porch, looking exactly like Borka. In fact it was Borka—not the old one, but another hog with the same name (he couldn't possibly have any other). Nyura was not aware that some sensitive patriots might denounce her and even put her name on a list of Russophobes for giving Russian human names to animals. But owing to her limited level of literacy, Nyura did not know any other English, German, or Jewish names for animals, so she had no name for her hog but Borka, and she called all her pigs of the female variety Mashka. She called the she-goats Mashka too, and the cows, apart from the one she had before the war which the Germans stole from her. That cow, the only exception, had been called Beauty. The house was locked, and the padlock on the door looked like the same one that had hung there before the war—heavy and black, with a touch of rust round the edges and a little gewgaw covering the keyhole. Chonkin had a mischievous, stupid, and rather frightening idea: if nothing here had changed, then maybe Nyura had stayed the same as she was—young, beautiful, and sturdy, with an ample, curvaceous figure? He sat down on the step of the porch and lit a cigarette. Chickens strolled around the yard and the hog grunted sweetly as it dug a pit beside the fence, obviously without any practical purpose, purely for its own enjoyment.

"Borka!" Chonkin called to it, sure that he had the name right. "*Come here!*"

Borka raised his head and gave Chonkin a rather dubious look, wondering if the invitation might not be addressed to some other creature of the same name.

"*Come here!*" Chonkin repeated.

And although Borka could hardly have known English, he interpreted the intonation correctly and took a few steps toward the inviting party. He walked halfway and stopped.

"Come on, come on," Chonkin encouraged him, slapping himself on the shin. Eventually Borka came up and thrust his snout trustingly against Chonkin's sneakers. Chonkin scratched Borka behind the ear and the hog grunted contentedly, tumbled over onto his side, and allowed himself to be petted and stroked. Then Chonkin remembered the other Borka, and he remembered a few other things from that life too, including the place where Nyura hid the key. Not daring to trust his own premonition, he stuck his hand under a plank in the floor and there, of course, was the key. In the same place where it used to lie almost fifty years earlier.

"*Funny*," Chonkin said to himself as he opened the lock. "Weird!" he thought, translating into his native tongue.

When he took his sneakers off in the hallway and went in, he saw that everything there was still the same. There was nothing new in the house apart, perhaps, from two chairs with curved backs and a Horizon television in the corner, covered with a lacy napkin.

There was one other thing that caught his eye, though—a large double portrait of a man and a woman, hanging directly above the television. The woman, in a black jacket and a white blouse, had her braid coiled around her head and was slightly colored, with a high bloom on her cheeks. That was Nyura, of course, Chonkin guessed. But the man, pressing up against her and gazing straight out at Chonkin, was a handsome colonel in an airman's cap, with the star of a Hero of the Soviet Union and three rows of decorations below it. It seemed to Chonkin that the colonel (no doubt the one that Lyoshka Zharov had blabbed about back then) was watching him with the contemptuous grin of a successful rival.

There, that's human nature for you!—the thought flared up like a flame, searing his soul with jealousy. He realized himself that this was stupid and ridiculous: life had passed by, for many years he hadn't even remembered his prewar love—what right had he to be jealous? But even though he realized that he had no right, he was unable to control himself and strode around the room, casting baleful glances at the colonel and muttering angry reproaches to Nyura for not waiting, for being seduced by stars on shoulder straps and a star on a uniform tunic and casting a simple private with no stars out of her heart. He walked about like that, waving his arms and muttering nonsense, not even realizing what he was saying, completely forgetting that he hadn't been a soldier for a very long time and that, in terms of social standing and prosperity, he probably stood higher than even a Soviet general. But once he had worked himself up, he couldn't restrain himself and carried on walking until he noticed a bundle of papers tied around with a rubber band on the sideboard. He picked them up and saw that they weren't just papers, but old, very old letters, folded into triangles, the way letters used to be folded during the war. They were all postmarked and addressed to Anna Alexeevna Belyashova, and the return address was simply "N command" and nothing more.

It's not right to read other people's letters, of course, but, in all honesty, Mr. Chonkin had not been brought up well enough to be concerned about such subtleties. He opened the first letter and started creeping along the lines, which was not easy, because although he had come across printed Russian letters on occasion in various places, he hadn't seen handwritten ones for a long time. Fortunately the author of the letters proved to have legible writing: "Greetings from the N command!" Chonkin made out, moving his lips. "Hello, Nyura! Good day or evening to you. This is your Ivan with a frontline army hello."

"Another Ivan," Chonkin noted, and that reconciled him somewhat with the author. He started reading further, something started bothering him and, without finishing the letter, he looked at the end of it, raised his eyes to the portrait, and guessed at a few things. But no, he didn't look like this handsome fellow in the picture.

After he had made out a few more lines, he grew very agitated and started running around the room, casting glances at the portrait, first from one side and then from the other. He looked at himself in the mirror, too, and acknowledged reluctantly that although he was young-looking for his age and his false teeth had been skillfully contrived, he couldn't bear any comparison with the colonel now, and probably never could have.

He went back to the letters and started reading them one after another, carefully unfolding them and then folding them back together. Twice he was unable to hold back a tear. He wanted to see Nyura immediately, hug her, hold her against him, stay with her to the end of his days. But on thinking it over, he realized he had probably been wrong to come here. It wasn't him that she had been waiting for during the war, or his image that she had carried in her memory after it. The one she had waited for was far better than him, and not at all because he was an airman or a colonel.

Chonkin glanced out the window. The sun was still high above the Tyopa River; if he hurried he might be able to get back to the station while it was still light. He folded up the letters, stretched the rubber band around them, put them back where they had been, and looked to see if he had left any signs of his presence.

No, he hadn't.

He put on his sneakers, put the key back in its place, and set off.

19

NO SOONER HAD HE MOVED AWAY from the house than she appeared.

She was walking along with two shopping bags, a poorly dressed old woman. And thin. There was nothing left of her plump cheeks, full breasts, and other generous curves. As she drew level with Chonkin, Nyura looked up at him as if he were a stranger—an indifferent glance in passing—but following the old village tradition that still lingered in some places, she greeted him and walked on. He carried on along his way too, but after a few steps he looked around. And he saw her standing there, looking at him.

He smiled at her with his full set of porcelain teeth. She smiled back, then realized what she was doing and put her hand over her toothless mouth. Then she put her bags down on the path and started walking slowly toward him. When she reached him, she held out her hand and said: "Hello, Vanya!" She said it as if there were nothing unusual about this meeting. And he replied: "*Hai!* Really nice to see you again."

After that they sat in her house and drank tea with caramel candy.

Or rather, he drank and Nyura watched him.

"So where have you just come from, then?"

"From Ohio," said Chonkin.

"Is that far away?"

"Very far," said Chonkin.

"In Siberia?"

"Further than that."

Nyura couldn't imagine how anything could be further away than Siberia, so she didn't say anything.

He realized that she couldn't imagine it and told her: "I've come from America, Nyura."

"From America," Nyura repeated mechanically and then seemed suddenly to realize: "How do you mean, from America? From the real America?"

She had a high opinion of Chonkin, she assumed that he was capable of many things, but for her America had always been somewhere up above the clouds or in the next world—she couldn't even imagine that the man sitting in front of her was capable of existing in America.

"From the real America," Chonkin assured her.

She was even more surprised when she understood that Chonkin hadn't just flown there for a minute or two, but had been living there since 1946, and when he started telling her the details of his real life, it was all too much to fit inside her head.

She told him a few things too, about the lives of her fellow-villagers, what she knew herself and had heard from others . . .

Chairman Golubev had never come back from the camp. Lyoshka Zharov had worked as a tractor driver after he was demobilized and drowned when he was driving his tractor across thin ice on the Tyopa. In 1948 Kuzma Gladishev, still officially in exile, had taken the risk of traveling illegally to Moscow, where he managed to reach Academician Lysenko and introduce himself as a loyal Lysenkoist. He complained to the academician about the district agricultural officials who, being root-less cosmopolitans (that is, Jews) stood in the way of all things progressive. In particular, they wouldn't let him conduct scientific experiments to cultivate a hybrid of the potato and the tomato. Lysenko listened to him attentively and reprimanded him for collaborating with the Germans, but concluded that the attempt to provide the country with high-yield varieties of hybrids was praiseworthy and deserved to be encouraged. As a result of his efforts, Gladishev was exempted from further punishment and he returned to his native village. But he went back to Moscow, this time with a valid passport, to participate in the famous conference of the Lenin All-Union Academy of Agricultural Science, where, as one of the invited representatives of the common people, he stamped his feet when the geneticists spoke and shouted: "Fly-catchers!" Lysenko promised to let him have a large field for his experiments, but fell into disfavor before he could do anything about it. Gladishev had died in the early 1970s and been buried in the local cemetery.

Nyura made up the bed for Chonkin for the night, and she slept on the stove. In the morning they had breakfast together and he gave her a photograph of himself, in color, standing in front of a white two-story house with a small balcony. He promised to send her an invitation to come to America, then they shook hands and he left.

20

THE NEXT SUMMER NYURA RECEIVED an outlandish-looking delivery by mail. A thick envelope, with seals indented into the paper, with
Nyura's name and address printed on it in non-Russian letters—the kind
that she had learned so long ago in school and then forgotten. Nyura
examined the envelope for a long time against the light without opening
it and then, for lack of any better advisers, she ran to Ninka Kurzova,
another solitary old woman just like herself. Ninka's son Nikodim had
left to join the army in 1960 and never came home again. He went off
to Vorkuta to earn some good money and was stabbed to death in a
drunken fight there. Nyurka once used to envy Ninka because she had
gotten married in time and known the happiness of motherhood, but
in time fate had evened out their circumstances. And now it seemed to
Nyura that it was better not to have a child than to have one, raise it, and
lose it.

Ninka also twisted and turned the envelope for a long time, examining it and feeling it, and she advised Nyura not to open it but to take it to
the Right Place immediately: let them take a look at it, she said, and see
what's what. Because who could tell what there might be in an envelope
like that? Ninka had heard on the radio that an envelope like that could
hold lots of those Colorado beetle grubs, and now they even had bombs
they could send to people in the mail. But Ninka was really very curious,
and Nyura even more so, especially since she had rather more realistic
expectations, which were not altogether disappointed.

When she opened the envelope, she found an invitation, witnessed by
a notary (it was in English, but there was a Russian translation), which
said that Mr. John Chonkin, a citizen of the United States of America,
invited Anna Belyashova, a citizen of the Union of Soviet Socialist
Republics, to visit him in the state of Ohio and stay as his guest for one
month and undertook to pay the cost of his guest's travel in both directions, her living costs, and her medical insurance. And there was also a
Continental Airlines plane ticket.

When she saw that, Ninka, who was still as envious as ever, even at
her advanced age, was struck dumb at first, and then she asked: "Well
then, are you going to go?"

"Well, why not?" Nyura responded. "If Vanka's inviting me, of course
I'll go."

"And you'll fly in an airplane?"

"I will," said Nyura. "Vanka told me you can't get there on a train. It's too far—and there's the ocean."

"Well yes," agreed Ninka. "Well, all right. Only make sure those black people there don't gobble you up."

"They won't gobble me!" Nyura assured her. "I'm old, my meat's too tough to chew."

21

IT'S HARD EVEN TO IMAGINE how Nyura got through all the difficulties involved in making a trip abroad, but somehow she managed to surmount them all. She went to Moscow and lived with Seryoga, Lyushka Myakisheva's son, who charged her three rubles a day for a camp bed in the kitchen. Moscow seemed like an absolutely vast city to her, inhospitable and frightening. Hordes of people, and all in a bad temper, all dashing, dashing to get somewhere or other, they just couldn't stop.

It took her a week and a half to sort things out, but she got a foreign passport in the Visa and Registration Office and then stood in line at the American embassy. With the help of some charitable individual who took fifteen rubles from her, she filled out a form in which she agreed that in the case of her death, seven thousand dollars of the sum of her insurance would be spent on transporting her body back to Russia. Then a woman in glasses, with a thin, impassive face, asked her questions, all of which baffled Nyura completely and almost threw her into a panic.

"What is the inviting party's relationship to you?"

She said: "He doesn't have one."

"If he has no relationship to you, why is he inviting you? Do you intend to work illegally? To conclude a fictional marriage? Are you a member of the Communist Party?"

Nyura didn't know how to lie. She answered no to all three questions, realizing that every answer reduced her chances of getting a visa. She wasn't planning to work, she didn't want to marry, she wasn't a member of the Party.

The next question was: "Are you planning to engage in prostitution?"

"Do I have to?" Nyura asked, losing heart completely. "I'm old, what good am I?"

She started thinking that at least they could give her passport back. But they didn't. The woman in spectacles said: "Come back next Wednesday." The next Wednesday a Chinese woman with brightly painted lips was sitting at the little window. She handed the passport out through it without speaking. Realizing that she had been refused a visa, Nyura didn't even want to glance inside it.

Back at home Seryoga asked:

"Well, Aunty Nyur, did they give you your visa?"

"Oh yes," Nyura sighed. "They couldn't wait to let me have it."

"They didn't give you it?" asked Seryoga, understanding her correctly. "But what did they say?"

"They didn't say anything, they said it all the first time. I have to join the Party and engage in prostitution."

"You what?" Seryoga asked incredulously.

"I told you what. And they asked about narcotics too, where am I going to get them from?"

"Aunty Nyur, you're talking plain nonsense. Come on, give me your passport. Look. There's your visa, that's it!"

Everything was new to her. She had never been in Moscow before, she had never flown in a plane, of course, and she had never been abroad. But now she was flying, and where to? Straight to America!

Soon after take-off two stewardesses with a trolley appeared in the aisle between the seats and one of them asked Nyura what she would like to drink: whiskey, gin, Irish liqueur, vodka, wine, beer, orange juice, water?

"How much will it cost?" Nyura asked.

"It's *complimentary*," the stewardess replied.

Nyura decided that if it was complimentary, it must be expensive, and she asked how much the water was.

"Everything's *complimentary*," the stewardess repeated. And then, after looking at Nyura, she explained:

"It's all free."

Nyura was still afraid of taking too much and she asked for tomato juice.

She was given a complimentary dinner too, but was so excited that she didn't eat even half of it.

She had a seat by the window and she gazed through the thick glass at the white snowdrifts heaped up one on top of another, completely hiding the ground. Nyura knew that airplanes flew quite high, but she had never imagined it was possible to look down on the clouds. The plane flew smoothly, sometimes it seemed to her that it was simply standing still, that it would hang there like that forever and never land. Somewhere above the ocean another plane appeared, just as big, and hung alongside, neither moving closer nor moving away. Nyura looked out the window and saw it flying, then she fell asleep and dreamed that she was flying. She had often dreamed of flying before, not in a plane, just on her own: she simply lifted up off the ground and soared like a bird, with her arms held out to the side or in front of her. Sometimes these dreams were so clear that when she woke up she wanted to repeat the flight in the waking world and it was hard to accept what she knew, that this was impossible.

Near the end of the flight they started giving out some forms that had to be filled in. She was helped by the man sitting next to her, an American doctor flying home after an international conference of oncologists in Moscow. The doctor, who spoke good Russian, translated the questions for her and put the checkmarks in the little boxes that signified "yes" or "no" in accordance with her answers.

The questions were strange again:

Do you suffer from any serious infectious disease that is dangerous to people around you and are you an inveterate drug addict?

Have you ever been involved in criminal activity, been imprisoned for such activity for more than five years, and is criminal or immoral activity the purpose of your visit to the United States?

Have you ever engaged in espionage, sabotage, or terror? During the years 1933–1945 did you take part in acts of genocide? Are you engaged in any of these at present and do you intend to engage in espionage, sabotage, or terror in the United States?

Are you seeking illegal employment in the U.S.A. and is your visa counterfeit?

Have you ever abducted and detained children in the care of American citizens and do you intend in future to abduct and detain American children?

Have you ever been refused an American visa and have you ever been deported from the U.S.A.?

Naturally, her answer to all these questions was no, but she couldn't understand why such questions were asked at all. She asked the doctor if there really were any Nazis suffering from incurable diseases, or terrorists or kidnappers of children who were stupid enough to answer these questions honestly.

"No," said the doctor. "Of course, they'll all answer no. But when one of them gets caught out because he has AIDs, or it turns out that he served in the SS or he wants to blow up the Brooklyn Bridge and steal a child, he'll receive additional punishment for providing false information, for lying."

Nyura's nerves were so taut that during the ten hours of the flight she didn't go to the restroom even once. She felt she needed to go for a number one only after the plane had already landed at O'Hare. It was just her luck that it took so long trundling along all those little roads and even across two bridges over highways, which Nyura also found absolutely amazing.

The first person she came into contact with was a black officer at passport control. He didn't eat the people passing by his desk, he just checked their documents and slammed a big seal down onto them. She gave him her passport and the forms she had filled out in the plane, but he got angry for some reason and started shouting: tikkit-tikkit-tikkit! The oncologist standing behind her explained that she had to show him her return ticket, which was the proof that she wasn't planning to stay here forever. Then there was another checkpoint, where another black man asked her to open her suitcase. When he saw her present for Ivan— a ring of Odessa sausage and a jar of salted cucumbers—the customs man was as horrified as if he had found a bomb. He abused Nyura for a long time but she couldn't understand why and then said *okay* but took the sausage and the pickles, probably for himself, handed her a ballpoint pen, gestured for her to sign her name, and let her go after all. At the exit from the customs hall she was finally met by Chonkin—grayhaired, thin and tanned, wearing jeans, a white shirt with short sleeves, and white sneakers.

"*Hai*, Nyura!" he said and picked up her suitcase with both hands.

"Just a moment," she replied and dashed through a door that had an image of a one-legged woman in a skirt on it.

By the time she came out, Ivan had found a cart somewhere and they walked along some corridors with it, then rode in a strange train with no driver and got out at another airfield with little airplanes standing on it.

Ivan led Nyura across to one of them that looked like a car with wings and opened it as simply as opening a trunk. He threw the suitcase onto the back seat, tied it down with a belt, and put Nyura in the front seat.

She wasn't surprised, this was how it ought to be, he was an airman after all. Chonkin put on a pair of white leather gloves with holes for ventilation and flicked a few switches.

"Not afraid?" he asked.

"No," said Nyura. She wanted to say, "I'm not afraid with you"—but she felt too shy.

"Well, if you're not afraid, *lets gou,*" he said and turned the ignition key.

This flight wasn't like the one before it.

It was a hot day for autumn. Steam was rising from the heated earth. The rising currents of air grabbed at the little plane, tossing it up and down. Nyura was frightened and squeezed her knees in her hands, but when she glanced at Chonkin and saw how confidently he held the control column, she calmed down. They landed on a strip of concrete and then taxied briefly along narrow tracks through a field where stalks of corn that had been cut high were sticking up. Chonkin taxied up to a white two-story house as simply and naturally as if he were driving up to it in a wagon, switched off the engine, and said:

"This is my *haus.*"

23

THE GREEN AREA AROUND THE HOUSE was like an oasis in the midst of fields of corn laid waste by harvesting. Stunted maples surrounded the house and the outbuildings, which had two automobiles, two tractors, and a combine standing beside them.

The house was far more spacious than it looked from the outside: seven rooms, one of which—fully furnished with a television, telephone, separate toilet and shower—was intended for guests. Chonkin had once occupied it, and now it had come in handy for Nyura. We may suppose that Nyura was not actually hoping but, on the contrary, rather apprehensive that he would invite her to stay with him as his wife and suggest that they sleep in his big bed on the second floor: in that case she simply wouldn't have known what to do. And it wasn't just that she was already well advanced in years, there was also the difficulty that for the last fifty years, ever since the old days, she hadn't slept with any other man and had even forgotten how to imagine herself in such a situation. But, for better or for worse, Chonkin didn't suggest anything of the kind.

Although the harvest was over, he rose early like a peasant farmer, never later than six, and after drinking a glass of orange juice, went out to his machines and tinkered with them. She tried to make him lunch, but he thrust some kind of convenient ready-mades at her and taught her how to heat them up in the microwave oven. Sometimes they went to the small town nearby for lunch—there were all sorts of restaurants there, including Chinese, Italian, and Japanese. Nyura had never even been in the tearoom in Dolgov, let alone a restaurant, and at first she was afraid she would hold her spoon or fork the wrong way and people would laugh at her. But no one took any notice of her. She would have been glad to do some washing for Chonkin, but he said she ought to learn how to use the washing machine so that she wouldn't spoil her hands. And there wasn't even any need to wash the dishes, because there was a machine for that, too. He himself cooked an omelette or something vegetarian for their supper and they washed it down with water with the little cubes of ice that were produced in great quantities by the refrigerator and came tumbling out as soon as you put a glass in. During supper and sometimes afterwards they watched the TV, which was always showing chases and murders. Chonkin sometimes translated a few phrases for her, but the plots were simple and obvious enough without any words.

On Sunday they drove to the nearby town of Springfield, where the building that several farmers regarded as their church was located. In fact it was an ordinary one-story house just like all the others standing beside it—walls faced with wooden planks that were painted white. The only thing that distinguished it from other, similar houses was the cross set above the door, but the cross didn't really mean a thing.

On the way there Chonkin explained to Nyura that it wasn't a Christian church or a Muslim church or a Baptist church or a Buddhist church or any other kind of church, but a church, pure and simple. And for them God didn't have any definite form or name. He was simply God.

"But why's that?" asked Nyura, perplexed.

"That's because we don't know who He really is," said Chonkin, "Yahweh or Jesus or Allah, and if we call Him by the wrong name, He might take offense and get angry. So we just call Him God, and that's all."

Nothing inside reminded her of a church either. The walls of the large room weren't decorated with icons, but with photos of the local area and local people. One middle-aged man was shown most often, in the company of various people who Chonkin told her were famous celebrities. Nyura only knew one of the celebrities, that is, she didn't really know him, but she'd seen him somewhere and she asked who he was.

"President Reagan," said Chonkin.

Then the man who was in the photograph came up to Nyura—not the president, that is, but the man talking to him. He turned out to be the local preacher, Father Jim. Like his predecessor, Father Michael, he also had a day job, working as an orderly in the local hospital. He asked Nyura who she was and why she had come. Chonkin told him everything himself and Nyura only smiled bashfully, with her hand over her mouth. In addition to all the other information, Chonkin also announced that two days earlier Nyura had visited the local dentist, Mr. Dan Horowitz, who had taken an impression and promised to make her false teeth very soon for a good price, about six thousand dollars.

The preacher also enlightened Nyura concerning their special religion, the essential point of which was that they did not know God, either His essence or His image, and all the descriptions of His appearance and intentions had been invented by people and were fundamentally blasphemous. They could not know God, because His secrets were unknowable. They doubted that He was like a human being, let alone like an old man, because an eternal being could not be either old or young. They doubted that He was like a human being since, if He was like a human being and had eyes and ears, He could not see everything, especially what was happening behind His back. And He could not hear everything, because the range of hearing was limited. They doubted that He had lungs, because lungs were for breathing oxygen and, as they understood it, God could exist in any environment. They doubted that He had a mouth, teeth, and a stomach, for if He did, He would have to eat, digest food, and so forth. They believed that God existed, that He was eternal, that He guided people's lives, thoughts, and actions, that He saw and heard everything, but people did not know what He looked like or if He even looked like anything at all.

When he saw that the people had already gathered, the preacher broke off his lecture with obvious reluctance, stepped up onto a dais, and gave a sermon that Nyura didn't understand, but which went approximately like this.

"We have gathered here today," he said, "on the day when we rest from our labors, in order once again to offer up thanks in prayer to our Lord for His constant mindfulness of our welfare and constant care to make our affairs go well. Oh Lord, forgive us for not calling You by name and not praying according to the precepts that people regard as sacred. We do not observe these precepts because we do not know if they really are so sacred. We do not know in which religion to trust, but we know that You do exist, You are merciful, and You forgive our ignorance. We thank You, oh Lord, for all the good things that You do for us all the time. We thank You for a good harvest this summer and a warm fall. This year our parishioners have worked well and earned well. Bill Jackson bought a new combine and Freddy Lancaster bought two hundred acres of land from Tony Romain. Last week, as You know, there was a bad storm in the nearby states. Thank You, Lord, for making this storm pass us by. On Friday night Deborah Simpson was killed in an auto accident. She left a husband and two little children. You have gathered Deborah to Yourself, may Your will be done, You know best what to do with Your foolish children, but we have a big favor to ask of You: be with the Simpson family in these days, do not abandon them in their distress, help them to survive this terrible loss, and I know they will thank You with all their hearts. Alex Carpenter, as You know, had an accident, he jumped down off his combine and hurt his leg. Please, we entreat You, help make his leg better. And also help Pamela Brickson to be delivered of a child. (He glanced at his list and continued.) And finally. Anna, a fine Russian woman, has come to visit us at the invitation of John Chonkin. She has come from a country where great events are taking place, but people are poor and have no money for the dentist. Oh Lord, help Anna to enjoy her time here and help the dentist Dan Horowitz to make Anna a good set of teeth. So that when she gets home she can smile broadly and chew her food."

WHILE THE DENTIST WORKED ON NYURA'S FALSE TEETH, the term of her visa drew to its close. She was glad to go back home, for she had missed her motherland, her village, her goat, her hog, and her chickens.

At home she astounded the neighbors with her new teeth, two suit-cases full of all kinds of junk, and albums of colored photographs of a strange and beautiful life that was beyond the villagers' comprehension. And from then on everyone in the village started calling her Nyura the American.

25

THE VILLAGE OF KRASNOYE, having been founded two or three hundred years earlier or even before that, had remained basically un-changed throughout its existence. Apart, that is, from the electric power that had arrived here in Soviet times, then radio, and then television. But since the Soviet regime had collapsed and the laws of free trade had come into effect, a great deal had changed here. Especially after min-eral water springs were discovered in the vicinity. No sooner were the springs discovered than certain enterprising individuals called "New Russians" showed up. And then the local area was transformed, and vil-las and palaces of red brick, surrounded by brick walls, sprang up, some even with barbed wire along the top and security cameras turning their heads this way and that, like snakes. One of the newcomers wanted to buy Nyura's little house and demolish it; he offered her big money, and threatened to arrange a fire if she didn't agree. She didn't agree, but he didn't carry out his threat because he himself was burned to death in his own jeep.

Chonkin wanted to send Nyura money for a new house, but she wouldn't take it, saying she would live out her time in the one that she had. However, her life in general has changed for the better. Every year she stays with her former lover for a month, or even two, returning home with presents for all her fellow-villagers and then living in anticipation of her next trip. At any time during that period letters can arrive from Ohio, letters that are almost impossible to read because the sender's handwriting is so appalling and he confuses Russian letters with Latin ones. Chonkin once sent her a portable computer and suggested she should connect to the Internet, but she hasn't figured out how to do it yet and the computer is still in its box under the bed, waiting for the right time to come. Maybe that's for the best, because letters in the Internet aren't on paper, they're different, and she treasures paper letters more.

She puts the letters from Chonkin beside the ones composed during the war, although they're written in different handwriting. She has different feelings for them too, just as she has different feelings for their authors, imaginary and real. The first was a part of her, but the second is something like a duckling that has been hatched out by a hen—he looks like a duck, but he doesn't act like one. Nyura expresses this sense of strangeness instinctively, in the polite way she addresses Mr. Chonkin. But even so, she's always glad to go to see him.

As for our hero, although he is now extremely old, he doesn't really feel his age. Well, sometimes he gets an ache in his lower back or is overcome by drowsiness on the combine, but apart from that he remains in rude good health. Even so, he has hired two helpers.

One of them is a former Soviet spy and the other, just imagine, is Kuzma Heraclovich Gladishev, son of the agronomist, grandson of the plant breeder, and himself a plant breeder and geneticist. He married the Jewish girl Nelly Matveichik and they came to America, but he couldn't find any work to match his education and accepted Chonkin's invitation to act as something like an estate manager. He works well, makes a real effort, and is considerate and attentive with his boss. Chonkin, who has no heirs, sometimes even thinks about leaving everything to Gladishev, who doesn't drink much, doesn't smoke, understands the work of a farmer, and, in his spare time, continues the work started by his grandfather, from whom he has inherited an inquisitive mind and an inclination to transform nature. He recently managed to produce a hybrid of the potato and the tomato, not by selective breeding, however, but by combining the characteristics of the two crop plants at the genetic, or cellular, level. He has called his hybrid Amedra, which is an abbreviated form of the full name—American Dream. He grows Amedra in two hothouses and sells individual plants to lovers of exotic flora by advertising on the Internet (anyone interested can find the advertisements at the site www.potato-tomato.amedra.com). He doesn't distill moonshine from shit, though: he's quite content with American corn whiskey—bourbon.